About the Authors

Kat Cantrell read her first Mills & Boon novel in third grade and has been scribbling in notebooks since then. She writes smart, sexy books with a side of sass. She's a former So You Think You Can Write winner and an RWA Golden Heart® Award finalist. Kat, her husband and their two boys live in north Texas.

Janice Lynn has a Masters in Nursing from Vanderbilt University, and works as a nurse practitioner in a family practice. She lives in the southern United States with her husband, their four children, their Jack Russell – appropriately named Trouble – and a lot of unnamed dust bunnies that have moved in since she started her writing career. To find out more about Janice and her writing visit janicelynn.com

Paula Graves, an Alabama native, wrote her first book at the age of six. A voracious reader, Paula loves books that pair tantalising mystery with compelling romance. When she's not reading or writing, she works as a creative director for a Birmingham advertising agency and spends time with her family and friends. Paula invites readers to visit her website, paulagraves.com

Friends to Lovers

Friends to Lovers:
Always You

KAT CANTRELL

JANICE LYNN

PAULA GRAVES

MILLS & BOON

First Published in Great Britain 2024
by Mills & Boon, an imprint of HarperCollins*Publishers* Ltd,
1 London Bridge Street, London, SE1 9GF

www.harpercollins.co.uk

HarperCollins*Publishers*
Macken House, 39/40 Mayor Street Upper,
Dublin 1, D01 C9W8, Ireland

Friends to Lovers: Always You © 2024 Harlequin Enterprises ULC.

An Heir for the Billionaire © 2016 Harlequin Books S.A.
Friend, Fling, Forever? © 2019 Janice Lynn
Fugitive Bride © 2017 Paula Graves

Special thanks and acknowledgment are given to Kat Cantrell for her contribution to the *Dynasties: The Newports* miniseries

ISBN: 978-0-263-32488-4

AN HEIR FOR THE BILLIONAIRE

KAT CANTRELL

One

If there was any poetic justice in the world, Sutton Lazarus Winchester had gotten his.

Nora sagged back against the wall of the sterile hospital room, unable to process the inescapable fact that her seemingly infallible father was indeed dying of inoperable lung cancer. She should feel relieved. His tyrannical reign was nearly over. The man who couldn't be bothered to walk her down the aisle at her own wedding lay pale and gaunt in a hospital bed, as if a bit of his spirit had already fled for hell in advance of the rest.

The relief didn't come. Nora had traveled home to Chicago with the barest hope she might find a way to reconcile with her father in his last days. And now that she was here, the sheer difficulty of that task nearly overwhelmed her.

"I had to see it for myself," Nora murmured to her sisters, Eve and Gracie, who flanked her as she faced down their father. None of them had gotten too close to the bed in case Sutton had more gusto than he seemed to have. Right now he appeared to be asleep but that didn't matter.

Like a snake, he waited until you were within striking distance and then sank his fangs into the tenderest place he could find, injecting poison and pain until it suited him to stop. It was how he'd always operated, and Nora had no doubt he'd find a way to do it from the grave.

"We all did," Eve murmured back. "The doctor wasn't too happy with me when I asked her to allow another doctor to review the oncology reports. But I had to make sure."

Methodical to her core, Eve never missed dotting an *i* or crossing a *t*. As the oldest Winchester sister, she'd always been large and in charge and seldom let anything stand in her way.

"Wanted to see the death sentence with your own two eyes, hmm?" Nora said without malice.

Sutton had terrorized all three of his daughters, but Nora was the only one who'd grown so sick of the constant drama surrounding her father that she'd moved halfway across the country to Colorado, effectively— and gratefully—turning her back on the money, the glitter and the heartbreak of the lifestyle she'd been born into.

Eve glowered. "Wanted to make sure it wasn't manufactured. I wouldn't put it past that Newport scum to have paid off a doctor to produce a false report."

"Do you really think Carson could find someone willing to do that?" Gracie asked, and it was clear she had no ill will toward the man the sisters had recently learned was their half brother.

The total opposite of Eve, Gracie always saw the best

in people. Nora's younger sister had such a big heart, even in the midst of the huge scandal caused by the recent revelation that during one of his past affairs, Sutton had fathered a son—none other than his business rival Carson Newport.

Now that Nora had seen her father, she could turn her attention to Carson, who was her second order of business while in Chicago. Oh, Nora didn't give two figs about Sutton's money and whether Carson Newport had a legal claim to any of it. Eve and Grace could fight that battle. But the man was her brother. She *was* curious about him. And she didn't appreciate the idea of her sisters losing out on their inheritance; it meant something to them, even if it came down to nothing more than a just reward for the years of being Sutton Winchester's daughters.

"I wouldn't put anything past him. There are a lot of unethical things people will gladly do for money, including doctors. And especially Newport," Eve responded, tossing her honey-blond hair over her shoulder impatiently. It was longer than Nora remembered, but then, they hadn't seen each other in quite a while. Not since before Sean had died.

The grief over her husband's untimely death, never far from the surface, bubbled up; coupled with the shock at seeing the larger-than-life head of the Winchester real estate empire laid out in a stark white hospital bed, it was too much.

One, two, three… Nora kept counting until she reached ten. That was all the time she was allowed to feel sorry for herself. Sean was gone. Nora wasn't and she had adult things to handle that wouldn't get done if she spent all her time curled up in a ball of grief as she had after the grim-faced army liaison had brought her the news that Sean had been killed in Afghanistan.

He'd never gotten to meet their son. It was the cruelest travesty in a litany of truly terrible circumstances. But Nora still had that tiny piece of her husband alive and present in their little boy, and no gun-toting terrorist could ever take that away.

A woman with thick-framed glasses and hair swept up in a no-nonsense bun appeared at Sutton's bedside, the tablet in her hand and white lab coat indicating she had medical business at hand. She checked a few things on her tablet and then glanced at the knot of Winchester women.

"I'm Dr. Wilde. We haven't met." The doctor rounded the bed to shake Nora's hand. "You must be the nonlocal sister."

"Nora O'Malley," she affirmed. She'd shed the Winchester name as fast as she could after she and Sean tied the knot, and it would take an act of Congress to get her to ever change it to anything else. "So it's true? My father is dying and there's nothing you can do?"

Dr. Wilde bowed her head for a moment, her discreet diamond earrings sparkling in the light. "As much as I hate to admit defeat, yes. It's true. I couldn't operate, due to the tumor's location, and then the cancer spread too fast to employ chemotherapy. He probably has another five months, tops. I'm sorry."

Five months. It was way too fast. How could she find the will to forgive her father for not loving her in such a short period of time?

"Don't be," Nora insisted, even as the doctor's prognosis hit her sideways. "It's his own fault. We all told him to stop smoking but he thought that deal he'd made with the devil would keep him alive forever, I guess."

She'd known that's what the doctor would say. But it was so different to hear it from her mouth personally. That was partly the reason she'd forced herself to get on a plane to Chicago, though traveling with a two-year-old had been exhausting.

And now it was shockingly final. Sutton would be dead by New Year's Day.

Sutton's personal assistant, Valerie Smith, poked her head in the door, not one ash-blond hair out of place. "Is your father awake yet?" she asked. "I was going to bring Declan in if you wanted."

Third order of business: to finally let her father meet his grandson.

It had been a difficult decision. The poison that Sutton managed to infuse into everybody around him couldn't be allowed to affect her son. But his grandfather was dying. Nora had hoped that on his deathbed, her father might have an epiphany about his character, his choices, his closed heart—*something* that would allow all of them to make peace with Sutton's passing and go on.

"No, he's still asleep." Nora couldn't help but feel grateful for the reprieve. She'd steeled herself for this moment of reckoning but nothing magical had happened to the disappointment and hurt inside upon seeing her father in person. "But I'll take Declan so you can have a break."

Valerie had offered to take the cranky and bored two-year-old to the cafeteria in search of Jell-O or saltine crackers, the only two things he wanted. He refused to eat the fruit snacks and banana chips Nora had shoved in her carry-on bag—the only two things he'd wanted when she'd been packing back home. Reason was not in the wheelhouse of a toddler, so holding out the packages and telling him that was the snack he'd picked hadn't worked.

The little boy popped into the room and Nora's heart lurched, as it always did when she caught sight of his curly mop of red hair. He looked like Sean, of course, and it was both a blessing and a curse to have the visual reminder of what she'd lost. "Hey, Butterbean. Did you find some Jell-O?"

Nora extracted herself from her sisters with a hand to Gracie's arm and a smile for Eve, guilt crowding into her chest that she'd opted to take the out of caring for her son instead of sitting here with her family. They'd all been by Sutton's side from the beginning, supporting each other, showing solidarity to outsiders, but Nora just…couldn't.

Declan nodded. "Jell-O."

It came out sounding more like *je-whoa*, but Nora had never had any trouble interpreting Declan-speak. The shiny machines of the hospital room caught his attention and he weaved toward the nearest one, finger outstretched. Nora scooped him up and kissed his head. "Not so fast, Mr. Curious. Have I told you the story about the cat?"

"Cat." Declan made a sound like one, except it was more of a yowl than a traditional meow. He was so funny and precious and her heart ached that his father wasn't here to see how he'd grown, how fast he learned things, how he slept with one foot stuck out from the covers—just like Sean had.

As quickly as she could, Nora bustled her son out of the hospital room before anyone saw the tear that had slipped down her face. Sean had died nearly two years ago. She should be ready to move past it. Ready to date again, find someone to ease her loneliness. But she couldn't imagine being with someone other than Sean, who had been the love of her life, the man who had thoroughly captured her heart the moment she'd met him at a football game during her junior year of college.

Seeking a quiet place to regroup, Nora spied an alcove with two chairs away from the main hospital corridor. She and Declan settled into the chairs, or she did. He sat in the opposing one for a grand total of four seconds before he squirmed to the ground and scooted around like his pants were on fire. Nora laughed.

"Problem with your diaper there, Butterbean?"

That had been Sean's nickname for the boy the moment he'd seen the ultrasound pictures she'd held up to the camera during one of their Skype calls. She'd kept the name, even after he was born, because Declan still resembled a bean when swaddled in the brown blanket Sean's mother had bought for her grandson.

Of course, Nora didn't do much swaddling these days, not with an active two-year-old.

Declan didn't answer, too preoccupied with his task of cleaning the hospital floor with his butt. Thirty more seconds and she'd use hand sanitizer on every inch of exposed skin, before he got around to sticking a random body part in his mouth. Midwest Regional was a highly acclaimed hospital, but sick people came through these halls all the time. A mother couldn't be too careful.

"Ms. Winchester?" A young hospital worker in plain clothes stopped near Declan. Her name badge read Amanda.

"O'Malley," Nora corrected. "But yes, formerly Winchester."

And she didn't choke on it. There might be hope for her yet to work through all her anger and disillusionment with her father.

The worker smiled. "There's a private room set up for the family if you'd like me to show it to you."

"Oh, yes. Of course."

How could she have missed that Sutton's wealth and influence had extended even to the hospital? It had been a long time since Nora had lived the life of a socialite, and even longer since she'd wanted to. But the lure of a private place, away from the crowded hospital, called to her.

Amanda punched in the code on the keypad outside the room and then promised to write it down for her. Nora pushed open the door and nearly gasped, but not over the sumptuously appointed room. Her mother's house had far more antique rugs and dark, heavy furniture than this place. No, her attention was firmly on the long table lining the wall that held enough food for four Winchester families. The empty bags under the table sported the logo for Iguazu, a new, trendy Argentinian fusion restaurant so hot that Nora had even heard of it back home in Colorado. A couple of uniformed delivery people were still setting up the warming mechanisms for the silver serving trays, so the food had obviously just arrived.

"What is all this?" Nora asked Amanda.

"Someone sent it for the family. Oh—" Amanda rummaged in her pocket "—there's a note for you."

Intrigued, Nora accepted the envelope and scooped up Declan with her other arm as he eyed the blue flame under the rolltop chafing dishes. "Thank you."

Amanda wrote down the keypad code on a sticky note and cheerfully waved as she exited behind the delivery people. Nora sat in one of the overstuffed wingback chairs and wedged Declan in tight so he couldn't squirm away, then ripped open the envelope.

The typed note was short and to the point: *Good food can make anything more bearable.*

In closing, the note contained only a simple state-ment—*Cordially Yours*. No signature.

Nora's eyes narrowed as she read over the phrase again. It tickled the edges of her memory and then came to her all at once. It was a phrase that had been a bit of a joke between Nora and a friend—Reid Chamberlain.

Wow. That was a name Nora hadn't thought about in years. Reid, his brother, Nash, and his sister, Sophia, had gone to the same private schools as the Winchester girls, practically since birth. Reid and Nora were the same age and had often been in the same class. Their parents ran in the elite circles of Chicago society, so it was only natural that they'd seen each other socially, and at boring grown-up events. What else was there for kids to do but bond?

It would have made more sense for Nora to become friends with Sophia, but it hadn't happened that way. Reid had always been the object of her fascination.

They'd spent a good bit of time getting into trouble together, playing make-believe in the cupboards of each other's kitchens until the servants chased them out, or getting up a game of hide-and-seek across the expansive Chamberlain estate grounds with their siblings. She'd loved it when they hid in the branches of the same tree, giggling quietly behind their hands when Nash or Gracie stood directly below, frustrated over not being able to find them. For a while, she'd had a bit of a crush on Reid.

But that had been before he grew into his looks and body, both of which put him firmly in the sights of every teenaged socialite-in-training in the greater Chicago area, shoving Nora to the back of the pack. Then Reid had started running with a crowd that worshipped at the altar of money, prestige and fast cars. She didn't blame him. Ninety-nine percent of the people in her life subscribed to the philosophy of *whoever has the most toys at the end wins*. They'd grown apart. It happened.

Last she'd heard, Reid Chamberlain had only increased his wealth and prestige through a series of brilliant moves in the hotel industry. He dominated the Chicago market along with a host of other cities.

Surely Reid wasn't the one who'd sent the smorgasbord. They hadn't talked in years and the joke involving *cordially yours* hadn't been a code of any sort, just something they'd said to each other when they mimicked how grown-ups talked when trying to impress other grown-ups. Lots of people could use the phrase on a regular basis.

Nora texted Eve and in a few moments, the rest of the Winchesters barreled into the private room to see the anonymous gift for themselves. Since she hadn't eaten in forever, Nora fixed a plate for Declan with a few French fries, his favorite and likely the only thing from the table he'd eat, and then took full advantage of the generosity of their unknown benefactor for herself. The dishes held layers and layers of steaming, mouthwatering food: Argentinian asado-style steak thick with chimichurri sauce, a tray of empanadas, a variety of grilled vegetables and cheeses.

Nora took a bit of everything, intending to go back for more of the dishes she liked the best. Eve and Gracie followed suit as they chatted about the identity of their anonymous friend, but even after a round of seconds, the spread looked like it had barely been touched.

"This food is delicious," Nora commented. "But it won't last long and there's so much of it. We should share it with the staff."

"That's a great idea," Gracie said enthusiastically. "They all work so hard. I wonder how often any of them get to eat at a place like Iguazu, where you have to know someone to get a table. I've only been there once and that took some doing. I'll mention it to Amanda so she can spread the word."

You needed an "in" to eat at Iguazu? Nora's intrigue meter shot into the red. Who would have sent food to the Winchester family from such an exclusive place? One of Sutton's associates? People tolerated Sutton because he was powerful, and sure, lots of them had sent impersonal gifts over the years, but rarely did anyone go out of their way to do something difficult or thoughtful. Even more impressed with the gesture, Nora fingered the note in her pocket.

Nurses, doctors and hospital staff streamed into the room in short order, exclaiming over the feast and thanking the Winchester women for their generosity. Crowd noise increased as people found seats and socialized. Nora's temples started to pound as the long day of travel caught up with her.

On the other side of the room, Declan had climbed into Gracie's lap, and she laughed as he stole French fries off her plate, apparently not having stuffed his little face enough with those his mother had given him. Declan was in good hands with his aunt, providing Nora with the perfect opportunity to grab a few minutes to herself.

Nora caught Gracie's eye and nodded to the door, then held up her palm with her fingers spread, mouthing, "Five minutes?"

Gracie smiled and waved her off.

Gratefully, Nora ducked out and went to the ladies' room to splash some water on her face. Belatedly, she realized there was probably a private bathroom in the area she'd just left. It had been a while since Nora had lived in her family's wealthy orbit. She'd never really embraced the privileged lifestyle anyway, even choosing to go to the University of Michigan, a public college, much to her mother's chagrin. But that was where she'd met Sean, so she'd considered it fate.

Out of nowhere, Reid popped into her head again. He'd gone to Yale, if she recalled correctly. Not that she'd spent a lot of time keeping track of him, but the private high school they'd attended had been small enough that everyone knew everyone else's business.

As she fingered the note in her pocket again, Nora's curiosity got the best of her. What if Reid had sent the catered spread? She should thank him. Gracie and Eve had known Reid, of course, but they'd never been close with any of the Chamberlain siblings, not as Nora had.

But why would Reid have done something so nice without signing the note? Suddenly, she had to know if her childhood friend had been behind the gesture. If for no other reason than to satisfy her curiosity.

Nora was nothing if not resourceful. After all, she'd walked away from her family's money and lived a simple life in Colorado on the monthly Dependent Indemnity Compensation payment that the government sent Nora as a surviving spouse of a military serviceman killed in the line of duty. Creativity came with the territory.

She pulled out her phone and tapped up the restaurant's website, then called. A cultured female voice answered. "Iguazu. How may I help you?"

"This is... Ms. O'Malley from Mr. Chamberlain's office." Nora crossed her fingers. She hated lying, but the ends justified this little white one. "Mr. Chamberlain would like confirmation that the food he ordered to be delivered to the Winchester family at Midwest Regional was delivered."

"Absolutely, let me verify."

Music piped through the speakers as Nora was put on hold. She grinned. That had been way too easy.

The music cut off as the Iguazu employee came back on the line. "Ms. O'Malley? Yes, the food was delivered and as specified, the note given directly to Nora Winchester. Please let Mr. Chamberlain know we're pleased he's chosen Iguazu for his catering needs and we look forward to his next event."

Somehow Nora squeaked out a "Thank you," though how she'd spoken when her tongue had gone completely numb, she'd never know.

Reid had not only sent the food, he'd specified that *she* should receive the note? Why? The signature *had* been some kind of code. One he'd clearly thought would mean something to her. And it did. She'd been besieged by memories of an easier time, before Sean, before she'd really understood what an SOB her father was.

Reid had wanted her to figure it out. She had to know why.

After the long trip and the blow of seeing her father so ill in that hospital bed, yet not feeling the rush of forgiveness she'd hoped for, Nora should have *wanted* to go home and shut out the world. But she'd been doing that for two years and all it had gotten her was a severe case of loneliness and a crushing sense of vulnerability.

Very little had happened lately that she'd had any control over. Her life had been spinning without her permission and all she'd been able to do was hang on. It was time to do something affirmative. Something decisive. Like thank an old friend for his kindness.

Two

On the way to Reid Chamberlain's downtown Chicago office, Nora pulled up a few articles about him on her phone. If she was going to beard the man in his den, she should at least know a few things about who he'd become over the years.

Gracie had volunteered to take Declan back to the Winchester estate, where Nora would be staying while in Chicago, and then insisted on calling for a car to take Nora on her mysterious errand. Being secretive wasn't second nature to Nora, but she didn't want to bring up Reid, at least not until she knew the purpose behind his kind gesture.

Especially when all of the articles she'd managed to find about Reid pointed to a very different person from what she'd expected. There were almost no pictures of him, save one very grainy shot that showed Reid rushing from a dark car to the covered doorway of one of his hotels. He'd turned his face from the camera, so the angle showed only his profile, but even that little bit clearly conveyed his annoyance at the photographer.

The caption underneath read "Reclusive billionaire Reid Chamberlain."

Reclusive? *Reid?* He'd been the life of the party as long as Nora could remember. Heck, that was the reason they'd grown apart—he'd become so popular, his time was in constant demand.

Doubly intrigued, Nora glanced up as the car slowed to a stop and the uniformed driver slid out to open the back door for her to exit. She got out and found herself standing in front of the brand-new Metropol Hotel in the heart of downtown Chicago.

A study in glass and steel, the hotel towered over her, reaching to the heavens. *Good grief.* This was Reid's office? She'd read that Nash Chamberlain had designed the Metropol, and it was nothing short of breathtaking, rising several dozen stories high and twisting every so often. The architectural know-how required to design it must have been great, indeed.

Impressed, Nora swept through the door opened by a uniformed attendant and approached the concierge, glad she'd opted for heels and a classic summer-weight pantsuit today. The concierge glanced up with a ready smile. Her mind went blank. Lying to the woman from Iguazu had been one thing, but this man was right in front of her, staring at her expectantly. She should have thought this through.

What if Reid wasn't here? Or hadn't really wanted her to seek him out? She'd only assumed he'd meant for her to figure it out. He might actually be mad that she'd tracked him down.

So what if he was mad. This trek had been about

something greater than a mere thank-you. *Taking control here.* Nora squared her shoulders. No apologies.

"I'm here to see Mr. Chamberlain. Tell him Nora O... Winchester is here." And she didn't even choke on the name. "Nora Winchester. He'll see me right away."

Wow. *Brazen* should be her middle name. The articles had called Reid reclusive and she'd waltzed right in to demand that he admit her without question? This was a dumb idea.

The concierge nodded. "Of course, Ms. Winchester. He's expecting you."

Nora picked her jaw up off the floor for the second time that day. "Thank you."

The concierge tapped a bell and a young man in a discreet rust-colored uniform that mirrored the hotel's accents appeared by Nora's side before she could fully process that Reid was *expecting her.*

"William will show you to the elevators and ensure that you reach Mr. Chamberlain's office," the concierge said.

Meekly, she followed the bellhop to the elevator bank, her heels sinking into the plush carpet that covered the rich dark hardwood floors. When they got on the elevator, the bellhop swiped a badge over the reader above the buttons and pushed one for the forty-seventh floor.

"Forty-seven and forty-eight are secure floors," William explained with a smile. "Only VIPs get to see Mr. Chamberlain. It's been quite a while since we've had one."

VIPs only. And Nora Winchester was one. What would have happened if she'd introduced herself as Nora O'Malley? Would the concierge have politely booted her out the door?

Nervous all at once, she discreetly checked her hair

and makeup in the mirrored paneling of the elevator. She'd twisted her blond hair up in a chignon this morning before her flight, and several loose strands had corkscrewed around her face. Not a bad look.

Silly. What did it matter how she looked? Reid had thrown her all off-kilter by telling his staff to expect her.

The elevator dinged and within moments William was ushering her into a reception area populated by a stately woman with steel-colored hair, who closed her laptop instantly as Nora entered.

"You must be Ms. Winchester," she said. "Mr. Chamberlain asked for you to be shown right in."

Far too quickly, the receptionist steered her through a set of glass doors and to an open entryway at the end of the hall, then discreetly melted away.

The man behind the wide glass desk glanced up the moment Nora walked across the threshold of his office.

Time fell off a cliff as their eyes locked.

Nora forgot to breathe as Reid Chamberlain's presence electrified every nerve in her body. And then he stood without a word, crossing to her. The closer he came, the more magnetic the pull became. He was all man now—powerful in his dark gray suit, a bit rakish with his brown hair grown out long enough to curl a bit on top, and sinfully beautiful, with a face that became that much more devastating due to a five o'clock shadow that darkened his jaw.

And then he was so close she could see the gold flecks in his brown eyes. A dark, mysterious scent wafted from him, something citrusy but mixed with an exotic spice that wholly fit him. She had a feeling she'd be smelling it in her sleep that night.

"Hi, Nora."

Reid extended his hand. For a moment, she thought

he was reaching for her, to hug her, or…something. But instead, he closed the door and leaned into it, his arm brushing her shoulder.

The *snick* of the door nearly made her jump out of her skin, but she kept herself from reacting. Barely. Did he have something in mind that was so intimate and private that it wasn't fit for prying eyes?

Her pulse jumped into her throat. "Hi, Reid."

He crossed his arms and contemplated her. "You got the note."

"Yes." Impulsively, she put out her palm, intending to touch Reid on the arm to express her thanks.

But at the last minute, something in his expression stopped her. Something dangerous, with an edge she didn't understand, but wanted to. Touching him suddenly held all kinds of nonverbal implications, maybe even an invitation she wasn't sure she meant to extend.

Goodness. How had a simple thank-you become so… *charged*? She let her hand drop to her side and his gaze followed it, marking the action.

"What can I do for you?" he asked simply.

He was not the same boy she remembered. She could see hints of his teenage self in the way he held his body, and small things such as the length of his lashes were the same, but his gaze had grown hard and opaque. It was almost as if he'd grown an extra layer between himself and the rest of the world and no one was allowed to breach it. One of the things she'd always liked about Reid Chamberlain was his smile. And that was noticeably absent.

The man was—according to the news articles—reclusive, and wealthier than King Solomon, Croesus and Bill Gates put together. But it didn't seem to have made him happy.

What could he do for her, indeed? Probably not much. But maybe she could do something for him. "You can smile for me, Reid. It might actually break this awkward tension."

Against all odds, the corners of Reid's mouth twitched. He fought to suppress the smile because he didn't want to encourage Nora Winchester into thinking she could command him into doing her will five minutes into their renewed acquaintance.

Besides, Reid didn't smile. That was for people who had a lightness of spirit that allowed for such a thing. He didn't. Normally. Nora had barreled into his office and the moment he'd seen her, it was like a throwback to another time and place—before all the shadows had seeped into his soul.

Which sounded overly dramatic, even to himself. That was why he never thought about his own miserable existence and instead worked eighteen hours a day so he could fall into bed exhausted at the end of it. When you slept like the dead, you didn't dream. You didn't lie awake questioning all the choices you'd made and cursing the genetics that prevented you from doing a simple thing like becoming a father to your orphaned niece and nephew.

Nora's presence shouldn't have changed anything. But it had. She'd breathed life into his office that hadn't been there a moment ago and he was having a hard time knowing what to do with it.

It was troubling enough that she'd tracked him down in the first place. And more troubling still that he'd been anticipating her arrival in a way that he hadn't *anticipated* anything in a long while.

"Smiling is for politicians and people with agendas," he finally said.

The air remained thick with tension and something else he wasn't in a hurry to dispel—awareness. On both sides. Nora was just as intrigued by him as he was by her. Reid was nothing if not well versed in reading his opposition. And in his world, everyone was the opposition, even Nora Winchester, a woman he hadn't spoken to in nearly fifteen years and who'd apparently interpreted his note as an invitation to invade his privacy.

He should be annoyed. He wasn't. That made Nora dangerous and unpredictable. Unexpectedly, it added to her intrigue. The heavy pull between them tingled along his muscles, heating him to the point of discomfort. He hadn't been this affected by a woman's presence since he was a teenager.

"Oh, really. And you don't have an agenda?" Nora crossed her arms in an exaggerated pose he suspected was designed to mimic his. "What was with the note, then?"

"It's polite to include a note with a gift," he replied as he fought a smile for the second time. He hadn't expected to like the grown-up version of Nora as much as he did. What was he supposed to do with her?

When his admin had called Iguazu to check on the delivery, imagine his surprise to learn that a mystery woman from "his office" had already called. A quick check-in with the hospital told him that Nora had indeed received his note. It hadn't taken much to guess she'd figured out that he'd sent the catering and would be along to see him in short order. He'd been right.

"Uh-huh. And is it customary to use a private joke in said note and then pretend you didn't intend for me to figure out you sent it?"

Her wide, beautiful mouth tipped up at the corners and communicated far more than her words did. She was toying with him. Maybe even *flirting*. Women didn't flirt with him as a rule. Usually they were much more direct, wrangling introductions from mutual acquaintances and issuing invitations into their beds before he'd learned their last names.

He'd taken a few of them up on it. He wasn't a monk. But he'd never held a conversation with one or called one again. Not since the day when his father had killed more than half of his family, including himself.

Nora was a first. In more ways than one. His body's awareness dialed up a notch. She was close enough to touch but he didn't reach out. Not yet. Not until he got a much better handle on his reaction to her. And maybe not even then. Nora certainly hadn't dropped by to be seduced by the CEO of Chamberlain Group. But that didn't automatically mean she'd be averse to the idea. It just meant he needed a clearer sense of the lay of the land before he made a move on a childhood friend.

"Are you…*accusing* me of deliberately trying to get your attention with a throwaway signature line on a note?" Reid hadn't enjoyed interaction with a woman this much in so long, he couldn't even *say* how long.

Her gaze narrowed. "Are you denying it?"

Cordially Yours. He hadn't uttered that phrase in over a decade. How had she remembered that joke? Or maybe a better question was: why had he put it in the note?

Maybe he'd intended for this to go down exactly as it had.

When he'd heard about Sutton Winchester's terminal diagnosis, Reid's first thought had been of Nora. They hadn't spoken in a long time, but she'd played an important role in his youth, namely that of a confidante for a boy trying to navigate a difficult relationship with his parents. He remembered Nora Winchester fondly and had never even said thank you for the years of distraction she'd provided, both at school and at parties.

The gift had been about balancing the scales. Reid didn't like owing anyone anything.

He certainly hadn't sent the food for Winchester's benefit. The old man could—and most definitely would—rot in hell before Reid would lift a finger to help him. The man had more shady business deals and crooked politicians in his back pocket than a shark had teeth. Reid wouldn't soon forget how Chamberlain Group had been on the receiving end of a personal screw-over, courtesy of Sutton Winchester.

"The food was for old time's sake. Nothing more." Nor should he pretend it was anything more. "Let's just say I wasn't expecting a personal thank-you for the catering, and leave it at that."

She laughed and it slid down his spine, unleashing a torrent of memories. Nora *was* an old friend, and for a man who didn't have many, it suddenly meant something to him that he had a history with this woman. A positive history. She'd known his sister, Sophia, and that alone made her different from anyone else in his life except Nash.

Yeah, letting her walk away untouched wasn't happening. Reid had long ago accepted his selfish nature and he wanted more of Nora's laugh.

"Obviously you *were* expecting me." Nora's gaze raked over his body as she called him on it. "Your staff couldn't have been clearer that they'd been waiting for me to arrive. How did you guess I'd be coming by?"

"Oddly enough, you tipped me off. My admin called

Iguazu and learned that Ms. O'Malley from my office had already inquired after the status of the delivery."

Guilt clouded Nora's gaze and she shifted her eyes to the right, staring at a spot near his shoulder. "Well, you didn't sign the note. How else was I supposed to figure out if you were the one behind the nice gesture?"

"I don't make nice gestures," he corrected her. "And you weren't supposed to figure it out. Is Ms. O'Malley a fake name you use often to perform nefarious deeds?"

He couldn't resist teasing her when it was so obvious she hadn't a deceptive bone in her body. Flirting, teasing and smiling—or nearly doing so anyway—were all things he hadn't indulged in for a very long time, and all things he'd like to continue doing.

But only with Nora. All at once, he was glad she'd tracked him down.

"Yes," she informed him pertly. "It's a name I use often for all my deeds. I got married."

Genuine disappointment lanced through his gut. Where had that come from? Had he really been entertaining a notion of backing Nora up against the door and taking that wide mouth under his seriously enough that learning she was married would affect him so greatly?

Ridiculous. He shouldn't be thinking of her that way at all. She was an old friend who would soon walk out of his life, never to be heard from again. It was better that way. It hardly mattered whether she'd gotten married. Of course she had. A woman as stunningly beautiful and intrinsically kind as Nora Winchester wouldn't stay single.

Some of the sensual tension faded a bit. But not all. Nora's smile did interesting things to him and he didn't think he could put a halt to it if he tried.

"Belated congratulations," he offered smoothly. "I hadn't heard."

"You wouldn't have. Sean was stationed out of Fort Carson in Colorado. We got married on base, much to my mother's dismay. It was a small ceremony and it happened nearly seven years ago." She waved it off. "Ancient history. I'm a widow now, anyway."

"I'm sorry for your loss." The phrase came automatically, as he did still have a modicum of manners despite not spending much time in polite company.

But Nora—a *widow*? Dumbfounded, he zeroed in on Nora's face, seeking…something, but he had no idea what. She'd said it so matter-of-factly, as if she'd grieved and moved on. How had she done that? If it was so easy, Reid would have done the same.

The specters of Sophia and his mother still haunted him, which didn't mix well with polite company, and he doubted he'd ever be able to toss off the information that they'd passed as calmly as Nora had just informed him that her husband had died.

Death was a painful piece of his past that shouldn't be the thing he had in common with Nora. The loss of his mother and sister *should* be the reason he showed Nora the door. Nonetheless, it instantly bonded them in a way that their shared history hadn't. He wanted to explore that more. See what this breath of fresh air might do to chase away the dark, oily shadows inside, even for a few moments.

"Thank you," she said with a nod. "For the condolences and the food. I want to thank you properly, though. Maybe spend some time catching up. I'd like to hear what you've been up to. Let me take you to dinner."

That bordered on the worst idea ever conceived. He cultivated a reputation for being a loner with practiced ease, and didn't want to expose their new rapport to prying eyes. And there would be plenty if he took a woman to dinner in a small town like Chicago.

"I don't go out in public. Why don't you come back for dinner here? I live in the penthouse, one floor up. My private chef is the best in the business."

No, *that* was the worst idea ever conceived. Nora, behind closed doors. Laughing, flirting… It didn't take much to imagine where that would lead. He'd have her in his arms before the main course, hoping to find the secrets deep in Nora's soul. Especially the one that led to moving past tragedy and pain.

But the invitation was already out and he wasn't sorry he'd issued it. Though he might be before the evening was out. No one had ever crossed the threshold of his home except very select staff members who were well paid to keep their mouths shut about their boss's private domain.

That didn't stop the rampant speculation about what went on in his "lair," as he'd been told it was called. Some went so far as to guess that all sorts of illicit activity went on behind closed doors, as if he'd built some kind of pleasure den and had lured innocent young girls into his debauchery.

The truth was much darker. Racked with guilt over not being able to save his mother and Sophia, he wasn't fit for public consumption and the best way to avoid people was to stay home.

The distance he maintained between himself and the rest of the world was what kept him sane. Other people didn't get that part of his soul was missing, never to be recovered. The hole inside had been filled with a blackness he couldn't exorcise and sometimes, it bubbled up to the surface like thick, dark oil that coated everything in its path. Other people didn't understand that. And he didn't want to explain it to them.

"You don't go out in public?" Curiosity lit up her gaze. "I read that you were reclusive. I thought they were exaggerating. You being all shut up away from other people doesn't jibe with the person I once knew."

"Things change," he countered roughly. "I have a lot of money and power. People generally want a piece of both. It's easier to stay away from the masses."

His standard answer. Everyone bought it.

"Sounds very lonely." Somehow, she'd moved closer, though he hadn't thought they were all that far apart in the first place. Her wide smile warmed him in places he'd forgotten existed. Places better left out of this equation.

"Expedient." He cleared his throat. "I run a billion-dollar empire here. Not much time for socializing."

"Yet your first instinct was an invitation to dinner. Seems like you're reaching out to me."

Their gazes caught. Held. A wealth of unspoken messages zipped between them but hell if he knew what was being said. What he wanted to say.

"It's just dinner," he countered and he could tell by her expression that she didn't believe the lie any more than he did. They both knew it would be more. Maybe just a rekindling of their friendship, which felt necessary all of a sudden. Nora was someone from before his life had turned into the twisted semblance of normal that it had become.

"Oh, come on, Reid." She laughed again. "We're both adults now. After the note and the rather obvious way you shut the door half a second after I walked through it, I think it's permissible to call it a date."

He glanced at the closed office door and just as he

was about to explain that he valued his privacy—nothing more—he discovered his mouth had already curved up in a ghost of a smile, totally against his will. "A date, then."

Yet another first. Reid Chamberlain didn't date. At least not since his father had murdered the most important people in Reid's life—and Reid had been forced to reconcile that he shared a genetic bond with a monster.

Three

The dress Nora had chosen for her date with Reid—or rather the dress Eve and Gracie had bullied her into wearing—should've been be illegal.

Actually, if she moved the wrong way, it would be.

The plunging neckline hit a point well below her breasts and the fabric clung to every curve Nora had forgotten she had. Simple and black, it was more than a cocktail dress. It was a dress that said: *I'm here for what comes after dinner.*

Nora was not okay with that message. Or maybe she was. *No.* She wasn't.

"I can't wear this," she mumbled again.

"You can and you are," Eve countered. Again. "I've only worn it one time. No one will recognize it."

As if committing a fashion faux pas was the most troublesome aspect of this situation.

Part of the problem was that Nora liked the way she

looked in the dress. The other part of the problem was that Nora didn't have the luxury of sticking around for what came after dinner, if she even had a mind to be available for...*that*. She had Declan. Her son made everything ten times more complicated, even what should have been a simple dinner with an old friend.

A friend whose very gaze had touched places inside her that she hadn't known existed. Until now, she hadn't realized how very good it felt to be the object of a man's interest. Sean had loved her and of course had paid attention to her, but this was something else. Something with a tinge of wicked. Purely sexual. It was exhilarating and frightening at the same time.

She practiced walking in front of the full-length mirror affixed to the closet in the master suite of her father's guesthouse. Yep. If she stumbled, her bare nipples would peek out with a big ole hello. So she wouldn't stumble.

Eve fastened a jewel-encrusted drop necklace around Nora's neck. "Perfect. It draws attention exactly where it should. To your neckline."

"It's like a big arrow that points to my boobs." Nora tried to shorten the chain but Eve took the necklace out of her hands and let the stone fall back into place in the valley between her breasts.

"Yes. This is not a date with a guy you met at church," Eve advised her. "Reid Chamberlain has a well-earned reputation. He doesn't invite women into his private domain. What few he's spent time with are very hush-hush about it, and it doesn't take a rocket scientist to figure out that he's giving these women a ride worth keeping their mouths shut over. You are beautiful and have something to offer. Make him aware of it and then make him work for it."

Gracie nodded as Nora swallowed. "It's not like that. We're old friends."

Eve took a flatiron from the vanity to their right and fussed a bit more with Nora's hair. "Yeah, well, I've known Reid a long time and he's never asked me to dinner."

Eve and Reid hadn't been friends, though.

Nora's history with Reid gave her one up on all these other women whom he *hadn't* asked on a date. When Nora had labeled it as such, she'd hoped that would dispel some of the confusion. It was always better to call a spade a spade, and it was clear—to her at least—that there was something simmering between herself and Reid. And dinner was A Date, she had no doubt.

Nora didn't date. She hadn't dated anyone since she'd met Sean nearly ten years ago. The only reason she had even agreed to this one was because Reid was a friend. It afforded her a measure of comfort to think about jumping back into the pool with someone she knew. Someone she'd always had a crush on.

Except the way he looked at her… She shivered. There was a lot more than friendship in his dark, enigmatic gaze. Tonight was a chance to finally see what it was like to be with Reid and not think of him as "just" a friend. The real question was whether she'd act on the undercurrents or chicken out. Nora hadn't had sex in over two years. What if she'd forgotten how?

"Reid is not some mysterious guy with a shady reputation," Nora insisted, but it was mostly to convince herself.

He *was* different. She'd definitely noticed that earlier today. Darker, more layered. But she'd gotten the distinct impression he needed to connect with someone—*her*. Perhaps for the same reason she'd agreed to the date in the first place. They had a history. Being in his presence today had brought back some good memories. No reason that couldn't continue.

"Nora, honey, you've been away from Chicago for a long time." Eve wrangled the same lock of hair until she got it the way she wanted it. "Trust me, I've crossed paths with him a few times now that I'm taking a more active role in the inner workings of Elite. He was short with me, all business. He's like that with everyone. Except you, I guess."

"He runs a billion-dollar company," Nora said faintly. "You of all people should know that means you can't be Mr. Pushover, especially not in meetings."

Gracie shook her head and added, "Just be careful. The girl who does my nails is convinced he pays off the women he dates. Word is that he's got some very unusual…tastes. Things he prefers in the bedroom. Things that are not fit to be discussed among polite company. That's why they never talk about it. They're well paid to keep quiet and probably don't want anyone to know they participated."

"That's just speculation," Nora scoffed as her pulse jumped.

What kind of things? Unfortunately, she had a good enough imagination and some of what she envisioned couldn't be unseen. It was a delicious panorama of poses, featuring Reid Chamberlain in splendorous, naked glory. Not that she'd ever seen him without clothes, but Reid was devastating and gorgeous in a suit. It wasn't a stretch to assume he'd look good out of one, too. Throw in this new dark and mysterious side? It only added to his appeal. And heightened her nerves.

"Besides, it's dinner between old friends," Nora continued, her voice growing stronger as her resolve solidified. Whatever his predilections were in the bedroom, she'd probably never find out. "That's all. I'm a mom. We don't incite men's fantasies."

And she had to keep Declan forefront in her thoughts. There were no grown-up sleepovers in her future, not when she had a two-year-old who still woke up calling for mama in the middle of the night. This was a thank-you dinner, nothing more. An escape from her father's scary health problems and the scandal of the inheritance drama.

Eve's brows quirked as she spun Nora to face the mirror. "Honey, that body is every inch a man's fantasy, and by the way, you're a strong, entertaining woman. A man can and will be as attracted to what's up here—" she tapped Nora's temple "—as by what's down here."

All three Winchester sisters followed Eve's gesture as she indicated Nora's torso. Even Nora couldn't argue that the dress did highlight her curves. Nor could she argue that any man who was worth her time would be attracted to her brain.

"Regardless, I'll be home by ten," Nora promised. "Ten thirty at the latest."

She kissed Declan and left him in Gracie's capable hands. They settled in to watch cartoons, waving to Nora as she left, nervous as ever.

On the way over to the Metropol, Nora sat ramrod straight in her seat, too edgy to relax. The driver didn't try to talk to her, which was a blessing.

Her imagination went into overdrive again. If Reid did have unusual tastes…did that automatically mean she'd say no? The thought of being a bit more adventurous than normal with someone she trusted got her a little hot and bothered. Because of course Reid was still Reid. There was nothing anyone could say to convince her that he'd turned into a monster who incited women into submitting to his twisted sexual practices.

Besides, her heart belonged to Sean. Anything that took place with Reid could be left behind once she went home to Colorado. It was freeing to not have the slightest worry about what might happen in the future.

When the concierge snapped for a bellboy to escort her to the penthouse—a different bellboy from last time—she forgot to breathe for a moment as the elevator doors slid shut. This was a one-way ticket to something she had no idea if she was *really* ready for.

You're being silly. You have no idea if the rumors are true. No idea if Reid even planned to do anything more than eat dinner. Also? He wasn't going to hold her prisoner. If she didn't like where the evening was headed, all she had to do was leave.

Of course, there was always the possibility that she would be on board with more than dinner. Maybe. The jury was still out.

The elevator doors parted, leading to a small alcove with a dazzling white marble floor. She stepped out and faced a closed unmarked door directly opposite the elevator.

"Have a good night, ma'am." With a silent swoosh of the elevator doors, the bellhop disappeared and then there was nothing left to do but knock.

Except the door opened before she could. Reid stood on the other side, wearing a different suit from earlier. This one had more closely cut lines and a darker hue and showcased his broad shoulders in a way she couldn't quite ignore. His jaw was shadowed with stubble that lent his handsome face a dangerous edge. Or perhaps she was imagining the edge after her conversation with Grace and Eve.

"Hi, Reid." Her voice came out all breathless and excited, turning the short phrase into something else entirely.

His gaze slowly traveled down her length, stopping every so often as if he'd run across something worthy of further examination. She felt the heat rise in her exposed chest but she refused to cover herself by crossing her arms. Still, her muscles flexed to do exactly that three times in a row.

"That dress was worth waiting for," he finally said, his voice as smooth as it had been earlier.

"Waiting for?" She scowled to cover her excitement. Two seconds in and he was already starting the seduction part of the evening, was he? "I wasn't late. I'm right on time."

His dark eyes took on a tinge of amusement, but his smile still hadn't returned. "By my count, I've been waiting fifteen years."

Oh, my. She fell into the possibilities of that statement with a big splat. Had he harbored secret feelings for her way back, as she had for him?

That couldn't be what he meant. He hadn't exactly been sitting around pining over her. "What are you talking about? You forgot I existed the second you turned sixteen and your parents gave you that Porsche for your birthday."

He crossed his arms and leaned on the door frame. "Would you like to continue this argument over a drink, or stay in the hall?"

"You haven't invited me in yet."

"I was busy."

He gave her another sweeping once-over that pulled at her core. And still, he didn't step aside to allow her to enter his private domain.

She could not get a handle on him, and only part of that stemmed from her sisters' warnings swirling around in the back of her mind. He'd invited her here, yet didn't seem to know what to do with her. Maybe she should help him out.

"Well, I'm thirsty," she informed him with a touch of frost. "So I choose the drink over the hall. You must not entertain much or you'd have already poured me a glass of wine."

A ghost of a smile played at his lips. "Forgive me, then. I *don't* entertain often and my manners are atrocious. Please come in, Ms. O'Malley."

With that, he stepped aside and swept his hand out. Clearly, she was supposed to take it. So she did.

The moment their flesh connected, awareness sizzled across her skin, raising goose bumps. A bit overwhelmed, she let him lead her into his penthouse.

With a whisper, the door shut behind her, closing her off from the world. And then she saw Chicago lit for the night beyond the glass wall at the edge of Reid's enormous living room.

"Oh," she gasped and his hand tightened on hers. "That's an amazing view."

Neon and stars, glass and steel, as far as the eye could see. The world was still out there, but they were insulated from it up here, high above the masses.

"I totally agree," he said quietly and she glanced at him.

His gaze, hot and heavy, was locked on her. Unblinking. Unsettling.

"You're not even looking." And then she realized what he meant and heat flushed her nearly exposed breasts again. "Um, didn't you promise me a drink?"

"I did. Come with me."

Apparently loath to let go of her hand, he led her to a wet bar where an uncorked bottle of wine stood next to two wineglasses. From that vantage point, she could see into the dining room, where a long table was set for two.

"Your servants have been busy," she commented as he finally dropped her hand to pour the red wine, filling each glass far past the line she'd have said would be an acceptable amount for a lightweight drinker such as herself.

But then, Reid didn't really know that about her.

"I gave my servants the night off." He handed her a glass and when she took it, he held his up in a quick toast. "To old friends."

She nodded and tossed back a healthy swallow. How she got the wine down her throat was beyond her; he hadn't taken his eyes off her once since she'd walked through the door and her self-consciousness was so thick you could cut it with a knife.

They were alone in this penthouse where no one could enter unless they had a special key for the elevator. Blessedly, deliciously *alone*. Should she be frightened? She wasn't.

Reid had gone to some trouble in anticipation of her arrival. The ambiance was sensual, edgy and quite delicious. All hard things to come by as a widowed single mom. Maybe she was far more wicked than she should be, but Reid made her feel beautiful and desirable and she wasn't going to apologize for liking it.

"Tell me something," she said impulsively, suddenly interested in picking up the thread of their conversation from the hallway. "You said you'd been waiting fifteen years for me to show up. What did you mean?"

He cocked his head, tossing a few curls into disarray, and she liked that he wasn't one of those men who used a ton of hair products. She could slide her fingers through his hair easily.

The thought warmed her further. That would be bold, indeed, if she just reached out and touched him. But that didn't mean she couldn't—or wouldn't—do it.

"Our friendship means something to me. I…didn't ever tell you that."

"Oh." A bit thunderstruck, she stared at him as the lines around his mouth grew deeper, expressing more than what his words had. Was he disappointed that he'd never told her for some reason? "That's okay, Reid. We developed other friendships and went on."

"You did. I didn't."

His cryptic words perplexed her. "You mean you didn't make other friends? But you were always with the popular crowd, piling into each other's cars after school and leaving dances or football games together to go someplace more exciting. Or at least that's always how I imagined it."

Reid shrugged slightly. "I passed the time with them. That's all."

Things weren't as they appeared back when they'd been in high school? Her heart turned over with a squish. "Sounds like you were a recluse in training, even then."

If things weren't as they appeared back then, what's to say the same wasn't true now?

His expression darkened. "In a way. I've never had much luck connecting with people."

"Except me."

Bold. But she didn't take it back. They'd been dancing around each other and she wanted to get on with the evening, whatever that entailed.

Their gazes met and he watched her as he sipped his wine, neither confirming nor denying the statement.

Go bold or go home. It was her new mantra, one she wanted to embrace all at once.

"Is that why you invited me to dinner?" she asked with a small smile. "Because you're lonely?"

"There's a difference between being lonely and desiring to be alone," Reid countered.

"That doesn't really answer my question, now does it?"

Nora was so close, Reid could easily count the individual strands of hair—honey wheat, warm sand, a few shoots of platinum—draped over her shoulder. He suspected it would be cool to the touch if he slid a strand through his fingers.

Dinner had been a mistake.

He'd wrongly thought that he and Nora would catch up, talk a bit about the past, that it would be an innocent opportunity to reminisce about an easier time. Before his world had crashed around his feet. He'd craved that with blinding necessity.

Instead, he'd spent the ten minutes she'd been in his penthouse trying desperately to keep his hands occupied so he didn't pull her into his arms to see if she tasted as good as she smelled. To see exactly what was under that black dress that showcased a body he hadn't remembered being so difficult to ignore.

You didn't seduce an old friend the moment she crossed your threshold. It was uncivilized and smacked of the kind of thing a man with his reputation would do. He'd done his share of perpetuating the myths surrounding his wickedness, mostly because it amused him.

Nora deserved better.

The problem was he had no interest in eating. At all. He'd developed an intense fixation with the hollow between Nora's breasts, which were scarcely contained by the bits of fabric that composed her dress.

You didn't stare at an old friend's rack, no matter how clearly she was inviting you to.

There were probably some other rules he should be reciting to himself right about now, but hell if he could remember what they were.

It had been too long since he'd had a woman in his bed; that was the problem. Nora Winchester O'Malley shouldn't be the one inciting him to break that fast. If he wanted to make the evening about catching up with an old friend, that was in his power to do.

"You're right," he allowed with a nod. "I didn't answer the question. I invited you to dinner because I wanted to thank you for being a good friend to me. The scales were unbalanced."

"Oh." Disappointment shadowed her gaze but she blinked and it was gone. "So dinner was motivated by the need to say thank you. For both of us, it seems."

"It seems."

That should have dispelled the sensual, tight awareness between them. That had been his intent. But she smiled and it lit up her face, inviting him in, warming up the places inside that had been cold since the plane crash that had changed everything.

"I feel properly thanked. Do you?" she asked.

"For what?" he nearly growled as he fought to stop himself from yanking her into his arms.

"For the food, silly." Her hands fisted on her hips. "That's the whole reason I asked you to dinner, remember?"

Yes, he did. They were two old friends. Nothing more. He had to remember that her labeling it a date might not mean the same thing to her as it did to him.

"Everyone has been properly thanked." He drained his wineglass and scouted for the bottle. The bite of the aged red centered him again. "Are you ready to eat?"

"Depends on what you've got on the menu."

His gaze collided with hers and yes, she'd meant that exactly the way it sounded. Her smile slipped away as they stared at each other, evaluating, measuring, seeking. Perhaps he'd been going about this evening all wrong and the best course of action was to let their sizzling attraction explode.

But he couldn't help but think that if that happened, he'd miss out on the very thing he'd craved—friendship.

Four

Somehow, Reid dialed back his crushing desire and escorted Nora into the dining room. Maybe eating would take the edge off well enough to figure out what he wanted from this evening. And how to get it.

Since the servants had the night off, he played the proper host and served the gazpacho his chef had prepared earlier that day.

"This looks amazing, Reid," Nora commented and dug in.

A woman with a healthy appetite. Reid watched her eat out of the corner of his eye, which wasn't hard since she was sitting kitty-corner to him at the long teakwood table that he'd picked up on a trip to Bangalore.

The hard part was reminding his body that they'd moved on to dinner. It didn't seem to have gotten the message. Friendship or seduction? He had to pick a direction. Soon.

"I trust it's sufficient?" he asked without a trace of irony as Nora spooned the last bite into her candy-pink mouth. Not only had she actually eaten, she'd done it without mussing her lipstick.

That was talent. Of course, now his gaze couldn't seem to unfasten from her mouth as she nodded enthusiastically.

"So great. I'm jealous of your private chef." She sighed dramatically. "I wish I had one. I have to cook for myself, which I don't mind. But some days, it sure would be nice to pass that off to someone else."

"Why don't you hire someone?" he suggested. "It's truly worth it in the end to have control over the fat and sodium content of what goes into your body."

"When did you become a health nut?"

"When I realized I wasn't going to live forever and that every bad thing I put in my mouth would speed me on my way to the grave."

It was a throwaway comment that any man in his thirties might make, but he actually meant it. When you spent a lot of time alone, you needed a hobby. His was his health. He read as many articles and opinion pieces about longevity as he could, tailoring his workouts and eating habits around tried-and-true practices. At one point, he'd even hired a personal dietician but fired him soon after Reid had realized he knew more than the "professional."

Staying healthy was a small tribute to his late mother and sister. They'd had their lives cut short, so Reid had decided he'd live as long as he could. And he wanted to be in the best shape possible for that.

"Good point. I wish it was as simple as you make it sound." She smiled wistfully. "But my bank account doesn't allow for things like private chefs."

He did a double take. "Did something happen to your father's fortune?"

Surely not. The scandal of Carson Newport's parentage wouldn't have reached the epic proportions that it had if Sutton were broke. Word was that Newport wanted as much of Winchester's estate as he could get his hands on. Though they'd crossed paths a few times, Newport wasn't someone Reid spoke to about private matters, so he could only speculate. But he didn't think Newport was in it for the money. Vengeance, more likely. Which was a shame. Winchester had it coming, but that meant Nora would be caught up in the drama, as well.

Perhaps Newport had already gotten his mitts on Nora's share?

But she shook her head. "Oh, no. Dad's money is well intact. I just don't have any of it. Walking away from Chicago meant walking away from everything. Including my trust fund."

Reid blinked. "Really? You renounced your inheritance?"

"Really. I don't want a dime of that money. It's tainted with the blood of all the people my dad has hurt over the years anyway. Plus, money is the root of all evil, right?" She shrugged one shoulder philosophically. "I've been much happier without it."

"*Love* of money is the root of all evil," Reid automatically corrected. Nearly everyone got that quote wrong. "It's a warning against allowing money to control you. Allowing it to make you into a terrible person in order to get more."

"Is that a dig at my dad?"

It had actually been a dig at his own father, not hers. Reid contemplated her before responding truthfully. "No. But it applies."

Sutton Winchester was cut from the same cloth as John Chamberlain, no doubt. Nora's father just hadn't had the courtesy to rid the world of his evil presence the way Reid's father had. Not yet anyway.

"Oh, have you dealt with my dad, then?"

Her slight smile said she knew exactly how much of a bastard her father was, but that didn't mean she deserved the full brunt of Reid's honest opinion of the man. Whether this evening consisted of two friends reconnecting or two friends connecting in a whole new way remained to be seen, but he imagined bad-mouthing Nora's father wouldn't benefit either scenario.

"Let's just say that we've got a solid truce and as long as he stays in his corner, I stay in mine."

That was a mild and very politically correct way to put it. Because when it came to business, Winchester fought dirty. His misdeeds had included paying off a judge to rule against a Chamberlain Group rezoning request, planting a spy at a relatively high level in Reid's organization and—the pièce de résistance—attempting to poison Chamberlain Group's reputation in the media with false allegations about Reid's ties to the mob. Winchester had gall. Reid had patience, influence and money—he'd won in the end.

"Well, I'm sure my father is the poster child for what happens to people who love money more than their own family," she said without hesitation. "It's part of the reason I left. I got tired of living the life of a socialite, doing nothing more meaningful than being photographed in the latest fashion or showing up at a charity event. Money doesn't buy anything worthwhile."

He topped off both wineglasses and served the main course, cold lamb and pasta, then picked up the thread of the conversation. "When used correctly, money is a tool that makes life better."

"Doesn't seem to have done that for you," she pointed out, tilting her wineglass toward him in emphasis. "You shut yourself up in this billion-dollar prison. I've been in your presence twice now, and I have yet to see any evidence that money has made you happy."

What would she say if he agreed with her? If he said that money had done nothing but give his father the power to rip away Reid's soul? First by never being any kind of a father figure and then by taking his family with him on his journey to judgment day. The elder Chamberlain had picked his three-million-dollar Eclipse 550 as his weapon of choice, crashing the small jet deliberately and killing his wife and daughter.

Reid hadn't been on board. He'd been too busy chasing that next dollar.

Scary how alike he and his father were. You could run, but you couldn't hide from genetics. That's why Reid hadn't hesitated to say no when Nash came looking for someone to take in Sophia's twins. Reid wasn't father material. Reid was barely human material.

Money hadn't insulated him from heartache; it only afforded him the means to create what Nora called a prison. To him, it was a refuge.

"I like being alone," he finally said. "Having more money than the Bank of Switzerland allows me the luxury of kicking people out of my presence whenever I deem it necessary."

"Is that a warning?" Her smile bloomed instantly, zapping him in the gut. "Play nice or you'll see the backside of the door lickety-split?"

No, that wasn't what was on his mind, especially not when she treated him to the full force of her smile. Because now he was wondering what that mouth would feel like under his. She had to be a hell of a kisser—among other things.

"It's a fact," he said hoarsely as his throat went dry. "Take it as you will. Though in all fairness, few people ever cross the threshold in the first place, so all bets are off as to how quickly I might show you the way out."

"Hmm." Her gaze warmed as she perused him with an undisguised once-over, which raised the tension a painful notch. "So you're saying this is a bit of a unique experience?"

"Extremely."

She wasn't eating now. Neither was he. He was busy trying to keep his hands in his lap; even reaching for a fork might end up becoming a reason to abandon dinner entirely for a shot at experiencing Nora's kiss for himself.

"I've heard quite the opposite." She leaned an elbow on the table, drawing closer to him and wafting the scent of vanilla and strawberries in his direction.

That nearly pushed him over the edge. Other women smelled like thinly veiled invitations to carnal pleasures. Nora smelled like something he hadn't experienced in a very long time—innocence. He wanted her in a way he hadn't wanted anything he could recall in his life.

"Really?" he murmured. "What have you heard?"

Lies, exaggerations and wishful thinking, if it was any of the crap he knew was being passed around regarding his sex life. If she'd come here expecting an introduction to the forbidden side of pleasure, she'd leave disappointed.

"Nothing that I believed."

Her guileless blue eyes found his, warming him in a totally different way from anything she'd done thus far. "Really?"

She shrugged. "I know you. Those who are spreading rumors don't."

And perhaps that was true. They'd been friends, confidants and sometimes partners in crime. She seemed to still get him in a way no one else ever had. It thickened their connection and he liked that there was more here than just physical attraction. Liked how her innocence and strength of spirit promised to heighten their unique experiences.

All at once, he found himself in the middle of a paradox. The question here wasn't whether this evening would end in friendship or seduction, but how in the hell he'd gotten to a place where he wanted both.

Nora couldn't get over the jumpy, fluttery sensation in her stomach that Reid's intense stare produced.

Otherwise, she'd eat the exceptional lamb and pasta he'd placed in front of her instead of indulging in a third glass of wine that was probably going to get her into trouble before too long.

Because all she could think about was kissing Reid until he smiled.

He had hidden depths that he wasn't sharing with her. She could sense there was so much more behind his enigmatic brown eyes, so much pain she hoped to banish. She wanted to make him happy again. Was it so bad to be imagining that she could?

As he picked up his wineglass, she noted he hadn't eaten much, either. Too caught up in the conversation or just not hungry? Swirling the red wine, he watched it settle and then glanced at her, his gaze hot and full of something she wanted to explore. But she didn't know how to get to the next level.

"You might well be the only person in the world qualified to say you know me," he finally said, his voice huskier than normal, as if he had a catch in his throat the wine couldn't quite wash down.

She tried to laugh it off but the shock of his words wouldn't let her. "I was expecting you to argue with me. You know, say something along the lines of 'that was a long time ago.'"

"It was," he acknowledged with a tip of his head. "But not so long ago that I've forgotten how much I enjoyed our friendship. We never pulled punches with each other. I could always be honest with you about everything. We had something real that I foolishly let slip away."

Wow. That nearly knocked her flat. She'd moved on, but that didn't mean she hadn't mourned the loss of their friendship.

"It was a long time ago," she repeated inanely. "We can let bygones be bygones."

"You give me a lot of grace." He stood and held out his hand. "Since I'd like to continue the tradition of being honest, I've lost interest in eating. Come with me."

Nora's pulse rate shot into the stratosphere. Was this the part where he planned to take her up on the invitation of her dress? The part where she got to find out what came after dinner?

Only one way to find out. She reached out and clasped his hand, allowing him to draw her to her feet. Awareness bled through her, tightening her breasts and heating her from the inside out. Her knees shook a bit, causing her stilettos to wobble in the deep pile of the runner that led from the dining room to the living room, where the breathtaking view of the Chicago skyline was eclipsed only by the sheer beauty of the man lightly caressing her knuckle with his thumb.

He stopped near the window and dropped her hand

in favor of placing his palms on her shoulders. Then he positioned her directly in front of him so she faced the city. Their reflections blurred the neon lines of the buildings. She watched as he bent his head toward her neck.

"I like the picture you make," he murmured in her ear. "You and the vibrant city together."

His breath fanned across her sensitized skin, raising goose bumps and heat in an impossible mix of responses. But she couldn't have controlled her reaction if she'd tried. Okay, part of the excitement came from feeling safe, from feeling that she could trust Reid. But it also came from having those handy images from earlier pop back into her head. The X-rated ones.

His heat burned her back but she must have forgotten all the warnings she'd ever heard about staying away from fire because all she wanted to do was press backward into it. Let the power of attraction and desire sweep her away into an experience she suddenly wanted more than her next breath.

"I like you in that picture, too," she informed him. "In the spirit of being honest, I'm thinking about what that picture might look like if you kissed me."

The subtlest shift of his body toward hers was the only outward sign he gave that he'd heard what she said. Then she felt his fingers in her hair, lifting it away from her back, to be replaced with his lips at the hollow of her shoulder.

The shock of his kiss buckled her knees and she threw her hands up to steady herself against the window with a moan she couldn't bite back. She watched his reflection in the glass as he worked his way up the column of her throat, nibbling at her skin. She let her head list to the side to give him better access, but couldn't stop watching their reflections.

It was stimulating. Unreal. Unique.

He flattened his palms against her arms, sliding them upward until they covered her hands, pinning them against the glass. His torso aligned with her back and his hips nestled against her backside, nudging his thick erection into place at the small of her back.

Oh, my. That hard length spoke of his intent. If she wasn't ready for this, now would be the time to say so.

Her mouth opened. And then closed.

Didn't she deserve a night of passion with a man who made her feel alive for the first time in a long time? There was no shame in two people coming together like this, as long as everyone understood it was a fling, and nothing more. Her heart was permanently closed, but that didn't mean her body was, too.

Or was she trying to talk herself into something because she'd decided it was time to move on and had chosen Reid as the barometer of her success or failure? After all, who'd established that this was a fling? No one. They'd just had a conversation about their connection, their prior friendship and Reid's admission that he'd let her slip away, only to regret it.

"Reid," she breathed and he answered the plea with a firm full-body press that she felt all the way to her core.

One of his hands raced down her arm, tangled in her hair to cup the back of her head, turning it. And then his lips found hers. The kiss overwhelmed her, sucking her down a rabbit hole of pleasure even as her fingers curled against the glass, scrabbling for purchase against the slick surface.

There was none to be had. Reid took her deeper still, so she was even more off balance. He slowly drew her head backward as he added his tongue to the mix, licking in and out of her mouth in a sensuous rhythm that she responded to instantly, meeting him in the middle in a clash.

Obviously he didn't want to talk.

The kiss raged on as they tasted each other. The glass under her palms kept her upright, but barely, as Reid shoved a knee between her legs, his thigh rubbing near the place that needed his touch the most. The angle wasn't good enough. She arched her back, thrusting her hips backward, seeking relief for that sweet ache.

Cool air swept along her backside and she realized he'd hiked her dress up to her waist. His palm smoothed down the globe of her rear and she found enough of her brain was still functioning to be thankful Eve had talked her into a thong. The heat of his hand against her bare skin made her quake. Coupled with the friction of his thigh, she nearly came apart then.

"So responsive," he murmured, his lips moving against her collarbone as his hands explored her uncovered lower half. Helpless, she let him as sensations knifed through her.

His hand slid around to caress her abdomen and then lower and lower still, toying with the waistband of her panties until his fingers disappeared inside to cup her intimately.

She gasped as one finger slid between her folds, exactly where the flame burned the hottest.

This was all upside down and backward—literally. When making love to a woman, you started at the top and worked your way down. And you faced each other.

Reid had completely redefined seduction. She couldn't stop herself from reacting heavily to it, especially as she watched herself being pleasured in the reflection from the window. This must be what they meant when they whispered of his unusual tastes. She was an instant slave to it.

As he relentlessly drove her higher, she spiraled her hips against his hand and moaned his name. Her lids drifted shut for a brief moment until he drew off one shoulder of her dress, peeling it away from her breast. Her nipple hardened as it popped into view and he pushed her forward until it touched the glass. The shock of the cold surface against her heated flesh, coupled with his hand between her legs... It was too much.

She crested and cried out as the powerful orgasm overtook her. She would have collapsed if he hadn't snaked a hand around her waist, holding her tight against him, giving her a ringside seat to watch her half-naked reflection as she came, his fingers still deep inside her.

It was the single most erotic encounter of her admittedly tame life and she wanted more, with a fierceness she didn't recognize.

"That was amazing," he murmured in her ear as she settled. He withdrew and finally turned her in his arms to back her up against the window again.

"I think that's supposed to be my line." Breathlessly, she blinked up at him, suddenly shy now that they were facing each other. She'd just had the orgasm of her life, almost fully clothed, and he barely seemed ruffled. What had started as a ploy to get a smile out of him had swiftly become something else, something she'd been helpless to stop.

Now she wanted to return the favor. Without waiting for his okay, she curved her fingers around his jaw and pulled him down into a scorching kiss.

He met her and then some, the kiss spiraling into the stratosphere as they picked up where they'd left off a moment ago. She let her hands wander down his chest and found his waistband, then yanked his shirt from his pants so she could burrow underneath. The smooth skin of his back felt like heaven under her palms and she touched him to her heart's content.

Reid groaned into her mouth, even as he deepened the kiss, changing the angle, tongue hot and hard against hers.

Beep. The sound registered…somehow…and she pulled back from his drugging kiss. "Was that my phone?"

Reid blinked. "Mine is on silent."

Of course it was. He'd clearly set aside this evening to focus on her, but she wasn't in the position where she could do the same. Declan could be hurt or sick. Dismayed, she stared at Reid as reality came rushing back. "I'm sorry. I have to check that."

She stepped out of his arms, nearly weeping with need, not the least of which was a desire to make him feel as good as he'd done for her.

Scouting around for her clutch—which she hadn't seen in who knew how long—she finally found it at the wet bar, leaning up against the granite backsplash. She fished her phone from the depths and her heart plunged into her stomach as she saw Grace's name on the screen.

Nora had been letting her carnal side come out to play while something bad had happened to her son. A single mom shouldn't be dating, not while her kid was still so young. It was unforgivable. But then she read the text message and breathed a sigh of relief.

"Sorry," she called over her shoulder. "Declan is staying in an unfamiliar place and my sister just wanted me to know that he went down for the night without any fuss."

Thank God. Her pulse still thundered in her throat as she tapped back a quick message to Grace, noting it was nearly ten o'clock, the hour she'd said she'd be home. Grace had probably thought her timing was impeccable, that Nora was no doubt already in the car on her way back.

Good thing they'd been interrupted. This craziness with Reid—it wasn't her. She had responsibilities that she'd forgotten instantly the moment he'd touched her.

She slipped her phone back into her clutch and stood. When she faced Reid again, something had shifted in the atmosphere.

"Who's Declan?" he asked smoothly, his expression frozen into a mask she didn't recognize.

The hot, exciting man of a few moments ago had vanished. The one in its place had a hard, merciless outer shell that warned her to back off.

"Declan is my son. He's two."

Reid's expression didn't waver as a shadow fell over it. "You failed to mention that you were a mother. Deliberately?"

"What, like I was trying to hide it?" She laughed self-consciously. Hadn't she mentioned Declan? He was the light of her life. But then she and Reid hadn't really talked, not the way two old friends did who were catching up on each other's lives. "It never came up. I was married for almost five years before Sean died. We had a son together. It's relatively normal."

"Dinner was a mistake." Reid swiftly crossed to her and put an impersonal hand under her elbow, guiding her toward the door. His touch nearly made her weep— because it was so different from the way he'd touched her moments ago.

Stung, she pulled her arm free. "What's wrong with

you, Reid? I'm suddenly no longer attractive because I have a kid?"

"Yes."

He offered no further explanation as Nora stared at him, her mouth hanging open. "That's a pretty ridiculous statement. Lots of women who are very attractive have children."

"I'm not dating any of them," he countered. "Nor am I dating you. Kids are a deal-breaker."

"I didn't know we had a deal." She crossed her arms over her midsection, very much fearing she was about to throw up. "I thought we were reconnecting while I was in town. I never expected this to go any further than one or two nights, tops. What does my son have to do with that?"

Everything, apparently, but Reid had said his piece. His mouth was a firm, grim line as he extended his hand, indicating the door she was supposed to be disappearing through. The connection she'd felt, the attraction and good memories of the past, all of it fled instantly. Nora suddenly felt both cheap and ripped off at the same time.

Her Achilles' heel—vulnerability—nearly overwhelmed her. But she didn't have to take what he was dishing out. She was in charge of her destiny. This shadowy, unfathomable stranger wasn't the man she'd known once upon a time.

"Nice. I guess your reputation *is* quite overblown." She whirled and marched toward the door before he caught glimpse of the hurt that was surely spreading over her face. "Don't worry. I won't tell anyone you're too obnoxious to sleep with," she called over her shoulder, slamming the door behind her.

Five

All of Reid's employees gave him a wide berth for two days.

Which was relatively normal, but usually it was out of respect for his preference to be alone. Lately, it was to avoid his wrath as he found fault with everyone in his path.

For the fourth time since his morning coffee, Reid was confronted with yet another example of ineptitude as he exited the elevator on the forty-seventh floor. The meeting he'd just attended across town had been full of pompous blowhards who wouldn't know compromise if it bit them in their butts. Traffic had been impossible and now this—the sign in the vestibule, the one that was supposed to greet visitors, had fallen over. And not even the right way. The front lay facedown on the short pile carpet, its blank backside displaying a whole lot of nothing in the direction of the ceiling.

He stormed through the door into the reception area of Metropol's administrative office. "Mrs. Grant."

His admin glanced up from her computer. "Mr. Chamberlain."

He rolled his eyes. Mrs. Grant was the only person he'd ever allow to speak to him with that kind of snarkiness and that was only because she was irreplaceable. "Call building maintenance. The welcome sign has fallen over. And while you're on the phone with them, ask them whether they like their paychecks. It's inexcusable to have a hotel with this shoddy of an appearance. Guests can stay in a lot of hotels that aren't mine. We want them... What are you looking at?"

Mrs. Grant stared at him as if he'd grown another head. "Are you finished?"

"Just getting started," he shot back.

She tsked. "Not with maintenance, you're not. Unless you'd like to run this hotel all by yourself?"

"What are you talking about? The Metropol has a maintenance crew that employs a hundred people—"

"And those numbers will dwindle down to one surly CEO if you keep it up," she interrupted mildly. "We've already had two resignations today alone. I'm not calling maintenance, so you can forget all that bluster and nonsense. Watch and learn."

Mrs. Grant stood and skirted him, jerking her head toward the vestibule. Was everyone determined to extract their pound of his flesh? After that disappointing meeting that had been a colossal waste of his time, all he wanted to do was go to his office, where he could decompress by himself.

She pushed open the frosted glass door and held it open, refusing to budge until he followed her. With a long-suffering sigh, he did.

Pointedly, she widened her eyes as she bent over and righted the sign. "See? No maintenance crew required, Mr. Chamberlain. No small children were harmed in the fixing of this problem."

Small children. It wasn't a dig, as Mrs. Grant had no idea what had transpired between Reid and Nora two days ago. But it felt like a strong reproach of his behavior all the same.

He didn't like it. He'd been doing his level best to forget about Nora Winchester—or Nora O'Malley, or whatever she called herself these days—and the reminders were not welcome.

"You're right," he acknowledged gruffly. "I could have resolved that one myself, but the rest of the issues—"

"Are a normal part of doing business." She crossed her arms over her nondescript suit and eyed him. "What's wrong with you lately? Something's bothering you."

How did she know that? Suspicious, he eyed her back. "I have no idea what you're referring to."

"Save it, dear. You and I both know that you're a pussycat under that grumpy exterior. Someone got you all worked up and you're going to have to fix it before too long. Even you can't do it all yourself."

Want to bet?

He almost said it out loud. But that wouldn't make Mrs. Grant any less right.

He deflated under the sympathetic gaze of his admin. "Sorry. I've been a bit beastly, I admit."

"Why don't you take the rest of the day off?" she suggested. "It's nearly five anyway. I know you like to work monstrously long hours, but I promise your empire will not collapse if you leave the helm a couple of hours early."

Working long hours prevented his mind from wandering. That's when the grief crept up on him, whacking him the hardest—when he wasn't prepared.

He nodded, but only because the idea of getting out from under Mrs. Grant's all-too-shrewd gaze had a lot of appeal. "Have a good night, then."

She would handle his email and take calls on his behalf. Such was the benefit of having an admin who was so well trained; he could disappear for a few hours and she'd steer the ship in the right direction.

But when he walked in through the door of his penthouse, he caught the faintest scent of vanilla and strawberries, and the memory of Nora in his arms, as she'd looked while reflected in the window, exploded in his mind. The image of her—hot, unrestrained, pleasured—appeared as if by magic in the glass, multiplying exponentially across all the panes until she surrounded him.

Yeah, he couldn't blame his bad mood on anything except the disappointment of really connecting with Nora the other night only to find out the truth about her: she had a kid. It was fine. He preferred being alone anyway. A woman would only complicate his life to the nth degree and he didn't need that.

Grimly, he turned his back on the floor-to-ceiling windows and sought out a bottle of fifty-year-old Dalmore. The scotch burned down his throat but even the heavy scent of toffee and alcohol couldn't overpower the memories of the woman he'd nearly bedded two nights ago.

Nearly bedded, but hadn't, thanks to the fortuitous interruption that had revealed Nora's lies.

Oh, she'd had no problem mentioning she'd been married. A widow, he could deal with. A mom, he could not. And she hadn't bothered to inform him that she had a kid in tow. He couldn't handle kids, couldn't handle the guilt of not having the ability to care for one. If he'd wanted to find out how crappy of a father he'd be, he'd have taken Sophia's twins when offered the chance, thank you very much.

The scotch had done the opposite of what he'd hoped. Instead of dulling his thoughts, it sharpened them as they drifted to Phoebe and Jude. His niece and nephew were fraternal twins, but they looked a lot alike. Because they resembled Sophia.

His mood fell off a cliff.

Sick of his own company, and tired of battling the pile of remorse on his shoulders, which weighed more every day, he yanked his phone out and called Nash. His brother answered on the first ring.

"Reid. Is everything okay?"

Worry tinged Nash's voice, thickening the ever-present guilt swirling around in Reid's gut along with the scotch. Guilt that he hadn't saved his sister and mother. Guilt because Nash had stepped up where Reid had failed. Guilt over how hurt Nora had looked after Reid had unceremoniously shoved her out the door. And then he still had some guilt left over for how he'd treated his staff these past few days.

"Yeah. Does something have to be wrong for me to call?"

Nash didn't hesitate. "Uh, usually. But if this is just a random drive-by call, that's okay. How are you?"

Lonely.

Reid cursed to himself. Where the hell had that come from? Nora was not right about that. He liked being alone. Except he'd enjoyed her company. She'd made the darkness inside…bearable. More than bearable. She'd eased it. Especially when she'd kissed him, when she'd opened up, inviting him into her warmth. Disappointment about Nora's pint-sized complication didn't begin to describe it.

"I'm fine," Reid lied. "How are the twins?"

"They're three. It's an extension of the terrible twos, which apparently lasts until they're eighteen." Nash's chuckle rumbled across the line. "Gina has been threatening to put them in military school, but of course they've latched onto the idea like it's some big game. 'Will we learn how to shoot guns?' they asked. Both of them."

"Phoebe, too?" Reid fell onto the sofa that faced the view of the Sears Tower, propping the phone up against his shoulder so he could retrieve his drink from the coffee table. "That seems odd for a girl."

Nash's shrug was nearly audible over the line. "Last week, she wanted to be a ninja. Lest you forget, Sophia never cared about quote-unquote 'girl stuff.' Phoebe wants to do whatever Jude is doing. You should visit. See them for yourself."

He should. They were his blood, too, same as Sophia. But he couldn't. The twins were one more huge reminder of how he hadn't been able to be what those kids needed. How he couldn't be a father because he lacked...*something*. There was a big, gaping hole where the ability to nurture and care about other human beings should be, a hole formed by genetic predisposition and further hollowed out when the family he loved had been ripped away. No way would Reid ever care about someone again. Not to that degree.

He couldn't risk it. Not with Sophia's kids, not with Nora's. Not even with Nora herself.

"Chamberlain Group is in a transition stage, so it would be difficult to get away," he explained even as his gut churned over the fabrication. Chamberlain Group always came first, regardless of what was happening internally at his company. It was safer that way. He controlled what happened and that would never change.

"Yeah, that's what you always say." Nash spoke to someone else in the room, his voice muffled as if he'd covered the speaker with his hand. Then, more clearly, he said, "Gina says hi and wants to know if you're seeing anyone."

"What? Why would she ask that?" Reid scrambled for an explanation as to how his brother's wife would have heard about Reid's date with Nora. Had Nora told a bunch of people? Surely she wouldn't be so indiscreet. "I'm not seeing anyone and the media likes to exaggerate stories of my love life anyway. Has Gina heard something? Tell me who's talking about my—"

"Relax. She didn't hear anything in the media. I would have told you so, as I know how much you value your privacy. Gina has a friend she thought you might like and wanted to introduce you since you're not seeing someone. That's all."

Reid's conscience kicked in as he envisioned having dinner with this new woman the way he'd had dinner with Nora. A different woman would sit in that chair kitty-corner to his at the big table. A different woman would drink from his wineglass, peering up at him over the rim.

No. Those memories belonged to Nora. He never brought women home in the first place and now Nora was stamped all over his penthouse. Irrevocably. This was why being alone was better.

"That's nice. Tell her thank you, but no. I'm pretty busy right now."

"So you *are* seeing someone." Nash laughed. "I

thought your protests a minute ago were a little too ve-
hement for a simple question. Who is she?"

"I'm not." Reid sighed. Who was he kidding? He'd
been in such a bad mood because he didn't like how
things had ended. Because he'd secretly wished for a
different outcome and couldn't see a way around the
cold, hard facts. "But only because it turned out she
has a kid."

"Still sticking to that stupid rule I see. You have no
idea what you're missing out on. Kids are great and
if you like this woman, you should spend more time
with her and her child before drawing such a hard line.
What's the worst that could happen? You find out you
can't stand children and you tell her it's not working out.
But at least you tried."

"It's not that simple."

But it could have been. If he hadn't been so brutally final about motherhood being a deal breaker. If he
hadn't freaked out as he had. Things had gotten intense
and maybe he'd been looking for a way to break it up
before something happened that he couldn't take back.

No kids was his rule. But he'd wielded it like a blunt
instrument, desperate to reel back an encounter that had
exploded into something much more than he'd expected
it to be.

His guilty conscience roared to the forefront. If nothing else, he owed Nora an apology. The way he'd acted
was inexcusable, especially given that neither of them
was looking for anything permanent. Nora had even
said one, two nights tops, and she didn't live in Chicago. He'd drawn a line that didn't matter in the long
run because her kid wasn't a factor if they didn't even
live in the same city.

"Why not?" Nash asked.

"I said some things that I probably shouldn't have. She probably wouldn't even take my call."

"So don't call her," Nash advised. "Go to her with as many flowers as you can carry, tell her you're sorry you're such a jackass and then make it up to her."

Reid bit back a self-deprecating laugh. "Really? That works?"

"Gina's nodding her head so hard, it's about to fly off."

His bad mood eased a little. "Thanks. I'll try it."

Nora made him feel alive. He wanted more of that, and if he handled the apology right, maybe he could have it. What was the worst thing that could happen?

Sutton Winchester was awake.

Nora liked it better when her father was asleep. Then she could pretend the reconciliation she'd secretly hoped for when she'd decided to come back to Chicago might actually happen. When he was coherent and could speak? Forget it.

After her father had demanded to meet Declan—a first for them both—she'd patiently waited for something akin to grandfatherly love to surface. And of course she'd gotten exactly what she should have expected: a comment about how her son looked nothing like a Winchester, which was somehow the fault of her marrying someone with strong Irish genes. Then came a scolding over the fact that she hadn't cashed the six-figure check Sutton had sent her so she could educate his grandson properly. Apparently private schools offered the only acceptable education for a Winchester. And so on.

Having her hopes dashed was exhausting. And after the debacle with Reid, Nora was sick of being disappointed. Since taking control of a bad situation had become her new mantra, she'd walked out of her father's hospital room without another word, taking Declan with her.

Medical personnel dressed in scrubs rushed by on both sides as she caught her breath in the hall. Not wanting to be in the way, Nora ducked into an alcove. From this vantage point, she glimpsed a similar alcove down the way and a familiar face popped into her field of vision.

Eve. And she wasn't alone. A man occupied the alcove with her. He had his back to Nora so she couldn't be certain of his identity, but his longish blond hair and authoritative stature gave her a big clue that it was either Brooks or Graham Newport, one of Carson's twin half brothers. Nora had met them all briefly yesterday for the first time and hadn't spent enough time with the brothers to tell them apart yet.

Her sister's expression made it clear they were having a heated conversation. Intrigued, Nora watched them for a few moments. She had zero prayer of hearing what they were saying since a good fifty yards and a sea of people separated them. But their body language told an interesting story: namely, that the two were far more comfortable with each other than Nora would have guessed. Their torsos and hips nearly met at least three times in the tight alcove and neither of them seemed inclined to shift away.

What in the world? Was Eve playing coy with one of the Newport twins to get dirt on Carson? Her sister had been furious over the inheritance grab Carson had initiated. Maybe she was trying to influence whichever brother she'd cornered into getting Carson to back off. That had to be it. The sparks between the two must be her imagination.

Declan tugged on Nora's skirt and held up his chubby arms, silently asking to be picked up in his little-boy language. She complied and hugged him close. This was all that mattered. The most important thing in her universe sat encased in her arms and she'd fight to shield Declan from the evils of the world as long as she could. Men like her father would corrupt him, and men like Reid would hurt him.

So she'd keep doing this alone. Nothing had changed. Then why had dinner with Reid felt like the beginning of something different, only to have it all crash down around her?

"Sorry Grandpa turned out to be such a mean man," she murmured into his neck. "We'll figure out how to be the better person here. Somehow."

"Home," Declan told her.

"Yeah, soon," Nora promised, her heart aching at the thought of the empty house waiting for them both back in Silver Falls.

All she'd wanted from her night with Reid was companionship. A few moments of being treated like a woman again instead of a mom and widow. Over the years, he'd obviously become someone else, someone she didn't like, and she mourned the loss of her starry-eyed childhood vision of him the most.

When she stepped out of the alcove, Gracie appeared from around the corner.

"Oh, there you are," she called and halted. A harried nurse nearly plowed into her, so they both shuffled to the edge of the corridor. "I was looking for you to see if you wanted to watch a movie with me and Eve tonight. This bedside vigil is killing me. I could use a girls' night."

"Yes, absolutely." It sounded heavenly all at once, not to have to face a long evening alone. "Come to the guesthouse so I can put Declan to bed and we'll watch something there."

"Sure, that sounds great." Gracie glanced around the brightly lit hallway. "Have you seen Eve? I texted her but she hasn't responded."

"I'm here." Breathless, Eve skidded to a stop near Nora, the color in her cheeks high. "I was...um, on a conference call. What's up?"

Nora's brows lifted involuntarily at her sister's bald-faced lie, but she didn't call her on it. Instead, she tucked the information—both the cover-up and the fact that her sister had been cozying up with a member of the enemy camp—into her back pocket in case she needed it later. "Gracie and I were just organizing a movie night. You in?"

"Great, great." Eve nodded, but her gaze shifted over Nora's shoulder, obviously distracted by something. Or someone. "Eight o'clock?"

They all agreed on the time and Nora slipped away from the hospital with the excuse that Declan needed to take a nap. Which was true but Nora really needed to regroup after dealing with her father's domineering attitude.

Once she arrived at the guesthouse, Nora found herself too restless to lie down, though her body screamed with fatigue. She thought about how she should find a job when she got home. It had been nearly two years since Sean died and her dream of being a stay-at-home mom to a brood of children had died along with her husband. Before she'd married Sean, she'd dabbled in web design, but hadn't built up a freelance business worth hanging on to. Gracie was the Winchester sister with all the natural design skill, which she put to use in the fashion industry. Nora had just enough to get by. So maybe something else would present itself.

The day dragged and Nora was looking forward to movie night more than she'd have anticipated. She and her sisters had always been close before she'd left for Colorado, but they'd drifted apart as their circle of friends changed and the distance made it too difficult to spend quality time together. It was nice to pick up the threads of their relationship as if no time at all had passed.

Dinner was a somber affair for two and Declan picked at his food more so than usual.

"Eat your carrots," Nora said and nodded at the fruit snack pack she'd placed out of reach but within his line of sight as incentive. "Dessert is only for boys who finish their dinner."

"No. Now." Declan's stubborn little lip came out, signifying his Irish temper had started a slow simmer, threatening to boil over if he didn't get his way.

"Carrots. Then fruit snacks."

Nora forked her own microwavable mush into her mouth. The box might have been labeled Asian Noodles with Chicken but it sure didn't taste like much. Reid's nonchalant mention of a private chef drifted into her head. *As if.* That was just one more reason why it was better for them to have parted ways. The man had too much money and it had shaded his view of mere mortals. Not everyone got to hire staff to cater to their every whim.

If Nora had wanted to be a slave to the all-mighty dollar, she'd have taken Sutton Winchester's dirty money and lived high on the hog without a thought of the stipend the military sent her every month. To do so felt like a betrayal of Sean's sacrifice for his country. That money was hers, sent from beyond the grave by the man she'd loved.

Even though Declan exhibited more drama than a group of high school cheerleaders at prom, the carrots ultimately disappeared into her baby's mouth. Fruit snacks finally in hand, Declan calmed down. Later, he even took a bath without objection, then went straight down in his crib, leaving Nora tired but victorious.

Movie night could officially begin.

Except when she emerged from the back of the guesthouse where the bedrooms lay, she saw her phone was flashing. She had a message. It was from Eve. Have to cancel tonight.

What in the world? She texted her sister back: Hot date?

The return message came back so fast, Nora wondered if her sister had been sitting on her phone: No, of course not! Why would you think that? That's ridiculous. Gracie and I decided to stay at the hospital with Dad.

At the hospital...where whichever Newport twin she'd been having such a heated conversation with had last been spotted. Nora sent a follow-up message: Seems like the scenery there is pretty good. Sure you don't have extra motivation to stick around? Maybe in the form of a MAN?

No.

Well. That was a clipped response if she'd ever heard one, and Eve's caginess only increased Nora's curiosity. But she let it slide, too disappointed in the lost movie night to worry about it for the time being.

But why Gracie had also canceled—that remained a mystery. One Nora would like to solve. Experience told her she had a long night ahead of her, heavy with reflection and loneliness. This was when she missed having a significant other the most. She should be used to it by now, especially since she'd pretty much decided that she'd be single the rest of her life. How could she possibly ever let herself fall in love again? She couldn't. So she'd be alone by default.

Mostly, she was okay with it. But not on a night when she'd expected to have company.

Nora tapped up Grace's contact info, intending to send her a message to ask what was up, when the speaker near the front door beeped. George, her father's gatekeeper, called out, stating she had a visitor.

Relieved, Nora couldn't press the intercom button fast enough. "Yes, I'm expecting someone."

Gracie wasn't canceling after all. Eve must have been using Grace as a cover and forgotten to actually get their stories straight before their youngest sister bailed on her. Too bad. Maybe Grace had the dirt on Eve's shenanigans.

Whatever the case, Nora was happy she wasn't going to spend the evening alone. Again.

Nora swung the door open, smile in place. But it instantly slipped.

Reid Chamberlain stood on her doorstep, holding a red tricycle in one hand and what had to be five dozen of the most amazingly full and beautiful flowers she'd ever seen.

Nora blinked but the image didn't change. "What are you doing here?"

"Apologizing."

Their gazes met and he pulled her into the moment, just as he'd done the first time in his office. And the second time at his door. *Mesmerizing.* That was the only word she could come up with for his mahogany-brown eyes. A sharp, quick memory of the last time she'd seen him, of what his hands had done to her body, weakened her knees.

She straightened them, refusing to be affected. Reid was mercurial, talking about connections and friendship in one breath and then turning into an implacable wall the next. This man wanted nothing to do with her son and therefore, he wanted nothing to do with her. He was moody and morose and far too complex. She'd let him hurt Declan over her dead body.

Reid held out the tricycle. "This is for your son. If you'll accept it. No strings attached."

The fact that he'd offered that first, before the flowers, knocked away a chunk of Nora's ire, quite against her will. She took it from his outstretched hand, but she had to use both of hers. The tricycle was much heavier than it appeared and he'd been holding it one-handed. "Thank you. He'll love it and he needs activities to keep him occupied. This was a nice gesture."

"I don't make nice gestures," he reminded her. She realized that she had no idea what motivated him, what governed his thoughts, why he shifted moods like quicksilver.

She set the shiny red tricycle inside the house, just to the left of the door where it was out of the way.

"That's right." Crossing her arms over her chest to ease the ache caused by the sound of his smooth voice, she eyed him. "You must want something. What is it?"

Her body hadn't gotten the message that Reid Chamberlain wasn't on the menu, apparently.

"For you to forgive me. I behaved badly the other night. I'm sorry."

A hint of the smile she'd once craved played at his lips as he stood there waiting for her response.

"For which part? The orgasm or for kicking me out?"

The ghost smile vanished. "I would never apologize for pleasuring you. It was an experience I'll never forget. One of the best I've ever had."

Oh, my. His gaze sharpened on hers and heat arced between them as she flooded with longing. "But we didn't even get to you. We were interrupted."

As if either of them needed the reminder.

"Make no mistake. It was just as good for me as it was for you. I'd do it again, anytime, anyplace."

She shuddered. She excited him and he'd enjoyed watching her as he touched her, aroused her, awakened her. It shouldn't be so stimulating. Not when they still had so much unsaid between them.

"I don't understand why you're here," she said faintly. "You said you didn't date women with kids."

"I'm making an exception if you'll let me."

His gaze bored into hers, communicating far more than his words did. He wanted her and was willing to break his rules. Only for her. She was ashamed that her soul latched onto the lovely thought so quickly.

She had to clarify what was and wasn't happening. Before things got out of hand. Again.

"Well, I'm not making any exceptions. Not when it comes to my son. I need to understand your intentions."

She needed to understand *Reid.*

He held out the flowers and waited until she took them. Merciful heaven, they were beautiful and smelled divine. She kind of wanted to throw them on the bed and roll around in them. Maybe with Reid—*after* he assured her he'd gotten over his aversion to moms. Declan was a part of her and Reid couldn't separate her from her son even if he tried. Nor would she let him.

"I intend to apologize," he repeated. "I can also explain why I don't date women with children. And why I'm standing on your doorstep, despite that. If more comes out of the evening, that's your choice."

Her heart tumbled a little at his sincerity. In a life where she mourned the loss of choices, being given one tipped the scales.

"Come in, then. But in the interest of full disclosure, my son is here. Asleep. But very much in the house and prone to waking up in need of a drink, crackers, his frog blanket, a missing stuffed animal and quite possibly a book that he'll have to have right that minute. Sometimes all of the above."

"I'll consider myself warned."

To his credit, Reid didn't hesitate to cross the threshold when she opened the door wider in invitation. He glanced around the lavishly appointed guesthouse with apparent appreciation for the priceless art on the walls and rare marble-inlaid floor. But he didn't comment and instead turned to face her in the foyer, which suddenly got a lot smaller despite the twenty-foot ceilings.

"Your son's name—it's Declan?" he asked out of the blue. "I want to refer to him appropriately."

"Yes." As an afterthought, she added, "O'Malley." But only because Reid had her all tripped up and sideways by making such a sweet effort.

"I remember. His father was killed in the line of duty."

Since the sudden lump in her throat wasn't conducive to talking, Nora nodded. She couldn't for the life of her recall telling him that.

"That's a legacy your boy should never forget." Reid

pursed his lips. "I have some things I want to talk to you about. Do you mind if we sit down?"

"That sounds so somber." She tried to laugh it off but his expression didn't change. It almost made her wish they could slide back into the place they'd been a minute ago, when the atmosphere grew heavy with implication and attraction the longer they stared at each other. "Should I open a bottle of wine?"

He inclined his head. "Sure. A little liquid courage couldn't hurt."

"Feeling shy?" she teased, a little desperate to get things back on even ground as she crossed to the wine refrigerator behind the small bar in the great room. "Surely we're past that stage at this point."

"The wine is for you."

There came that ghost of a smile again and it did funny things to her insides. What would happen if he really let go? Did she want to find out? The last time they'd been in close proximity, she'd ended up hurt and confused. She didn't want to give Reid an opening to do that again. But after his apology and comments about Declan and his father, maybe she could trust him.

She popped the cork on the wine that she'd planned to share with Grace and Eve. At least she wasn't alone anymore. But whether that turned out to be a good thing or not remained to be seen.

Six

Reid accepted the wineglass from Nora's outstretched hand and downed a healthy sip. Despite what he'd told her, the wine was for him, too. The darkest period of his life wasn't an easy thing to spell out, but he owed her an explanation and he planned to give it to her.

Except he'd never talked to anyone about this stuff. Sure, lots of women had tried to dig into his moods and tendency to be a loner, usually with disastrous results—for them. He was more than happy to let them be disappointed. No one got to see inside him.

But for the first time, here he was about to spill his guts to a woman he'd hurt and then driven away. She should've been furious and full of righteous indignation, not settling in next to him on the leather sofa, her T-shirt stretching nicely over her gorgeous breasts.

When she'd arrived at his penthouse the other day in that little black dress, he'd had a hard time unsticking his tongue from the roof of his mouth. He'd have said that version of Nora was his favorite. He'd have been wrong.

Dressed for a night at home, Nora had a tantalizing, comfortable air about her that invited him to get cozy. He ached to take her up on that invitation. The woman vibrated with sensual, fresh energy 24/7, and he couldn't look away. Nor did he want to.

"Also in the interest of disclosure," Nora said before he could open his mouth, "I appreciate that you're leaving the direction of the evening up to me. I've become a bit of a control freak in the last little while and like to know that I'm driving the bus."

And instantly, that bit of information jump-started his libido again. He didn't mind a woman in control one iota and his imagination exploded with ideas designed to help her get there.

Starting with her on top of him—fully naked, because that was a bridge he'd yet to cross—head thrown back as she used her fingers to pleasure them both to her heart's content. Nora had painted her half-inch-long nails a whimsical purple and he couldn't stop imagining them wrapped around his erection. That picture wasn't going to work, at least not if he hoped to be honest with her instead of using sex as an excuse to avoid intimacy. Until now, that had been his usual go-to method.

"Noted." He cleared his throat. "I appreciate that the theme of the night is full disclosure. In that vein, I admit, I was upset about what I considered an omission on your part about your son."

Her brows came together as she processed that. "I didn't not tell you on purpose. It just never came up and honestly, it never occurred to me that it would be an issue. Lots of people in their thirties have kids. Personally, I'd find it more surprising to learn that a married couple didn't have kids. Wait." She reached out and placed a hand on his arm, her expression turning grave. "You *do* know how babies are made, right?"

A smile raced across his face before he could catch it and she lit up instantly. Which both aroused him and made him uncomfortable because he still didn't know if they were headed toward a reconciliation that might include sex.

He'd be happy if she accepted his apology and they acted like friends, just talking for a little while. Because he wanted that, too.

"You so rarely smile, Reid." Her hand didn't move from his arm and warmth bled through him as she talked. "I've missed it. That's one of your best features and I've always liked your smile. Do it more often."

"I would have sworn I'd permanently lost my smile." The fact that she'd dredged up something from his depths that he'd assumed was gone forever somehow made all of this easier. And harder. "I came to deliver flowers, a gift for Declan and an explanation. Smiles weren't included in the deal."

"Then I'll consider it a bonus." She sipped her wine, watching him over the rim. "What is the deal, then? You're going to give me your song and dance about how you like your freedom and a kid would only cramp your style and then what? We pick up where we left off in your penthouse?"

"Is that what you think this is about?"

She blinked but it was the only outward reaction she gave. "Of course. I'm a big girl. I can take it if kids are not your thing, as long as you're honest about it. I don't have stars in my eyes about some rosy future between us. We're hot for each other, and given the preview of what sex is going to be like between us, why dither around?"

"Because," he growled, "it's *not* like that. I'm not... There's nothing wrong with kids. It's me."

His throat tightened up so fast he couldn't breathe. A sip of wine didn't help.

"Hey."

She squeezed his arm and waited until he glanced at her before she continued.

"If it's not like that, I'm sorry." She peered up at him from under her lashes and the sincerity in her hazel eyes sucked him under. "Tell me what it's like, then. If you want to."

He wanted to. But how did you explain something so deeply flawed about yourself to another person? Nora might be the kindest person on the planet, but she wouldn't easily accept what he had to tell her. And he couldn't stand the thought of that light in her eyes being snuffed when she found out just how messed up he truly was.

No. He actually *didn't* want to tell her. He'd operated out of pure selfishness for so long, he scarcely knew how to put someone else first. But Nora deserved to know the truth.

"You heard about Sophia?" he choked out. He might as well start at the beginning.

Nora's hand froze on his arm. "No."

"She died." Blunt. There was no other way to say it. Death was always blunt. And brutal. "About two years ago. My whole family was involved in a plane crash. I was the only one not on board."

"Oh, Reid." Her eyes filled with unshed tears. "I hadn't heard. I'm so sorry."

"Nash survived. Barely."

That hardly covered the emotional angst Nash had battled when he'd awoken in the hospital, in pain and facing months of recovery, only to realize he was the sole survivor. Guilt had burdened his brother for a while. But he'd eventually gotten over it. Reid never had.

"But no one else did?" Nora asked softly and her stricken expression said she already knew the answer.

"No. Everyone is gone. Sophia had two children who weren't on board, either. Twins, a boy and a girl. Her ex-husband isn't in the picture, so her kids were essentially homeless."

Nora shook her head as the tears finally cascaded down her cheeks. "How awful for them. How old were they when it happened?"

"Babies."

His throat closed. Tiny, helpless babies, only a year old. And he'd ignored them in their most desperate hour. Never mind the turmoil he'd been thrown into while mourning the loss of his mother and sister—but not his father. The investigators at the scene had told him that the black box had recorded John Chamberlain confessing a multitude of sins and a desire to take his family to the grave with him.

Nora slid her hand down his arm, then threaded her fingers through his and clasped them tightly. He stared at their joined hands and something welled in his chest, squeezing it pleasantly. Providing wordless comfort that he didn't deserve.

He yanked his hand free before he came to rely too much on her warmth. He owed her the unvarnished truth and he wasn't close to done. "Nash and I fought about what to do. We were both single men with demanding careers. What did we know about raising kids? I... Well, we agreed we didn't want them to go to strangers, but the whole idea of becoming a father didn't sit well with me."

That was way too kind a way of putting it.

"Of course it didn't!" Nora's staunch support rang out in her tone. "You'd just lost your family, and grief is a terrible place to be in when trying to make decisions. I know. Trust me."

"No." Bleakly, he met her gaze and forced out the words that would destroy that fragile, brave sympathy in Nora's expression. "You don't know. You can't possibly understand. I abandoned them. I didn't want to be a father. I'm not loving and nurturing, nor do I have any desire to learn. My company is my life. I chose that over my sister's children and forced Nash's hand."

Nora's expression didn't change. It should have. She should have been scowling at him and blasting him with ugly words about what a horrible person he was. Because *that* would be the unvarnished truth.

Instead, she smiled as two more tears splashed down her cheeks. *Smiled*, and the smile held more understanding and grace than he could fully comprehend. Combined with her tears, it wrenched something open inside him and tears he almost couldn't contain pricked at his own eyelids.

Mortified, he blinked them back. Sorrow had no place here; he had no right to feel anything other than condemned. This was a recitation of his sins, plain and simple.

"What happened after that?" she murmured softly.

"Nash took them in," he admitted hoarsely. "He was the bigger man. I…couldn't. I'm selfish. I work eighty or ninety hours a week because my empire makes sense to me. That's why I wasn't on board the plane. I was in a meeting that I couldn't miss."

He should have been on that plane. Nash had insisted he'd tried to overpower their father with no success, but if both of them had been there, things might have turned out differently.

"Guilt is a killer," she said simply, and that nearly put him on his knees.

How had she zeroed in on that? She saw too much, understood too much. *She* was too much.

"Reid. Look at me," she commanded, and God help him, he did.

She took his wineglass and placed it next to hers on the low coffee table near the sofa. Slowly, she cupped his jaw in both of her hands and brought his lips to hers for a sweet, unending kiss that had nothing to do with sex. It was absolution.

And he didn't want it.

But he couldn't stop the freight train of his pulse as her goodness and light filled the cold places inside. Greedily, he soaked it up even as his own arms came up to encompass her, drawing her closer.

She broke off the kiss and touched his cheek with hers. "It's okay," she murmured. "I'm not going anywhere."

"You should," he said roughly even as he tightened his arms. "You should be kicking me out as unceremoniously as I did you the other night."

"Why? Because you made a decision you regret?" She tsked. "Who hasn't?"

It wasn't the same. But oh, dear God, he wanted it to be. Wanted to latch onto the simplicity of what she was trying to convey. That kind of liberty wasn't available to him. "You're making this out to be something it's not."

"Stop arguing with me!" She drew back and *now* she was scowling. "You listen to me. You are not a bad person because you didn't want to take in Sophia's children. Kids are a huge responsibility and more people should think about their capacity for parenthood before jumping into it. You want to know something? I think it's honorable that you don't let things go too far with a woman when she has a child."

Dumbfounded, he stared at her as his hands fell to the couch on either side of her. "What?"

"You heard me," she shot back fiercely. "A mom has more to think about than herself. You got that and immediately shut things down between us, even though I was all about the moment. It was nothing but fun and games to me. *You* were the bigger person in that scenario."

He shook his head but it didn't erase the spin she'd put on his actions. "That's—"

True. Yeah, he'd been selfishly thinking of himself the other night but in the end, he had found the force of will to step away, even though it had been the last thing he wanted to do. And that was the only honorable thing he'd done. "You're not listening to what I'm saying. I turned my back on my blood, on my sister. It's unforgivable."

She waved it off as if he'd admitted to taking the last cookie. "Are they being beaten at Nash's house? Starved?"

"No. He hired a great nanny and then fell in love with her. Gina is the best mom to those kids." Which was totally not the point. "I would have botched it."

"See?" She threw up her hands. "It all turned out like it should have. Some people call that fate. You, on the other hand, have moped around about it far too long."

"Moped?" Reid Chamberlain had a reputation for being dark and brooding. Reclusive and mysterious. He did not *mope*.

Her wide smile lessened a little of the sting. That mouth... He was a huge fan of it. Some guys called themselves leg men and Reid had always thought that sort of attitude was so limiting when a woman had many attributes worth praising. But he got it now. When she smiled, he felt it in his gut. He was officially a mouth man.

"Well," she murmured, smoothing a finger over one of his knuckles. "Maybe *moping* isn't the right word but you're doing something. Carrying around a lot of guilt over the plane crash and what came after, I guess. Would Sophia be angry with you for how it turned out? If she was standing in front of you right now, would she punch you in the face and tell you that you're a crappy brother?"

"Maybe." When Nora's brows snapped together in frustration, he shrugged. "Maybe not. I think she'd approve of Gina. It doesn't make me any better of a person."

It also didn't make him any less selfish or any more of the kind of guy who could be a dad. A woman like Nora wasn't for him for a lot of reasons. She deserved better. She'd skipped right over that piece of the puzzle and nothing she said could change that.

"You can't think like that."

"Like what? That it's my fault?" He shook his head with a dark, unamused chuckle. "But it is. I could have done something. I could have saved Sophia and my mom. If only I'd been there instead of at the Metropol."

What had been his passion had become his refuge. The place he hid from his crimes. The world seemed to be spinning on without him, so obviously he'd made a good decision for once to remove himself from polite society.

Sympathy flooded Nora's gaze, weighted her touch as she squeezed his fingers. "Or you could have died along with them. Also fate. Because if you had, you wouldn't be here now. With me."

Something shifted in the atmosphere as they stared at each other.

"No. I wouldn't be." But he wasn't so sure that was a good thing. While he'd hoped she'd accept his apology and then perhaps they could move on to more intimate activities, he hadn't expected that she'd uncover all his raw places with her understanding and pointed questions. "I should go."

"Don't you dare run away." Her grip tightened on his hand, pinning it to the leather cushion. "We're just getting started. I'm happy you're here, in case that wasn't abundantly clear. I don't get out much. I haven't been on a date since before Sean was deployed over two years ago. I'm enjoying this."

"You're...enjoying this? Which part? When I made you cry or when I admitted how I put my company ahead of my family? I'm a selfish workaholic who can never be a father, which means you should kick me out before I hurt you, too."

A noise of disgust burst from her throat. "Stop it. You say that like working a lot automatically makes you a bad father. Declan's dad was stationed overseas. How often do you think they would have seen each other? But we had a plan to make it work. That's what you do when you have kids. You improvise. Compromise. Figure things out. Because they're so worth it."

Nora's face had taken on a sharp, sweet expression as she talked about her son. *That's* what was missing, what Reid's DNA had skipped over when building his soul. Reid had never felt that way about Sophia's children. They were cute, sure. But he didn't love them unconditionally, the way Nora obviously felt about Declan. Sacrifice wasn't in his tool kit.

"I'm not father material," he said.

She needed to understand this before anything else happened between them. She could spin his decisions in a way that made it seem like forgiveness might be possible, but there was no happily-ever-after where he filled in the holes of her and Declan's lives.

"You underestimate yourself," she countered. "When it matters, you find a way to be more than you ever thought you could."

"Chamberlain Group comes first," he said flatly. Brutally. "I have no desire to be a father and so I didn't become one, nor do I plan to ever do so. That's why I don't date women with children. Where could it possibly go?"

Nora's mouth flattened. "You might as well say you don't date women *without* children, either, because all of them might someday want to have one, so you're out from the get-go."

That was one of his worst fears. "Fair enough. Then it might be better to describe my current state by saying I don't typically date anyone."

"Except me."

He nodded. "You are the exception in more ways than one."

"That seems quite implausible given your *reputation*. It may not be one hundred percent true but the rumors have to start somewhere." She couldn't have infused more innuendo into the statement if she'd tried. If he didn't miss his guess, the whole idea intrigued her.

Normally, the subject of his prowess in the bedroom pissed him off because it almost always came from uninformed gossipmongers who latched onto a titillating topic in hopes of spicing up their own boring lives.

With Nora, it might well be an opportunity to push the boundaries with a willing partner whom he already knew how to play like a well-tuned piano. The whole idea intrigued *him*, as well. Against all reason.

"Make no mistake." He caught her chin with his palm and guided it upward in order to meet her gaze. She didn't balk, staring him down without blinking, making him think that her spirit might be his favorite thing about her. "I have plenty of sex. A few hours of pleasure now and again is one of life's basic necessities. But I always make sure my lovers know the score and I rarely come back for seconds."

A saucy smile bloomed on her face. "So you being here tonight. Is that considered seconds?"

"Yes. And thirds."

Heat gathered in her expression as she absorbed that. Awareness built on itself, stretching the moment into a charged encounter that shouldn't have aroused him as much as it did. At least not so fast. But his body reacted of its own accord. He had a hell of an erection even as his pulse raced double time.

"I'll consider myself schooled on the score, then," she murmured. "Full disclosure. I'm not looking for anything more than a few hours of pleasure. I'm going back to Colorado soon and I won't be coming back to Chicago. Tonight, you need me. I need you. There's nothing more complicated about us than that."

So it seemed as if he'd freaked out over nothing. And now he felt like whacking himself in the head with a hammer. He'd missed out on the culmination of his dinner with Nora the other night over his own stupidity. A hot, willing woman had surrendered herself to wherever the mood took them and he'd *kicked her out*.

Being alone suited him. Mostly. Tonight it felt right to be with Nora.

* * *

When Nora had expressed a desire to better understand this complex man, she'd never dreamed she'd get her wish in such a deep and irrevocable fashion. The pain radiating from his beautiful brown eyes... It was almost too much for her to bear. Too much for her to internalize.

Because she identified with it far more easily than she wanted.

"You need me?" he repeated.

So much.

"Yes." The answer floated from her throat on a whisper. "You're not the only one who's still dealing with loss."

Wordlessly, he held out his hand and she took it. The contact sang through her, vibrating along all her nerve endings. The moment stretched as they shared a near-spiritual sense of unity. *Connection.* It had been present almost from the first but she hadn't recognized it for what it was: two souls finding each other, finding what they'd both so desperately sought. Someone to ease the pain and loneliness.

It was so much more than reconnecting with an old friend. Because neither of them was the same person as before. That was okay. Tonight, they had connected on a whole new level.

The way Reid was looking at her was...*delicious.* Nora let the feeling flow all the way down into her core, where it burst open in a heated shower of desire.

She should have been ashamed. She'd never dreamed she'd be the kind of woman who could indulge in a wicked encounter with a man she had no intention of marrying, no desire to fall in love with and no plans to even see again. But she'd not only already done that the other night, her body was gearing up to do it again.

Except when Reid reached out, cupping her cheek with one hand, his touch blew that lie to pieces. This wasn't a one-night stand with an anonymous man. It was *Reid*. As she absorbed his heat, the hugeness of what he'd shared settled over her. *She needed him*—to salve her own loneliness, to feel alive. To connect with him on a higher level than just over mutual pain.

She wanted to connect through mutual pleasure. And afterward, to know they'd helped each other heal in some small way. They had no future together, but what they experienced tonight might change their individual futures. Oh, she genuinely hoped it would.

Reid's curls begged for her fingers so she reached out to sink her fingers into them all the way to the knuckle. The moment she touched him, he came alive, reaching back, yanking her into his arms. Their lips met hungrily, without hesitation. His essence spilled into her as he kissed her. Filling her. Beating back the weight of life as together, they experienced something good and wonderful.

They both deserved the peace to be found only in each other's arms.

Except, in her mind, the pleasure scale remained completely unbalanced. She owed him one unbelievable, mind-blowing orgasm, the kind he'd dream about for several nights to come.

Masterfully, he gripped her jaw and shifted her to take the kiss deeper. His powerful, thrilling tongue worked its way farther into her mouth to claim hers, taste it. Heat engulfed her, radiating along her skin, diving under it to boil her blood. Her pulse hammered as his hand snaked under her T-shirt to fan across her bare back.

She was drowning in him, in the sensations of his

hands on her flesh, his lips on hers. Who was doing the giving here?

Before he stole her ability to think completely, she pulled away and threw one leg over his lap to straddle him and...*oh*. His hard length nudged her core and he gazed at her without speaking, his eyes hot and heavy-lidded with desire. For her.

"Better," she murmured.

His hands settled at her waist and he pulled, grinding her harder against his erection. Sparks burst at the contact point and her head tipped back automatically.

"It's getting there," he growled, and fused his lips to her throat.

First he nibbled, then sucked hard on the tender skin at her neck. There would be marks in the morning. Good. She wanted this man's brand on her body. A physical reminder that they'd shared something.

But she wasn't ready to surrender to him, to the sensations she knew were in store for her at his hands. Somehow, she pulled his mouth from the hollow of her neck and forcefully manacled his wrists, pinning them to the couch on either side of his shoulders.

"You. Be still."

His brows rose. "Because why?"

"The other night, I was the star of the show. You were behind me and I couldn't see you in the window. This time, it's your turn. "

Intrigue filled his expression. "I'm dying to find out what that means. And how you're going to stop me from touching you as much as I please."

Challenge accepted.

Seven

Nora contemplated the man at her complete mercy. Of course, that state of affairs would last only as long as it amused him to allow such a thing. She had no illusions about whether or not he could break free of her hands if he wanted to.

But he wouldn't.

"You're going to do exactly as I say and like it," she instructed, rolling her hips forward to notch his erection deeper into her recesses. Exactly where she wanted it most. "I've had precious few things I can control in my life lately. If I say you don't get to touch me, you'll obey because you want me to be happy."

"Yes," he murmured, his voice thick with passion that made her shiver. "I do want you to be happy. What would you like me to do, then?"

It was a total turn-on to have his agreement, to have complete control over a man's body, especially one as powerful and commanding as Reid Chamberlain's. Especially one she'd dreamed about as a teenager. Of course, her harmless young fantasies had included a kiss under the mistletoe hanging from the center arch at her parents' house one Christmas. Or holding hands at a football game.

Having permission to do whatever she wanted to a man who had grown up to be sinfully gorgeous and masculine, one who had gained a reputation for unusual tastes, was a far cry from that.

It should frighten her. It didn't.

"Let me undress you," she said.

Bold, decisive. She liked it.

He held out his hands in surrender, one to each side, and she watched him as she worked on the first button. It popped free and she traced a line down his torso to the next one, delighting in the feel of his crisp chest hair against her fingertip.

His eyelids shuttered as she touched him, and that was a turn-on, too. She'd barely gotten started and she'd already pleased him. And there was more where that came from.

She spread his shirt wide, drinking in the curves and valleys of his well-defined chest, sucking in her murmur of appreciation because it sounded childish to be so impressed by a man's physique. But he was gorgeous, muscled and bronzed, as if he'd spent hours honing his body strictly for her viewing pleasure.

"I like it when you look at me," he told her unnecessarily. She could feel the evidence between her legs as his hips strained forward, seeking her hungrily.

What else might he like? She had precious little experience with men other than the one she'd been married to. Sure, they'd had a good relationship in the bedroom, but this was different.

Reid was different. And that meant she could be different, too. This was her chance to be as experimental as she wished, with no fear of judgment. No worries about where their relationship was going, whether he'd be good for Declan, none of that. Because this was one night only.

There were no rules.

It was freeing and exciting.

Pulling him forward by his shirt, she dived into a kiss with gusto.

Instantly, his hard lips softened under hers as he surrendered to her completely, allowing her to explore to her heart's content. She traced the line of his closed mouth, forcing her tongue inside, opening him wide so she could taste him. Wine and man melded together, delicious and tempting at the same time.

More. She deepened the kiss, drawing a groan from him that vibrated against her breasts. Her nipples hardened under her bra, aching to be free of the confines of her clothes. *Not yet.* This initial round was about Reid and his pleasure. Not hers.

Going on instinct alone, she broke off the kiss and yanked his shirt free from his arms, then slid to the floor between his legs. He watched her as she unbuckled his belt, and the unbanked fire raging in his gaze turned her fingers numb. Somehow she got the leather strap untangled and pulled, then worked on the button and zipper holding his pants closed.

His erection strained against the fabric and she accidentally grazed it with her fingernails. He sucked in a strangled breath, and that's when her nerves completely disappeared.

This was his turn. She had the power to make him come and she planned to.

Slowly, she drew down the zipper and then hooked the waistband of his briefs with her forefingers to slide them down just a bit, just enough. His erection sprang free, gorgeous and thick, and so close to her mouth she couldn't resist a small taste.

It pulsed under her tongue. She wrapped one hand around the base to hold him still as she took the rest between her lips. Groaning, he slid a hand to the back of her neck, holding her head in place, which thrilled her. She shut her eyes, concentrating on the flesh filling her mouth as she sucked.

His hips bucked, driving him deeper, and she worked him relentlessly, shamelessly, until he froze and uttered a guttural expletive, then came in a glorious, salty burst that left her quite pleased with herself.

She cleaned up, giving him a few minutes to collect himself, and then she settled back into a spot near him on the couch. "That was amazing."

His brown eyes filled with amusement. "I think that's my line."

Still no smile. She'd have to work on that. "Let me know when you're rested up. I've got a few more things on the agenda."

"I'm done."

Lightning quick, he hauled her into his arms and devoured her whole from the inside out with nothing more than a kiss. Lips burning against hers, his tongue demanded entry. Heat skidded across her skin as he swirled into her mouth, flesh on flesh. Relentlessly, he deepened the kiss again and again, winding his fingers through her hair to slowly draw her head backward until she was helplessly caught in his powerful embrace.

His mouth raced down her throat and cool air caressed her bare skin an instant before she realized he'd yanked her shirt and bra strap down to reveal one shoulder. The bite of his teeth as they sank into her flesh made her flinch, but then he rested the palm of his hand against her shoulder blade, soothing her as he held her in place, pleasuring her with his whole mouth.

And it was pleasurable. She had never thought her shoulder could be an erogenous zone, but she wouldn't make that mistake again. Moaning, she leaned into his lips as his tongue laved over the spot where he'd nibbled, which still smarted a bit. It was an intense experience. Unique. Much like watching herself come the other night.

The memory blasted through her, dampening the juncture between her legs. Desperate for relief, she rolled her hips against the crease of her jeans but it wasn't enough.

Reid paused long enough to notice her discomfort and with a wicked gleam in his eye, he sat back. "Don't forget, your wish is my command."

How *could* she have forgotten? If she wanted him to touch her, all she had to do was say so. With two fingers, she flicked open the button of her jeans and unzipped them. Wiggling free of her panties at the same time, she lay back on the couch. "I want that mouth on me. Here."

She rested a hand on her mound. His trademark ghost of a smile curved his lips as he swept her with a heated glance.

Wordlessly, he put a hand on each knee and pushed, opening her up. And then…she bucked as his tongue connected with her center. A thick wave of pleasure radiated outward to engulf her whole body.

Those gorgeous lips nibbled at her flesh at the same

moment he plunged his fingers into her core. Again. Deeper. He twisted his fingers inside her. Sucked at her. Higher and higher she soared as his talented mouth treated her to the hottest experience of her life.

When she came, she thrust her hips upward against his mouth and he bit down. Lightly, but enough that she felt it. The combination of sensations ripped through her, and she cried out as her vision dimmed.

Reid's fingers drew out the orgasm, draining her. Filling her. His mouth on her was the sweetest paradox. They were fully connected, yet not. She wanted more.

"Take me to your bed," he demanded hoarsely before she'd fully recovered. "I need to be inside you."

She needed that, too. *Now.*

Urgency Reid didn't recognize coiled low in his belly as he scooped up the still-quivering woman from the couch and carried her across the room. He followed Nora's breathless directions until he found the bed. Gently, he laid her out on the coverlet, fished two condoms from his back pocket and stripped.

She watched him, her gaze sensual and expectant.

With reverence, he sat her up so he could remove her T-shirt. They had a bad habit of getting way too hot, way too fast, and clothes seemed to be the least of their concerns.

No more. He wanted to see her. The creamy swell of her breasts fell loose as he unhooked her bra and he couldn't stop himself from thumbing one nipple. It felt like silk. He fondled the other one in kind and she arched her back, moaning as he circled them, squeezing gently.

"Reid," she gasped.

"Yes? Something you want?"

"You."

Nonsensical sounds poured from her throat as he sucked a pert, hard nipple into his mouth. Heaven. He rolled the tip along the ridges of his teeth. She liked it when he got a little rough, as evidenced yet again when she shifted against his lips, shoving her nipple deeper into his mouth. He liked obliging her. Her responses to the slightest bite…unbelievable.

He couldn't wait to see what else she'd like.

On a whim, he flipped her over and drew her up on her knees, shoulders down against the coverlet, her legs spread wide to reveal all her secrets.

"I want to see you," he murmured and knelt between her thighs to trace his tongue along the crease he'd so thoroughly acquainted himself with mere moments ago. But then he'd been focused on pleasuring her. This perusal was purely for his own benefit.

And it was hot. So hot, his erection flared to life again. Faster than he'd have anticipated.

Her hips rocked, pressing her folds against his mouth, and he indulged her by driving his tongue straight into her wet center. She filled his taste buds and he fingered her bud until her head was thrashing against the coverlet.

Nora was so wet for him. It was the most arousing taste he'd ever had.

"Reid, please," she sobbed, and as he was about to lose his mind anyway, he rolled on a condom and gripped her hips.

She was so gorgeous spread out like this. Her backside was legendary, lush. He watched as his tip nudged her entrance from behind and then he sank into her slick, tight center. Instantly, she accepted him to the hilt and she gasped as he held her in place, savoring the feel. Slowly, he withdrew and plunged in again, and the angle was amazing.

She was amazing.

Something snapped in his chest and spilled warmth all over him. But it wasn't the heat of lust. It was something else, and his frozen, dark places evaporated as if they'd never existed. There was only Nora.

Watching them joined like this... The image heightened the urgency of his lovemaking. He couldn't hold back and didn't have to. She met his hard, quick thrusts and then some. They came together again and again until they both cried out in tandem. As she closed around him like a snug fist, he emptied himself.

He snaked an arm around her chest and rolled, taking them both to the mattress, her hot body spooned tight against his.

He didn't let go. Might never let go. His torso heaved against her spine. Spent, he lay there unable to move, unable to collect his scattered thoughts.

How did they top *that*?

Of course, the beauty of it was that they didn't have to. He could leave and never call her again. A few hours of pleasure had been delivered, as specified.

He didn't pull away, jam his legs into his pants and scout for the exit as he had so many times in the past. Instead, he pressed his lips to Nora's temple and pulled her closer, still inside her and not the slightest bit interested in changing that. He should be. He should leave. She snuggled deeper underneath his arm, and he couldn't have pulled away if his life depended on it.

"I have another bottle of wine," she murmured. "And several chick flicks bookmarked on Netflix. Wanna watch *Bridget Jones's Diary* with me?"

"Sure." That was a mistake. What the hell was he doing agreeing to stick around?

"Really?" She half rolled and eyed him over her

shoulder as if he'd started speaking Swahili. "*Bridget Jones* isn't the kind of thing men usually go for."

He cursed. She'd expected him to leave, too. They weren't a couple who lay around post-sex and had wine, falling asleep in each other's arms. She'd probably just offered out of courtesy.

Smooth, Chamberlain. "Maybe I should take a rain check. Early meeting."

Her face fell. "Oh. I was looking forward to it. Grace and Eve canceled on me and, well… Never mind. We agreed this was—"

Capturing her wide, unsmiling mouth, he kissed her nonsense away. "Forget I mentioned anything about a rain check. I'll get the wine. You get the movie."

"Okay. Let me check on Declan. Back in a flash."

And that was how he found himself wrapped up in Nora, sitting up against pillows in her bed, watching a movie about a British woman played by an actress he'd swear wasn't British. But Nora laughed every so often, and it thrummed through his torso in a thoroughly pleasant way. He'd do it again in a heartbeat.

When the credits rolled, Nora glanced up at him. "This is the best date I've ever had."

At her sweet admission, something unfolded inside him, and he didn't know what to do with it. This had been a date? He had precious little to compare it with, but she'd been married, which meant she'd probably gone on a lot of dates with the guy she'd eventually tied the knot with. What had Reid done that was so much better?

"You need to get out more."

"Or less." She snuggled up against his chest and his arms tightened involuntarily. "I'm not a fan of crowds. Staying in like this is perfect. It's exactly what I needed."

It suited him, as well. She fit him far better than he'd

have guessed. The sex had been off the charts. No holds barred. Meaningful, when it shouldn't have been.

But that didn't change facts. The evening had been the best date of his life, too.

Too bad they weren't dating. "I should go."

She sat up. "You keep saying that. And then not doing it. In case there's any confusion, I'd be more than happy if you stayed the night."

As in *all night*? His throat pinched with something that felt a lot like panic. "That's not really my thing."

"Trust me, it's not my typical thing, either. But..." She trailed off, looking so frustrated and forlorn that he couldn't stand it.

Tipping her chin up, he forced her to meet his gaze. "What is it?"

"I just don't want to be alone. Not after the spectacular evening we've had so far." She crossed her arms over her stomach, vulnerability practically bleeding from her pores. "Stay."

"I'm not going anywhere."

The instant he said it, he wished he could take it back. What the hell was wrong with him? It was as if his brain and his vocal cords had never met. They certainly weren't on the same page.

But then she smiled and he forgot why it was a bad idea to stay. She didn't want to be alone and for the first time in a long time, neither did he. At least until she fell asleep. Then he could dash for the door without her being the wiser.

He pulled her back into his arms, content to just be with her, for now. Who could blame him, when the scent of vanilla and strawberries and sex lingered in the air? She was just as sweet dozing against his chest as she had been against his tongue when he pleasured her. He almost hated to leave. But he had to. That way, there would be no morning after, no opportunity for regret, for what-ifs, for *maybe we should think about a second date…*

Just one night. And it was over.

Reid turned off the TV and settled Nora's head against the pillow as he eased out from under her. She shifted, drawing her palm up to rest a cheek on it, but she didn't wake. He pulled the covers up over her naked form, hiding the faint marks on her shoulder and neck.

What they'd done behind closed doors was private. And he liked that he'd left her with something of a reminder that would fade into memory, just like their night together.

Which was over, he reminded himself yet again. Why was he still standing here soaking up the gorgeous vision of Nora sleeping in her bed, replete from his lovemaking? Because he wanted to curl up next to her again. Wake up with her in the morning and do it all over again.

That wasn't the deal. Nor was the deal open to alteration. It wasn't as though he'd had to talk her into one night only. She'd been the one to insist on that, which fit him to a T.

Reid went out into the living room and found his pants, underwear and shirt, but his belt was nowhere to be seen. Glancing back toward the hall that led to Nora's bedroom, he risked turning on the light in hopes of locating it.

"Mmmair. Mmmair."

What the hell was that? Reid's hand froze on the light switch he'd just flipped.

He whipped around. A tiny redheaded boy dressed in pajamas with a picture of a dinosaur on the chest stood in the dead center of the living room. Looking at him.

Reid's pulse jumped. "Um, hi."

Declan. Obviously. Reid did a mental sweep for the information he'd gleaned from Nora about her son. He liked books and blankets and was…how old? Two? Wasn't the kid too little to be wandering around in an unfamiliar house at night? By himself?

"Mmmair."

"Hey, buddy. You go on back to bed. Nothing to see here."

Not one muscle in the boy's body moved. Now what? Reid edged toward the door, eyeing it. Couldn't he still just leave? An ocean of Oriental carpet stretched between him and freedom. One small twist of the doorknob and he could—

"Mmmair."

Reid sighed. He'd be frustrated by the lack of communication, but Nora had probably drilled "Stranger Danger" into her son's head so well that he wasn't about to talk to some unfamiliar man who happened to be present in the living room at—Reid glanced at the clock on the mantel—1:45 a.m.

That's when Reid noticed the boy had tears welling up in his eyes. He cursed and then nearly bit off his tongue. You weren't supposed to talk like that around kids.

"What's wrong… Declan?"

Maybe if he called him by name, it would ease some of the tension, most of which seemed to be in Reid's legs, weighing them down. Rooting him to the spot. He couldn't leave, not now. Not in the middle of whatever crisis was going on with Nora's son. Besides, Reid couldn't walk out the door until he could be sure Declan wouldn't follow him outside or turn on the oven or order an X-rated movie with the universal remote lying on the couch.

The door was so close, and yet so far.

"Mmmair. Mmmair," Declan insisted, the tears spilling down his little face.

Nora. Nora could fix this. The kid obviously needed his mom, who could interpret this foreign, little-boy language with practiced ease.

But she was asleep. If Reid woke her up, there would be a whole…thing about whether he was going to stay the night. He couldn't do that, no matter how much he inexplicably wanted to. It wasn't fair to anyone.

Reid glanced at the door and then back at the hallway where Declan had come from. "Let's find your room, okay? We can handle that."

Wonder of wonders, Declan nodded. But he didn't move. Cautiously, Reid approached him the way he would a feral dog: hand outstretched, lots of eye contact and soothing noises.

The kid watched him unflinchingly. The moment Reid got within two feet, Declan's little arms stretched out and latched onto Reid's leg. Tight. Like a barnacle.

Oh, hell no. Reid groaned. What was he supposed to do now?

"Come on, kid. Give me a break," he muttered, wondering if it was okay to pry him off.

But he might hurt Declan. He had literally never touched a child in his life. Okay, well, not as an adult. He'd punched Nash plenty of times when they were growing up. But that was different. They'd been pretty close to the same size at the time.

Reid shook his leg. Gently. Declan did not magically detach.

"Declan." Reid waited until he looked up, and then spoke to him as he would anyone else who was being unreasonable. "You have to let go or I won't be able to walk."

Actually, that wasn't entirely true, as Reid discovered when he dragged his leg toward the hall—and Declan moved with him. So that was the secret. Reid shuffled. Declan shuffled. Eventually they got halfway down the hall, where Reid paused to get his bearings.

Which one was the kid's room? Nora's was at the end of the hall, as Reid well knew, but he'd failed to do an inventory of the rest of the house since it had never occurred to him that he'd be scouting for a place to deposit a two-year-old with stickier arms than an octopus.

Faint light spilled from one of the open doors. That seemed like a good candidate.

Reid did a few more shuffle-drag steps and peered inside the room. A white crib sat against one wall, with an antique writing desk against the adjacent wall. The floor was covered with a patchwork quilt sporting blobby animal shapes, and a night-light glowed from one of the plugs.

It looked as if the room had been repurposed for the little boy, but he didn't immediately untangle himself and toddle inside the way Reid had hoped.

"Here's your room, Declan," Reid whispered, ever mindful of Nora's open door not too far down the hall.

Declan tightened his arms. *Okay, then.* Looked like he was all in. Reid dragged Declan into the room and closed the door. "We'll just have us some men time, then."

Reid eased down onto the quilt. The moment his butt hit the ground, Declan's did, too, and he finally released his death grip. And he wasn't crying. So it was a win all the way around.

"Maybe we can get back in bed?" Reid suggested casually, eyeing the crib. How did one maneuver such a contraption? Clearly Declan had gotten out of it. Did he know how to get back in by himself?

This would be one of those times when it would be beneficial to have a manual. Reid fished his phone from his pocket and googled "How to put a baby in a crib."

Holy crap. An ungodly number of results appeared on the screen. But as he scrolled through them, most seemed to be about keeping the kid there once you got him into the thing.

"Yeah, already figured out that was a problem," he told his phone sarcastically as he thumbed past "15 Tips to Help Your Child Sleep through the Night."

Declan crawled over and peered at the screen with his head cocked, and then promptly plopped into Reid's lap, as if they'd done this a hundred times.

Reid groaned. The boy had put all his weight right on Reid's ankle bone. No problem. He could stand it. Probably. The seconds ticked by as together, they knocked out this task of reading useless articles debating the benefits of laying a baby on his back, stomach or side.

Nora's son wasn't even in the bed yet. How to position him on the mattress didn't matter a hell of a lot at this point in time.

Reid's leg started tingling. There was no helping it. He had to shift the child's weight. Dropping his phone, he gingerly gripped Declan's upper arms and pulled up, resituating his own legs, the boy's legs, and trying whatever else could be done with what felt like a fifty-pound sack of potatoes in his grip.

And then somehow, the boy half squirmed, half rolled and ended up cradled in Reid's arms. Huh. He'd have sworn Declan was too big to fit like this, but there you go. It seemed like a good next step would be standing and maybe he could ease the boy into his crib.

Should have thought of that, moron. What a simple solution.

Reid stood. Apparently he owed his personal trainer an apology for cursing the man out for the last three months over that exercise designed to hone his glutes. Reid hated that exercise. But it had worked.

He carried Declan to the crib and eased him onto the mattress. Maybe Reid should have actually paid attention to the article on the pros and cons of putting a baby on his stomach or back because hell if he knew whether this was the right way to do it.

Declan rolled and stood up, hands gripping the side of the crib. "Mmmair."

And…never mind. Reid sighed. "Seriously? Come on, lie back down. Please."

"Mmmair."

"What does that even mean?" Frustrated, Reid scowled at Declan. "Is that the name of your stuffed animal or something?"

Declan threw a leg over the side of the crib, clearly intent on repeating his escape.

"Oh, no. Not that again." Reid pushed back on Declan's leg and pointed to the mattress. "We're in the bed. We're not getting out until morning."

Which would be here much sooner than Reid would like, at this rate. If he didn't get this sorted out, he and Nora would be having a lovely conversation over coffee about how Reid had been the go-to substitute daddy during the night.

Ice coated Reid's lungs and they refused to fill with air. He wasn't father material. He'd told Nora this. And this situation was a case in point. Maybe Reid should just pretend he'd never heard Declan and get out while the getting was still good.

Declan stuck two fingers in his mouth. "Mmmair."

For whatever reason, the word sounded different than the other nine hundred times the boy had uttered it. Different enough that it was suddenly a word that had meaning. Reid frowned. "Did you have a nightmare?"

Two tears flung loose from Declan's face as he nodded. Progress. Except now everything was so much worse. A *nightmare*. As Reid had experienced his fair share of those, he fully sympathized. Poor kid. Only a heartless bastard would walk away after that kind of brave confession.

And while Reid would have labeled himself exactly that every day of the week and twice on Sunday...that little tear-filled face stabbed at something inside and there was no other recourse than to work through his reluctance. But what was Reid supposed to do?

Before he could think twice, Reid scooped the kid from his prison and stretched out on the floor, situating Declan near him on the patchwork quilt. His elbow landed somewhere in the middle of an elephant as he propped his head up on his hand.

Somehow, the words to a long-forgotten song filtered through his head. A song his mother had sung to him when he was young. Soon Reid found himself singing and stroking Declan's back. The way his own mom had done.

His throat seized up, cutting off the song midhum.

God, he missed his mother. She'd had her flaws but she'd loved Reid unconditionally and he'd forgotten what that felt like. Here on the floor with no one else but a near-mute little boy as his only witness, he let the memories flow and didn't check his monumental grief as he normally did.

Acute sadness welled up in him. It was almost too

much to bear. He had to get out of here before he became a blubbery mess. Besides, memories of his mother came part and parcel with memories of his father…which reminded Reid all over again what lurked in his DNA.

Darkness. Maybe even a deeper brand than Reid had already experienced. What if *becoming* a father brought out the worst traits of his bloodline and he found out too late? He should leave for that reason alone. No one under this roof deserved to be subjected to the murderous, suicidal tendencies that had lurked in his father's soul and surely lurked in Reid's, too.

But he forced himself to lie there with Declan until the boy fell still, his lashes flat against his cheeks and his chest rising and falling rhythmically. Surely the boy could sleep here on the floor, right? There was no way Reid could put him back in that crib, not with how clearly Declan had expressed his preference to be out of it. He'd probably wake up and climb back out again anyway.

Now he could leave with a clear conscience.

As Reid ducked out the door, he breathed deeply for the first time in what felt like a million years. It had been pure beginner's luck and only his intense desire to let Nora sleep had motivated him to succeed. No way could Reid ever deal with something like that again. It was way too intense.

Eight

What in the world?

Nora pushed open the door of Declan's room. It had been wide open when she checked on him last night before watching the movie with Reid. She always left it open so she could hear him if he called for her in the middle of the night.

Declan lay on the floor in the middle of his quilt, head pillowed on one chubby arm. Asleep.

Hands on her hips, her pulse hammering in her throat, Nora watched her son sleep. He'd started climbing out of his crib at home a couple of weeks ago but then he'd stopped and she'd—wrongly—assumed he'd had his fun doing it, then lost interest.

Guess not. He must have closed the door but how he'd done so without waking her up was baffling. It wasn't as though he could reach the doorknob, so he'd have to have pushed it shut. But she hadn't heard it, and her razor-sharp hearing had never failed her.

Good thing he hadn't come into her room last night.

Her cheeks warmed. Yeah, some of that might have traumatized Declan for life. And wouldn't that have been a disaster if Declan had run into Reid. One sight of her pint-size wonder would have sent Reid screaming for the hills.

No matter. Reid must have left well before Declan had performed his Houdini act. And that was perfect. Exactly as she'd expected. Their one night was over and she had several great memories to keep her warm for a good long while. Yeah, the sex had been *wow* and then some. No surprise there. But the way he'd made her feel…treasured. Beautiful. Exciting. That had been totally unexpected. Wonderful. Reid Chamberlain was so much more than a talented lover.

And if she'd been a little sad when she woke up and realized Reid had already left—without saying good-bye—no one had to know. She'd take that secret to the grave. She shouldn't have asked him to stay in the first place and she appreciated that Reid had figured out a way to let her save face, but not give in. Waking up together would have opened up their relationship to further speculation and there was nothing to speculate about.

Declan's eyes blinked open. "Daadee."

"What's that?"

Her son had added a new word to his vocabulary apparently. She loved the discovery process, where she got a chance to learn more about what went on in his head and communicate with this amazing little creature she'd been gifted with.

"Daadee."

"Daddy? Oh, honey." Nora shut her eyes for a blink. That was the one word she'd dreaded him learning. "Your daddy is in heaven. It's just you and me now."

A travesty. And what she wouldn't give for it to be different. But it was the cold, hard truth. If she'd loved Sean a little less or wasn't so worried about Declan being hurt by future loss, she might consider dating a nice man who could eventually fill that daddy-shaped hole in her son's heart.

After all, Declan would know Sean only from pictures. He'd never be held by his father or play baseball with his dad cheering on the sidelines. Nora had no doubt there were men out there who could love a kid who wasn't their blood. She just didn't have any interest in opening herself or her kid up for anything less than a sure thing. Which didn't exist. The odds favored an eventual breakup, more loss, more tragedy. Something other than a happily-ever-after—because that was Nora's reality.

"Daadee," Declan repeated and pointed at the door.

"Sorry, Butterbean. There's no daddy on the other side of that door."

Declan took it upon himself to make sure, doing a thorough search of the whole guesthouse, while Nora followed him, perplexed by his dogged determination. It rubbed at her the wrong way. Something had to have jump-started all of this.

Had Declan caught a glimpse of Reid last night and let his little-boy imagination go wild? Surely not. But then Nora hadn't ever brought a man around Declan. What if he had seen his mother kissing a man? Maybe he'd latched onto the idea of having a daddy of his own.

Nora's heart nearly squeezed out of her chest as Declan gave up his mysterious quest, finally plopping down on the Oriental carpet in front of the TV with a frustrated scowl. He refused to eat breakfast, refused the stuffed animals Nora tried to entertain him with, refused to watch any of his favorite shows. It was like trying to deal with a brick wall.

By 10:00 a.m., Nora was ready to pull her hair out. Her sisters had called from the hospital twice, wondering where Nora was. She'd intended to go by this morning but all the daddy talk had sidetracked her time frame.

"Okay, Butterbean. Enough with the theatrics. We're going to see Grandpa and you're going to be on your best behavior." Which was a little like telling the wind where to blow. Fruitless.

Somehow she got Mr. Impossible into the town car Eve had sent and buckled him into the car seat. Declan clutched a baggie of banana chips in lieu of breakfast, but it was food, so Nora considered it a victory.

The Chicago skyline unfolded outside the window and she was a little ashamed her eye shot straight to the twisted tower near the north end—the Metropol. Reid was inside the building somewhere. Was he thinking about their night together, remembering how amazing it was?

If so, that made two of them.

She shouldn't be thinking about him at all. He'd made it clear there was no future for them. If there was anyone more ill-suited to being that nice man who could fill the holes in her life, it was Reid Chamberlain.

Holes in *Declan's* life, she'd meant. Her own life had no holes. It was full of motherhood and dealing with her father's health problems. While she would go home eventually, she might have fudged the time frame with Reid a little bit, making it sound like she'd be jetting off in a few days, when she'd really planned to be in Chicago for the foreseeable future.

Her father was dying. She'd never forgive herself if she left without reconciling with him.

When Nora entered her father's hospital room, his eyes shifted toward her but otherwise, he didn't move.

"Hi, Dad."

Gaunt and pale, her father looked twenty years older than the picture she carried of him in her head. Cancer had aged him and it was a visual reminder that it would eventually kill him. Grief sloshed through Nora's stomach over the years of pain this man had caused. She'd missed out on having a loving father. Her son would, too, a commonality she mourned, but she'd had no control over the circumstances of Sean's death.

Sutton had made his own choices that prevented Nora's childhood from being the one she'd imagined other children getting to have. And some of those choices would prevent her son from knowing his grandfather. Some widows had supportive fathers who stepped into the gaping hole where their husbands used to be. Nora wasn't one of them.

"Nora." Her father's voice had degenerated into a gravelly growl, but it still carried a sense of authority. "You're late."

There were so many things she wanted to say in response to that, but none of them were conducive to reconciliation. So she smiled instead because that was what she did best: pretend everything was fine.

She chatted *at* her dad, not with him, because letting him get a word in edgewise gave him too much of an opening to say something horrible, mean or manipulative. Or all three. She told him about the modest house she lived in and the small town of Silver Falls that she'd moved to after Sean died because she couldn't stand living in Colorado Springs anymore, where the memories were sharpest.

Declan climbed up on Nora's lap to peer at his grandfather. "Pa."

"You may call me Grandfather," Sutton informed the boy, his brows snapping together. "Or you may refrain from addressing me."

Apparently, when correcting someone, her father had plenty of energy.

"For crying out loud, Dad. Declan is barely two." Nora stood, hauling Declan up against her hip, which got harder every day since Declan grew like a weed. "Since both of us lack the ability to meet your exacting standards, we'll do you the courtesy of removing ourselves from your presence."

Shaking so hard she feared she'd drop Declan, Nora fled the hospital room, nearly plowing into Eve outside the door.

"Where are you going?" she asked with a frown. "You've only been here for an hour."

"Don't start."

But Nora felt guilty and wondered if she'd been too hasty in dashing out of her father's hospital room. Either she wanted to reconcile—which meant accepting her father as is, poisonous personality and all—or she had to wash her hands of him.

Neither option made her feel like bursting into song Rodgers and Hammerstein–style right there in hospital corridor. She sighed.

"Okay, yeah." Nora set Declan down to give her arms a rest. She'd need her strength if she planned to continue arm wrestling with her father. "I know. We don't have long with Dad. I get it."

She marched back into the room and gritted her teeth. She lasted ninety-two minutes this time, which felt like an eternity. To Declan, too, apparently, as he had upended a tray of medical equipment, turned off the room's lights—twice—and called the nurse's station. The tittering women on the other end of the speaker didn't help. They thought talking to Declan was a riot and encouraged him to keep pushing the button as much as he liked.

Sutton, in a rare act of mercy, managed to fall asleep in the middle of the hubbub.

"I need to…" *Jump off a tall building.* Nora pinched the bridge of her nose. "Use the ladies' room. Be right back."

Eve distracted Declan by opening and closing her mirrored compact, nodding at Nora over her shoulder. "Who's that boy in there? Oh! Where did he go?"

Seeing how Declan instantly loved the game of peek-aboo, Nora decided to veer off in the opposite direction from the ladies' room and instead sought out some much-needed coffee. The lack of sleep the night before had started wearing on her.

But the reason for it—that made it all worthwhile.

Exhaustion must have had her seeing things because she could swear the cause of it had just stepped off the elevator with a stuffed horse the size of Declan under his arm.

Reid's gaze met hers across the corridor. And a slow smile spread across his face.

Her knees went weak. Oh, no. Reid had gotten under her skin when she wasn't looking.

"What are you doing here?" she whispered furiously as Reid caught up with her in the hall. Weak knees and hospital visits weren't part of the deal. Her resistance was down and there was nothing good that could come of this.

Reid pulled Nora out of the middle of the corridor and

into an alcove that afforded them a measure of privacy. "I was concerned about your father."

"Sure you were."

The irony of having recently seen Eve and one of the Newport brothers squashed into a similar alcove wasn't lost on Nora. If anyone who knew her happened by, the speculation would be rampant because this little space was scarcely big enough for one person, let alone two.

Which meant that Reid's arms obviously would fit only if he slipped them around Nora's waist. Since that was where she secretly wanted them, that worked for her, too.

His beautiful face still wore a hint of that amazing ghostly smile, and his wholly masculine scent, much stronger here in closer confines, nearly made her weep.

Somehow, her head tipped up and she landed in the middle of a sweet kiss that seemed to surprise Reid as much as it did her.

He simply held her close as the connection they'd shared last night lit up like an electrical circuit had been completed by the act of joining lips. All the angst and disappointment and hurt from the last few hours at her father's bedside melted away. The difficult morning with a stubborn two-year-old vanished instantly.

And the darkness she sometimes sensed inside Reid—that was gone, too.

This was precisely what she'd needed. *Reid.* Only him. He energized her, enlivened all her nerve endings with a tingle that she couldn't pretend was anything other than the thrill of his presence. Despite all the promises she'd elicited, from him and from herself, he'd come anyway.

It meant something to her. What, she couldn't say yet. Especially since he wasn't supposed to be here. Especially since they were all wrong for each other. Especially since she suddenly couldn't let go of him.

But he didn't deepen the kiss the way she half expected. She appreciated his discretion. They were within sight of her father's hospital room.

When Reid broke off the kiss—far too soon, in her opinion—he nuzzled her ear and she found about a hundred reasons to like that, too.

"No, really," he insisted and his breath warmed her neck. "Sutton is a fixture of Chicago business. Everyone is aware of his health situation and anyone with a pulse would be concerned. I wanted to check on him. And you. See how you were holding up."

"I'm fine."

His brows rose. "Try that on someone who didn't just spend hours learning how to read your subtle nuances, sweetheart. You can give me the real answer."

Something crumbled inside her under the dual spotlights of his brown eyes. "He's a beast, what do you expect? Cancer didn't magically make him into a nice person or a better father."

"Shh." Reid tightened his grip on her and one hand came up to cradle the back of her head as he pressed it to his shoulder.

And that's when she realized she was shaking. Of course he'd misinterpreted that as her needing comfort. But now that she was here, his shoulder was strong and she didn't mind leaning on it. It hid the fact that a couple of tears had worked their way loose and his dark suit jacket absorbed them easily.

"You were gone this morning."

Why had she brought that up? He'd left for really good reasons. None of which she could recall at this moment, but there were some.

"Yeah."

"But you came to the hospital. You don't like being in public."

"No."

His fingers tangled in her hair, stroking across her scalp, comforting her. These one-word responses weren't cutting it. Not when the ground was sliding away at her feet and she couldn't catch it. "You came for me. Why?"

He pulled back enough to capture her jaw with his hands, holding her face up so he could look into her eyes. "You know why. We're not finished. I want to see you, even if it's just for a few more days until you leave. Don't tell me to go."

No way. Her will wasn't that strong. Not with that kind of an admission. So she'd have to push him to leave on his own. "We agreed, Reid. One night. You said it yourself. Where could this possibly lead?"

He blinked and when he opened his eyes, she saw a vulnerability she didn't recognize in their depths. "We did agree. But the problem is, I don't think I can stick to it. I thought we were working through our attraction and that would be that. I've been useless at work for hours. I can't stop thinking about you. Can't we find a way to spend a few days together and *then* answer the question about where this is going to go?"

She was already shaking her head. "Reid, we've been through this. But maybe I wasn't clear enough. I have a son. He has to be at the root of all my decisions. I don't have a few days to play hooky with you while we run around like teenagers having sex in elevators."

"Well, that wasn't what I had in mind at all. But it is now."

She felt the heat rise in her cheeks. "You know what I mean."

"Yeah, but you don't know what I mean."

The corners of his mouth lifted in his ghost of a smile again. But she'd just basically told him to get lost, after he'd pleaded with her not to. Why was he forcing her to be the one making all the hard choices here? It shouldn't be like that.

"It doesn't matter what you meant. I'm a mom. You've got zero interest in kids." Nora had zero interest in finding someone permanent, even if he wanted a dozen kids. "We might as well be from different planets."

"Even if I meant I wanted to spend time with Declan, too?" Reid picked up the stuffed horse, which Nora had forgotten he'd dropped to the floor of the alcove because she was too busy leaning on his strong shoulders. Which she shouldn't have done. It was confusing her.

He was confusing her. "What are you talking about? You want to spend time with me *and* my son?"

Reid nodded as if this was the answer to all their problems. "I'm not trying to turn you into someone who's not a mom. Let me take both of you to Lincoln Park Zoo. They have giraffes. Declan might like to see them."

Oh, no. Declan couldn't be allowed to latch onto Reid as the answer to his "Daadee" quest. After the heartbreaking scene this morning, she couldn't afford to even introduce them to each other. There was no telling what her son would do with it.

"He would like that." What was wrong with her? *Say no. Right now.*

Except Reid's face transformed as he treated her to his rare megawatt smile and she forgot her own name and how to breathe.

The problem was *she* would like to spend more time with Reid, especially after he'd gone to such lengths to ask. Especially after he'd so sweetly included Declan.

Even if it was just for a couple of days, an extension of their one night. She could handle that. Probably.

"Tomorrow, then? We'll make a day of it. I'll take you both to lunch."

She nodded, though she'd have sworn she'd been about to tell him she had plans. *Oh, goodness.* What had she just agreed to?

Nora should have told Reid to take a hike when he'd accosted her at the hospital yesterday. He still didn't understand why she hadn't. It would have saved them both the trouble of ending it later on, because he knew good and well they were living on borrowed time.

No one, least of all Reid, had any illusions about what this was: he was dragging out their one night because he was too selfish to let Nora fade into memory. So selfish that he'd manipulated her into an actual date that included her son.

She should have said no.

Instead, she'd agreed to his impulsive invitation. It was insanity. And felt like the smartest thing he'd ever conceived. The best of both worlds. No one expected him to sign up for Fatherhood Duties and he got to breathe in the scent of vanilla and strawberries while easing the tension and fatigue on Nora's face.

Surreptitiously, he watched Nora as she directed his driver in how to install the car seat the man had carefully placed in the rearmost seat of Reid's limousine. It should look odd, or refuse to fit right. Obviously his driver either had experience at this sort of thing or the gods had blessed this zoo trip—because the seat went in like a charm and Nora got Declan into it with no fuss.

Which was good. Reid wiped his clammy hands on his khaki slacks. Nerves? Really?

But it made a whacked-out sort of sense that foreboding was prickling along the back of his neck. After all, he rarely went out in public. And he'd already tempted the fates by going to the hospital yesterday. Thus far, he'd escaped any sort of media attention, but the odds of that continuing, when he'd be very visible at a huge tourist attraction such as Lincoln Park Zoo, were zilch. The press would work itself into a fever pitch over this and expose Nora to the joys of Chicago's fascination with its "most mysterious bachelor," as well.

He should have thought this through a bit more.

Except then Nora settled in next to him against the creamy leather seat and brushed his thigh with hers. He pushed the negatives to the back of his mind. *What's done is done.* If the media clued in to the fact that he had invited a woman and her son on a date, so be it.

Nora handed Declan a chunky book. He took it immediately and turned it over a couple of times with a little noise of satisfaction. Could the kid read already? Somehow Reid had the impression kids learned to read when they were like five or six. Maybe Declan was one of those Mozart-genius types who would become a prodigy.

Fascinated, Reid watched as Declan stuck the corner of the book in his mouth. Ah. So he didn't actually *read* it. The book was more of a chew toy. Honestly, Reid would have batted the cardboard out of the kid's mouth with an admonishment that books were for looking at, not eating. Which showed what he knew.

"Thank you," Nora murmured to Reid.

He glanced at her, though he kind of didn't want to miss a minute of observing Nora's son so he could keep demystifying little-boy things. "We haven't even gotten to the zoo yet. Maybe Declan will hate it. You should save your thanks for later."

Nora's warm hazel eyes caught and held his, refusing to let him weasel out of her gratitude. "You gave me an alternative to sitting at the hospital, where I'm forced to watch my father die bit by bit. Anything else will be a great time by comparison, unless the giraffes try to eat us."

Reid couldn't help the smile that flashed over his face. He'd been doing a lot of that lately and couldn't seem to find a reason to stop. "Well, there are some rules on this outing."

She pursed her wide, sexy lips. "Oh, really? Rules like make sure you know where your field trip buddy is at all times?"

As if he needed a rule for that. There was no danger of losing track of her. When she did stuff like that with her mouth, she got his full attention. A Victoria's Secret model could strut by in the tiniest lingerie the company made and he'd never notice.

"Yep. That's the first rule," he replied anyway. He slipped his hand in hers and threaded their fingers together. "So we're going to hold hands the whole time just to be sure we don't lose each other."

Her touch burned his palm, heightening the awareness inside the limo. Reminding him that handholding was the extent of the intimacy available to them when a pint-size audience sat a few feet away. How did people with kids ever find time alone?

"Might be hard to push the stroller if we're holding hands," she informed him pertly. "Can't wait to see how you navigate that."

"I run a billion-dollar hotel conglomerate," he countered. "I can push a stroller and keep up with my field trip buddy at the same time."

He hoped. Actually, he'd forgotten all about the

wheeled contraption his driver had loaded into the limo's trunk. But this had been his idea; he'd figure it out.

And somewhere along the way, maybe he'd figure out what he'd hoped to accomplish with this zoo outing. He'd only been trying to take Nash's advice. No one was extending marriage proposals—nor was anyone confused about whether one was forthcoming at some point in the future. It wasn't. Reid and Nora were spending time together without any pressure, without any expectations, until one or both of them decided they were done.

Until then, it gave him a chance to be in her orbit, a place he'd discovered suited him, and also afforded Reid an opportunity to be around Declan without the white-knuckle panic that had accompanied their first interaction. If this trip to the zoo turned out to be a disaster, then Reid could in good conscience tell Nora it wasn't working out...as Nash had said.

But Reid fully intended to give it the college try, especially if he could somehow find a way to get Declan asleep and contained so he could strip Nora naked later on. The zoo trip had been designed to grease those wheels and he wasn't ashamed to admit it.

"Rule number two is everyone has to have fun," Reid advised her. "So be warned. Anyone who doesn't have fun is banished to the car."

"I'd like to know how you plan to gauge that," she said with a laugh. "Do you have a fun meter in your pocket?"

"Why so many questions?" He squeezed her hand. "You don't trust me?"

Her gaze lit on his and grew heavy with implication. With awareness. With a hundred other things that he should do something to stop. But couldn't.

"I would trust you with my life, Reid. But you'll forgive me if I'm a little skeptical about all of this. Every conversation we've ever had has included your no-kids disclaimer. So yeah, I'm hesitant to embrace the zoo wholeheartedly."

That stung more than Reid would have expected, given that it was true. But it wasn't the whole picture. "I'm…trying something new. Because you're worth it."

Her gaze warmed. "You have no idea what that does to me, do you?"

"What, telling you how special you are?" He shook his head, a little off balance at the direction of the conversation. How had things veered into the realm of significant so quickly? "I hope it makes you ready for fun because that's rule number two, if you recall. Rule number three—"

"You're not changing the subject." She rubbed a thumb over his knuckle in apparent apology for cutting him off. "Humor me. I've been on my own for a long time and then was plunged into my father's health drama. Unwillingly. You're distracting me from both, with style. I appreciate it. This is the second-best date I've ever had."

He wanted to brush it off, to deflect all the *significance* because she had it all wrong. She was the one distracting *him*, treating *him* to an escape from his everyday world where the black swirl of tragedy colored everything. But to say so would only add to the implications, which were already far too deep to ignore.

He shifted uncomfortably but didn't let go of her hand because he liked the feel of it in his. "You're far too easy to impress. Not only has this date not even started yet, I haven't begun to treat you to the date you deserve."

"Well, I can't wait for the follow-up, then. My calendar is suddenly very clear."

"Mine, too," he lied. Or rather it wouldn't be a lie

once he told Mrs. Grant to call everyone he'd ever met and tell them he was busy for the next year.

An overreaction. But warranted. The things Nora made him feel… He never wanted it to end. He was so tired of not feeling. Of being forced to bear his burdens alone. Granted, he'd brought it upon himself, but only because no one else understood. Nor did he want to burden anyone else. Nora blew all of that away.

It would suck when this ended, as it surely would, despite his wishes to the contrary.

Reid's driver pulled up to the entrance of the Lincoln Park Zoo and scurried around to the back to unload Declan's stroller, unfolding it with ease on the sidewalk. Reid waited for Nora to unbuckle the little boy from the car seat and then he helped them both out of the limo. Once Declan was seated, they rolled toward the entrance, Reid pushing the stroller, and he fully appreciated that Nora didn't make one crack about how it actually took two hands to maneuver.

Nine

The third time Declan said, "Jraff," Nora almost burst into tears.

His vocabulary had exploded the last few days. It was miraculous, considering he'd been a slow starter in the speech department. Apparently a trip to the zoo had unleashed the kid's vocal cords.

Reid strolled ahead with Declan, pointing to the black howler monkeys that Nora recalled from trips to the zoo in her youth. Of course, her father had never taken her to the zoo. Not that she was casting Reid in the father role in this scenario. But he was a man and Declan was a child. It wasn't a stretch to think how nice it was to have someone around with strong, masculine arms to push the million-pound stroller that only got heavier as the day wore on.

For goodness' sake, it wasn't just nice. She'd been doing this single-mom thing from day one and it sucked. Only she hadn't realized how hard it had been to be the sole parent until there was someone else around to pick up some of the burden. Was it so bad to wallow in it for a minute?

Reid had already done more with Declan in this one excursion than Sutton had done with Nora in the whole of her life. Her gratefulness knew no bounds. What had started out as reconnecting with an old friend had become something else. Something she hadn't seen coming. *What* that was, she couldn't say. Or rather didn't want to say. Especially when Reid laughed—*laughed*—at something Declan said.

The darkness she'd sensed in Reid from the first moment hadn't returned. It was powerful to think she might have had something to do with that.

She realized he was getting too far ahead of her. How had that happened? This was her day of fun, too, but she'd been too busy soaking in the gorgeous sight of a man pushing her baby in a stroller. The same man who had rescued her from a day of withering away at her father's bedside. Rescued her from the guilt of not trying harder to forgive.

Nora caught up and ignored the flutter in her chest when Reid glanced down at her, his brown eyes full of mirth.

"What's so funny?" she asked.

"Declan would like the monkey to henceforth be named George." Reid ruffled Declan's head as the boy craned his neck to see the people behind him. "He's rather insistent, too."

Nora smiled. "That's the name of the monkey in one of his books. Curious George. Declan can be a bit stubborn when he latches onto something. I have no idea where he gets that from."

They pushed through a knot of people outside the

primate house and Reid lit up as he saw the sign for a nearby enclosure. "Zebras. We have to go."

He took off and, breathlessly, she followed. The day was every bit as fun as Reid had commanded it to be but not because she'd done anything special to follow his rules. Reid made it that way. His phone had stayed in his pocket except for a brief thirty seconds at the tail end of lunch when he scrolled through it, but then it disappeared again. Up until that point, she hadn't even realized he'd brought it.

His sole focus had been on Declan. Surprisingly. She'd half thought he'd invented this zoo trip as a way to butter her up so she'd say yes when he tried to charm his way into her bed again. If so, she would have been happy to tip him off that no zoo was required for that. Their whole relationship centered on what happened in the bedroom…and sometimes the living room. But that didn't change facts. They were sleeping together but that was it. All she'd let it be.

Which made this whole excursion that much more mystifying.

When they finally fell into the limo, exhausted and happy at the end of a long day, Reid captured her hand again and held it tight. "Navy Pier. Tomorrow. Don't make me beg."

"What?" She stared at him, trying to make the words fit the agenda she'd swear he had, but couldn't figure out. "You want to take us to an amusement park? Tomorrow? You have work."

I have another long day at the hospital. All at once, she didn't want to go back there, not on the heels of the alternative Reid had supplied her with.

"I do not have work. Oh, I mean, I do. The hotel industry doesn't sleep, no pun intended." He flashed that gorgeous smile he seemed to pass out rather freely now, and yet it still affected her exactly as it had in the hospital corridor yesterday—as if she'd been hit in the solar plexus by a freight train. "But I don't have anything that can't wait," he continued. "You're leaving soon. I'll catch up later."

Guilt coated the back of Nora's throat. She definitely wasn't staying in Chicago. Nothing could convince her to come back to this hellhole permanently, not even the death of the man who'd made it so miserable for her. But as she'd been using her imminent departure as an excuse to push away any hint of this thing between her and Reid blossoming into something more, she should correct his assumptions.

"My schedule is pretty open-ended. I wasn't sure what was happening with Dad, so I didn't buy a return plane ticket in case…well, I ended up having to help organize a funeral." Quickly, she rushed on. "So there's no hammer going down anytime soon. You certainly don't have to take off work to entertain us."

"Nora." Reid tipped up her chin so she met his gaze squarely. "I'm not entertaining you, like you need a tour guide for the city you grew up in. Don't be so silly. I'm spending time with you and Declan because I want to."

Oh. His sincerity convinced her and since there was nothing she wanted to do less than sit at the hospital, she found herself nodding. "Then we'd love it. Right, Declan?"

He nodded drowsily, his forehead resting against the padded car seat lip. He fell asleep on the way back to her father's guesthouse and in another surprising move, Reid insisted on carrying the sleeping toddler into his room, placing him gently on the crib mattress with ease.

"You'd think you'd done that a million times," Nora

said with a laugh as soon as Reid shut the door to Declan's room.

"I might have googled it," he admitted with a chagrined expression. "I guess some people are born with the parenting gene, but I have to depend on technology to figure out how to get a kid into a crib."

"No one is born with the parenting gene. We all have to struggle through it and figure things out." Her heart tightened, wringing out some emotions she'd have sworn were dead and buried.

He'd done research on how to put a baby to bed? Reid didn't want to have anything to do with kids. Why, in all that was holy, would he have done that—unless he'd planned to be in a position to need the information? Something had changed fundamentally and she scrambled to wrap her mind around it.

"And now for my follow-up," he murmured and swept Nora up in his arms, Rhett Butler–style.

Breathless, Nora clung to his neck, but that was strictly to steady herself. There was no danger of Reid dropping her as he carried her to her bedroom without one hitch in his stride. He kicked the door behind them and placed her on the bedspread. The sudden heat in his gaze left no room for misinterpreting what he'd meant by "follow-up."

"Did you google 'getting a mom into bed,' too?" she asked with raised eyebrows, her hands fisting against the bed in search of something to hold on to as the look in his eye told her she was in for a wild ride.

"That's one I didn't have to research."

In a flash, he stripped off his khaki pants and button-down shirt, treating her to the best sight of the day—Reid in all his naked splendor. She sucked in a breath as everything went liquid inside.

Just as quickly, he got her out of her clothes and rolled her into his arms, murmuring against her neck. They'd had some pretty inventive sex thus far, and Nora geared herself up for something that could rightly be called a "follow-up."

But in another surprise after a long day of them, Reid seemed intent on something different still: slow, languorous lovemaking.

She fell into the sensations, savoring them as he kissed her long and deep, touched her everywhere with a kind of reverence. When he finally pushed into her with a maddeningly unhurried glide that threatened to drive her off the edge, the perfection of it squeezed a tear loose from her.

A *tear*. It was only sex, for crying out loud. But when she focused on Reid as he withdrew, then repeated his torturous reentry, he caught her gaze. That smile spilled over his face, transforming him from the inside out.

Transforming *her*. This wasn't old friends becoming something more. It was a spiritual joining of two people, and she couldn't hold back any longer. Her heart exploded with so many unnameable things at the same moment as her body did. Things she needed to shut down—*immediately*. But couldn't. She was lost to this man.

Reid tensed with a low groan, experiencing his own release on the heels of hers, then gathered her close as if he'd never let go.

But he had to. Eventually. Nothing lasted forever and Nora was tired of losing things. It was better to never grab onto them in the first place.

Reid knocked on the door of the Winchester guesthouse for the third time in three days.

It was a habit he'd been trying to think of a reason to break and had failed miserably. He liked Nora. She always had a quick smile, her wry sense of humor matched his and she'd learned exactly how to use that wide mouth to drive him to the brink.

Sometimes, he let her push him over the edge because it was just that amazing when she took it upon herself to pleasure him. He always made it up to her later, though, usually twice. If he played his cards right, hopefully that would be on the agenda later tonight after they made an appearance at this pesky Foundation for Education fundraiser he'd agreed to attend.

Since he was on the board—because doing charitable works for kids should assuage his guilt over his niece and nephew, and yet, did not—he felt obligated to go. And for some reason he'd yet to fathom, Nora had agreed to be his plus-one. She shouldn't have. A public appearance together at a black-tie event was sure to get the tongues of Chicago wagging. But he could imagine only Nora at his side. Which had also become a bit of a habit that he couldn't figure out how to break.

When Nora swung open the door, Reid nearly forgot how to breathe.

"Wow." That was all that he could squeeze out around the sudden lump in his throat.

"It's okay?" she asked.

She spun around, sending the floor-length skirt of her dress flowing. It was the color of deep sapphire, strapless, with little folds of fabric over her breasts that highlighted one of her best features. She'd put her hair up in a loose bun, leaving tendrils to fall around her face. A glittery collar of blue stones that matched her dress circled her throat, winking in the low light of the setting sun.

But that sparkle paled in comparison with the woman.

"No," he murmured, not quite trusting his voice. "It's the opposite of okay unless you want to skip this black-tie shindig and go lock ourselves in your bedroom for a few hours. If that was your goal—bingo."

She laughed and waved over her shoulder at her sister Grace, who was just visible beyond the foyer playing with Declan on his patchwork quilt. "We're off. Back by ten."

"As if," Grace called. "I brought an overnight bag. Don't even bother acting like you didn't see it. I'm here till morning. Don't waste the opportunity."

Well, then. Grace might have just moved into the number one spot as Reid's favorite relative of Nora's. Or maybe she shared that spot with Declan. Imagine Reid's surprise as he'd developed a fondness for the kid over the last few days.

Of course the boy still scared the bejesus out of him with his fragile little body and inability to communicate in something other than short words and phrases that were impossible to decipher. Reid spent half his time in Declan's presence making sure he didn't do something wrong, which was stressful and frustrating. But the other half of the time, the kid was amazing. Funny, inquisitive, fearless.

Nora shut the door and it was just the two of them on the front steps. Reid swallowed as the reality hit him. This wasn't an excursion to the zoo or to Navy Pier that he could blow off as spending time with an old friend and her son if anyone questioned him. Or that he could justify to himself as nothing special. This was a real date in public with Nora Winchester O'Malley on his arm. The paparazzi would be there in full force as the whole point of the fundraiser was to get publicity for the foundation. There was nowhere to hide. No excuses.

He was dating Nora. And vice versa.

Maybe going public wouldn't be as invasive as he was envisioning.

That hope smashed into little pieces as the limo snaked toward the entrance of the Field Museum. The number of people in the throng of onlookers, most armed with cameras sporting telephoto lenses, was truly frightening.

"Sure you're ready for this?" he asked Nora.

"Not really, no," she admitted. "I practiced my dance steps all day but I'm relatively hopeless. I'm probably not going to enhance your reputation any."

"Ha. That's a lie. You enhance my reputation just by being on my arm," he shot back. "And I was talking about being ready for a public splash."

He hated the idea of their privacy being invaded, their lives raked over by strangers who had never spoken two words to either of them. There would be photos flung across the internet far and wide with ridiculous captions like Reclusive Billionaire Corrupts Chicago Real Estate Mogul's Daughter.

So far, they'd managed to avoid attention but that wouldn't last forever. In fact, judging by the frenzy of the crowd as his driver pulled to the curb, parked and came around to let them out, they'd just become very visible in the public eye.

"Oh. Yeah, I'm sorry, but you're the one who's mainly affected by that. I'll go home and no one will even remember my name." She waved it off. "That was part of the draw in vacating Chicago, after all. I also removed myself from the limelight. The socialite scene wears on you. I don't miss it."

What would it be like to just walk away? That was a scenario he'd never considered—but should have. All at once, it sounded heavenly. What better way to avoid all the gossip and speculation and people he didn't want to be around than to go somewhere else?

Of course, he couldn't run his empire unless he was in the middle of it. Other people might be able to handle working remotely, but not Reid. He breathed his hotels like air and liked it.

But the idea of chucking it all stuck with him as he helped Nora from the limo and hooked her hand on his arm to tread the red carpet lining the roped-off area leading to the entrance. Flashes bathed them as a hundred photographs were snapped in under a minute. Reid was grateful when they finally made it inside the museum. All the street noise was cut off instantly.

Faint strains of Mozart piped through the great hall from hidden speakers. Two dozen tables with white cloths and tea lights had been strewn about the cavernous space; one corner housed an elephant statue and a grand piano. A couple hundred of Chicago's elite worked the room, wheeling and dealing. More money would change hands under this roof than on the whole Magnificent Mile the weekend before Christmas.

"Eve's here somewhere," Nora commented as she craned her neck to scan the crowds. "She made me promise to say hi so she could see how the dress turned out. She had it sent over."

"There she is." Reid nodded as he spied Nora's willowy sister. "Dancing with Graham Newport."

Very cozily, as a matter of fact. The dance floor had been set up a good hundred yards from the entrance, but even at that distance, Reid could see the possessive slant to Newport's hold on Eve Winchester. Surprising, given the drama going on with the Winchester fortune, that Eve would fraternize with a Newport, but she didn't seem terribly put off by the proximity of her dance partner. They were so close, you couldn't wedge a sheet of paper between them.

It looked as if Nora wasn't the only Winchester sister making a public confession about her love life this evening.

"Huh." Nora zeroed in on her sister, a speculative look in her eye. "There's something going on there, which she has thus far refused to admit to. She's being very cagey about it, but there's no way she can shrug it off now."

"Especially not if we go dance near them." Which suited Reid's purposes as well, since he had a strong need to get Nora into his arms. The scent of vanilla and strawberries was particularly alluring this evening and it had been driving him nuts since the moment they got into the limo. "Assuming you want to dance?"

Nora's wide smile answered that question.

"Sure that's Graham?" she asked as Reid took her hand to lead her to the dance floor. "I don't know the twins well enough to tell them apart."

"I do," Reid said curtly, without explanation.

He'd crossed paths with the brothers more than once; they got around. That one was Graham for sure. He had a reserved demeanor about him you couldn't miss, a wait-and-see approach that was the opposite of his brother's. Brooks had a hot head and a quick mouth that sometimes got him into trouble as he leaped without looking more often than not.

Which made it all the more perplexing that Graham

was the one making time with a Winchester sister. If there was some nefarious intent behind their interaction, Reid would have put money on Brooks being involved.

Then everything else slid away as he swept Nora into his arms and held her close.

"This is the first time we've danced," he murmured. "I like it."

"Me, too." She peered up through those matchless hazel eyes, which had gone a bit soft and warm, and everything good in the world was right here. In his grasp.

Not for the first time, his gut knotted. She would leave soon. He did *not* like that. This thing between them wasn't burning itself out and he was in a bit of a quandary over the next steps. Mostly because he didn't see any miracles popping up that would fix all the roadblocks between them.

Neither of them had any business thinking of next steps.

He was going to have to say goodbye. Soon. He flat out didn't know how he was going to do it. Usually, that was the easiest word in the English language to utter. It should have been the easiest here, too, especially given Nora's permanent plus-one.

But goodbye wasn't happening tonight. Grace had given them a pass on what time they returned, which didn't even have to be until morning. Reid intended to take full advantage of it.

Eve and Graham finally noticed Reid and Nora dancing near them, though how they'd yanked their attention away from each other was beyond him. The couple sprang apart as if they'd been caught spray painting graffiti on the Cloud Gate sculpture in Millennium Park.

"Oh, hey, Nora," Eve called and crossed her arms,

then uncrossed them to let them dangle at her sides. "I didn't know you'd arrived yet."

"Yeah, you seemed pretty busy." Nora nodded at her sister's dance partner. "Hi, Graham. Nice to see you again, especially outside of the hospital."

There was a hint of frost in Nora's voice that Reid didn't recognize. He was glad it wasn't directed at him as her warmth was one of the things he craved in the middle of the night, when he woke up, alone and freezing, after a particularly vivid nightmare about Sophia and his mom.

Eve blushed, which seemed out of place on a no-nonsense, confident woman. Even as a kid, she'd been authoritative and decisive, with a take-no-prisoners approach. He'd always admired that.

Another couple nearly collided with the now-stationary group in the center of the dance floor.

"Well, I'm headed to the bar," Eve said brightly. "Thanks for the dance, Graham."

Reid nodded to Eve and Newport as they edged away, clearly uncomfortable with the audience. But as Reid was still dancing with Nora and loath to stop, he didn't worry about the dynamics of whatever was going on with Eve and Newport.

He just wanted to soak up as much Nora as he could and worry later about the screeching halt to their relationship, which loomed on the horizon.

At dinner, he and Nora predictably ended up at a table with Eve and Graham, as well as Brooks and his date, a bombshell model from Hungary who spoke little English. Brooks and Graham scarcely noticed her lack of conversation once they got going on what appeared to be a hot topic—their opinions about Nora's father, his money and the half brother they shared with the Winchester sisters.

The rib eye and lobster weren't bad, so Reid ate his dinner and stayed out of it until Brooks mentioned that he'd called an old friend who was a lawyer to help with his case against Sutton.

Nora flushed and laid down her fork. "You called a lawyer to fight my father? What on earth for?"

"Because Winchester's up to something. When the paternity test came back negative for us, he admitted he wasn't our father but then clammed up. He knows who our father is. I need him to spill his guts," Brooks explained. "And Carson has a stake in ironing out details, too, since he's an heir. An impartial lawyer can only help both situations. We can't be too careful."

"Carson is not an 'heir,'" Eve insisted with exaggerated air quotes and a hearty scowl. "He's nowhere in Dad's will and Winchester blood doesn't automatically earn Carson the right to anything."

Nora's mouth turned down and it was clear the conversation was upsetting her. Reid squeezed her hand under the table as everyone else forgot about eating in favor of jumping into the argument full steam.

"We say differently," Graham retorted. "Our friend Josh Calhoun is stopping by here on his way home to Iowa. He's a legal expert who should be able to shed some insight and then we'll see what's what. You can't block us from getting what's rightfully ours."

"What about what's rightfully *ours*?" Eve glowered at the man she'd just been dancing with so cozily. "Carson didn't have the pleasure of growing up as a Winchester. Our dad's estate belongs to those of us who suffered for years at his hands."

Brooks nearly came out of his seat. "You don't think

Carson's suffered over Winchester's selfishness? That SOB knew he'd fathered a kid and never bothered to claim him."

"He's lucky," Eve shot back. "Some days, I wish I'd never been claimed. But trust me when I tell you that the billions Carson thinks he's due belong to me, Grace and Nora. Period."

"Stop it!" Nora pushed back from the table and stood as the other diners at nearby tables began to murmur about the drama. "Fighting like this doesn't solve any-thing. We can't stop you from getting additional legal help, so you boys do what you think you need to do. But leave me out of it. It's only money and I don't want any of it."

With that, Nora spun and fled the hall. Reid nodded to the other stunned guests and followed her. He found her in the lobby, huddled in a corner. When he gathered her up in his arms, his stomach clenched as the tears running down her cheeks caught the light.

But then she clung to him and gave a soft little sigh that thrummed through him, winnowing under his skin, making everything better just because they were to-gether. A dangerous fullness in his chest spread and it felt so good, he couldn't find a reason to stop it.

"I hate to ask, but would you mind if we left?" Her voice was muffled against his shoulder. "I know my family is ruining your party, but—"

"No one's ruining anything," he broke in. "If you want to leave, we're leaving."

He was the last person to argue with the idea of get-ting the hell out of Dodge, especially when the flip side meant that he got to have Nora all to himself. This surely wasn't his scene and if anyone didn't like that he'd left early, they could make an appointment during business hours for some time in the next century to complain about it.

"Thanks." She took a deep, shuddery breath and flashed a watery smile. "You've developed a habit of rescuing me from bad situations. I've kind of grown fond of it."

"I'm happy to be your knight in shining armor," he said gruffly, as the gratitude radiating from her eyes added to the already heavy moment. There were things going on here that couldn't be ignored. But they were not things he felt equipped to deal with.

Because at the end of the day, anything other than saying goodbye could only be described as selfish, selfish and even more selfish.

But as the night was still young and he'd never claimed to be a saint, he took full advantage of Grace's pass and ferried Nora back to his penthouse. They made love in his bed, and he surprised himself by asking Nora if she'd stay. Which he desperately wanted all at once. He'd been breaking all his rules left and right. What was one more? Especially when he felt the end of their relationship snapping at his heels like a rabid dog.

But she shook her head. "I've never slept apart from Declan. I'm sure I'll have to eventually but I'm not rushing it."

Reid let her go through an act of sheer will. He slept alone in his bed after all, his rules still intact, but not by his own choice.

But the morning news brought a healthy reminder of the situation.

Front and center in his newsfeed was a photograph of Nora on his arm as they exited his limo. But the caption didn't include the usual sexual innuendo, or allude to his playboy reputation and his status as a recluse. Instead, it asked a question that shocked him to the core: Is Chicago's Most Eligible Bachelor off the Market?

Had everyone clued in that he was falling for Nora before he had?

Ten

The days after the fundraiser dragged miserably. Nora didn't hear from Reid other than a slew of funny text messages at odd hours. While she appreciated that Reid was clearly thinking about her as much as she was thinking about him, she felt his absence keenly. More than she would have anticipated.

Declan played his game of searching for "Daadee" at least once a day and it killed her every time. She found herself daydreaming of a life free of complications, heartbreak and terminal diagnoses. Of course Reid had to get back to work and she had to get back to the reason she'd come to Chicago, though.

She'd done her duty by her father and gone to the hospital every day, even though it meant wading through hordes of media mongers who had begun following her constantly. Apparently, the scandal regarding Carson's parentage coupled with the photograph of Nora on

Reid's arm at the fundraiser had thrust her back into the limelight, the last place she wanted to be, the place she'd fled to Colorado to escape.

"I'm going to get some coffee," she announced to Sutton's personal assistant after a particularly long afternoon when her father had been awake more than usual.

It wore on her to listen to the endless lectures about how she should be raising Declan and her father's imperious demands that she move back to Chicago and "act like a Winchester."

Her counterargument—that she was an O'Malley and therefore not subject to patriarchal tyranny—hadn't gone over well.

Valerie nodded to acknowledge Nora's announcement. "Eve's been in the lounge for an hour. You might want to check on her to see if she's okay."

"Sure."

Nora sighed as she punched in the code for the family lounge area and pushed open the door. The smell of freshly brewed coffee nearly made her weep. She'd been dragging lately, sleeping fitfully and waking in a bleary-eyed stupor. It wasn't like her and she'd chalk it up to being back in Chicago to anyone who asked. But she had a feeling it was deeper than that and had Reid's name written all over it, which she did *not* want to examine.

The feelings she'd been ignoring seemed like a betrayal of Sean, and she wasn't dealing with that well. Nor did ignoring them make them go away.

Eve sat in a wingback chair near the window, staring out at the hospital parking lot as she nursed her own cup of coffee.

"On the lookout for loverboy?" Nora said by way of greeting.

Eve's head whipped around and the scowl on her face could have peeled the paint off the walls. "What's that supposed to mean?"

"Wow. I should call Grace and tell her she lucked out in volunteering to stay with Declan at the house instead of subjecting herself to the bad moods around here. But then, if she's drinking the same Kool-Aid, I'll just get my head bitten off."

"Maybe you should look in the mirror for the reason people are particularly touchy today," Eve advised her with a smirk. "You're rubbing everyone the wrong way. What's the matter? Reid finally stop calling? It was bound to happen. Women bounce off him like he's a trampoline. No one gets his attention for long."

"Hey. Leave Reid out of this." Was that what had happened? Their relationship had run its course? Sadness crowded into her chest all at once. She'd kind of thought they'd have a few more days together at least.

Somehow, the fact that Eve had clued in on it before Nora had made it worse. Her sister had obviously seen Reid's dating habits up close and personal since they ran into each other at least a few times a year. But it didn't matter. Nothing had happened that Nora hadn't already been preparing herself for. Things were going to end eventually. Why not now?

"Besides, it's not like that," Nora said a little more forcefully. "We're just old friends. Nothing more."

"Sure. That's why you're in a crabby mood."

"I'm not in a crabby mood! You're the one who's being weird about your love life."

Eve flinched and then tried to cover it by nonchalantly sipping her coffee. "I don't know what you mean."

Nora latched onto her sister's deflection with a bit of desperation. "Want me to spell it out? G-R-A-H—"

"There's nothing going on between me and Graham Newport," Eve shot back furiously, but not before Nora noted a heaping ton of guilt in her gaze. "I danced with him one time at a stupid fundraiser. Sue me. I'm not the one whose photograph is burning up the gossip sites as we speak."

Nora laughed but it sounded forced. Because it was. "That's old news. You're mistaken if you think anyone cares about a photograph of me and Reid."

Silently, Eve picked up her phone, tapped it a few times and scrolled through the plethora of hits on Nora's name, some as recent as a few moments ago. *Ridiculous.*

Nora's pulse jumped into her throat as she read page after page of perfect strangers commenting on her love life, including theories on whether she was into kinky sex or just put up with it for a shot at landing someone as mysterious and reclusive as Reid. There were also guesses as to whether Nora might next appear with an engagement ring on her finger.

She shook her head. "People need something better to do with their lives than speculate on something as inane as whether Reid is off the market. Besides, as you just pointed out, he's probably already forgotten about me. There isn't much to gossip about."

Nora crossed to get that much-needed cup of coffee and was shocked to see her hands were shaking.

If Reid did find some time in his schedule to see her again, she'd say no. She had to. She had no desire to expose Declan to this level of scrutiny, and that was surely next if the media chose to pick up on her status as a single mom. They'd have a field day with captions about whether Reid had hung up his handcuffs in favor of a baby carriage.

Actually, she'd be hard-pressed to say which idea was more ludicrous—Reid's reputation as a man with unusual tastes, or Reid as a father.

When her phone beeped, she almost didn't pull it from her pocket. She wasn't in the mood for another random text message from Reid with a noncommittal joke about chickens crossing the road.

But that wasn't the message.

I'm downstairs. I need to see you.

Yes. She needed that, too. So desperately. Thank goodness he was here. Her fingers flew to respond: Where?

In my car. Come down? I don't want to give anyone a chance to photograph us.

Brilliant, brilliant man. A smile spread across her face before she could catch it and then she was halfway out the door before she remembered to tell Eve to go back to their father's room. "I've got to go. Can you go sit with Dad?"

Nora shut the door on her sister's groan and hightailed it to the elevator. Once the doors slid closed, common sense wormed its way to the forefront. This wasn't a chance to get hot and heavy in his limo, though that was probably exactly what was on his mind. And hers.

Dang it. She'd have to take the high road and inform him it was over. They couldn't keep doing this. Disappointment settled low in her belly, but once again, she had to take control of the situation before it got out of hand. She still had the final word about what went on in her life.

When she got outside, she dived into the limo, head down and face shielded from the lenses of the paparazzi who seemed like a permanent fixture at the entrance to Midwest Regional these days. The moment the door closed, Reid swept her into his arms before she could squeak out a protest. And then her brain drained out the moment his lips touched hers.

Oh, yes. She'd missed him, missed his taste, missed his hands in her hair. And she couldn't pull away. She just needed one more second. Which turned into two and then three…and his hands drifted to her waist, where his clever fingers sought her bare skin.

Through some force of will, she surfaced and slapped a palm on his chest to push him back.

"Wait," she commanded breathlessly even as she curled her fingers into the soft cloth of his shirt, almost dragging him back to finish what he'd started. "I have a few things to say before my clothes end up on the other seat."

Reid smirked. "You're going to do a striptease? All right, if you insist. Carry on."

She bit back a laugh. How did he make her laugh so easily as she was about to embark on a difficult conversation? "I meant before *you* start taking them off. We have to talk."

"I know." He threw up a hand, a chagrined expression on his face. "I'm sorry I've been incommunicado but I had some things I needed to handle. I should have called."

She waved it off as if it was no big deal and all was forgiven. Really, that should be the case. The disappointment and heartsick moments at 3:00 a.m. were her fault, not his. "It's fine. It was a good breaking point for us anyway. The gossipmongers have been out in full force, as I'm sure you're aware. That's what I wanted to discuss. We shouldn't see each other anymore."

"I thought so, too," he admitted. "I tried to stay away. I really did. It didn't work for me."

Oh, it *so* hadn't worked for her, either. But that wasn't the point. "Well, we'll have to try harder. Between the media breathing down my neck and my dad—"

All at once, the horrific day came crashing down on her and broke her voice into pieces.

Instantly, Reid gathered her up in his strong arms and she let him because…well, there was really no excuse except she needed someone to care and he did. It was in his touch, in the soft words he murmured into her hair. The tears she'd been fighting didn't seem so weak after all. A few squeezed out, falling onto his gorgeous suit.

She was crying all over Reid Chamberlain and he wasn't pulling away. The way he should. *Good.* She was so tired of being an adult. She'd done about all the adult stuff she could handle for the day. His fingers slid across the back of her neck, cradling her against him, and it was the most peace she'd felt in days.

"What happened with your father?" he asked and the concern in his tone nearly undid her.

If nothing else, Reid was her friend and she had precious few of those. "The usual Sutton Winchester stuff. I guess I'm just particularly affected by it today."

"Because I haven't been around," he finished for her and guilt laced his flat statement. "You can say it. I left you high and dry and didn't call. But I'm here now. Let me take care of you."

With a really spectacular orgasm? She didn't know whether to laugh or cry some more. Mostly because it sounded like the best plan she'd ever heard in her life.

"That's not your job, though I appreciate the sentiment. I've been taking care of myself for a really long time."

He pulled back and pierced her with his brown eyes, which were still swimming with concern. But he didn't let go of her and she started to wonder if he ever would.

"You need to get away from all of this. I'm not kidding. You're letting your father get to you. You don't owe him anything and this bedside vigil is killing you. Why are you still here catering to your family's demand that you come back to Chicago?"

"Because—" All at once, she didn't have an answer. Why *was* she still here? Certainly not for her father, who wasn't going to turn into someone new so she could magically forgive him, as Reid had just painfully helped her remember. Oh, goodness. Had she been waiting for Reid to come around? "Because…"

Gently, he smiled. "Why don't you go home?"

Home. The word permeated her mind. Yes, that's where she wanted to go. "I can't go home. My dad is dying. My family—"

"Will be fine. You said he has until New Year's. That's months away. It's not like sticking around is going to cure his cancer, Nora." His fingers caressed her neck, warming her, and she was a little ashamed she leaned into his touch. "You said you didn't have a return plane ticket. Let me take you home. I have a private jet that's just sitting around."

She swallowed the *yes*. Now was not the time to crumble under the premise that Reid was—once again—rescuing her from her life. The fantasy world he'd drawn her into needed to be over. "That's not necessary. I can fly commercial."

"But you don't have to. Let me take care of you," he

insisted. "I want to. Let me. If not for you, then for Declan."

She hadn't seen that trump card coming. Her will melted away as if she'd left it in the rain. The lovely thought of not having to fly in a crowded plane with a two-year-old grabbed onto her and wouldn't let go.

She could go home, get away from the media's fixation on her relationship with Reid, remove Declan from the reach of their sharp claws—and avoid the hospital, where nothing in the form of reconciliation seemed to be happening.

How could she pass up what was simply an act of kindness from an old friend?

"What if my dad needs me?" Even she heard the feebleness in that argument, and Reid didn't let her get away with it.

He snorted. "Sutton needs a swift kick in the rear. And that's all I'll say about that. If anyone needs you, they know how to use the phone. Get away for a while and then come back, if that's your concern."

"You make it sound so easy." She smiled to take away the sting. "Some of us don't have access to a private plane to jet around whenever the whim strikes us."

"Then I'll stay until you're ready to come back," he replied nonchalantly.

"What do you mean, stay? As in *stay*? In Colorado?" Her voice had just entered the decibel range where only dogs could hear her, but *really*? "Reid, that's crazy."

And exactly what she wanted. Oh, yes, she did. Crazy, wonderful togetherness. Not an empty bed and even emptier heart.

"No crazier than trying to live my life here in Chicago with the media firestorm going on. I hate that you're affected by it, too. Besides, I told you. Staying away wasn't working for me. This affords us an opportunity to spend time together without all these eyes on us. So we're solving all our problems at once."

"But we're not... That is, you and I—" She couldn't even put a label on what she and Reid were. How did they get to a place where they were talking about continuing their relationship instead of ending it? A place where she *wanted* to talk about it?

"Stop thinking so hard, Nora." Without taking his eyes off her, he took her hand in his and held it to his lips. "Escape with me. Just for a little while. Let's be crazy and indulgent and ignore the outside world. Fall into the moment. Neither of us do that enough."

The beauty of his suggestion wrapped itself around her like a web, ensnaring her firmly. Real life had beaten her down so much that she'd forgotten how to seize the moment. Reid understood that and was offering her a chance to learn again.

Do not say yes. Do not say yes. But then...why shouldn't she?

He wasn't proposing. He wasn't saying he was staying forever. It was an extension of their wild, wonderful affair far away from those who were trying to turn it into something else. She could put off saying goodbye to the man who had become far more important than he should have.

"Okay. Take me home."

She'd have to deal with saying goodbye soon. But not today. And hopefully the fallout wouldn't include any broken hearts. Well, she'd just make sure of it.

When Reid woke, the smell of vanilla and strawberries clued him in that the cocoon he'd fallen into while in Colorado hadn't vanished while he slept.

His eyes blinked open and sure enough, Nora lay firmly encased in his arms, exactly where she'd been last night. Naked, lush, beautiful. He couldn't recall the last time he'd slept with a woman until morning. He liked it.

Kissing her awake had become as necessary as breathing and he didn't hesitate to indulge. That's what this little foray into craziness was about after all. Doing what felt right. Ignoring the voices in his head that said he was letting this woman hook him far deeper than he had any right to allow.

As he turned her head to take her mouth, she responded instantly, her body coming alive against his, sensation rushing along his skin as her backside drew flush with his raging erection. His hands flew to her breasts. He was desperate to touch, desperate to enflame her in kind.

She tilted her hips backward, adjusting herself against him. Groaning with the effort to stop from sliding right into her, as he ached to do, he half rolled over to blindly fumble for the condoms he'd hidden in her dresser the moment they'd arrived yesterday.

Finally, finally, he sank into the heaven of Nora's body. She took him deep and then deeper still as they moved in tandem, driving each other to the peak of bliss and back down the other side. The release was so much more than physical. He had no way to describe the way she filled him so there was no room for the misery that had lived inside him for so long.

How he'd convinced her to let him follow her to her home in Silver Falls, Colorado, he'd never know. All he knew was that he couldn't stand being away from her. He wanted to explore these new feelings for her that were so big and so important he could barely articulate

them. So he'd shot for the stars and had been richly re-
warded. So far.

They'd only just started down this seize-the-moment
path and he liked not knowing what came next.

Eventually, they rolled from bed and got dressed,
then saw to breakfast, which they ate sitting around the
distressed pine table in Nora's kitchen. Her whole house
was quaint, with a farmhouse style that absolutely fit
her. He just hated that she was living here alone, without
the benefit of her father's money to make her life easier.

Good thing he was here and could fill in the gaps.

As Reid finished his coffee and scrolled through
the morning's headlines on his iPad, Nora ate cereal
and chatted. Declan sat in his high chair, his gaze fastened firmly on Reid as if evaluating this new element
in his environment. Once he focused his attention on
the breakfast his mom had given him, she stood and
announced she had about a million loads of laundry.

It was all very domestic. He liked that, too. He'd never
had anything like this experience, which suddenly felt
like a shame. There'd been a huge hole in his life that
he'd only just discovered.

"Need some help?" he asked.

She snickered. "Do you even know what a washing
machine looks like?"

"Sure, I've seen them lots of times," he returned easily. "In TV commercials. How hard can it be?"

"It would be a much bigger help if you sat here with
Declan and made sure that he doesn't tip his high chair
over." Nora tugged on one of Declan's red curls affec-
tionately. "He's becoming quite the climber, aren't you,
Butterbean?"

"Bean," Declan echoed and shoved a few more dry
cheerios in his mouth.

"You can get him down when he's finished eating, right?" Nora called over her shoulder as she headed toward the bedrooms.

Reid and Declan eyed each other. "It's you and me, sport."

Declan nodded. "Daadee."

Reid blinked. "Uh…"

Clearly, this was not one of those times when the kid lacked communication skills. How had he never realized that Declan might draw some conclusions about Reid's presence in his life and interpret all of this in his own way?

"No, I'm not your dad. Though he was a great man. He fought for our freedom in a very dark place and wasn't able to come home."

For some reason, that choked Reid up. It was a raw deal for Nora and her son, but she'd handled the challenges of becoming a widow with grace. She'd created an amazing house that was every inch a home, with crayon scribbles posted on the refrigerator and toys strewn around the living room.

Despite the darkness of her circumstances, she hadn't let it affect her. It was amazing. He wanted to learn from her example.

"Daadee," Declan repeated, and pointed at Reid.

Reid shook his head. "No, bud. Just because we hung out that night doesn't mean I can do it again. I'm really good at telling other people what to do but they're adults and paid to listen. I—"

He broke off because it wasn't as if Declan could understand how difficult this whole subject was for Reid.

Especially when he didn't understand it himself. He stared at the redheaded pint-size human in the high chair less than two feet from Reid's chair. The kid had wormed his way into Reid's limited circle of people he cared about, and that made all of this worse. Declan and Nora needed someone with far more to offer than a brooding loner who was marking the days until he could return to his lair and shut himself away from the world again.

Except the concept didn't seem as appealing as it had in the past.

Reid's penthouse didn't have the same feel as Nora's house. His style leaned toward sharp, modern, stark. He would have insisted that he preferred it right up until the time he walked through Nora's door and felt the difference between the two.

At Nora's house, her warmth emanated from the very walls. He wanted to soak it up as long as possible. As long as she'd let him. There was nothing in his penthouse or his work at Chamberlain Group that could compare with having a lover and a friend rolled into one. As Nora had often said, money didn't buy happiness and he got that in a way he never had before.

Nora bustled back into the kitchen. "First load is in the machine and it's not even nine o'clock. That's a personal record."

Her sunny smile felt like a reward that he eagerly accepted.

Nora's phone beeped and they both glanced at it where it lay on the long island that separated the kitchen from the dining area. She frowned. "It's Eve."

She picked up the phone and thumbed up the message, then shook her head and made a little noise of disgust. "She says my dad wants to talk to me and would I please Skype her. That's just like him. It's not like he can pick up the phone himself. He's got to make it as difficult as possible on everyone else."

"So don't do it," Reid advised and Declan threw a Cheerio on the floor as his vote in the matter.

"Then he'll just take it out on Eve and Grace. That's how he operates." Her mouth tightened. "Better to get it over with, which I honestly think is part of his strategy."

She retrieved her small, off-brand laptop from the built-in desk near the kitchen and set it on the table to boot it up. Eve answered a few seconds after Nora clicked Call, and her sister appeared in the chat window.

"Thanks, Nora. Here's Dad." Eve shifted her own laptop to aim the video lens toward Sutton.

Sutton Winchester's gaunt face filled the screen. *Wow.* Reid had known the man was sick. Dying. But his appearance had so degenerated, it was a bit of a shock. He was pretty sure her father couldn't see him sitting near Nora because of the angle of her laptop, but Nora could, so he kept his alarm to himself. She knew her father didn't have long. She didn't need Reid to add to her burden.

"Nora." Sutton's imperious voice rang out in the small breakfast nook. "I'm very disappointed you've chosen to abandon your family in this time of need."

Reid bit his tongue. Emotional blackmail? The man had nerve.

Nora scowled. "Is that why you called, Dad? We've been over this. I told you I'd come back if there was a real emergency, but I have myself and my son to take care of. That's the most important thing right now."

Sutton coughed, prolonging the fit past the point where Reid had any concern left. It was clear Winchester was milking it.

When he'd recovered, Sutton glared at Nora. "And where exactly does the Spawn of Satan fit into that, may I ask?" This was the nickname her father had used for Reid ever since discovering that she was spending time with him.

"His name is Reid and you can leave him out of this conversation." Nora's gaze shifted toward Reid, as he stood, crossing behind Nora's chair to rest a hand on her shoulder.

"You rang?" he commented to Winchester mildly.

Reid would be the first in line to agree with the moniker Spawn of Satan. His own father was no doubt in hell trying to dethrone the devil as they spoke. But the fine, pinched lines around Nora's mouth were not okay. Just because she was related to this cruel, miserable man didn't mean Reid would stand by and allow her to be abused.

"Chamberlain," Winchester fairly barked. "Since warnings to my daughter have gone unheeded, I'll appeal to your sense of honor, whatever little of it you may have. Stay away from Nora. Your bad blood will only lead to pain and suffering. If she won't give you the boot, take it upon yourself to remove yourself from her house."

"Dad, that's enough!" Nora was fairly bristling under Reid's palm. "You have no idea what you're talking about. How dare you intrude on my life and then make demands of a man who's shown me nothing but kindness?"

Kindness? That was laying it on a bit thick but just as Reid was about to tell the old man to go to hell, Winchester cleared his throat. "You're obviously not thinking this through, Nora. You have a son to be concerned with. You do not want him to be negatively affected by your poor choices, do you?"

"The only poor choice I've made lately is making this call," Nora retorted darkly. "And asking this is probably the second one, but I have to know. What, exactly, do you think is going to happen to Declan by being exposed to Reid?"

Nothing good could come of that question, but now that she'd asked, Reid was interested in the answer, too. Not because he had any respect for Winchester's opinion, but simply because Reid had already arrived at the conclusion that he was bad news for mom and son. It couldn't hurt to solidify that fact in both his and Nora's minds.

That the answer came via her father stuck in his craw, though.

"The man is ruthless," Winchester announced as if Reid wasn't standing right there listening. "In his business dealings and his personal relationships, such as they are. Hasn't anyone explained his distasteful reputation to you? He's corrupt, soulless and cold. A man like him cannot be around my grandson. I forbid it."

Hearing it spelled out like that without a filter, without any pulled punches, was brutal. But it didn't make it any less true. He wasn't father material and Winchester saw it as clearly as Reid did.

"Reid," Nora said without turning around. "Tell my father Declan's favorite animal."

"Giraffe." Or at least it was now. He slept with the stuffed giraffe Reid had bought him at the zoo and carried it around as if he'd been gifted with the Hope Diamond.

"What time does he go to bed?"

"Eight o'clock. If you mean for the night. He also takes a nap after lunch." As Reid well knew since he'd taken complete advantage of the all-adult alone time on more than one occasion.

Nora cocked her head at her father, staring him down as she addressed Reid. "What did he eat for breakfast?"

"Cheerios." This was a fun game, especially since Winchester's complexion got grayer and grayer the longer Nora kept it up.

"Now it's your turn, Dad." Nora folded her hands. "If you can answer at least one of those questions about me from when I was two, I'll take your advice about Reid. Wait, I'll make it even easier. Answer it about me, Eve *or* Grace. Go ahead. Wow me."

Winchester sputtered as Reid's mouth flipped up into an appreciative smile that he didn't bother to hide. God, she was amazing.

"That's what I thought," Nora concluded. "You know how Reid answered those questions so easily? Because he spends time with Declan. He makes an effort. He's already a better father figure to my son than you ever were to me. And you're *my* blood. This conversation is over."

Nora clicked the lid shut to her laptop and put her head down on it.

Reid lightly massaged her shoulders in hopes it would be comforting and tried to unstick his tongue from the roof of his mouth. A *father figure*? That was... What was that? He had no context for the definition of the term, what she'd meant when she'd said it and whether the fifty-pound weight on his chest had landed there because the concept scared him or because it didn't.

After all, he did care about Declan. The kid had grown on him when he wasn't looking. He was funny, innocent and a piece of Nora. What wasn't to like?

Regardless, as far as all those things she'd asked him were concerned, his ability to answer didn't give him any special skill to do something as huge as be a father. Yet Nora seemed to think so or she wouldn't have made that point so well to her own father. Confusion clogged his throat.

"Sorry," she mumbled. "You shouldn't have been subjected to that. I—"

"No problem." This conversation needed some spin control before more things came out of her mouth that tilted his world. "You were brilliant, by the way."

Declan kicked his legs against the plastic footrest of his high chair and said, "Daadee."

And Reid didn't know what he was supposed to do with that, either.

Eleven

That afternoon, Reid tried to shake off the weirdness of the Skype conversation with Sutton Winchester and talked Nora into letting him rent them a sailboat for a spin around Chatfield Reservoir. Nora's small town of Silver Falls lay to the southwest of Denver, right at the foothills of the Rockies, and made for amazing views.

The skyline of Chicago had its own beauty but Reid appreciated the diversity of the vistas here, including the gorgeous blonde at his side as they boarded the fifty-foot cruising sailboat that he'd chartered for their fun afternoon. The captain welcomed them aboard and went over a few safety precautions while Declan explored the small seating area designed for the guests. The captain handed them all orange life vests and Nora actually got Declan to stand still for four seconds while she strapped him into his. A full crew scurried about the deck, making the sails ready for departure.

The wind kicked up and blew through Nora's hair as they headed out toward the center of the reservoir. It streamed out behind her and she laughed as Declan put his face up to the breeze like a dog sticking his head out the window.

This was the perfect distraction from the heaviness that had weighed Reid down all day. Not that Nora had noticed his reticence, or if she had, she'd elected not to say anything. Maybe she'd been thinking about the conversation, too, wondering if she should take back what she'd told her father. But she hadn't. Probably because she didn't realize that Reid had faulty genetics that prevented him from being the father figure she'd described.

Declan wandered over to the edge of the boat and gripped the railing, watching the water rush by with a happy smile. It jabbed Reid right in the stomach. What a rush to put that kind of expression on a kid's face. The poor guy had it tough with losing his dad and having a sick grandpa. If any of the excursions Reid had planned made his life a little easier, that was fair compensation for how much warmth Declan and Nora had brought to him.

Nora leaned in toward Reid, her eye still on her son. "Thanks for this. It's nice."

He smiled back in response. "Thank you for what you said to your dad."

"You're welcome. You aren't going to argue with me about what I said? I've been waiting for you to bring it up all day."

The seat cushion under Reid's butt grew uncomfortable and he sought a different position. But no amount of fidgeting changed the fact that she was right. He had been avoiding the subject. "You didn't have to say that about me just to get your dad off your back."

"I didn't. It's true." Her hand drifted over to clutch his. "You've been an amazing influence on Declan and he likes you. I know you think you're not father material, but it's obvious to me that you are."

Reid went cold. This was the part where he had to come clean with her. Where he had to be so very clear that answering a few questions about breakfast cereal didn't erase the Chamberlain genes from his makeup. "It's not that I hate the idea of being around kids. Declan is great. It's that I…have a lot of internal stuff to overcome."

"Don't we all?" She dismissed his comment with a wave of her hand. "Besides, I've told you before, I think it's admirable that you stop and think about these things before jumping into the deep end. That's part of what makes you father material, Reid. Because you care so much about doing the right thing. My dad never did. You're already better just in that one respect."

Reid opened his mouth to categorically deny every last word she'd said. And couldn't do it. Because all at once, he got her point. He did care about Declan. And Nora. How had that happened? He'd have sworn he didn't have the ability to nurture and love, that tragedy had ripped that away from him. Apparently, he'd been wrong. What else had he been wrong about?

He cleared his throat. "Thanks. I'm sorry your father is such a piece of work."

There was so much more he wanted to say but he couldn't get the swirl of emotion in his chest to stop long enough for him to form coherent speech.

"You'd think it would be easier to hate him. But I can't." Nora caught her lip between her front teeth, worrying it as she glanced at Reid. "He's still my father despite all the crappy stuff he's done over the years. Despite the horrible mandates he threw around this morning about you. He's my dad and I still love him. Am I insane?"

"No." He yanked Nora into his arms, simply holding her, because the break in her voice had echoed through the hollow cavity inside his chest and he needed her warmth just then.

He needed *her*.

She'd just described the very essence of unconditional love, something he scarcely understood, but wanted to. Nora had opened up a whole world of possibilities by breathing life into Reid's stale world. By shedding light on all the darkness of his existence. By presenting new ways to view old, set-in-stone beliefs.

If Sutton Winchester had been a horrible excuse for a human being and yet still had managed to retain his daughter's love, perhaps the fatherhood bar wasn't as high as Reid had always assumed it was. Hadn't he been successful at everything he'd ever tried? Why had he always categorically dismissed his weaknesses as bad DNA? Nora had overcome her genetics. She was a great mom. Surely if he tried, he could do leagues better than her father. Or his own.

And if that was true, maybe it wasn't a sin of the highest order to imagine that he'd found something in Nora Winchester O'Malley that was worth hanging on to with both hands—a family. He wanted that.

"I'm glad you're here," she said and pulled back a bit from his embrace. Not all the way, which was fortunate, because he'd just yank her back. "I really didn't expect anything to come out of tracking you down that day after you sent the catering. But I've been carrying this load by myself for so long that I've forgotten how much I need someone to turn to when it gets rough."

Yes, exactly. Her thoughts so eloquently and perfectly mirrored his, it was almost spooky. Or maybe it was just fate.

Hope filled him to the brim and he cleared his throat to tell Nora that something miraculous was happening. Something that afforded them an opportunity to write a different ending to their affair. Grief and darkness had held him back from caring about anyone for so long... and he was sick of being alone. He had an opportunity to be there for Nora and Declan, to perhaps atone for what he'd failed to do for Sophia and his mother.

But at that moment, the winds shifted, billowing the sails backward. The boat lurched as if it had hit a brick wall.

Declan slipped.

Reid watched it happen in slow motion as if time had literally slowed down, allowing him to internalize every second of the little boy's feet sliding out from under him. Declan fell to the deck, his forehead slamming against the wood paneling with a sickening thud. His red curls lay still as the wind died down.

Nora cried out and wobbled to her feet, throwing herself toward the boy. Her hands rushed over her son, checking his crumpled, unmoving form.

Reid's heart jammed into his throat. *No air.* He couldn't move. His hands went numb and useless. He shoved himself off the bench anyway, rushing after Nora to do...something. Anything.

The captain shouted to the crew and the boat settled into the wind. One of the crewmembers knelt by Declan and spoke to Nora, gently checking the boy's pulse.

The crewmember motioned Reid out of the way, so he crouched on the opposite side to smooth a hand over Nora's back because he needed to do something and this was the best spot to monitor the situation. Someone had to make sure Declan was being taken care of and it should be Reid since he was responsible for the injury.

Blood smeared Declan's forehead. The crewmember asked Nora's permission to hold a bandage on it, explaining the risks of concussion as tears streamed down Nora's face unchecked.

Reid's gut clenched. This was all his fault. Declan was too young to be out on a boat this size. A real father would have known that. Would have known what to do when his kid was hurt. But Reid didn't because he wasn't Declan's father. Nor should he be.

Sutton Winchester could see Reid's unsuitability a mile away. Like recognized like in the end. Perhaps Nora had completely missed the point of her father's warning. Instead of resisting it, she should have realized her father had in fact only been looking out for her because he'd be gone soon and unable to do so any longer. In a way, it was a complete reversal of Winchester's typical method of operation.

And the old man's point hadn't been lost on Reid. If Nora wouldn't listen to reason, then Reid had to be the one to do the right thing. The thing he'd known would be the end result of this affair all along—he had to extract himself from Nora and Declan's world before he hurt them even more. Because he loved them both.

The boat butted up against the dock. An ambulance sat idling nearby and two EMTs in dark blue uniforms stood on the dock waiting until the boat was secured. The instant the ropes held, they clambered on board and went to work evaluating Declan.

Nora's gaze never left her son. As well it shouldn't. Though Reid felt her slipping away even as he made conscious effort to let her go. In reality, she'd never been his and he'd never had any kind of claim on her. So whatever connection he'd become so aware of, so dependent on, couldn't continue.

The EMTs explained that only family could ride in the ambulance to the hospital and Nora nodded, finally glancing at Reid as if she'd just realized he was there. The look on her face—ravaged, tear-stained—gutted him. He'd done that to her, caused her pain and worry for her son by being so clueless about safety.

He had reasons why he didn't know more about kids. But they weren't good ones. And definitely not excuses. When you didn't know something and it was important to learn, you learned. Why hadn't he done that?

Because he'd been trying to turn his brief affair with Nora into something meaningful to assuage his own loneliness. He was nothing if not self-serving.

It was time to change that.

"I'm sorry, Reid," she murmured, her voice just as ravaged as her face. "I'm going to ride in the ambulance with Declan, but they're saying you'll have to take separate transportation. I can't... Well, I have to go."

He nodded. "No problem. You do whatever you need to do."

Separating from Nora and Declan was perfect for his purposes, actually. He watched the EMTs load the still-unconscious boy onto the gurney and then roll it into the back of the waiting ambulance. He helped Nora into the cavernous space and squeezed her hand one final time before the driver shut the door. Then the ambulance drove away, taking with it the only people who had managed to coax a smile out of Reid in a very long time.

The oil slick in his soul bubbled up, crowding out all the good waking up with Nora this morning had done. He shouldn't have come here and allowed the darkness that lived inside him to harm others. And he surely shouldn't have bribed Nora with a private plane ride here in order to stay in her orbit. Because he selfishly wanted a family without giving anything of himself.

Easily fixed. He'd just leave his pilot and plane here and fly back to Chicago some other way. The trick would be not letting on to Nora how much it hurt to not be the man she deserved and the father Declan deserved.

Reid hadn't come to the hospital and Nora had a pretty good idea why. Exhausted, Nora pushed open the front door of her house with one hand and shifted a sleeping Declan higher against her hip, making sure she didn't jostle his brand-new stitches.

"Reid," she called softly and shook her head when he didn't answer. The man was a big, fat scaredy-cat and he needed to see with his own two eyes that Declan was fine. Which wouldn't happen if he kept hiding away from the frightening parts of life.

It was a step back. A small one. Slowly but surely, Reid had been coming around to the idea that kids weren't all that bad and then this had to happen. A bump on the head that would heal in time. Like all wounds. She'd thought maybe Reid had gotten to a place where he believed that. Where they could really talk to each other about their fears and setbacks, and yeah, maybe share in the triumphs.

She could have used his strong shoulder at the hospital. She was a little upset that he hadn't realized that.

First things first. She got Declan undressed and in his crib with his stuffed giraffe, then covered him with his frog blanket. The boy didn't stir, likely a combination of the late hour and the activity at the hospital. Then she went in search of Reid.

The house was dark and silent. Reid wasn't here.

Frowning, she glanced around her bedroom and immediately noted his suitcases were gone. In the kitchen, she found a handwritten note, folded, with her name on the outside.

Her stomach sank as she picked up the page. The flowing script blurred as she took in the contents. Apparently, it didn't take many lines to rip her heart out.

One, two, three... She let the pain take over until she reached ten. Then she cut it off.

He was gone. Without explanation. "It's my fault Declan was hurt. It's better we end things now before something worse happens," was *not* an explanation.

Anger bloomed, hot and fierce. That...*man.* How dare he leave her when she needed him most? She'd kept her panic and tears under control while watching the doctor stitch up her baby, but only because she'd had to. It didn't stop her from wishing Reid had been there to hold her in the hallway while she crumbled. She was so tired of not being able to crumble, of not having someone strong enough to catch her.

Why did she always have to fall for men who were determined to leave? First she'd fallen for a man with such deep wanderlust, he'd enlisted in the army to satisfy it. And he'd paid the ultimate price with his life. She didn't begrudge Sean his choices, nor blame him for dying, but she did wish she'd had an opportunity to say goodbye. It was her biggest unresolvable regret.

As for Reid, she could blame him all day long for his choices. Jetting off and leaving her a note. That was... unforgivable. And all at once, she didn't plan to stand for it. Sean had left her to go to a place she couldn't follow. But Reid hadn't.

The note indicated that Reid had left his plane at

the private airstrip not far from Silver Falls, which was available for her use to return to Chicago whenever she deemed it necessary.

It looked as though that time was now.

In the morning, she threw the load of laundry from the dryer back into the same suitcases the clothes had come from yesterday and zipped them up. Declan was a bit harder to herd as he was still tired and cranky from the bump on his head. But she prevailed and Reid's pilot took off for Chicago before lunchtime.

After an uneventful flight where Nora passed the time fuming over Reid's cowardice, she made a quick call to Grace, who dropped everything in order to take Declan. This was one showdown that didn't need an additional audience member.

Finally, Nora walked through the door of the Metropol business office and faced down Reid's admin. "I'm here to see Mr. Chamberlain. He's expecting me."

It wasn't a lie. He should be expecting her. If he thought she was going to take that BS note at face value, he had another think coming.

"Oh." Reid's admin's eyes rounded. "Yes, you should definitely go right in."

Nora was all too happy to comply, but when she stormed into Reid's office, the genuine shock on his face when he looked up from his desk brought her up short.

The force of his presence slammed into her, far more powerfully than it had the first time she'd come here. His brown eyes were full of secret pain and even more secret longing. His body, as she knew firsthand, was full of heat and tenderness. And her heart was full of him.

They'd come full circle. A few weeks ago, she'd been looking for an old friend. Today, she was looking for the man she'd fallen in love with. And had only just realized that was the root of her anger.

She loved Reid. How dare he treat that so casually? Didn't he realize how hard it was for her to open her heart again? How afraid she was of loss?

Her legs started shaking but she shrugged her nervousness off, marching forward to yank the phone out of Reid's hand.

"He'll have to call you back," she said and ended the call, tossing the phone over her shoulder. "You left. That note? Not going to cut it. Tell me to my face that we're through and I might believe you. But I don't think you can do it. Because you know we're not even close to finished."

"Nora." Reid's gaze swept over her hungrily, weakening her already-shaking legs. "What are you doing here? Is Declan okay? Or is it your father?"

"No, nothing's changed with my father's health and Declan is fine. I just told you why I'm here." Something broke inside as he stood, circling the desk to invade her space, drawing close, so close. But not close enough. There was an invisible barrier between them that she ached to destroy but first, she had to understand. "I deserve to hear from you personally what's going on in your head. We're not just sleeping together. We're involved, whether you like it or not. I thought…"

All at once, as his expression darkened with something she had no idea how to interpret, she faltered. What *had* she thought? That Reid accompanying her to Colorado meant something different from what it had? That he'd turned into someone who wanted a woman with a kid? His refusal to entertain the idea of ever becoming a father couldn't have been clearer. When she'd gently tried to help him see that he'd surely be a better father than most, he hadn't agreed with her. And he hadn't come to the hospital because that was too much for him to handle.

She'd run all the way back to Chicago to confront a man who wanted out from their affair. She should have left well enough alone.

"You thought what?" His voice dipped dangerously low. "That something was happening between us? That I might have developed feelings for you?"

"Yes." She couldn't look away. Couldn't lie. Even though she knew it was the wrong tactic, the absolute worst thing to admit to a man who had run away from her as fast as he could. The facts spoke for themselves after all. "Tell me I'm wrong. Say it. Out loud."

"You're not." The phrase reverberated in the air, settling across her skin. Raising goose bumps as his eyes bored into her. "That's why I left. Because I care about you too much to hurt you."

"What are you saying?" she whispered as everything inside her slid off a cliff. "You…left because you developed feelings for me?"

"I can't…" He shook his head. "That's why I left the note. It was supposed to keep you in Colorado. Where you were safe. Not drag you back to Chicago. Go home. I'm not good for you."

"Reid." His name bubbled up on a sob as she fought back tears. "That's ridiculous. You're the best thing that's happened to me in a long, dark couple of years. I need you. And you left. *That's* what hurt."

His gaze was raw as he nearly closed the gap between them. But didn't. "I'm sorry. I was trying to protect Declan. And you. I've caused enough pain."

"Protect us from what? You?" She tried to laugh it off but the sound got caught in her throat. "Declan is fine. Kids get hurt. They're not as fragile as you seem to think. But I don't buy that as the reason for all of this. I think you ran because of what's happening between us."

To her shock, he nodded. "Yes. Because it's the right thing to do. I never expected to fall for you and never expected to have to make the difficult choice to walk away."

She nearly groaned at the irony. The one time he'd elected to make an adult decision, and it was the wrong one. "Then don't walk away. Seize the moment. And the next one. For the next fifty or sixty years, let's be crazy together. I love you and I'm not leaving until you say yes."

To emphasize the point, she plopped down on his desk, crossing her arms. Nora Winchester O'Malley charted her own destiny and she wanted this man, with all his glorious complexities.

She wasn't leaving without his heart.

He hesitated for an eternity and then his fingers slid around her elbows, pulling her to her feet. For a half second, she thought he was going to throw her out. But then he swept her into his arms, kissing her with an intensity she could scarcely take in.

His essence swirled into her soul, joining them in a connection that couldn't be explained but didn't have to be. Because they both felt it. Both yearned for it. Both accepted it, despite all their objections to the contrary.

When he finally let her surface long enough to gulp in some much-needed oxygen, he murmured, "I'm sorry. I shouldn't have done that. It's not fair to keep drawing you back in. You should leave."

"No." She scowled. "And I'm not letting you make this decision for me. I want you in my life. And in Declan's. We both need you."

He pierced her with his deep, soulful eyes. "I don't know how to be a father. What if there's something wrong with me that I can't overcome? You're taking too big of a chance with your son on what's essentially a work in progress."

Even now, he was trying so hard to do the right thing and couldn't see that she accepted him as he was. "Since we're on the subject, I'm a work in progress, too. I know everything about being a mom of a one-year-old. But I've never been the mom of a two-year-old. It's a lot harder. I'm making all new mistakes. That's where you come in. Be there for me. As my sounding board. As my lover, to help the bad parts of the day melt away. As my partner. That, you know how to do."

Because he'd been doing it all along. And she'd been too blind to see that she needed to encourage it, nurture their blossoming relationship by telling him every moment how important he was to her.

"Guess we know where Declan gets his stubbornness from. Seems like his mom latches on to an idea and never lets go, either."

"I don't know what you're talking about," she countered primly, her pulse racing to keep up with all the things going on inside. "I'm not stubborn. I just know what I want. And you, Reid Chamberlain, are it."

He shook his head and her heart froze. But then he smiled, the real genuine one that made her feel like she'd won the Reid Chamberlain sweepstakes and everything was going to be all right.

"What if I just want to be friends?" he asked, even as his arms slid around her, possessively, intimately, drawing her so close there was nothing between them.

Everything inside yearned for this man. "Too bad.

You better get used to the idea of being lovers *and* friends. And one last thing. No more notes."

His lips toyed with hers, not quite completing the connection. "Not even 'I love you' scrawled in the steam on the bathroom mirror?"

She pretended to contemplate it but the thought of sharing a bathroom with Reid for the rest of her life made her a little giddy. "That one might be okay. But only if you promise to follow it up verbally."

"I do."

The sweetest words in the English language. "Then so do I."

Epilogue

Nora hid a smile as Reid picked up Declan and hoisted him to his shoulders, then galloped around the living area of his Metropol penthouse. The neighing noises Reid was making were her favorite. It was the kind of thing Reid did frequently without thought and Nora fell a little more in love with the man every time he came up with a new game to play with her son.

And soon, Declan would be Reid's son, too. They'd already filed adoption papers.

Reid had put Chamberlain Group on the back burner in favor of learning everything he could about being a father, claiming he had to catch up fast. Before it became official. He didn't seem to understand it had been official since the moment Declan had picked Reid as his "Daadee."

Nora's phone rang and she scooped it up when she saw Grace's name on the screen.

"Everything okay?" Nora asked anxiously. Every phone call from a family member could be the one where she got word that her father had died. When Dr. Wilde had given Sutton Winchester until New Year's to live, it didn't necessarily mean he'd make it until then.

Before Reid and Nora had gotten married, they'd agreed to split their time between Chicago and Silver Falls, at least until the first of the year. Eventually, they hoped to buy a bigger house higher up in the foothills of the Rockies, one that would accommodate the brood of children they both wanted. But for now, Chicago was where Nora needed to be.

"No, everything is not okay," Grace said. Nora could hear the scowl in her sister's voice. "You are not going to believe what those Newport scum have done now."

The call wasn't about her father. Nora breathed a sigh of relief and wandered into the kitchen to sit at the island. "Brooks and Graham? What have they done?"

More inheritance drama. But that came part and parcel with being a Winchester. Nora's patience with it had grown the longer she had Reid to lean on.

And when leaning on his strong shoulder wasn't enough, he just took her to bed and made love to her until she forgot about everything outside of the two of them.

Grace made a very uncomplimentary noise. "They hired a private investigator to work with that lawyer, Josh Calhoun."

"They went ahead with involving their friend in this?" Nora's stomach sank. The Newport twins were fired up about getting Carson his share of the Winchester fortune and honestly, she didn't get their passion for the quest. "I don't understand what a private investigator is going to add to the mix other than making more of a mess."

"Yeah. They want to find their real father, and I guess

a private investigator is supposed to help with that. But I didn't tell you the worst part. The PI is Roman Slater." Grace nearly spat out the name. "My ex."

"Oh, Grace." Nora still remembered how her sister had cried for the six months following her breakup with Roman. "I can't believe they would stoop to working with someone so underhanded."

The twins were obviously trouble waiting to happen, and must have been deliberately involving people they thought were going to put the screws to the Winchesters. It was unforgivable.

"Well, Dad is being so closemouthed about their parentage. I'm even starting to believe he knows something."

Nora secretly agreed. Since moving into Reid's penthouse, she'd tried to spend at least three days a week at the hospital and really talk to her father. Amazingly, her dad had completely reversed his stance on Reid with no explanation, only stating—very gruffly—that he'd heard Reid had appointed Nash as the interim CEO of Chamberlain Group while he spent time with his new family. Sutton approved.

None of it made up for the years of not having a father. But Nora was slowly letting go of her disappointment and grief. Reid's love helped with that, too. When her father finally passed, she felt more confident than ever that she would be at peace with it.

"I'm glad you're here, Nora," Gracie admitted. "I have a feeling this whole thing is going to get uglier before long."

"Yeah, me, too. Sorry. Let me know what I can do to help."

Nora disconnected the call and returned to the living room to find Reid and Declan in the middle of the floor, laughing so hard, neither of them could breathe. Her soul filled with the sound. How had she gotten so lucky to find a man who could love her son as much as she did?

"What's all of this?" Nora demanded. "Having fun without me?"

"Never," Reid said, his gorgeous grin spreading across his face. "Care to join us, Ms. O'Malley?"

He smiled all the time these days and she delighted in taking full credit for it.

"That's Mrs. Chamberlain to you, buddy," she corrected and the sound of her new name thrilled her. She'd sworn to never change her name again, but that was before she found it vitally necessary to be joined with this man in every way possible.

He was her friend. Her lover. Her husband. Soon to be the legal father of her child. And she would never let him go.

* * * * *

FRIEND, FLING, FOREVER?

JANICE LYNN

To Samantha Thompson, who puts together the best fundraisers ever!

Thanks for your big heart and all you do for others.

CHAPTER ONE

"BUY ME AT the charity auction."

Nurse Kami Clark didn't look up from the computer screen where she keyed in vital signs on the patient in bay two of the Knoxville General Hospital's emergency department.

Doing her best not to let her eyes veer in Dr. Gabriel Nelson's direction, she made a nurse's note on the normal results. "Not happening."

Wearing his favorite blue scrubs, Gabe moved into her peripheral vision. She didn't have to look to know the color paled in comparison to the brilliant hue of his eyes.

"You know you want me, Kam. Here's your chance."

"Right," she snorted, keeping her voice flippant despite how his accusation almost sent her into a choking fit. "Keep dreaming, lover boy."

Most straight women did want Gabe. Not that he typically encouraged their desire. He didn't have to. Not with his looks, personality, and quick intelligence. The fact he was a successful emergency-room physician didn't hurt. Women flocked to him.

But not Kami.

Oh, she thought he was all that and more. The man had the biggest heart of anyone she knew and seemed to always be able to make her laugh. But she knew better than to get caught up in his revolving-door love life that left a long line of broken hearts. She was immune to his love-'em-and-leave-'em charms. Mostly.

"More like I'm trying to escape a nightmare in the making." He gave a frustrated sigh that was almost believable as he plopped down into the chair next to hers. "Debbie is planning to buy my date."

Ah. Debbie. The latest ex-girlfriend who didn't want to admit it was over and had been finished for a month or so.

No wonder Gabe was in such a tizzy. Debbie had stuck like glue even after he'd told her point-blank on several occasions that their relationship was finished. The poor woman must be hoping to rekindle a spark. Good luck with that.

Gabe never dated the same woman for more than a couple of months and never went back to the same one. Not once. He was a move-on-and-never-look-back kind of guy.

"You have to rescue me."

"Says who? You got yourself into this mess," she reminded him, fighting back a small smile at her friend's overly dramatic tone. She could almost buy into his angst. "It's only right for you to face the consequences."

"I was roped into this charity fund-raiser and you know it. Not only do you know it—" he leaned close enough so that his words were just for her "—you're the one who convinced me to say yes."

"I meant the Debbie mess, not the auction," she clarified, fighting the urge to look his way. Better not to look into Gabe's eyes when he was trying to convince you to do something. Staring into those dazzling blues got women into trouble. Immune or not, she wasn't taking any chances.

"Besides," Kami continued, "even if you had to spend a *week* with your beautiful and persistent ex, if it raised money to help Beverly's family and others like her, then so be it."

Anything any of them could do to raise money for their coworker's seriously ill infant daughter needed to be done. Although their medical insurance was covering many of the expenses, there were still co-pays and deductibles. Not to mention Beverly had been out of work since giving birth, as had her husband, most of it as unpaid leave of absence. Even after Lindsey got her heart transplant, months would pass prior to Beverly leaving her baby's side to return to work. Their friend had enough worries without having to be concerned about how she and her husband were going to pay their bills.

"Easy for you to say," Gabe pointed out. "You aren't on the auction block."

Yeah, as one of the fund-raiser's organizers she'd dodged that bullet.

"I'll be working the night of the auction, but not by being auctioned." Thank goodness. Kami would have been a statue. Not her scene at all.

"Not the same," he pointed out.

"You love the attention and you know it," she accused, closing out the patient's chart. Fun-loving Gabe would work the stage and have a blast.

She glanced at him for the first time since he'd barged into the nurses' station located across from the patient bays.

Her incorrigible playboy friend actually looked a little frazzled.

"Fortunately for you, it's not a week, just one night where you have to show Debbie—I mean, whoever wins your date—a good time."

Okay, that was bad but she couldn't resist teasing him. It was so rare to see him off his game. Actually, she couldn't recall having ever seen him off his game. Not during any crisis that came through the ER doors. Given he was such a goofball at times, Gabe was one coolheaded dude.

Plus, she wasn't buying his woe-is-me-buy-my-date-package-so-Debbie-can't-act.

"You're real funny, Kam."

"Come on. That was a good one." Kami had thought so. He didn't look convinced. "I'm sure you'll manage one night with Debbie if needed."

After all, he dealt with situations and people a lot more

intense than the Z-list television actress he'd been involved with still obsessing over him. Debbie might be crazy over Gabe, but the woman didn't have any real psychiatric problems.

"And risk encouraging her nonstop calls and texts continuing?" He winced. "Thanks anyway."

Kami raked her gaze over his six-foot frame. "You're not *that* bad, Gabe." She patted his hand as if reassuring a small child. "There will be other bidders." Faking a look of uncertainty, she shrugged. "Well, hopefully."

One side of his mouth cocked upward. "Gee, thanks for the compliment, *friend*."

"Anytime," she assured him, her lips twitching. "What are friends for?"

Eyes sparkling, he gave a pointed look. "To rescue each other when one's relentless ex plans to buy her way back into your social life."

He had a point.

If Kami believed he was in real need, she'd probably empty her house-deposit fund to bail out his butt. Good thing he wasn't because she'd been hoarding every spare penny for years, had a hefty down payment saved, and would hate to have to start over to make her dream of owning a home come true just as she finally had enough saved to actually start looking for the perfect house.

"Just because Debbie plans to bid doesn't mean she'd be the winner," she said on a more serious note. "Stop worrying."

He didn't look assured. "Debbie doesn't like to lose."

Kami gave a semi-shrug. "Who does?"

He raked his fingers through his hair. "Come on, Kam. Place the winning bid and I'll show you the night of a lifetime." He waggled his brows. "We'd have fun."

Kami laughed. As if. "You must have me mixed up with one of the other women running around the hospital who actually wants you to show them a 'night of a lifetime.' I've better things to do than mess with the likes of you."

Looking as if she'd said exactly what he'd expected her to say, he chuckled. "Or maybe I want you to buy my bid because I know I can ask this huge favor and not worry about you freaking out down the road when I break things off."

Yeah, there was that. She wouldn't freak out over a man. Never had. Never would. She'd watched her mother do that one time too many.

This time it was she who gave the pointed look.

"If I ever gave you the privilege of dating me—" she stared straight into his blue eyes, held her chin a little higher than normal "—who says it would be *you* to break things off?"

Although she adored his friendship, his arrogance irked. Then again, was it arrogance if it was true he'd been the one to end every relationship he'd had during the time he and Kami had worked together? Probably his whole life?

Gabe chuckled, then surprised her by tweaking his finger across the tip of her nose."You might be right, Kam. Only a fool would break things off with you. Speaking of which, how is Baxter?"

Ha. Talk about turning the table.

"Our breakup was a mutual decision," she reminded him, not that she hadn't already told Gabe as much a dozen times previously. "We aren't talking much these days, but he's fine as far as I know."

Just as she was. Baxter had been sweet, only she'd realized continuing their relationship was pointless. When he kissed her, she felt nothing. No sparks. No butterflies. Nothing.

Kami wasn't so delusional she thought someone would come along, sweep her off her feet, and give her a fairy-tale romance. But she wasn't going to settle for *nothing*, either.

Good friendship and sparks—it could happen.

Not that it had, but she was only twenty-seven. There was plenty of time for someone special to come into her life.

And, if not, she'd rather be alone than like her mother and with the wrong man over and over.

"Keep telling yourself that he's fine. Dude was devastated last week when I bumped into him."

Baxter hadn't been devastated. When she'd broached the subject of their relationship not working, he'd seemed relieved. Obviously, he hadn't felt any sparks, either. On paper they were a good match. In reality, there had been little chemistry beyond their initial attraction.

"When did you run into my ex?" Baxter, an accountant for a law firm, and the usually laid-back man in front of her didn't exactly move in the same social circles.

"At the gym."

Kami's jaw dropped. "Baxter was at the gym?"

She shook her head to clear her hearing because she couldn't have heard correctly. Not once during the time she'd known Baxter had he ever gone to the gym. To her knowledge, he'd not even had a membership.

"Pumping the iron in hopes of winning you back." Gabe's eyes twinkled with mischief. "Too bad you aren't up for grabs at the auction 'cause he could buy a night to remind you of all you're missing out on. You, him, Debbie and me could go on a double date and reminisce about the good ole days."

Kami rolled her eyes.

"Baxter is a great guy," she defended the man she'd dated for over six months. He truly was. He'd been steady, quiet, dependable. She'd wanted to feel something, had tried to convince herself she did because he'd make a good husband and father someday, but *nada*.

"Just not the guy for you?"

"Exactly. Now, was there a reason you interrupted my work other than to whine about Debbie?"

"As if she isn't enough of a reason." He gave an overly dramatic sigh that should have put him up for an award or two. "I can't believe you're refusing to help, Kam. You know I'd do it for you."

"I wouldn't want you to." She curled her nose and shuddered at the mere thought. "Can you imagine the rumors that would start around the hospital?" She gave a horrified look. "Uh-uh. No way. I can, however, put out word you're hoping someone outbids Debbie at the auction. I'm sure there'll be a few takers."

He shook his head. "I'm disappointed in you, Kam. I was sure I could count on you to save me."

"You have the wrong girl, but no worries. You'll find someone over the next few weeks to outbid Debbie."

Gabe disagreed. He had the right girl. The perfect girl.

Kami wouldn't get happily-ever-after ideas. He always had fun when she was around. And, best of all, she already knew the real him. The him who had no intentions of settling down anytime in the near future.

But he changed the subject instead of pursuing the topic further. As she said, they had a few weeks before the fundraiser. A lot could happen during that time.

Like his convincing Kami to buy him.

Not that he couldn't deal with Debbie. He'd just rather not have to.

She was great, but had gotten too clingy too fast and he'd started feeling claustrophobic in their relationship by the end of the first month. At the end of the second, he'd been done. Too bad Debbie hadn't been.

"How is Racine Mathers tonight?" he asked to change the subject.

Apparently, the fragile elderly woman had arrived by ambulance in hypercapnic respiratory failure earlier that day. Yet again. She'd been admitted to the medical floor, which neither Gabe nor Kami had anything to do with, but he knew Kami would have checked on the woman prior to clocking in for her shift. She cared about people and that big heart was one of the things he liked most about the perky little blonde who'd quickly become one of his closest friends.

At the mention of their patient, her green eyes filled with concern. "Her arterial blood gases are still jacked up. Her CO_2 level remains in the upper fifties."

"I was hoping once they got her on BiPAP her numbers would improve." He logged in to the computer, began scanning messages in his inbox.

"That makes two of us, but apparently she hasn't wanted to keep the mask on and the day-shift nurse caught her with it off several times."

He shook his head. "Racine knows better than that."

Kami nodded.

The woman did. This wasn't her first respiratory failure rodeo. Then again, Gabe suspected the elderly woman was tiring of her inability to breathe and the medical community's failure to do much more than Band-Aid her back together until the next episode.

"I'm going to swing by and see her. If I'm needed before I get back, page me."

She arched a brow. "You think I wouldn't?"

Gabe grinned. No, he never doubted that his favorite nurse would do the right thing and get him where he needed to be when he needed to be there. Kami was an excellent nurse. There was no one he'd rather spend his shift working with. Fortunately, their schedules were on the same rotation and he got to spend several nights a week in the emergency department with her.

Whether it was busy, slammed, or on the rare occasion slow, he was never bored. Not with Kami around to keep him entertained with her quick wit and sassy mouth.

Which was yet another reason she should be the one to rescue him from Debbie. Not only would Kami not get the wrong idea, but Gabe would truly enjoy their "date." Not that they'd ever gone anywhere just the two of them, but when the work gang gathered, he gravitated toward Kami and they almost always ended up paired off.

There was just something about her that made him feel good on the inside.

She needed to buy his auction package and he intended to make sure she did.

* * *

"That is the most exciting thing I've heard in weeks."

While dropping in a urinalysis order for bay one, Kami curled her nose at the woman who'd been her best friend since they'd bonded during nursing school. "You would say that."

Mindy gave her a *duh* look. "The man is gorgeous and I saw that once-over you gave him. I think you should go for it."

Kami shook her head. "You misunderstood. That once-over was a joke and Gabe doesn't want me to buy his date so we can go on a *real* date. He wants me to save him from having to go on a date with someone else. Either way, no, thank you."

Mindy leaned against the desk. "I'm just saying, the most eligible bachelor in the hospital asked you to buy him at the fund-raiser. I think you should see that as a sign and go for it."

Go for it? Her friend had lost her mind.

"A sign of what?"

Mindy waggled her brows. "Your good fortune. Do you know how many women would kill for Gorgeous Gabe to ask them to buy his date package?"

Kami made a bleh motion with her tongue. "They can have him. He's too stuck on himself for my taste."

Mindy didn't look convinced. "That's not how I see him."

Kami didn't, either. Not really. Gabe was gorgeous, but he didn't seem to get caught up in his looks other than that he took care of himself and worked out regularly. Nothing wrong with trying to stay healthy.

Gabe was the picture of good health.

Great health.

Health at its finest, even.

Yeah, yeah. The man was easy on the eyes. No big deal.

"He's got a big heart and you know it," Mindy continued, oblivious to Kami's wayward thoughts—thank goodness. The last thing she needed was Mindy pushing her toward doing something she knew better than to do. She might be immune, but you didn't rub your face in germs to tempt fate, either.

"He doesn't mind getting his hands dirty. He's the first to jump in and help when someone needs something. I've never known him to pull the doctor card." Mindy gave a pointed look. "I'd be hard-pressed to name someone, male or female, who didn't like him."

"Since you're a walking, talking advertisement of his virtues, you bid on him," Kami suggested and wondered at the slight twinge in her belly at the thought of her friend buying Gabe's date.

Her two friends getting together would be a good thing, right? Well, except that Gabe would eventually break Mindy's heart and then Kami would have to bust his chops for hurting her bestie. That was what the issue was. She didn't want to have to dislike him for breaking Mindy's heart.

But Mindy's eyes lit at Kami's suggestion and a smile slid onto her face. "I might do that."

Kami's brow shot up. Her mouth opened, but she didn't comment as Gabe came strolling back into the emergency department.

"What have I missed?"

"Not much. Been a slow one so far," Mindy told him, all smiles and looks of all sorts of possibilities.

"Bite your tongue," Kami and Gabe said at the same time.

"Listen at you two," Mindy said, giving Kami a mischievous glance that said maybe her friend hadn't really veered from her original mission after all. "So in sync."

"Not wanting you to jinx our evening is common sense. Nothing in sync about that," Kami corrected, hoping her friend caught her warning tone. "Now, Dr. Nelson." She turned her attention to Gabe, ignoring his curious looks between her and Mindy. "Bay one is a urinary tract infection. Onset earlier today. Her urinalysis results are in her chart. Bay two is a fever and sore throat. I've swabbed for strep, but the results are pending. Both are pleasant, stable, and accompanied by their significant other. You want me to go with you while you examine them?"

Bay one was given an antibiotic, a bladder antispasmodic, a handout on the preventions of UTIs, and was sent on her way. The woman in bay two, however, looked worse than she had a few minutes before when Kami had last checked.

Her temp was just over one hundred and three, her throat beet red, and her conjunctivae injected. The woman was also now complaining of a severe headache, which she hadn't mentioned during triage or when Kami had done her nursing assessment.

The woman shivered as if she were freezing and looked miserable.

"Can you get her a blanket or something?" her husband asked, looking frustrated that his wife was getting worse.

"She doesn't need to cover up," Kami reminded him. She'd intentionally not given the woman a blanket. She directed her next comment to her patient. "It'll hold heat to your body and you're already too warm. We have to get your fever under control before we can even consider giving a blanket or doing anything that might make you worse."

Wincing with discomfort, the woman tightened her arms around her body. "I'm so cold."

They had to get her fever down and stable. Once they did, then she could possibly have a lightweight blanket. Certainly not before.

"When did the headache start?" Kami asked.

"She had a headache when she got here. It's just gotten a lot worse," the husband clarified. "It wasn't bad enough to mention."

Apparently not even when Kami had directly asked about a headache. Ugh. She really didn't like when patients said something completely opposite when the doctor was present than what they'd told her during their assessment. It happened almost nightly.

Gabe ran through a quick examination of the woman. "Some swelling in the cervical nodes and neck stiffness. I want a blood count and a comprehensive metabolic panel on her STAT, and has that strep finished running?"

"Should be. I'll log in and check." Kami signed in on the in-bay computer and the test result was back. "She's negative for strep."

"Ache all over," the woman told them, her eyes squeezed tightly shut. "Cold."

Gabe gave some orders, which Kami turned to do, but stopped when the woman said, "I'm going to throw up." Then did exactly that.

Gabe was closer than Kami and got an emesis pan in front of Mrs. Arnold just in time.

"Give her an antiemetic IM now." He named the one he wanted given and the dosage. "Then let's get a saline lock on her."

Kami drew up the medication and injected the solution. The woman was shaking and looked much worse than she had when they'd entered the bay.

"Do something," the husband ordered, sounding worried, as he hovered next to his wife's bed, gripping the woman's pale hand.

Gabe sent Kami a concerned look. "Get phlebotomy to draw blood cultures times three and the previous labs I mentioned. It's off season, but run an influenza test, just in case. Let's get a CT of her head, too. I'm probably going to do a lumbar puncture."

He was thinking a possibility of meningitis. Rightly so, given how rapidly her status was changing.

"Let's put her in isolation. Just in case," Gabe continued in full doctor mode.

The husband was talking, too. Kami didn't want to ignore him, tried to answer his questions while she worked, but he continued to fret.

Gabe gave an order to get IV antibiotics started and told her which he wanted. Kami rushed around making things happen. Although she'd really not looked like more than a typical sore throat patient, Mrs. Arnold had gone downhill scarily fast. In case she continued on the decline, they needed to act fast to get an accurate diagnosis as quickly as possible.

Linda Arnold's blood count came back showing a significantly elevated white blood cell count with a bacterial shift. Her headache and neck pain had continued to increase and the woman refused to even attempt to move her neck. Her strep and influenza were negative.

Lumbar punctures weren't Gabe's favorite things to do as there was always risk, but his concerns over meningitis were too high not to test her spinal fluid. As soon as he had the CT scan results back, he'd pull the fluid so long as the scan didn't show any reason not to. He didn't want to risk brain herniation by not following protocol.

From all indications, the woman had meningitis. Gabe needed to know the exact culprit.

He cleared out two other patients who'd come into the emergency department. Then, protective personal equipment in place, he went back to Mrs. Arnold.

The woman was now going in and out of consciousness and didn't make a lot of sense when she was awake.

Also wearing appropriate personal protective equipment, Kami was at her bedside. She'd already gathered everything he'd need for a lumbar puncture. They needed to move fast.

Hopefully, the antibiotics infusing into her body via her IV line would be the right ones for whatever caused her infection, but if they weren't, waiting around to see could mean the difference between life and death.

That wasn't a chance he was willing to take.

"Dr. Nelson?" Mindy stopped him from entering the area where Mrs. Arnold was. "Dr. Reynolds just called with her CT results. He is concerned about meningitis and recommends proceeding with lumbar puncture."

This was the call Gabe had been waiting for giving him the safe go-ahead.

Checking to make sure his respiratory mask was secure, Gabe nodded, then entered the area where Mrs. Arnold was isolated.

From behind her clear plastic glasses, Kami's eyes were filled with worry when they met his.

"She has gaze palsy and mild extremity drift now," she told him. "I thought you'd prefer her husband not be in here for this as he was getting agitated. I sent him to the private counseling room to wait for you to talk to him after we get this done."

That was one of the things he loved about Kami. She was always one step ahead of him.

Except when it came to the auction.

On that one, he planned to outstep her. Not planned to—he *would* outstep her, because the more he thought about it, the more he wanted to go on that "date" with Kami.

CHAPTER TWO

"WHAT A NIGHT," Kami mused at the end of her twelve-hour shift that had turned into over fourteen. She couldn't wait to get home, shower, eat whatever she could find in the fridge, and crawl into bed to pass out until it was time to come back and do it all again for night two of her three in a row.

"You look tired."

She glanced toward Gabe. "You don't look like a bowl of cherries yourself."

He laughed. "Not sure if that was meant to be an insult or not, but I'll go on record saying I'm grateful I don't look like a bowl of cherries."

Kami shrugged. "Too bad. Cherries would be an improvement."

"A cherry fan?"

"They're my favorite," she admitted with a quick sideways glance toward him.

"You one of those talented people who can knot the stem with your tongue?" he teased.

Kami had very few silly talents, but tying a cherry stem into a knot was in her repertoire. Rather than admit as much to Gabe, she shrugged again.

"I'll never tell."

"Because you prefer to show me?" he joked, not looking tired at all despite the fact he had to be exhausted.

It really had been a long night.

"Okay." He gave a dramatic sigh. "I'm game. There's a

pancake house a few blocks from here where you can get whipped cream and cherries."

She frowned. "You know this how?"

"A man has to know where he can get whipped cream and cherries twenty-four hours a day."

Kami scrunched her nose. "Ew. Spare me the details because I don't want to know."

Looking intrigued, he chuckled. "Your mind went to the gutter, Kam. I'm surprised, but I think I like it."

"Nothing to like about you grossing me out."

His brow arched. "My liking whipped cream and cherries on top of my pancakes grosses you out?"

She ran her gaze over his broad chest, down his flat abs that his scrubs failed to disguise. "Yeah, I can tell you regularly chow down on pancakes with whipped cream and cherries."

"You might be surprised."

Not really. She'd seen him put away a lot of food during their shift breaks. The man could eat. Not that it showed. Whether because of good genetics or his time spent in the gym, Gabe truly was the picture of good health.

"Doubtful," she tossed as she clocked out and grabbed her lunch bag. "Not much about you surprises me."

His brow rose. "Oh? You know me that well?"

"As well as I want to." She gave him a look that said she was well aware he had fallen into step beside her as she exited the emergency department. "Bye, Gabe."

"You have to eat, Kam. Let me take you to breakfast before I hit the gym."

Her brows knitted together. "You're going to the gym this morning after working over and having to be back here this evening?"

His eyebrows lifted. "Why wouldn't I?"

Kami stared at him as if he were the oddest anomaly. "Do you not need sleep?"

He grinned. "Not when I'm properly motivated."

"You that excited at the prospect of running into Baxter

again?" She glanced at her watch. "You should hurry or you may miss him. Wouldn't want that to happen."

Gabe burst out laughing. "Okay, I'll take a hint and a rain check on the pancakes with whipped cream and cherries."

That evening, Kami glanced at her cell phone and winced. Her mother. Should she answer? Guilt hit her that she considered not doing so. Her mother knew it was time for her to be at work. If she was calling, something must be wrong, right?

"Hi, Mom. I'm about to clock in at work, so I can't talk but a second. What's up?"

"I'm headed out of town," her mother answered. Then a male voice spoke in the background and, muffling the phone, her mother said something back. Then she said into the phone, "Can you feed my cat while I'm gone?"

Why her mother had gotten the scruffy cat, Kami had no clue. Most days she couldn't take care of herself, much less a pet. But at least she'd not left without making arrangements for the stray she'd taken in. Then again, her mother should have been an expert at taking in strays.

Fortunately, her mother didn't make a habit of asking Kami to feed them. At least, not since Kami had moved out the moment she'd graduated from high school and escaped the constant chaos of Eugenia's life.

"I'll swing by in the morning and feed her." Then she couldn't hold back asking, "What's his name?"

"Bubbles. You know that."

"Not the cat. The guy."

"Oh." Her mother giggled and the person in the background said something else, which elicited another giggle. "Sammy. He's a drummer in a band and so good."

Her mother tended to be drawn to artistic types. Especially unemployed ones who needed a place to crash while they waited on their big break. Not that any of them ever stuck around long. They stayed. They used. They moved on. Another arrived to fill the vacancy. It was the story of

Kami's childhood and was still ongoing. Would her mother never learn?

"Okay, Mom," she sighed, putting her lunch in the break-room refrigerator. "I'll feed Bubbles. Any idea when you'll be back?"

"A couple of days. I'll text to let you know for sure. Don't forget to love on Bubbles."

"Right." Because she wanted to stick around at her mother's apartment longer than she absolutely had to. Not. "Well, I'm at work, so I need to go. Bye, Mom. I'll feed Bubbles."

She'd probably love on the scrappy cat, too. Goodness knew that if her mother had a new man in her life, the cat would be ignored until his departure.

Kami had a lot of empathy for Bubbles.

"I was disappointed I didn't see Baxter this morning," Gabe teased as Kami came over to where he sat reviewing chart notes. Gabe loved his job, loved being a doctor, and loved knowing that, if the need arose, he could do everything humanly possible to save someone's life. Knowing he'd see Kami made the prospect of going to work all the sweeter. He never knew what was going to come out of that sassy mouth of hers.

"Maybe he's already given up his exercise kick," Kami mused, not looking as if she cared one way or the other.

Actually, she looked distracted and he wondered who she'd been on the phone with earlier. He'd been coming back into the department from the NICU, where Beverly and her husband had been sitting with their baby. He couldn't imagine the stress they were going through as each day was a struggle for their tiny baby girl to live. He'd been thinking on the fund-raiser, hoping it raised enough money to cover the couple's out-of-pocket medical expenses, not to mention all their day-to-day expenses that still had to be paid despite their being at the hospital instead of their jobs. Whomever Kami had been on the phone with, it hadn't been a pleasant conversation.

"Doubtful." Gabe leaned back in his chair and eyed the petite blonde nurse standing a few feet away. Were there problems with the fund-raiser? Or had the call been personal? "My guess is he was already there and gone by the time I got there. He's determined to buff up for you."

"Yeah, yeah." She didn't sound impressed. "Someone should tell him I'm not into buff."

Gabe arched a brow. "I thought all women were into buff."

She rolled her eyes. "Men are into buff. Any intelligent woman would rather have a man of substance than bulgy muscles."

"Can't a man have both substance and muscles?"

Kami shrugged. "Apparently not."

"You're overlooking the obvious."

Her forehead scrunched. "What's that?"

He waggled his brows. "I'm substance *and* bulgy muscles."

Giving him a critical once-over, she seemed to be debating his claim. "You're not that gross. You don't have that no-neck, bulgy-muscles look I can't stand."

Gabe wasn't sure if she'd insulted or complimented him. "That means I don't count?"

"You don't count, anyway," she said flippantly, handing him a piece of paper she'd jotted patient vitals on.

Ignoring the paper, he asked, "Why's that?"

"We're talking muscles and *substance*, remember?" she said matter-of-factly and gestured to the paper she'd handed him.

Gabe laughed. "Right. I forgot. Disqualified on all counts."

"Exactly. Now, are you going to go see the poor lady in bay three? Her blood pressure is crazy high at two hundred and fifteen over one hundred and thirty-seven."

"Slave driver," he accused, glancing down at the numbers on the paper she'd handed him as he headed toward the bay. "But rightly so."

* * *

Connie Guffrey's EKG was normal, as were her cardiac enzymes. Fortunately, after Kami administered IV medication, her blood pressure decreased to closer to the normal range, but Gabe decided to admit her for overnight observation due to her having developed some shortness of breath and mild chest pain just prior to plans to discharge her home.

Kami agreed doing serial cardiac enzymes overnight was in Ms. Guffrey's best interest and arranged the transfer to the medical floor.

"Don't look now," Mindy advised, "but you know who has been watching you all night. I think he really does want you to buy his date."

Kami immediately turned toward where she'd last seen Gabe. He was busy talking to a respiratory therapist who'd just administered a breathing treatment on an asthma patient.

"I told you not to look," Mindy reminded her.

"Doesn't matter that I looked because you're imagining things."

"Not hardly. And you know what?" Mindy looked absolutely smug. "He's not the only one who's been staring."

Realization dawning as to her friend's meaning, Kami frowned. "I have not been staring."

"Sure you haven't."

"The only time I've looked at the man is when we're discussing a patient or treating a patient." She scowled at her friend. "Don't you have something better to fill your time than making up stories?"

"You just looked at him, Kami."

She gave a *duh* look. "Because you told me not to."

"Exactly, and you immediately seized the excuse to look at him." Mindy bent forward and whispered, "I think you like him."

"Of course I like him. He's a nice guy who I work with. We're friends."

Mindy shook her head. "Not buying it. You should be more than friends."

Kami's gaze narrowed. "Says who?"

"Me." Mindy leaned against the raised desk area that provided a divider for the nurses from the examination bays. "Apparently he thinks so, too, or he wouldn't have asked you to buy his date."

"The reason he asked me to buy his date is because we're just friends and I wouldn't get the wrong idea."

"Which is?"

"That there could ever be something between him and me." Kami outright glared at her friend. "This isn't some television show where doctors fall for nurses and harbor secret feelings. This is reality and the reality is that he and I are just friends and that's all we want to be. Don't make this into something it's not."

"Maybe you should make it into something it's not."

"You sound like a broken record. Let it go," she ordered, then, frowning, added, "Besides, I thought you planned to bid on him."

Mindy crossed her arms, regarding Kami. "I should."

"Good. Buy him. He's taking his date to Gatlinburg for a fun-filled Saturday of visiting the aquarium, playing laser tag and putt-putt golf, riding go-karts, and topping the night off with a dinner show. You'd have a great time."

"I should hire you as my press agent. My bid might break records."

Kami jumped at Gabe's interruption. "I didn't hear you come up. I was...uh...telling Mindy she should bid on you."

"I heard." He grinned at Mindy. "She convince you?"

"I'm saving my pennies, Dr. Nelson."

He laughed. "Good to know."

Mindy looked back and forth between them, smiled as if she was in on a secret, and gave Kami a you-should-go-for-it look. "I hear the receptionist talking to someone. I'm off to see if it's a new patient and they're ready to be triaged."

Kami frowned at her retreating friend. She hadn't heard

anyone registering. Her friend had purposely left her and Gabe alone. Mindy had a distinct lack of subtlety.

"Good to know that since you don't plan to buy my package, you at least plan to save me by convincing others to bid."

"What are friends for?"

He met her gaze. "I've already answered that question."

"True." Still feeling irked at Mindy's comments, she gave him a tight smile. "And we've already established that I'm not bidding on you."

"I'd spot you the money. Imagine—you'd get a fun-filled day in beautiful Gatlinburg, my company, and you wouldn't even have to save your pennies."

"You're wasting your breath."

"Talking to you is never wasted breath."

"Don't try sweet-talking me, Gabe. I know you better than to buy into that garbage."

He held his hands up. "Hey, I was making a legitimate observation, not trying to woo you into bidding on me."

"Right."

He laughed. "Okay, you're right. I was trying to woo you into winning my bid. Can you blame me?"

She gave him a look she hoped said she sure could.

"Fine," he relented. "But I do enjoy our conversations, Kam. You make me smile."

He made her smile, too, but she wasn't convinced that was what he'd meant.

"How is Ms. Guffrey?" she asked to redirect the subject to work. "Any news of how her cardiac tests are holding?"

"She's stable. We're thinking she just panicked and that's where the new symptoms came in. I sure didn't want to send her home and her have an MI."

"Agreed. I'm glad she's doing okay."

He glanced at his watch. "Only another hour until the end of our shift. You want to go for pancakes with me?"

Surprised at his repeated offer from the day before, Kami frowned. "Why would I do that?"

"Because you didn't go yesterday and you have me curious."

"About?"

"You know what." He waggled his brows.

It took her only a second to realize what he referred to.

"Puh-leese. That's what this is about? You want to know how talented I am with my mouth?"

As the words came out of her mouth, Kami realized how her comment could be interpreted. Her cheeks flushed hot.

"That's not…" At his laughter, Kami's face burned even hotter. "You know what I meant, Gabriel Nelson, and what I didn't mean."

"Do I?"

She narrowed her eyes. "You know you do."

He crossed his arms and leaned against the desk. "Maybe, but saying I don't might be a lot more fun. Why are your cheeks so red, Kam?"

Deciding that ignoring him was the best approach, Kami grabbed a brochure and fanned her face. "It is hot in here, isn't it?"

Which was a joke if Kami ever heard one. The emergency department was notoriously cool—purposely so to help keep germs down.

But, for once, the area felt blazing.

"Not particularly." His grin was still in place. "Even better than you going for pancakes with whipped cream and cherries with me would be if you did that *and* went to work out with me. That would send Baxter the message that he was wasting his time, for sure."

"If I ate pancakes then tried to work out, I'd be sick, so, in that regard, you're right about sending a message."

He laughed. "We could have breakfast after we work out."

She looked at him as if he was crazy. "Again, wrong girl, Gabe. I'm not a gym rat and I'm not a girl who would work out on an empty stomach."

His gaze ran over her. "You look like you could be."

"Is that a compliment?"

One corner of his mouth slid upward. "It wasn't an insult."

Kami fought to keep heat from flooding her face again. "Either way, I'm not going to the gym."

"You don't want to see the new and improved Baxter?"

Not that she could go anyway since she had to go feed Bubbles, but Kami pointed out, "You don't even know he'll be there this morning."

"Then you do want to see him?" Gabe sounded surprised.

"No, I don't want to see Baxter. That's why I broke things off."

Gabe immediately seized on her comment. "I thought your relationship ended due to a mutual decision."

"It did. Mutual means I told him things weren't working and he agreed." She glared at Gabe. "Would you stop twisting what I'm saying?"

Feigning innocence, he put his hands up in front of him. "I'm doing nothing of the sort. I'm just trying to buy you breakfast. Quite friendly of me, I'd say."

"You just want to harass me into buying your bid," she countered, knowing it was true. Gabe was her friend, but he was a guy and guys had ulterior motives, right?

"Perhaps," he agreed. "But I was serious about buying you breakfast. We could discuss the fund-raiser."

"What about it?"

"I could help in ways besides the auction."

"Uh-uh." She shook her head. "You're not getting out of the auction, Gabe. We're auctioning off five men and five women and you're the big-ticket item."

Grinning, he asked, "You think so?"

Despite all her efforts to prevent the heat, her face went hot again.

"Women seem to think so." At his pleased look, she added, "Especially Debbie."

That ought to simmer his arrogance down. If not, the brilliant idea that hit her would.

"I'm thinking of asking if she'll use her television connections for local publicity to raise awareness of the fundraiser."

Rather than look annoyed, he looked impressed. "That's brilliant. You want me to check with her?"

A bit floored he'd be willing since he was making such a big deal of the woman planning to buy his date, Kami nodded. Garnering as much free publicity as possible was important and she should have thought of Gabe's connection to the local television station sooner. "Would you?"

His eyes danced. "For you?"

"For Beverly and her baby," she corrected.

"If it would help Beverly's baby get a new heart, I'd talk to the devil himself."

Kami didn't recall Debbie being anywhere near that bad, but she'd only met the woman a couple of times when she'd shown up at the emergency department to bring Gabe a late dinner or a cup of his favorite coffee. On television, she smiled often as she made over homes in the Eastern Tennessee area and seemed nice enough.

"Great." Kami rubbed her palms together. "Encourage her to pay plenty when she wins that Gatlinburg getaway. Sounds like fun."

"Obviously not fun enough. I can't convince you to bid."

"Can I go without you?"

He gave an offended frown. "That appeals more than the total package?"

Rolling her eyes, she clicked her tongue. "You're hardly the total package, Gabe."

Later that morning, Kami hit the drive-through and ordered a coffee to keep her going long enough to get to her mother's when all she really wanted was to go home and crash.

Within a few minutes, she was sitting on her mother's sofa, Bubbles walking back and forth next to her while Kami stroked the cat from her head to the tip of her tail.

Silly cat. Often, Kami wondered if the cat was happier

to see her during her short visits than her mother was. She glanced around the tiny, messy apartment. No family portraits lined the walls. No memorabilia from Kami's childhood. Instead, the walls were bare except for a Red Hot Chili Peppers poster. If there had been a photo, Kami wouldn't have expected it to be of herself, but of this latest guy.

Kami emptied the litter box, bagged her mother's overflowing trash, put in a fresh bag, and picked up the empty food containers and drink cans scattered around the apartment.

Making sure the cat had food and water, Kami grabbed the trash and headed out of the apartment to go home. Sleep had her name all over it.

Only, when she got back to her place and finally crawled into bed, sleep refused to make an appearance.

Perhaps she should have skipped the coffee. She didn't need anything interfering with her rest prior to going into the third night of her three-in-a-row work schedule.

Especially not thoughts of her mother, a silly cat who was home alone, and Gabe.

Why was Gabe even on the list of things running through her mind?

He was a friend. Nothing more.

Ugh. Sleep was not happening.

She reached over and grabbed her phone off her nightstand. Ten a.m. Still early enough that if she dozed off she'd get plenty of rest before going back to work. Not that sleep seemed anywhere near.

Maybe she should get up for an hour, then try again later to go to sleep.

Sometimes after the first night of her three-in-a-row, she struggled to get to sleep the next morning, but never after the second or third nights.

Ugh.

Gripping her phone, she hit the text emblem, then Gabe's number from her contacts.

So, was he there?

Why she asked, she wasn't sure. She didn't care if Baxter had been at the gym or not. She just couldn't sleep. It made no sense, but deep down she knew talking with Gabe—even via text—would take her mind off her mother and off Bubbles, whom she'd considered packing up and bringing home with her. She might have, had her apartment not had a restriction against pets.

Who?

You know who.

Ah, the ex. He was there. Looking better every day.

Good for him.

There was a long enough pause that Kami wondered if Gabe was going to respond again.
Come on, Gabe. I need you to take my mind to a better place so I can close my eyes and stop my brain from racing because I feel sorry for a cat who has my mother as a caregiver.

Want me to take a picture for you next time I see him?

The idea of Gabe snapping a shot of Baxter working out had Kami laughing out loud.

People might get the wrong idea, think you had a man crush on him.

Yeah, well, I'm the kind of guy who would risk it to help a friend.

Good one. I'm still not bidding on you.

She lay back, head sinking into her pillow as she stared at her phone screen.

So you keep saying.

You think I will?

Hoping you will. Spoke to Debbie this morning. She's talking to her producer about the fund-raiser, see what they can come up with to help.

He'd already talked to his ex about the fund-raiser? Then again, Gabe had said he would and she'd never known him not to follow through on something he'd said he'd do.

Awesome. Hope it wasn't too painful. Thank you.

Thank you for all you're doing to help Beverly and her baby girl. If it wasn't for you and Mindy putting so much into this the fund-raiser wouldn't even be happening.

Ha, I'm not sacrificing nearly as much as you. She was only doing what she thought needed to be done to help with the overwhelming expenses that come with having a seriously ill baby. I'm not the one being auctioned off.

So you admit you feel badly for me?

That you're going to have women fighting over you with their wallets? Sure, I'm heartbroken. Poor, poor Gabe.

You're a funny girl, Kam.

She could picture his smile.

Something like that.

Why aren't you asleep? You were clamoring to get home to bed when I asked you to have pancakes with me.

Yeah, she had been. Too bad sleep continued to elude her.

I had errands to run. I may or may not have drunk coffee. Just saying.

It's not too late for those pancakes.

Sure it is. I'm in bed.

Nothing wrong with breakfast in bed. You want syrup or cherries and whipped cream? I recommend the cherries and whipped cream, but I admit I'm biased.

Kami stared at her phone screen and shook her head. The man was incorrigible.

Good thing she knew better than to take him seriously.

A smile on her face, she snuggled into her covers and began typing a response worthy of his outrageous suggestion.

CHAPTER THREE

GABE STARED AT his phone. What was he doing?

Flirting with Kami, that was what. It didn't take a genius to figure that one out.

Question was, why?

He and Kami were friends. So why had he typed out the message and hit Send as if flirting with Kami were the most natural thing in the world?

They often bantered back and forth and he enjoyed their conversations a great deal. Talking with Kami was mentally stimulating. They'd texted before but always light or something about work.

This felt different, not quite all in fun and games.

How about both, Gabe? We can use the whipped cream and cherries for after the pancakes.

Gabe's eyes widened and he wondered if he'd fallen asleep while sitting on the sofa messaging with her. Not once during their friendly banter had Kami ever flirted. Usually she came back with something sassy to put him in his place.

Her comment had his throat tightening; had him swallowing to clear the knot that formed there; had him fighting to keep the image of Kami, cherries, and whipped cream out of his head.

Why did her comment have his heart picking up pace?

Have his breath hitching in his chest?

Have his… This was *Kami* texting him. His friend Kami. His coworker Kami. What was he thinking?

Obviously, he wasn't.

Because if he was he wouldn't be considering calling in a to-go order for pancakes with whipped cream and cherries.

His phone buzzed and he braced himself, drawing on all his willpower not to run out of the door to grab that order.

Only, can you just set them inside the front door? I'll let you know later what my company thinks of your thoughtfulness in delivering breakfast.

Her message dumped a mental bucketful of cold water over his being.

Sitting up straighter on the sofa, Gabe tensed. His teeth clenched and his heart pounded as he typed.

There's someone there? In bed with you?

Why did that bother him? She'd dated Baxter for months, had probably spent many mornings with the accountant. What did it matter who Kami spent her mornings with? It wasn't his business.

You didn't think I meant to share pancakes in bed with you, did you? Ew, Gabe. Get real.

Ah, there was the Kami he knew and expected. Still, for a minute she'd had him going.

Then again, the gutted feeling in his stomach that at this very moment Kami was in bed with some Joe Blow, well, he didn't like the thought at all.

Which didn't make sense. They were just friends, right?

"So, who is this mystery guy?"

Kami flinched. She'd hoped Gabe would have let her

ridiculous attempt to cover her comment go. She'd been meaning to take him down a peg, have him backtracking, but he'd taken her comment seriously and clearly hadn't known what to say back.

To which she'd been flabbergasted with embarrassment and had done what needed to be done to ease the tension crackling over the phone.

She'd made up a boyfriend.

No big deal. Women had been doing it for centuries. Not that Kami ever had, or even fully understood why she had that morning. Not with Gabe. It wasn't as if it mattered what he thought.

"No one you know." She refused to look at him, just kept staring at the computer monitor.

"Does Baxter know about him?"

"Shh." Kami glanced around, hoping Mindy didn't over-hear their conversation. The emergency department had been slow since they'd arrived, and her friend was chatting with a paramedic who'd brought in a non-emergent patient for direct admission just prior to shift change and had stuck around afterward.

"Your best friend doesn't know about a guy you're hav-ing sex with?" Gabe tsked, pulling up a chair next to hers.

"Would you keep it down, please?"

Gabe gave her a suspicious look. "What's wrong with this guy that you don't want anyone to know of his existence?"

"Nothing is wrong with him," she defended. There wouldn't be a thing wrong with him. If he actually existed, she thought. Too bad he didn't. She'd like to throw him in Gabe's face right about now.

"How long have you known him?"

She swiveled her chair to face him. "Since when do you have the right to question me on my love life?"

His expression didn't waver. "Since you invited me to breakfast in bed."

"I didn't invite you to breakfast in bed," she hissed, not bothering to hide her outraged horror at the mere idea.

"Technically, you did."

Technically?

Kami's temples throbbed as she thought back over their conversation. Technically. Ugh.

"This is the most ridiculous conversation I've ever had." She pushed back her chair, stood to walk away, but he grabbed her hand, his hold gentle but firm enough to stop her.

She glared at where he touched her. Anger. That was why her skin burned there.

"Be careful, Kami," he warned. "Don't jump into something so fast on the heels of your breakup with Baxter."

Kami didn't know whether to burst out laughing or to cry. That Gabe would say not to rush into a new relationship when he usually had a new girl on his arm the week following a breakup was comical. She and Baxter had called it quits five, no, six weeks ago. Had she been in bed with another man, she still would have logged more getting-over-it time than Gabe put in prior to jumping into another bed. She was sure of it.

Men were so hypocritical.

"Take note, Gabe." She pulled her hand free. "My love life is none of your business."

"I am one hundred percent positive I'd rather have been in on this conversation than the one I just had with Eddie Pruitt."

Ugh. Mindy would have to overhear that. No doubt her friend would jump to all sorts of wrong conclusions, but at the moment Kami just wanted away from Gabe. Far away.

"Then you're welcome to this conversation, because I'm done with it."

With that, she left Mindy and Gabe staring after her.

"You want to tell me what you said to my best friend that upset her?"

Gabe wasn't sure what he'd said that had put Kami on the defensive. He'd been concerned and her hackles had stood at full attention. Even if he had known why she'd gotten so irate, he doubted he'd discuss it with Mindy.

If Kami hadn't told her friend about this mystery guy, then Gabe wasn't going to be the one to spill the beans.

Mindy studied him a moment. Then her expression softened. "You trying to get her to buy your date again?"

"No." If Kami was involved with another man, she wouldn't be buying his date. Nor would he ask her to. That went beyond the call of friendship.

Only, something didn't feel right about the whole conversation.

Then it hit him.

"Excuse me, Mindy. Kami might have been done with our conversation, but I wasn't."

He found Kami restocking bay one despite the fact that the shelf wasn't low.

He wasted no time in asking, "If you were in bed with another man this morning, why were you texting me?"

Letting out an exasperated hiss, Kami turned toward him, pursed her lips, crossed her arms, and glared. "Fine. I wasn't in bed with another man."

He let that sink in, let the wave of emotions wash over him and sought to label the one beating him down.

Relief. Why was he relieved that she hadn't been in bed with someone?

Because they'd been flirting and he'd liked it?

"Why did you lead me to think you were?"

An annoyed sigh escaped her lips. "Because you shouldn't have said what you did about breakfast in bed."

Now she wasn't meeting his eyes, which made him all the more curious. "Why not?"

"Because you didn't mean it." She gave him a disgusted look. "No wonder women like Debbie don't let go if you make comments like those when you don't mean them."

"First off, I don't make comments like those to Debbie or any other woman. Second, who says I didn't mean my offer?"

She rolled her eyes upward. "Right."

"Right, what?"

Her hand went to her hip and she stared him down. "Right, you meant it when you offered to bring me breakfast in bed."

He had. It floored him as much as it did her.

He cocked a brow. "You're saying I didn't?"

Looking flustered, she huffed out, "Quit being ridiculous, Gabe. Of course you didn't."

He held her gaze, refusing to look away or back down. "Want to bet?"

"You'd lose," she returned.

The challenge in her eyes had Gabe knowing he'd do nothing of the sort.

"Guess we'll find out when I bring you breakfast in bed tomorrow, won't we?"

She let out a huff of air. "You aren't bringing me breakfast in bed tomorrow or any other day."

"You'll see. Tomorrow morning." He glanced at his watch, saw it was after midnight. "Technically, *this* morning. You're going to eat every bite and you're going to like it."

Annoyed at him and herself, Kami gawked at Gabe, not quite believing that she was arguing with him about breakfast in bed.

That he was arguing back.

Had they ever argued? Or raised their voices with each other?

Never.

That they were now, over breakfast in bed, was the most ludicrous thing she could imagine.

So ludicrous that, despite her tension of moments before, she burst out laughing.

His face tight, Gabe's gaze narrowed. "What's so funny?"

"You."

He frowned. "I see nothing funny about this."

"Really? You don't find the fact you just threatened to

make me eat every bite of my breakfast and that I was going to like it hilarious?" Another round of laughter hit her and she grabbed her stomach. "Oh, Gabe, I thought you had a better sense of humor."

His expression easing, a smile twitched at his lips. "Okay, so maybe a little hilarious, but don't think that gets you out of breakfast. You are going to eat up. Mmm…good."

"Yeah, yeah," she mocked, grateful the tension inside her had dissipated. "Keep threatening me and I'm going to report you to my nearest supervisor."

"I am your nearest supervisor," he reminded her, his tone back to its usual teasing.

"There is that."

"Hey, you two, we have incoming." Mindy stuck her head into the bay. "Motor vehicle accident. One dead at scene, two critical on their way here."

Their slow night morphed into total chaos as at the same time as the first ambulance arrived, so did a private vehicle with an overdose victim requiring multiple doses of Narcan administration prior to them being able to revive the woman and transfer her to the ICU.

The night flew by with one patient after another. By the time she'd given her report to the day-shift nurse taking her place, Kami was exhausted.

She clocked out, visited with an even more exhausted-appearing Beverly in the NICU for a few minutes, stopped by to feed and water Bubbles, fought guilt over leaving her mother's cat home alone while she drove home, showered, and was about to crawl into her bed when she heard knocking.

"Who in the world?"

Glancing down at her shorts and well-worn Ed Sheeran T-shirt, Kami headed toward the apartment door. She wasn't wearing a bra, but she wasn't overly endowed and doubted anyone would be able to tell.

"Who is it?" she called through the door at the same time as she stretched on her tiptoes to peek through the peephole.

Gabe!

Carrying bags displaying a local pancake house logo.

He hadn't.

He had.

"Delivery boy."

Heart pounding against her rib cage, she leaned her forehead against the door. Gabe was at her house. With breakfast.

Why?

Why was her pulse pounding in her ears?

"Wrong address. I didn't order anything," she called back.

What was he doing there? Why did she suddenly feel the need to go put on a bra after all? And a dozen other layers? Why was her heart racing as if something really good was happening?

"It's a special delivery."

"Sorry, I don't open my door for strangers."

"What's wrong, Kam? Someone in there with you?" he teased. "I could always leave the bags by the door."

Undoing the lock and dead bolt, she flung open the door. "That, Dr. Nelson, was a low blow."

He grinned. "You'd have done the same had the opportunity presented itself."

He had her there.

"Invite me in," he reminded her when she kept standing in the doorway, glaring at him.

"Because you're a creature of the night and can't enter unless invited in first?" She stepped aside, motioning for him to come in.

"Something like that," he tossed back, entering the apartment and glancing around. "Where do you want these?"

"Not in my bed." She closed the front door and followed him, not quite believing he was there, inside her home. With breakfast.

He laughed. "Ah, now come on. You're spoiling my fun."

"Right." She glanced around her mostly clean living

room, thinking it wasn't in too bad shape for the end of three nights on at the hospital.

"How about you set them on the coffee table?" Then, thinking it might be easier, she suggested, "Or on the table over there?"

The apartment, although not really big, had an open floor plan so that the kitchen, dining area, and living room were all visible to each other. It was one of the features Kami had fallen in love with when she'd first walked into the place. That and its close vicinity to both the hospital and the university. She'd started out there with a roommate, but the woman had married and moved away several months ago. Kami had never bothered to replace her since she'd been mere months from reaching her house-down-payment goal and would hopefully be buying her first home soon.

Someday soon she would own her own home and no one would be able to take it away from her. A place where she'd never have to move from because it would be hers. A place where if she wanted to bring her mother's cat to her home, she could.

With her next paycheck, she'd hit the target she'd set for herself years ago and she'd start the search to make her homeowner dream a reality.

"Either way is fine," she rushed on.

"Let's do the coffee table." He set the bags down on the laminated wooden table. "Less formal."

Still way more formal than her bedroom.

Her cheeks heated at the thought.

She stopped moving. "Why are you here, Gabe?"

"I'd think that was obvious."

She arched her brows and waited.

"I promised you breakfast."

"Actually, you threatened breakfast in bed."

He picked the bags back off the coffee table. "Point me in the right direction."

Kami had thought her cheeks had been hot before, but the heat coming off them now could melt the polar ice caps.

"You goofball. I ought to take you up on that." She rolled her eyes, trying to ease the twirling in her stomach. "That would teach you."

At his mischievous look, she shook her head.

"Or, more likely, not teach you anything at all." She sighed. "You're not going in my bedroom, Gabe. Not now or ever."

"Now who's threatening who?" he teased, putting the bags back down and unpacking the plastic containers. "Jeez, Kam, you're grumpy in the mornings. Now I know why you work night shift."

Eyeing the numerous containers he was pulling from the bags, she asked, "How is it that you're so cheery when I know you were up all night?"

He waggled his brows. "What man isn't cheery when he's been up all night?"

Rather than respond, Kami gave in to the smell coming from her coffee table. "Why do you have three drinks?"

He pulled out a milk carton and a plastic orange-juice container from one of the bags.

"Five drinks?" she corrected.

"I wasn't sure what you'd want, so I got a variety of choices. I aim to please, so I'll drink what you don't want."

"That was thoughtful of you."

He grinned. "I'm a thoughtful kind of guy."

Kami sank onto her sofa, suspiciously eyeing the man unpacking a third bag. "It's been my experience that when a man does something thoughtful he wants something in return."

He shot her a serious look. "Baxter has a lot to answer for."

Kami shook her head. "I wasn't referring to Baxter."

He continued unpacking plastic containers and setting them on her coffee table. "What was the guy's name before him? Kent or Kenny or something?"

Surprised that he recalled her previous boyfriend's name, Kami nodded. "Kent, but I really didn't mean him, specifically, either. Just was making a comment about men in general."

"I'm not like other guys."

"Sure you aren't," she said, although secretly she agreed. Gabe was unlike anyone she'd ever known. Although he never stuck around, just as her mother's numerous boyfriends hadn't, Gabe never made promises that he would. Plus, he was genuinely a likable person. She didn't recall liking any of the men her mother had brought in and out of their lives. "You delivered breakfast." She gave as mean a look as she could muster. "If you brought whipped cream and cherries, I'll know for sure you're up to no good."

Eyes sparkling with mischief, he popped the top off a plastic container. Sure enough, inside was a big dollop of thick whipped cream with six or seven long-stemmed cherries to the side.

Kami's breath sticking in her tight chest, she lifted her gaze to Gabe's. "Oh, my."

He laughed. "Am I in trouble?"

"I'm beginning to think you're always trouble," she mused, tempted to reach for a cherry. They really were her favorite, but no way would she stick one in her mouth while Gabe watched. Besides, as difficult as it was simply to breathe at the moment, she'd likely choke if she did.

"There goes my knight-in-shining-armor image."

"I've never thought you were a knight in shining armor," she scoffed.

"There is that." He placed the now empty and folded bags on the floor. "Which is one of the reasons I like you."

Ignoring his comment, she eyed the multiple containers as he popped off lids. "Which of those did you get for me?"

"The ones I knew you'd like."

She started to ask how he'd begin to know what she liked for breakfast, but asked instead, "What if I told you I didn't like pancakes?"

"I'd know you were lying." He scooted a plastic container toward her. "These are yours."

She eyed the contents. "Are those pecans?"

He nodded.

Rather than digging into the delicious-looking pancakes, she wrinkled her nose. "What if I told you I had a nut allergy?"

As if he knew she was purposely being ornery, his eyes twinkled. "I'd know you were lying," he repeated.

"Lots of people have nut allergies," she needlessly pointed out.

"But you don't." His smile said it all.

"How can you be so sure?"

He laughed, shaking his head at her obtuseness. "How long have I worked with you, Kam? Nuts are your favorite snack. Pecans, almonds, walnuts, cashews. I've seen you eat them all and don't recall a single hive ever."

He had her there.

"But if you suddenly develop an itch, I promise to scratch it."

Um, no. Gabe would not be scratching her itch.

"I don't have a nut allergy," she conceded, wondering that he'd paid attention to what she ate for snacks. Who knew?

"Or an aversion to pancakes," he added in case she went back to that.

She sighed. "Do you really have to hear me say it?"

He nodded.

She glanced upward, as if asking for help in dealing with the likes of him. "Fine. I love pancakes. They're amazing. My favorite carbs. Especially hot pancakes, which these aren't going to be if you don't quit talking and let me eat."

He laughed and popped the lid on another container, revealing bacon and sausage links, and held the tray toward her. "Help yourself."

She shook her head, then reached for a tiny bottle of syrup, unscrewed the top, and poured a generous amount over the plastic tray of pecan pancakes. Taking a bite, she couldn't contain the pleasure her throat emitted at the fluffy cakes coated with sticky sweet syrup.

"Mmm…you're forgiven for being a pain. That's good."

"Apparently."

Kami opened the eyes she hadn't even been aware she'd closed, met his gaze, and smiled. "Don't go being all smug just because this is amazing."

"Would I do that?"

"In a heartbeat."

He laughed and, rather than sit on the sofa next to her, he sat on the floor.

"You could have sat up here. I wouldn't have bitten you."

"Which is why I chose the floor."

"Seriously, Gabe, you need to quit that." She took another bite, enjoyed every morsel as she chewed, then added, "Someday it's going to get you into trouble."

"Possibly," he agreed, munching on a piece of bacon. "But life sure is fun in the meantime."

Still working on her pancakes, Kami eyed him. "It must be good to be you."

In between bites of the omelet he'd ordered for himself, Gabe stared from across the coffee table. "Why's that?"

She waved her empty fork in the air. "Women just let you do whatever you want and you get away with it."

His brow arched. "You're referring to me bringing you breakfast and you letting me?"

When he put it like that…

"Don't make yourself sound normal and me sound like the psycho."

"You said it, not me."

She laughed.

"Okay, so this was nice." It only hurt a little to admit that. "But I didn't really expect you to show with breakfast. I'd actually forgotten you'd threatened to do so."

"Good to know I'm so easy to forget."

She doubted any woman in the history of the world had forgotten him. Take Debbie, for instance. Had Gabe showered her with such attention—more, since they'd actually been dating—no wonder the woman was so desperate to get him back. Giving up a man like Gabe couldn't be easy even when one knew it was inevitable.

"Had you shown up fifteen minutes later, you'd have been stuck eating this all by yourself. I was about to go to bed."

He nodded toward her clothes. "Like your pajamas."

She glanced down at her T-shirt and loose shorts. It could have been much worse. "You should catch me on a good morning."

"That an offer?"

Good grief. If Mindy ever heard him making such over-the-top comments, Kami would never convince her Gabe was just teasing.

She shook her head. "No, Gabe, that's not an offer. Quit saying such things."

Kami was right. Gabe did need to quit saying such things.

But teasing her, getting a rise out of her, sure did tempt him.

"Afraid you'll get weak and say yes?"

She arched a brow. "Are you saying a woman saying yes to you is a sign of weakness?"

Gabe chuckled. "Never."

"For the record, you're leaving that whipped cream and cherries for me to eat later, at my leisure, without you."

"If I say yes does that make me weak?"

She laughed. "I'd say it makes you a smart man for not coming between a woman and her dessert."

"Point taken."

They ate in silence for the next few minutes. Then Kami stood and stretched, drawing Gabe's gaze to the expanse of skin on display, making him realize that he'd never seen her legs before.

Not unless they were covered by scrubs. But that couldn't be right because he would have seen her at the Christmas party and she wouldn't have had on her nursing uniform then.

He racked his brain.

"A black pantsuit."

Her brows veed. "Huh?"

"It's what you were wearing at the Christmas party."

She stared blankly. "What does that have to do with anything?"

"I was looking at your legs, and—"

"Hold up. Why were you looking at my legs?"

"I was thinking that I had never seen you out of scrubs," he continued, ignoring her question. "But that isn't right because you weren't wearing scrubs at last year's Christmas party."

"Which doesn't explain why you were looking at my legs," she reminded him.

"You have great legs, Kam. You should show them off more."

"Oh, yeah. I'll just roll up in the emergency room wearing a miniskirt."

He waggled his brows. "I wouldn't complain."

"I'm sure you wouldn't." She snapped her fingers and waved them in front of her face. "Eyes up here, Gabe. Not on my legs."

"You're such a party pooper, Kam."

She laughed. "You're crazy and did you really just call me a party pooper?"

"If the shoe fits."

Shaking her head, Kami gathered her leftover pancakes and the trash, using the empty bags to store them. "You're lucky I'm not wearing shoes or I might be throwing them at you."

His gaze immediately fell to her bare feet. "Are those emojis on your toenails?"

Kami's gaze dropped to her toes and the most secretive smile he'd ever seen lit her face. "Smiley faces, Gabe. Those are smiley faces."

"Now you've gone and done it. I'm never going to be able to look at you the same."

Her gaze lifted. "Because I have painted toenails?"

"Legs that go on forever and smiley faces on your toes. A man could do worse."

"Just you forget you ever saw my legs or my smiley faces."

He stood and helped gather the remaining food and drinks. "Not going to happen."

"They're burned onto your retinas for life? Like tragic scars?"

He followed her into her kitchen, took in the brightly colored walls and multicolored dishes on the counters. What was it called? Festive ware? That didn't sound quite right. Fiesta ware. That was it.

The room fit the barefoot woman opening a cabinet and tossing trash into a hidden bin.

"There's enough left for me to have breakfast tomorrow," she mused when she put the leftovers in the fridge.

"Or I could just bring you breakfast again in the morning."

She spun toward him and pointed her finger. "No."

"Now that I've seen those toes, I'm not going to be able to stay away, Kam," he teased, enjoying the color that rose in her cheeks. "You had to have realized that when you opened the door bare-legged and laid-back sexy."

"Yeah. Yeah. I have that problem all the time." Her gaze hit the ceiling, then came back to his. "Don't fool yourself, Gabe. I opened the door because you had food. No other reason."

He laughed. "I won't ever have ego problems with you around to keep me grounded."

"You don't need me to fluff your ego," she said. "You have a whole slew of women for that without me joining the fan club."

Something about the way she said it struck Gabe. Not that he had a fan club or that many women fluffing his ego. He'd always been blessed with an abundance of dates, but he had never seen himself as she was making him out to be.

"But you are a fan, aren't you, Kam?" he asked, curious as to her answer.

"Your fan?" she asked, turning from the refrigerator and leaning against it to stare at him. Her eyes flashed with something he couldn't quite read. "Yeah, Gabe. I'm a total groupie. You know it."

Her tone and expression were flippant, but something sparked in those green depths that he couldn't quite read, as if maybe there was a spark of attraction there, too.

"But, seriously, breakfast was nice. You'll understand if I throw you out because I'm ready for bed." When he started to say something, she jabbed her finger in his direction. "Don't even go there. Not if you value your life."

Yeah, his former thoughts had been nothing short of ridiculous. Gabe laughed. "So what you're saying is breakfast in bed with you doesn't start or end in your bed?"

She bared her teeth in an exaggerated smile. "Exactly."

"Anyone ever told you that you're a party pooper?"

"A time or two," she admitted with a small laugh. "Now, time for you to go so I can get some beauty sleep."

"You don't need it."

Her brow arched. "Pardon?"

"Beauty sleep. You don't need it."

She didn't. There was something inherently attractive about her air-dried hair pulled back in a braid with a few escaped strands framing her face, her brightly scrubbed skin with its faint spattering of freckles across her nose, her loose T-shirt and shorts, and those long legs and happy toenails.

"Right," she scoffed at his beauty claim, shaking her head. "What was in that milk you drank, anyway?"

"Calcium and vitamin D."

"Hallucinogenics, too, perhaps?"

Perhaps, because, looking at Kami, he was definitely seeing things he hadn't in the past.

She really was beautiful. Funny, he'd never thought about that before. Sure, if asked, he'd have said she was an attractive woman, but he'd never really looked at her before. Not in that way.

Not as he was looking at her. Not with the idea that he'd like to run his hands over those legs and…

"It's the toenails. They've cast a spell on me."

Kami wiggled her toes. "Lay off the toenails, dude. They make me happy."

"Since you didn't seem to think the bare legs thing would jibe, I could put in a motion to allow open-toed shoes."

Kami shook her head. "Yep, that'll go over so much better than the bare legs. Nothing like exposed toes, sharp instruments, and bleeding patients."

"You have a point," he conceded. "Maybe we just need to spend more time together away from the hospital."

Her smile slipped and she stared at her feet. "You really shouldn't say things like that."

She kept reminding him of that.

At first, he'd agreed. But the more he teased her, the more he wondered why he had to stop when their conversations usually made her smile and come right back at him. When she made him smile.

"Why shouldn't I say things like that?"

Seeming taken aback at his question, she pushed off from where she leaned against the countertop. "Because we both know you don't mean them."

She rubbed one foot across the other in what was likely a nervous gesture. The motion drew Gabe's attention, had him wanting to touch her there, kiss her there and work his way up.

"That's where you're wrong," he admitted to her and to himself. "I've had a great time. So much so, I want to do this again. Same time tomorrow morning?"

Her eyes widened. "No. Not tomorrow morning or the morning after that, either."

"Why not?"

She looked flustered, as if she wasn't sure what to say. "Because you being here is insane."

"What's insane about us having breakfast together?"

"We're not that good friends."

Did she not think so?

"We will be."

CHAPTER FOUR

GABE DIDN'T SHOW at Kami's house the following morning, but he did text a photo that made her burst out laughing and eased the tension she'd fought all night.

She texted him back.

That does it. You're officially a creeper.

Some things a woman just has to see to believe.

Some things a woman should never see.

Hey, you were the one who dated the guy.

Not for his gym skills.

Which leads me to wonder what skills you were dating him for. Do tell, Kam.

Never.

A girl who kisses and doesn't tell, eh?

You'll never know.

Keep flashing those smiley-face toenails my way and I'll prove you wrong.

Kami gripped her phone a little tighter as she reread his message. There went the butterflies in her belly again, so she reminded herself Gabe was just being Gabe and she shouldn't read anything into his comments.

She texted again.

Ha. Ha. I see you had your morning dose of calcium, vitamin D, and hallucinogenics.

A full glass. Want to meet me for breakfast?

Nope. I already ate.

Her heart wasn't racing because part of her wanted to say yes. Really, it wasn't.

A pity. What did you have?

Whipped cream and cherries.

Now, why had she gone and admitted that? She was as bad as him.

Forget the toenails. I want to see your knotted stems. Show me.

She shouldn't do it, but she was going to anyway.

Feeling completely giggly, she held out her phone toward the seven perfectly knotted cherry stems she'd left on a napkin because she'd not been able to bring herself to toss them. Silly. What was she planning? To save them as a keepsake?

A keepsake of what? Gabe bringing her breakfast? They were only friends. Had only ever been friends.

Would only ever be friends.

Yet, here she was sending a picture of her knotted cherry stems and grinning like a complete idiot.

Someday you're going to show me how you do that in person.

Keep dreaming.

I am. Of smiley toenails and talented tongues.

Pervert.

Leaning back against her kitchen countertop, she typed on.

Obviously you aren't working out nearly hard enough if you're able to keep up your end of this conversation.

Keeping things up has never been a problem for me. Nor working hard. I'm talented that way. Want me to show you?

Kami took a deep breath. She and Gabe had always gone back and forth at work, had occasionally texted each other funny little snippets, but this…this they'd never done.

This had blatant sexual overtones. It was a kind of sexual energy bouncing back and forth between them.

She didn't understand it, and the more she reminded him he shouldn't say such things, the more determined he seemed to say them.

Then again, how could she fuss at him when she'd been the one to bring up the whipped cream and cherries?

Gabe was a gorgeous man, a successful doctor. He had beautiful, successful women chasing him. His last girlfriend was a local television celebrity, for goodness' sake. What was he doing carrying on this conversation with Kami as if their relationship were blossoming into something beyond friendship?

He was just playing with her. Nothing more.

Why, she didn't know, nor did it matter. What mattered was her keeping things in perspective. Otherwise, she might get caught up in their play and end up hurt. Hadn't she learned anything from her mother's many mistakes? From the constant whirlwind of men who'd come in and out of her mother's life?

Gabe didn't run into Kami's ex at the gym the following morning.

Usually he put in an hour or so on his days off work, but today he had an excess of energy he needed to burn and he was hitting it hard.

Probably hard enough that he'd be sore, but he didn't slow his pace on the rowing machine.

Not even when his phone buzzed, indicating he had a text message. Hoping he'd be pleasantly surprised, he glanced down at his smartwatch, saw the name, and kept right on rowing.

The number hadn't been a pleasant surprise.

Although he didn't want to deal with Debbie's incessant efforts to get back together—efforts that had intensified since he'd contacted her about the fund-raiser—she wasn't the source of his restlessness.

Kami was.

He liked her, had liked her from the moment they met when he'd joined the emergency department in Knoxville the year before. She was dependable, fun, had a quick wit, and a sharp mouth that didn't mind putting him in his place.

And often.

He'd always found working with her refreshing, had always found himself seeking her company at the hospital and at the occasional work get-togethers they'd both been at.

Obviously, none of these had involved cherries as he wouldn't have forgotten had she tied a knot in a cherry stem.

An image of a knotted stem between her full rosy lips had a fresh trickle of sweat running down his forehead.

Now, where had that come from?

He didn't think of her that way. Not that Kami wasn't an attractive woman. With her sandy hair, heart-shaped face, big green eyes, and full lips, she was. Gabe had just always preferred tall, curvy brunettes or willowy blondes to petite women with smart mouths.

Since he'd seen that picture of those seven cherry stems with their perfect knots, his thoughts of Kami had changed.

Or maybe it had been the legs that went on and on.

Or the bare feet with their happy toenails.

Or the way her eyes danced when she countered him tit for tat and never let him have the last word.

Or the little happy bop she sometimes did when she put him in his place.

Or the...

Slowing his pace, Gabe wiped the sweat off his brow with the back of his hand and forced himself to begin cooling down.

He'd had enough for the morning. Time to go shower, eat, and not think about cherry stems, long legs, happy toes, or little dances anymore.

He liked their relationship, the camaraderie they shared at work. Why would he risk messing up a great working relationship? A great friendship? There were dozens of women to date, to fantasize about.

He wasn't willing to risk losing a friendship he valued.

Kami was off-limits as anything more than his friend, so maybe she was right to tell him he shouldn't say certain things and he needed to start heeding her advice.

Now, if he could only convince his body to go along.

"You didn't answer my text yesterday," Gabe accused the first moment he and Kami were alone during their next emergency-room shift together. He'd just finished suturing a fifteen-year-old kid who'd cut his hand on a broken glass and he'd followed her to the supply closet.

"I was busy." Rather than look at him, she kept gathering the supplies she'd come for.

Gabe frowned. "Too busy to answer my text?"

She glanced his way, arched her brow. "Did I answer your text?"

"No."

She gave a pointed look. "Then I was too busy to answer."

Right. Gabe studied her, taking note of the tension pouring off her. The unusual tension. Kami rolled with the punches. Nothing ever got to her too much. She was usually all smiles and sass. He knew he'd made the decision to back off from their flirting to preserve their friendship, but someone had put a bee in her bonnet.

Or had their flirting been the culprit and he'd not checked things soon enough? Regardless, he'd contacted her about business, not pleasure.

"Then you don't care that Debbie's producer wants to meet with us about the fund-raiser?"

Kami's dour expression took on new life, sparking her into her usual excitement. "That's awesome."

Glad to see the light back in her eyes, he wasn't quite ready to ignore her former cold shoulder. "But since you didn't answer my text, I wasn't sure when to tell her we could meet them."

Her eyes narrowed suspiciously. "We? Them?"

"Me, you, Debbie, her producer."

Her brows veed. "Why are you and Debbie going to be there? Couldn't I just meet with the producer?"

As if she didn't know. "You tell me, friend-who-refuses-to-bid-on-my-charity-date."

Okay, so he probably needed to quit with the poking comments, but he was irked that she'd ignored his message the day before and him for most of their shift thus far.

Kami's nose scrunched. "Oh."

"Yeah, oh," he agreed, then returned her sharp look. "Have I mentioned that you owe me?"

A tolerant smile twitched at her lips. "A few times."

"I'll expect you not to forget."

"I never forget when I owe someone something. You're

doing this because you're a good man and want to help our coworker raise funds to help cover her baby's heart-transplant expenses. This has nothing to do with me, so I owe you nothing."

Her comment had put him in his place and he couldn't argue with her, not even teasingly.

"Way to make a guy feel bad." He hung his head in mock shame, then looked up and winked.

She smiled, this time for real, and the tension within Gabe eased.

"I was complimenting you," she pointed out. "Can I help it if you had a guilty conscience?"

Eyes locked with hers, he took a step toward her, stared down into her wide green eyes. "First compliment that ever left me feeling reprimanded."

"That's because you don't get reprimanded nearly often enough," she countered, her gaze dropping from his scrutiny and landing on his mouth.

She sucked in a tiny sharp breath, then glanced away to stare at something behind him. He wanted to touch her face, to brush his fingers over the stray hairs along her face that had escaped her clip, to place his thumb beneath her chin and lift her mouth.

To his.

Gabe swallowed. "You volunteering for the job? Because I'm willing."

Her gaze cut back to his. "Gabe, I can't do this."

"This?" he asked, knowing the gap between them had somehow shortened because he was so close she had to feel his breath against her face. He could feel hers; he wanted to feel more.

"You. Me. This."

She closed her eyes, but rather than take advantage of the moment, he waited.

"We can't do this. We'd regret it forever."

"What would we regret forever?" He knew what she meant, but asked anyway. He needed to hear her say it out loud. Maybe then it would drive the message home because what she'd closed her eyes to hide hadn't been regretting what they might do, but what they wouldn't.

"Oops." Mindy opened the tiny supply room's door and spotted them. "Sorry. I didn't realize you were in here. Together. Alone."

Kami's eyes had popped open, had filled with guilt and so much more he couldn't label. Gabe wanted to pull her close, tell her it was okay, that he was positive Mindy would celebrate if she'd actually seen anything physical happening.

Gabe had wanted something physical to happen. Had wanted to kiss her. Maybe he shouldn't have hesitated. Maybe he should have covered her mouth with his and settled his curiosity of what Kami's mouth would feel like.

But probably not.

Her hackles were back up and she refused to look at him.

"Very alone," Mindy continued, looking quite pleased at what she'd interrupted. "I can come back later."

"No. Don't do that. I'm finished here." Kami stepped back, bumping against a shelf, then blushing at having done so. "I have what I need."

"I'm sure you do," Mindy teased, looking back and forth between them with a smile.

Kami winced. "As for Dr. Nelson, he was telling me good news about promoting the fund-raiser. Great news about the fund-raiser," she corrected, sounding breathy. "You should ask him about it, since you're the event's co-chair and are going to have to take my place on this one because I'm done."

With that, Kami rushed from the room.

"What did you do this time? And why do I have to keep asking you that?"

"Good question."

Mindy's hand went to her hip. "What's she done with?"

Gabe shrugged. He wasn't sure of the answer to that, either, but suspected she'd meant him and whatever was happening between them.

Mindy let out a long sigh and shook her head. "You convinced her to bid on you yet?"

He glanced toward his coworker. "You think I have a chance of changing her mind?"

Mindy shrugged. "I'd say you have a chance at anything you set your mind to, including my best friend buying that date package."

"I guess we'll see."

She sure didn't seem to have any problems pushing him away.

Or not answering his text.

Plus, the last thing he'd call the way his body had responded to her closeness, to her staring at his mouth, to the sparks that had been flying between them, was safe.

Unless playing with fire was safe, because he felt that hot under the collar.

"I'm sorry."

Not wanting to acknowledge Gabe, but knowing she should, Kami nodded and took another bite of the sandwich she'd packed for her after-midnight "lunch." They'd finally gotten a slow moment and she'd clocked out for her break.

Gabe had been tied up with discharging an asthma-attack patient who had settled down perfectly with a steroid injection and breathing treatment.

He sat down at the break table. "I don't want to lose your friendship, Kami."

"I feel the same," she admitted, wondering if it was already too late. She'd felt something in that room. Something that had been hinted at and building for days, maybe longer, but that she'd been able to tamp down.

Now she wasn't sure she was going to be able to safely tuck it back away. *It* being the chemistry she'd felt with Gabe as he'd zeroed in on her mouth.

She'd wanted him to kiss her.

To run his fingers through her hair and hold her to him and devour her mouth; to press his body to hers and… Ugh. Her brain had to quit going there.

"Good," he agreed. "As much as I love to tease you, I don't want to do anything that undermines our friendship."

Not sure what to say, she nodded again.

He sat next to her, quiet for a few moments. "Something's changed between us, hasn't it?"

She turned to him. "Do you really need to ask me that?"

He eyed her for long seconds before asking, "Are we going to be okay?"

Did he mean individually or together? Because for all her mind slips since their supply-room episode, she really couldn't see there ever being a "together" between them.

"We're going to be okay." They would be. He'd forget whatever this little blip of attraction was and move on to the next hottie who caught his eye. She'd go on being happy with her life, and if the right guy, a safe guy who wouldn't use her or leave her, came along, then she'd get involved again.

Baxter had been safe.

Now, where had that thought come from? Baxter didn't count. There had been no magic when Baxter had kissed her, touched her.

Gabe hadn't touched her or kissed her and yet the supply-room incident felt surreal.

"Well, as long as we're going to be okay. I really don't want to lose you, Kam." With that, he reached over and patted her hand much as an adult might pat a child's hand, then pushed back his chair and left her to stare after him.

Nothing awkward about that conversation, she thought as he left the small break room. Nothing at all.

Maybe she needed to stay away from Gabe for a while. At least until she got her head wrapped around what had happened.

Almost happened.

Because nothing had happened.

She closed her eyes, recalling the moment. Nothing physical might have happened, but something had happened.

Something intense and she didn't like it.

Gabe was messing with her immune system.

Maybe she needed to avoid him and pray her mother hurried home so she'd get another inoculation of all the reasons why messing with a man like Gabe was nothing but heartache waiting to happen.

CHAPTER FIVE

KAMI SUCCESSFULLY AVOIDED Gabe for the rest of that shift and most of the next night's. Unfortunately, she couldn't completely avoid him as there were times patient care demanded their interaction.

She was polite. He was polite. Everything was awkward.

A heart-attack patient came in by ambulance and coded minutes after arrival.

Under any circumstances Kami hated working codes.

Not that the medical demands were more than other emergency situations she encountered, but because a code meant someone's life was on the line, and if the code team failed, that person was gone forever.

And everyone who knew and loved that person would forever be changed.

The current code she was working, happening right at the end of her night shift, was no different and she silently prayed for the man and his family.

Gabe was doing compressions on the man's chest, while she delivered breaths via an air bag.

A unit secretary recorded the events and Mindy readied the crash cart for Gabe's instructions to defibrillate the man in hopes of shocking his heart into beating again.

"On the count of three, all clear," Gabe instructed, keeping the compressions going. "One. Two. Three. All clear."

Kami and Gabe both stepped back as Mindy pushed

the button and the man's body jerked from the electrical impulse.

Nothing.

Putting his interlocked hands back on the man's chest, Gabe went back to compressions and Kami to delivering precious air, watching the rise and fall of his chest from each squeeze and relaxation of the bag.

When the defibrillator had reset, Mindy motioned that it was ready.

"On the count of three, again, all clear," Gabe ordered. "One. Two. Three. All clear."

The man's lifeless body jerked. A bleep appeared on the cardiac monitor then went back to nothing.

Kami expected Gabe to call the code.

But he just kept compressing the man's chest in rhythmic pushes as the rest of the team did their jobs.

Gabe had Mindy defibrillate the man again. Nothing.

Still, rather than call the code, Gabe went back to his compressions.

Wondering why he hadn't called an end, why they were still trying to revive the man when too long had passed, she studied Gabe in between keeping a close check on their patient in hopes of a miracle. What did Gabe know that made him keep this code going so much longer than was usual?

"Want to swap places?" she offered.

He had to be exhausted. CPR took great effort.

Not glancing up from the man's face, Gabe shook his head, called for the defibrillator yet again.

Kami's gaze met Mindy's; she saw the same questions in her eyes that she was sure were in her own. She shrugged and stepped back when Gabe called all clear.

Nothing.

None of the crew hesitated to jump back into their spots, but they all knew the code had failed and were also all wondering why it was continuing. Still, Gabe was in charge and it was his place to decide when to stop.

"Time?" he asked, his voice sounding slightly off to Kami, but maybe she'd imagined it.

The recorder told them how long they'd been doing CPR.

Gabe winced, gave one last chest compression with arms that seemed to buckle, then called the code and hung his head.

Kami had worked codes with Gabe in the past, but wasn't sure she'd ever paid attention to him immediately after a code came to an end, when the adrenaline rush subsided and that deep sense of failure set in.

At least, that was how she always felt when a code hadn't worked. Unfortunately, statistically, few codes were successful, but the few that were made going through the many failures worthwhile.

Was that how Gabe viewed codes, too? As emotionally, physically, and mentally exhausting, but worth it if you revived a single person?

She studied the fatigue etched on his handsome face, the way his head bowed forward ever so slightly, the way he slumped making him seem several inches shorter than his six-foot frame actually was.

He looked defeated.

Vulnerable.

Very unlike the man who was usually teasing her.

He looked unlike any Gabe she could recall ever having seen before.

Emotion pinched her insides, making her want to do something to put his usual smile back on his face, to put that mischievous twinkle back into his eyes. Which didn't go along at all with her goal to avoid him for a while. Still, a man had just died and Gabe looked wiped out.

Despite all her crazy emotions, he was her friend. She cared about him as a person. She couldn't just walk away.

"You okay?"

Briefly glancing her way, he didn't make eye contact, just nodded. "Fine."

He didn't look fine. His eyes were watery, red, and her insides twisted up even more.

She wasn't sure what she should do, but knew doing nothing wasn't an option. Not for her. Not when Gabe looked so devastated.

What she wanted to do was grab hold of his scrub top, drag him somewhere private and make him tell her what had upset him so about the code.

Other than the obvious, of course.

What right did she have to do that? None. They were friends, but she couldn't demand he tell her what had upset him. Not really.

Full of tension, she moved about the emergency bay, doing her job, while Gabe disappeared to go tell the family of the man's death.

That she didn't envy him.

Maybe that had been the issue. Maybe the deceased patient had been someone he knew, the family he was about to sit down with a family he was familiar with. If so, that couldn't be easy.

The rest of the night was busy and she never got a chance to corner Gabe.

Giving report to the arriving day-shift nurse, Kami was glad to see the shift end. She clocked out, but before leaving searched out Gabe.

She'd seen him a few times after the code, but he'd been busy with patients. No smiles, no jokes, no silly puns, no waggles of his brows, no...

Kami shook her head to clear her thoughts. Suffice it to say, Gabe hadn't been himself.

It didn't take long to find him.

He sat in the small dictation room off the emergency room that served as an office for the emergency-room physicians on staff.

First making sure he wasn't in the midst of recording a chart note, Kami poked her head in. "Rough night, eh?"

Turning toward her, he nodded.

Something didn't feel right. Not about how he looked. Not about how her gut wrenched. Not about anything that had happened since that stupid code. Why did she want to wrap her arms around him and hold him until whatever was bothering him subsided?

Because he'd messed with her brain in that closet.

Before then, too.

"I'll show you my toes if you'll smile."

As she'd hoped, Gabe smiled. It wasn't much of a smile, but he did smile and the gesture did funny things to her insides.

"Okay, but remember you smiled for it," she warned, bending and untying her shoe.

His eyes gaining a little spark of light, Gabe laughed. "Keep your shoes on, Kam."

She put her hands on her hips and pretended to be miffed. "So much for you implementing an open-toed shoes policy."

"Not one of my better ideas."

"Perhaps not, but I was willing to do my part." When he went quiet again, she couldn't stand it. "Want to go eat pancakes with me?"

Surprise lit his eyes. "You're kidding?"

Yes. She was. She did not invite men to breakfast. Especially men like Gabe, who went through women as if they were disposable.

Then again, she'd already eaten breakfast with Gabe once, so what would it hurt if they went to breakfast again?

As friends, of course. She had a cat to feed, but she'd go by to feed and love on Bubbles after breakfast.

"I'm hungry and I don't want to eat alone." Her stomach growled to confirm her comment.

At first she thought he was going to refuse, but, standing, he nodded. "Let me tell Dr. Williams I'm out of here."

Out of here with her.

Because she'd asked him and he'd said yes.

Which made her uncomfortable.

But not nearly as uncomfortable as his forlorn look had left her feeling.

A teasing, flirty Gabe was one thing. A lost-looking Gabe quite another and not one she could turn her back on without doing what she could to help him.

That was what friends did, right?

They said everyone had a doppelgänger. Gabe had just performed CPR compressions on a man who could have passed for his father.

His father on whom he'd been too young to perform CPR and had watched die, helpless to do anything other than cry and wait for the paramedics to arrive and do what he should have been able to do.

Logically, he knew he'd only been eight years old. A kid. He'd known to call for an ambulance, but hadn't been able to do one other thing but sob while he watched his father take his last breath.

Even now the moment played through his mind as if it had just happened.

He wasn't dense enough not to have realized long ago that his drive to become an emergency-room doctor had been seeded in that experience. Nor was he foolish enough to think that had he been able to perform CPR he'd have likely made a difference in his father's outcome.

But he *might* have, and because he'd been a kid with no skills, he'd never know what might have been.

Roger Dillehay, the man Gabe had done a code on that night, had been his shot. He'd failed again.

Maybe that was a sign, an assurance that he'd done all that could medically be done and it still hadn't been enough to save the man who looked so much like his father.

That had his eight-year-old self had skills, then the outcome would have been the same and he'd still have grown up without his dad there to cheer him on, would still have had to listen to his mother's tears.

"In all the time I've known you, not once have I ever accused you of being quiet."

Gabe blinked at the woman sitting across the table from him. Her big green eyes held a softness he'd seen as she cared for her patients but of which he'd yet to be the recipient.

He'd never had a reason to be the object of her empathy.

Nor did he want it now.

She'd been avoiding him and he'd let her because he'd waffled back and forth between thinking he needed to step back rather than risk their friendship versus giving in to what he was feeling and kissing her until they were both breathless.

"I'm sorry, Kam." He raked his fingers through his hair. "I should have skipped breakfast. I'm not good company."

"Which is exactly why you shouldn't have. We're friends." Had she really put emphasis on that last word? "Something is bothering you and I want to help."

Kami was a fixer. She wanted to fix her patients and now she wanted to fix him. He didn't need to be fixed. He wasn't broken, just...

"Want to talk about it?"

"You were there."

"You're right. I was. You went above and beyond with that code."

Gabe gave a low snort. "Let it go for too long, you mean?"

Her brows veed in disapproval of his comment. "As long as you had medical reason to believe there was hope of resuscitating him, then you were right not to call the code."

"I'm not sure that was the case," he admitted, unable to look into her eyes for fear of what she might see in his. "It was more a matter of the code patient reminding me of someone I once knew."

Now, why had he admitted that? He didn't need to go spilling his sob story to Kami, didn't need the sympathy that people had always given to the little boy who'd been alone with his father and had watched him die of a heart attack.

He was a grown man and didn't need sympathy or anyone knowing his past.

He hadn't talked to anyone about his father in years. He sure didn't want to start back today.

Especially not with a woman who was already getting under his skin.

"Oh," Kami said, then reached across the table and touched his hand. "I'm sorry."

Kami's touch carried the intensity of a defibrillator machine, so much so that Gabe was surprised when his body didn't jerk from the electricity in her fingertips.

His heart certainly jump-started as if it had been struck by a bolt of lightning.

He stared at where her hand covered his. "It's no big deal."

"One of the things I've always admired about you is that you are bluntly honest," she said. "Now I know why you're usually truthful."

Gabe glanced up, met Kami's gaze in question.

"It's because everyone would know," she continued. "You're a terrible liar."

He'd been called worse. One corner of Gabe's mouth lifted. "You think?"

"After that big whopper you just told? I know."

Gabe gave an ironic chuckle. "You're right."

"You could've just said you didn't want to talk about it."

"Would you have let me get away with that?"

"Probably not," she admitted with a sheepish grin. "I know things have been strained between us lately, but I don't like seeing you without a smile on your face."

Her admission warmed Gabe's insides. "Why's that?"

"Because we're friends."

He'd had enough of his wallowing in the past and focused on the woman across the table.

"You're a good person to have as a friend, Kam." As if to prove his point, he shifted his hand, laced their fingers.

Holding Kami's hand felt right and did make him feel better.

"Who did he remind you of?"

Gabe winced. "It was a long time ago."

"Sounds like the beginning of an interesting story."

"It's not."

"I'll be the judge of that."

He frowned. "You're sure pushy, lady."

She arched a brow and gave a *duh* look. "You're just figuring that out?"

He gave a low laugh, then lowered his gaze. "If it's all the same, I'd rather not talk about it anymore."

"Okay." She squeezed his hand. "But know I'm here if you need me."

"Thank you, Kami. You really are a good friend."

Her expression tightened for a brief moment. Then she seemed to shake it and teased, "Don't think buttering me up is going to change my mind about bidding on you."

Giving her hand a little squeeze, he laughed. "Maybe if I'd been on my game I'd have taken advantage of the moment."

"Too bad you missed your chance." Her gaze dropped to their bound hands.

"I'm not so sure I have," Gabe said half under his breath as their waitress set their plates in front of them. A loaded omelet for Gabe and a stack of cinnamon pecan pancakes for Kami.

"Pardon?" she asked, freeing her hand to reach for her utensils.

"Missed my chance to butter you up, I said."

Before Kami had the chance to question Gabe, he reached across the table, took her knife, and slathered her pancake with butter.

She rolled her eyes.

"Now you can say I have literally buttered you up."

"My pancakes don't count."

As his comment hit Kami, she glanced up, met his gaze, saw that the mischievous twinkle was back.

"That an offer?"

"You know it isn't."

"Why do I know that?"

"Because we're friends. Nothing more."

"Who better to slather butter on each other with than a friend?"

"Maybe that's something you do with friends, but that's not the kind of friendship I usually have."

"So you don't rescue your friends from their exes and you don't slather them in butter. What else do you not do with your friends, Kam?"

Rather than answer, she dug into her pancakes, grateful for the delicious bursts of flavor that practically melted in her mouth.

"I think I ordered the wrong thing."

Kami glanced up at Gabe.

"You make that look as if it tastes amazing," he clarified.

"It does."

"Prove it."

Kami started to tell him to be quiet and eat his omelet, but instead forked up a generous bite of her pancakes and extended the fork to him.

His eyes locked with hers, Gabe's mouth closed around her fork, then slowly pulled back. After eating the bite, he nodded. "You're right. That is good. I'm going to have to do double time at the gym if I keep having breakfasts like these." He chuckled.

The sound warmed Kami's insides. She much preferred Gabe's smiles and laughter to the solemn man he'd been after the code. Not that it would have been appropriate for him to be all smiles after someone had died, just that she wanted him to bounce back into his normal self and he hadn't.

That had gotten to her in places she didn't want him or anyone to reach.

Good thing she knew his revolving-door history with women or she might fall for his brilliant blues, quick intelligence, and smile that encompassed his entire face because, as much as she'd like to think herself immune to his charms, she was quickly realizing that her heart had taken up a mind of its own and was feeling all kinds of awareness it had never bothered to feel with Baxter.

Or anyone, for that matter.

Just Gabe.

CHAPTER SIX

"What's up with you and Gorgeous Gabe?"

Kami frowned at Mindy. "What's that supposed to mean?"

"I've caught you looking at him more than a dozen times tonight, and don't think I've forgotten walking in on you two the other night."

Yeah, it was best her friend didn't find out she and Gabe had gone to breakfast that morning.

"So what?" She made light of the incident because she wasn't admitting to Mindy that something had shifted in her relationship with Gabe. Something had shifted? Something had been shifting for a while. The supply room had been a landslide. "I was getting supplies."

"And Gabe?" Mindy pushed. "What was he getting?"

Kami's face heated. "Not what you're implying."

"Not even a little smooch?"

"Get serious. He's not my type."

Much.

Well, not her brain's type. Her body and heart seemed to have come out of a lifetime of hibernation with a vengeance.

"Smart and sexy as all get-out?"

She couldn't deny her friend's claim. "A total playboy. We both know he never stays in a relationship more than a couple of months."

Mindy shrugged. "Maybe he just sees no reason to keep a relationship going once he realizes things aren't going to work long term. Maybe he's just being efficient in searching for the right one rather than wasting time with women he's realized aren't for him."

"Or maybe he gets bored once the chase is over and can't commit."

"I doubt Gabe had to chase any of them."

Probably not, but her friend was missing the point.

"Okay, so maybe he gets bored once the shiny newness of the relationship is over."

Mindy shrugged. "I like my theory better."

"Because you're planning to bid on him and want to think the best of him?"

"I don't have to *want* to think the best of him. I *do* think that and so do you." Mindy's expression dared Kami to deny her claim. "He's a good guy."

Kami started to reply, but halted her words when Gabe came over to the nurses' station.

"Bay one is ready for discharge home."

Kami gave Mindy a warning look not to say anything inappropriate to Gabe, then said, "I'll get her IV taken out and get her discharged. Any scripts you need me to send?"

Gabe shook his head. "I'll get them in the computer record and send them. Thanks, though."

"I'd be happy to do that for you, Dr. Nelson," Mindy offered, a big smile on her face.

Looking a little uncertain at her overly bright expression, Gabe glanced back and forth between them.

"Uh, sure. Go ahead." He told her the scripts and to which pharmacy. "Thanks."

"Anything for you, Dr. Nelson."

Gabe looked confused and Kami rushed to discharge the patient rather than stick around for whatever else was said.

The best thing that could happen would be if Mindy did make a play for Gabe. Dating one of her friends would no doubt kill this unwanted awareness of him. Mindy was welcome to Gabe.

Kami had even encouraged her to bid on him, would even donate to the cause.

Only... No, she wasn't jealous at the thought of Mindy with Gabe.

She just didn't want her friend to get hurt when Gabe moved on to his next conquest.

Unless Mindy was right and Gabe just went through women so quickly because once he knew the relationship wasn't going to work out, he ended it, and moved on to someone who might.

That didn't make him sound like a player, but someone who was smart.

Gabe was smart and efficient. He was also a player. Wasn't he?

He'd had dozens of girlfriends during the short time Kami had known him.

She'd had two boyfriends during the same time.

Two boyfriends she'd known weren't her forever guys but she'd stuck around with longer than she should have. Why was that?

Because she didn't want to be like her mother, so she stayed to prove she could hold on to a man if she wanted to? Because they'd both been safe, hadn't made her heart step outside its comfort zone?

Ugh. She so wasn't going to psychoanalyze her motives in staying with Baxter or Kent.

Nor did it matter why Gabe went through women so quickly, because Kami wasn't interested, regardless of the reasons for his revolving-door love life.

If Mindy believed her theory, then she could bid on his date, or, better yet, save her money and just ask Gabe out.

They could have breakfast together.

As a couple and not just as friends.

That would be wonderful.

Great.

Awesome.

So why did her blood turn a little green when she glanced back and saw Mindy and Gabe laughing?

"Debbie wants to meet with us tonight."

"Tonight?" Kami asked Gabe as she finished last-minute cleanup prior to shift change. "It's Friday night."

"You have other plans?"

"I'm off work. Of course I have plans." Not that she was admitting to Gabe that her evening plans consisted of vegging out in front of the television while she caught up on her favorite reality show. "Don't you?"

"Even if I did, I'd cancel them. The charity auction is just a few weeks away. Any promotion Debbie helps with is going to have to be put into motion quickly. If we wait, it might not happen."

Guilt hit. He was right. Still...

"It's a television station. They're used to reporting on things as they happen. Promoting a charity event to raise money to help a sick baby shouldn't be outside their capabilities."

"Does that mean you want me to have Debbie reschedule the meeting with her producer?"

If the producer couldn't meet at a later time, she'd feel horrible that the event might not reach its potential. Especially since she didn't have any grand plans.

"Did you check to see if Mindy could go?" After all, she'd implied he'd have to take her co-organizer. Had he forgotten?

A stubborn expression took hold, tightening his jaw. "No. Either you go or everything's off."

Kami frowned. "Fine. I'll put off my plans so we can meet with your ex and her boss."

He studied her a moment, then seemed to have a change of heart of his own. "If your plans are that big a deal, I can see if Mindy wants to go."

Kami bit the inside of her lip and tried not to look addled. Did he want to take Mindy instead? Was he hoping she'd say she wouldn't cancel her plans so he'd have an excuse to invite Mindy? Had their laughter earlier in the week been bonding toward a more personal relationship?

No, Gabe was a man who would ask a woman out if he wanted to ask. He wouldn't play games. If he wanted to take Mindy to dinner, he'd take her to dinner.

"Someone special?"

Kami arched her brow. "Who?"

"Whoever you have plans with."

"I didn't say I had plans with someone," she countered, refusing to slide back into that untruth.

"Baxter's workout program softening you up?"

"I don't have plans with Baxter, and if I did, it's not your business."

He looked duly reprimanded. "You're right. I shouldn't tease you."

"No, you shouldn't." Not that she minded his teasing. Not really. Just, she didn't want him to know that she had no plans for the first weekend she'd had off work in close to a month other than working on the fund-raiser.

"I'll pick you up at six."

"If you'll tell me where to meet you, I can drive myself," she countered.

"I'll see you at six," he repeated and walked away before she could pry more details from him.

What did one wear to a Friday night dinner meeting with a television show hostess, her producer, and a coworker who was just a friend but that your body had become painfully aware of in beyond friendship ways?

Especially when you didn't know where the meeting was being held?

Okay, so, logically, they'd meet at a nice restaurant.

She'd had no chance to find out the location so she could drive herself. Him picking her up from her house seemed too much as if they were a couple going on a double date.

Quit being ridiculous, she ordered herself. Friends picked each other up for meetings. It was no big deal.

Still, what was she going to wear?

She could text him, but stubbornly didn't, just studied the contents of her closet. Her gaze repeatedly settled on a blue dress that was the right mix of casual and dressy. No way did she want to feel overdressed for the meeting, but she also didn't want to feel frumpy while with Gabe's beautiful ex.

Debbie was a knockout.

Kami put her hand to her forehead. What was wrong with her? What Debbie looked like did not matter. Not in the slightest. She was not competing to take Debbie's former place in Gabe's life. Far from it.

Kami needed to get her butt into bed and get a few hours of sleep after being up all night. That was what she should be worrying about.

Not about what she was going to wear or how she was going to look in comparison to Gabe's ex.

On her best day she couldn't compete with the television personality and, seriously, she didn't want to. This was a business meeting to discuss advertising a charity event for a coworker's daughter. Nothing more. Nothing social. Nothing. Nothing. Nothing.

That evening, Kami was still telling herself that when Gabe drove them to an upscale restaurant and her nerves were getting the best of her.

She wasn't a nervous person. This was ridiculous.

Glancing his way didn't reassure her.

He was too good-looking for his own good in his dark trousers and blue button-down dress shirt with the sleeves rolled up to reveal a generous glimpse of his forearms.

His manly forearms. Strong and skilled. The urge to reach out and run her fingers over them hit her.

Yeah, that urge didn't help her nerves, either.

Obviously, tossing and turning in her bed half the day

hadn't done a thing to rest her brain because she was delusional. Sleep deprivation had to be the cause of this insanity.

"You look great, by the way."

Gabe's compliment didn't lessen her unease but she murmured a thank you.

"I like your dress."

"Because my legs are showing?" Now, why had she asked that? Just because he'd made a big deal of her bare legs the morning he'd brought breakfast didn't mean she had to point out her exposed limbs.

Putting the car into Park, he glanced toward her, then lower, letting his gaze skim slowly down her body, going lower to inspect her legs. Then, lifting his gaze to hers, he shook his head. "Nope, that's not why I like your dress."

With that, he turned off the motor and got out of his car.

Still trying to figure out his comment, Kami was even more stunned when her car door opened and Gabe extended his hand.

"You didn't have to open my door."

"My mom taught me good manners."

"Good to know, but this isn't a date, so you don't have to do things like that."

His brow rose. "Treating a lady right doesn't just extend to the woman you're dating. Ask my mom."

Good thing one of their mothers had taught good behavior. Kami's sure hadn't. Nor had she come home yet. Poor Bubbles. Kami put her hand in his and got out of the car. She immediately pulled her hand away and straightened her dress.

After Gabe closed the passenger door, his hand settled low on her back and he guided her toward the restaurant entrance. Kami wanted to pull free, to push away his hand, but would doing so be making a big deal out of nothing?

His palm burning into her flesh through her dress material didn't feel like something that was nothing.

It felt so not nothing it was a little scary after all her nothing relationships.

"I still think we could have done this with a phone conversation," she mumbled, feeling more and more self-conscious as they made their way into the upscale restaurant.

"No doubt, and you're preaching to the choir." He pierced her with his blue gaze. "I'm not the one who insisted on a dinner meeting."

"Right." Guilt hit her. He probably didn't want to be here any more than she did. "Debbie seized the excuse to spend time with you."

He feigned surprise. "You think that's what this is?"

"I only know her through things you've said. What do you think this is?"

He sighed quite dramatically. "Foreplay for my charity auction date."

Despite her nerves, Kami laughed. "You're crazy."

"Apparently or I wouldn't be here."

She paused. "Thank you, Gabe. I'm not sure I've thanked you for setting this up, but I do appreciate it. I know Beverly appreciates everything being done to help ease the burden of Lindsey's expenses, too."

A genuine smile slashed across his face. "You're welcome, Kam, and so is she."

"Worth the sacrifice you're about to make?"

He grimaced. "Ask me again after dinner."

CHAPTER SEVEN

IF GABE WASN'T enjoying himself, he was putting on a good show.

However, his attention wasn't focused toward the model-perfect woman who left Kami in awe of her beauty, grace, and poise.

Gabe's focus was on Kami.

Overly so.

As in, if she didn't know better, she'd think she and Gabe were a couple. She knew better and her head was still spinning.

Was that what he was trying to make Debbie think?

His little smiles, winks, and frequent touches of her hand and arm were getting to her.

To the woman sitting across from them, too.

She'd gone from super friendly to regarding Kami with suspicion.

Not that she wasn't nice.

Kami believed the woman was inherently pleasant and that was part of her television viewer appeal. She had a wholesome goodness that shone as brightly as her beauty. Plus, intelligence glimmered in her big brown eyes.

The woman wasn't buying that Gabe would be interested in Kami. What sane man would be when Debbie wanted him?

Tall, willowy, blonde, smart, successful.

"Gabe says you work with him at the hospital?"

"I'm a nurse." Kami took a sip of her water. She'd ordered a glass of wine but had yet to take a sip. She needed all her wits for this meal and didn't want to risk lowering her inhibitions even the slightest bit.

Especially not when Gabe gave her a fond look and said, "My favorite nurse."

"Every female nurse is your favorite nurse," Kami countered, knocking her knee against his leg in hopes he'd take the hint and stop with the cheesy comments.

"You know there's no one like you," he came right back, his leg brushing against hers. Only, rather than a cut-it-out knock, the grazing of his leg against hers was more an awakening of her senses as the material of his pants teased her thigh.

"You mean someone who doesn't fall at your feet?"

"Something like that." Gabe's expression said Kami had fallen at his feet a time or two despite her denials.

She decided to ignore him and finish this meeting as quickly as possible before she made a complete fool of herself over Gabe's attention.

"We appreciate your offer to help with the Smiths' fund-raiser." There, see, that sounded competent. "As your show is about home improvements, I don't know a possible angle for us to promote the fund-raiser for Lindsey's medical expenses. What were you thinking?"

Eyeing Kami and Gabe closely, the woman slid into professional mode.

"That's where Jerry comes in." She turned to her producer and smiled.

The slightly overweight man's entire persona brightened.

In that moment, Kami realized the producer was totally besotted with the woman. As in, head over heels. He'd probably jumped at the offer when Debbie had requested he meet with them just so he'd have an excuse to spend time with her outside work.

"He's going to arrange a segment on our late-night news that will run over a few days. Then—" Debbie's smile conveyed real enthusiasm "—we're going to do a home improvement for your coworker."

"The baby needs a new heart, not updated curtains and carpet," Gabe pointed out.

Debbie tsked. "There's going to be medical equipment and such, so it'll be a renovation to make their transition from hospital to home easier."

"I don't know if Beverly and her husband want their home renovated, but it's a generous offer. Certainly, I'll discuss it with them," Kami assured them, thinking the new family might need a lot of things. She didn't know. "I'll admit I worry the added stress of a home remodel during all the craziness of Lindsey's medical issues isn't a good idea."

"Obviously you've not watched my show," Debbie scolded with a pout of her full pink lips. "There will be no lengthy remodel. We'll time the remodel for while the baby is having her heart transplant. Everything will be done and waiting on them when they bring Lindsey home from the hospital." She glanced at Jerry, excitement practically seeping from her barely existent pores. "It'll be an amazing show."

"It sounds wonderful," Kami admitted. "But they don't have the money for a remodel."

Debbie smiled again. "There's no cost to them. This is our pleasure. We'll just want to film their story, of course, and especially when they return to the home the first time after the remodel, and maybe a quick shot or two of them in their new, improved home."

"I don't even know if they own their home," Kami confessed. "They may rent… We should have had them here with us."

"I'm sure Gabe can arrange a meeting."

Of course he could.

But he immediately passed. "Kami is organizing the fund-raiser, not me."

"Gabe, darling, the remodel has nothing to do with the fund-raiser," Debbie corrected. "We'll do a news piece for that, something we'll refer back to in the episode for their home improvement."

"It's a great idea for a show and ratings." Kami could have bitten her tongue when the words came out of her mouth.

However, Debbie didn't look offended. Instead, she and her producer nodded. "It's a win-win all the way around. Your coworker gets a renovated, state-of-the-art home free of charge. We get a phenomenal episode. Right, Jerry?"

The man beamed at his hostess. "It's rather brilliant."

"I'll give your information to Beverly," Kami assured them. "Anything beyond that will be up to them. Our purpose is to generate awareness of the fund-raiser so we can raise as much as possible. Everything will need to be between you and Beverly and her husband directly."

"Sounds perfect. Now—" Debbie flashed a smile that truly was Hollywood-worthy "—let's set aside shoptalk and enjoy our meal."

Kami looked at Gabe, gave him a look that hopefully conveyed for him to get her out of there as quickly as possible, then said, "Let's."

The meal was delicious. The conversation not too horrible as Debbie came across as a genuine, albeit ambitious, person. Jerry was probably a killer businessman, but this softened whenever he looked at Debbie—which was all the time.

Something she seemed oblivious to as she zeroed in on Gabe.

Who in return zeroed in on Kami in a move to deflect Debbie's attention.

Kami was exhausted from it all.

"Are you two seeing each other?" Jerry asked after their entrées arrived.

"Yes," Gabe answered at the same time as Kami said, "No."

"I see," Debbie said.

Kami was glad the woman saw, because Kami didn't.

Ignoring the couple, Gabe asked, "What was breakfast this week?"

Kami glared at Gabe. What was he doing?

Actually, she knew what he was doing and that was what irritated her.

"A meal because I was hungry."

His gaze searched hers. "Both times?"

Kami's glare intensified. He was purposely trying to make them think breakfast had involved a lot more than food.

Gabe wanted Debbie to think they were a couple so it would deter her from bidding on him during the auction.

He didn't mind using Kami in the process.

"Sorry, Gabe. I shouldn't have used my status as your favorite nurse to get a free breakfast," she said in an overly sweet tone, all the while shooting mental daggers at him.

"True, but since you paid the second time, it all balanced out."

Ack. She should have known he'd point out that she'd paid when they'd gone to the restaurant on the morning of the code. Not that he'd liked it, but she'd insisted since she'd invited him. Eventually, after she'd snagged the ticket and refused to give it to him, he'd relented.

His expression was smug. "Guess that makes me your favorite doctor."

She rolled her eyes. "Don't count on it."

Debbie and Jerry watched them curiously and Kami became more and more self-conscious. This was ridiculous.

"Don't let Gabe fool you." She leaned toward Debbie. "He's not my type and I'm not his. We enjoy our friendship and being coworkers. This is all a game Gabe plays. Nothing more."

There. That should settle any doubts and teach him not to trifle with her.

But rather than look repentant, he put his fork down on the table and stared at her, a confused look on his handsome face. "Who says you're not my type?"

Kami turned toward him and willed him not to have this conversation in front of the couple. "I'm not."

"Says who?" he persisted, oblivious or not caring that she didn't want to continue.

"You've never dated anyone like me," she pointed out, very aware of their curious audience.

"That doesn't mean I wouldn't like to."

He was laying it on thick for Debbie's sake. Kami didn't like it.

Then again, who liked being used?

Besides her mother, who seemed a glutton for punishment, that was.

"Thank you so much for meeting with us about Lindsey's fund-raiser," she told Jerry and Debbie, ignoring Gabe's last comment. "I'll give Beverly your business card." Despite only having eaten about half her meal, Kami pushed her chair back. "Now, if you'll excuse me, I've recalled that I had other plans tonight that really can't wait, after all."

When Gabe went to rise, Kami shook her head. "You stay and enjoy your meal. I'll catch a taxi."

Gabe joined Kami on the sidewalk outside the restaurant. "You didn't really think I'd let you take a taxi home, did you?"

A crowd had gathered, waiting for their turn to be seated inside the restaurant, but Gabe had had no difficulty spotting where Kami stood near the curb.

"You didn't really think I'd let you get away with using me like you were, did you?" she hissed without looking his way.

That had Gabe pausing.

"I'm sorry if that's what you thought. Let me take you home."

"What I thought?" she scoffed. "You know you were acting as if we were an item to put on a show for your ex."

"Aren't we an item?"

Risking escalating her wrath, he put his hand on her

lower back and guided her toward his car. Whether out of a desire to get away from the waiting restaurant patrons or as a testament to how upset she was, Kami let him.

"You know good and well we aren't," she insisted, turning on him as they stopped at the passenger side of his car.

"We have a good relationship, have been flirting with one another, have had breakfast twice this week, and dinner together tonight. It's not illogical of me to imply there's something between us when there is something between us."

"Friendship," she spit at him, her eyes a vivid green. "That's what's between us."

"Yes. We're friends."

"Nothing more." She opened the car door, slapped his hand when he tried to help, climbed inside, and slammed the door.

Gabe stared down at her through the passenger-door window.

Friends. Nothing more, she'd said.

They were friends.

He drove her home, contemplating the night and what she'd said. He had flirted with Kami heavily during the meal. Had he been doing so to deflect Debbie?

Flirting with Kami had felt right.

Not because Debbie had been there, but because he enjoyed the back-and-forth between them. Enjoyed the chemistry he felt when he was with her.

He pulled into Kami's apartment complex parking area and turned off the motor. "I'm sorry, Kam."

She stared straight ahead. "Because you know I'm right?"

"Because I don't want you upset with me."

She sighed, touched her temple. "What does it matter?"

"Because you really are my favorite nurse."

She closed her eyes. "Fine, but don't use me ever again."

"Okay."

Kami was obviously surprised at his quick acquiescence, judging by the way her gaze shot to him.

"I won't ask you to rescue me at the auction again, if that's what you want." He crossed his heart.

"You won't ask me to rescue you from a beautiful woman? Oh, thank you," she said with great sarcasm and an eye roll. "Thank goodness I won't have to go through that."

He didn't come back with anything, just got out of the car, went around and opened her door.

She got out without taking his offered hand. Stubborn woman.

Gabe stared after her as she headed toward her first-floor-apartment building entrance, watched her fumble with her keys, then unlock her front door.

She was going to go inside without saying another word. Life was too short to let her go that way. He knew that all too well.

He sprinted after her.

"Kami?" he said from right behind her as she pushed open her door.

Standing half in, half out of the apartment, she turned.

"Why are you so upset with me over this?"

Rather than answer, she looked away.

Needing to know, Gabe lifted her chin, trying to get her to meet his gaze.

Finally she looked up, staring for long moments with her big green eyes, then dropping her gaze to his mouth.

"I don't like you pretending we have a relationship that we don't. It's as confusing to me as it was to our dinner companions."

Gabe was confused, too. He'd admit that. How could he not when Kami staring at his mouth had his brain turned to mush?

Obviously that was the case.

Because Gabe gave in to what felt like the most compelling thing in the world, but might be his most foolish move ever if she never forgave him.

He leaned forward and pressed his mouth against Kami's warm, sweet lips.

At the contact, her eyes widened.

One light kiss became two.

Still, she didn't push him away, nor did she tell him to stop.

Instead, she searched his eyes as his mouth explored hers, tasted her, and grew hungry for more.

Lots more.

Gabe wasn't holding her. She could pull away at any time. She wasn't.

Quite the opposite.

She was kissing him back.

Slowly at first, uncertain and unsure, then with a mounting urgency that fueled his own.

He moved forward, bringing them both inside the doorway, and closed the door behind him as he pulled Kami against him so he could kiss her more deeply.

Her fingers went into his hair and she pulled him closer, her body now flush with his.

Her amazing body that still wasn't close enough.

He brushed his hands over her back, lower, cupping her bottom. Lifting her against him, he kissed her deeper, his tongue making its way into her mouth.

A soft sound emitted from her throat. She shifted against him, her fingers massaging his scalp, pulling him toward her as the kiss went on and on. As their bodies melted together.

He wasn't sure how long they kissed, touched, how long their bodies pressed so tightly against each other, moving, feeling. He wasn't even sure which one of them pulled away.

It had to be Kami. Only a fool would stop kissing her.

Kami's kiss had been tender, passionate, hot.

Had demanded his all, that he hold nothing back, but give everything he was to her.

He wanted to kiss her again. To sweep her off her feet and carry her to her bedroom and kiss her all over until she cried out in release.

Until he felt her release. His release.

Nothing pretend about that or his body's very obvious reaction to their kiss.

But Kami's mind and body obviously weren't at the same place as his.

She pulled away and stared up at him with confusion shining in her eyes.

"Kami, I..." he began, not sure exactly how to explain to her since he didn't fully understand himself what had just happened between them, not wanting to say the wrong thing, but wondering if there even were right words he could tell her.

Shaking her head, she held up her hand and pushed against his chest. "How could you? You promised not to use me again."

"Use you?" he asked, puzzled by her accusation and still more than a little dazed by their kiss.

"As a substitute or just someone handy or whatever it was that possessed you just then."

"What possessed me just then," he admitted, "was you."

That was when it hit Gabe.

What probably should have hit him months ago. He'd sought out Kami's company, laughed with her, flirted with her. They were friends, but he wanted more.

Lots more.

He'd been wanting more for months. Why hadn't he seen his feelings for what they were?

Because she'd been in a relationship with Baxter.

When Kami had ended things with the accountant, Gabe's interest in anyone other than her had dissipated. He'd wanted Kami.

Correction—he wanted Kami, and now that he'd admitted that to himself, he wasn't sure he could go back to how things were. He didn't want to.

Kami looked thrown off kilter by his claim, her eyes narrowing. "I did no such thing."

He raked his fingers through his hair, over the spots on

his head that still tingled from her touch, and fought the stunned feeling in his brain, his body. "I think you did."

She shook her head as if to deny his claim. "What are you talking about?"

"This." He leaned forward and pressed a gentle kiss to her parted lips again.

Immediately, she softened against him, kissing him back.

Sometimes words just didn't cover what needed to be conveyed.

"That is what I'm talking about," he whispered against her mouth. "What I want and what I hope you want, too. You say we're just friends, Kam. I think you're wrong. We're so much more than that. But if not, then you're the only friend I want to date, to spend time with, to have sex with, and those things I want more than you might believe."

CHAPTER EIGHT

DESPITE HER RACING THOUGHTS, Kami had finally settled into sleep and crashed for a good ten hours before rousing the next morning.

Upon waking, she assured herself the events of the night before had been a dream.

Reaching up to touch her lips, she knew better.

Gabe kissing her hadn't been a dream. It had been real.

Gabe had kissed her, had said he wanted to date her and have sex with her.

How crazy was that?

How crazy was his kiss?

A fervent, hungry kiss that was like the wildest spice she'd ever tasted. Something so good, so addictive you had to keep tasting even when it was setting your mouth afire.

Gabe's kisses had lit infernos, had melted her down to the core.

His had been the most amazing kiss of her life.

Comparing Gabe's kisses to Baxter's or Kent's or any of the men she'd dated was like comparing a firecracker to a stick of dynamite.

Being anywhere near something so explosive was dangerous.

Kami got out of bed, went about her normal day-off routine, spent an hour at her mother's playing with Bubbles, then headed toward the hospital where the board had volunteered the use of a conference room to store the donated items that would be auctioned off at the fund-raiser.

Kami and a few others were inventorying everything, gathering the smaller items, and making up baskets to be auctioned.

Working on the fund-raiser would hopefully distract her from the night before.

Or not.

The first person she saw when she walked in was Gabe. Gabe in a blue T-shirt and jeans that outlined his body in an oh-so-yummy kind of way.

Or maybe it was his smile that was yummy.

He was laughing with Mindy and didn't look as if he'd given her a second thought since she'd thrown him out of her apartment.

Of course he hadn't. If he wanted, he could crook his finger and have any number of women running to do his bidding.

Something gripped her belly.

Good grief. She was not jealous. Not of Gabe crooking his finger and women doing his bidding. Not of Gabe laughing with Mindy. Not of Gabe or anything he did.

She had no claim.

Despite the fact they'd kissed and he'd destroyed her brain circuitry with the way his hard body had felt.

That hard body, she thought, not able to pull her gaze away from how his T-shirt stretched over his chest, his shoulders. Not too tight, not too loose. Just right.

Like what was beneath the material.

Heat flooded at the memory of running her hands over those shoulders, of pulling him toward her as he kissed her.

At how he'd leaned down to press one last kiss to her mouth, almost as if he'd had to have one last touch, told her to think about what he'd said, and then he'd left.

As if she'd needed him to tell her to think about what he'd said.

She'd thought of little else.

She was surprised she'd slept at all considering the emotional surge his lips against hers had caused.

A tsunami of adrenaline and emotions had flooded her senses and knocked out all common reason.

Getting all worked up over Gabe was a mistake.

He ate women's hearts for breakfast and yet they invited him back for lunch and dinner and said, "Here you go," handing their entire beings to him on a platter.

She didn't want Gabe gobbling her up, even if his kiss had been out of this world. She didn't want to be so desperate for a man that nothing else mattered. Hadn't she learned anything from her mother's mistakes?

He turned, met her gaze, then smiled. One of those smiles that was uniquely him and encompassed his whole face, lit up his eyes, and made the room brighter. Like the sun coming out from behind a cloudy sky.

Listen to her, thinking sappy thoughts.

Gabe was not a man she needed to have sappy thoughts about.

As if nothing monumental had happened the night before, he winked and went back to what he was doing.

Her heart took that moment to skip a beat.

Oh, good grief. If she weren't careful she'd be hand-feeding Gabe her heart for breakfast, too, and asking if he'd like the rest of her for lunch, dinner, and dessert.

No, no, no. She was not on the menu.

There were more than a dozen volunteers making inventory lists and baskets for the fund-raiser. Kami had expected to spend the biggest portion of her day working on the project, but, thanks to everyone's enthusiastic efforts, they finished after only a couple of hours that had felt more like fun than work—aided by the fact that Gabe had been on his best behavior and kept everyone smiling, her included despite all her attempts to avoid and ignore him.

One by one the volunteers left.

All but Mindy, Gabe, and herself.

"You want to go to lunch?" Mindy invited Kami as they put away the last of the baskets.

Thank goodness. Going to lunch with Mindy meant no opportunity to be alone with Gabe. It would happen, but she wasn't ready for that this afternoon. Not when she felt so rattled from his kiss.

"Sure." She beamed at her best friend. "That would be great."

Lunch with Mindy sounded like heaven and gave her the perfect excuse not to stick around to talk to Gabe—assuming that was why he had stayed until the end. No doubt, despite his smiles and friendly behavior, he wanted to reiterate that what had happened the night before meant nothing, that he didn't look at dating and sex the same way she did.

As if she needed him to tell her that.

It wasn't *her* bedroom door that was in a constant spin from the women going in then being pushed out.

Gabe cleared his throat.

Mindy glanced his way, her brows lifted, and then with a barely contained smile, she recanted. "Oh, wait. Sorry, I can't go to lunch with you today. I forgot I'd made other plans."

"Um…maybe we can get together tomorrow," Kami suggested, not quite sure what Mindy had seen in Gabe's face that had her changing her mind about lunch. Regardless, it didn't take a genius to know what had taken place.

Mindy's smile broke free as she said, "You should take my bestie to lunch, Dr. Nelson. She deserves it after all her fantastic work this morning."

"I could do that," he agreed, all innocent-looking.

Ha, neither of them were innocent. She was going to have to have a serious talk with Mindy. The last thing she needed was her friend playing matchmaker.

"I thought you might be able to." She gave him an approving look, then glanced toward Kami. "You have to go to lunch with Gabe. Otherwise, I'm going to feel guilty for bailing."

Rather than wait for Kami to answer, Mindy hugged her and promised she'd talk to her later.

"Go," she ordered, "have lunch with Gabe, and have fun."

When her friend was gone, the conference room seemed a lot smaller than it had when filled with Mindy and the dozen or so volunteers. Or maybe Gabe's presence just seemed that much larger than life when she was alone with him.

She'd been alone with him before. This was no big deal.

Just because he'd kissed her the night before didn't change anything.

Not really.

Just everything. Because before she hadn't known what all the fuss was about.

Looking at Gabe, she recanted. Well, yeah, she'd known he was a great guy and that women were crazy about him. It was just that she hadn't personally experienced that greatness on a physical level.

Gabe on a physical level changed things.

Changed her.

Changed how being alone with him made her feel.

How could it not when every cell in her body throbbed with awareness of him?

Snap out of it, Kami.

She glanced around the room at the baskets and items that filled the table and that were pushed up against the wall. "I need to lock up."

He moved closer. "Anything I can do to help?"

Disappear so I don't have to deal with this right now.

Ha. Somehow, even if she had spoken her thoughts, she didn't think he'd comply.

Forcing a smile, she shook her head. "Thanks, but this is it for today. Later, we'll finish putting together items donated between now and the fund-raiser and move all this stuff to the convention center the day of the event."

Gabe nodded, followed her out of the conference room, then stood beside her as she locked the exterior door. Pheromones exuded from his pores. Had to. How else could she be so aware of him?

They walked down the hospital hallway.

"I didn't realize you'd be here today." She glanced toward him, then quickly refocused on watching where she was walking. The last thing she needed was to trip over her own two feet in front of him.

"There was an open call for volunteers. I volunteered." He sounded nonchalant, as if it had been no big deal. Why wasn't she buying it?

"The more help, the better, right?" Kami smiled at a couple of nurses they passed in the hallway, then walked through the hospital door Gabe held open for her.

When they were headed toward the employee parking lot, he asked, "Can I take you to lunch, Kam?"

She supposed they needed to talk, to work past this awkwardness, because she didn't like this new apprehension she felt being near him.

This underlying nervousness.

This awareness of just how hot he was. How was she ever going to look at him and not remember what his body had felt like pressed up against hers?

"Okay, so long as it's not something heavy." She imagined their conversation would be heavy enough when she told him that, although she hoped to date again soon, she didn't plan on him being the one she dated.

Or kissed.

Or pressed her body up against as if it were a contest to see just how much of her could be touching him.

Sure, he'd been a great kisser. Would be great at other things, too.

Of that, she had no doubt.

But she wasn't going to have sex with someone she didn't envision herself having a long-term relationship with. Someone who would be no different than one of the guys who came in and out of her mother's life. Gabe wasn't a long-term relationship kind of guy. She wasn't a quickie relationship kind of girl. Better to nip whatever this was in the bud.

"Dinner date?"

As she stepped off the sidewalk, she cut her eyes toward him. "What?"

His blue eyes stared straight into hers. "Not wanting to eat heavy with me because you have a dinner date?"

She'd let him think that there was someone else when he'd offered to bring breakfast, but she wanted to be honest. Their friendship was tense enough without throwing in deceit.

"You know Baxter and I broke up some time ago," she reminded him. "I've not been on a date since."

Her response put a pleased expression on his face.

"Not counting me."

"You don't count as a date," she corrected and took off toward her car.

Falling into step beside her, he pretended offense. "Says who?"

"Me."

"I want to count."

She frowned. "Because you kissed me and have decided you want to do more than that with me?"

"I find you attractive and want to have sex with you. Is that so terrible?" His expression was full of mischievousness, one that said if she was smart she'd want to kiss him, too.

She did want to kiss him, but wouldn't risk being just another woman who came in and out of his life. More than that, she wanted to protect their friendship. Gabe meant more to her than just a good-time romp in the sheets. She didn't want to lose the special bond they shared. Sex would change everything.

Giving him a look of challenge, she asked, "I don't know. You tell me. Is sex with you so terrible?"

"I've not had any complaints."

Kami wasn't sure whether to laugh or groan at the way his cocky grin slid into place. "I bet not."

Although the sparkle was still in his eyes, so was something more, something that hinted that, despite his teasing, Gabe cared about her response. "Because you enjoyed my kiss?"

She wasn't going there. Not in the hospital parking lot where anyone could overhear. "I didn't say I enjoyed your kiss."

Not looking one bit fazed, he grinned. "But you did."

"What makes you so sure?"

"You walked to my car rather than yours."

Kami blinked. He was right. She'd walked right past her car and gone to his. Heat flooded her face.

"That only means I planned to conserve gas by taking one vehicle instead of two." After all, she had planned to go to lunch so they could talk. "Not that I enjoyed you kissing me."

He opened the passenger door and she climbed into the car.

She glanced up at where he stood, his hand on the open door. The sun shone on him, making his eyes dance with light, making his hair glisten, and his skin glow. No woman in her right mind would have not enjoyed his kiss.

He was a kissing Adonis. Beautiful and talented.

He closed her door, came around and got into the driver seat.

She sighed. "You make me want to say just forget this."

He glanced her way. "Lunch, you mean?"

Although she wasn't sure she just meant lunch, she nodded.

"Because you want to go straight to your place and kiss me all over?"

Images of doing just that, of stripping his T-shirt off him and trailing kisses over his chest, his abs, filled her mind.

Yeah, so a part of her, a carnal, feminine part that probably had something to do with good old-fashioned nature at work, did want to go straight to her place and kiss him all over. Fortunately, she'd evolved enough to have the good sense not to give in to those urges.

Rolling her eyes, she shook her head. "Not what I meant and you know it."

"Sorry." But he didn't look repentant. Not with one corner of his mouth crooked upward and his eyes searching hers for things she didn't want him to see. "Wishful thinking."

"Truly?" she asked, frustrated that he wasn't taking her seriously and that her good intentions seemed to have come to a screeching halt, because all she could do was look at his mouth and wonder if those lips had really felt as good as she remembered. "If I said yes, I want to go to my place and have sex, you'd drive us there and go at it? Just like that?"

"Sounds crude when you word it that way," he complained, his smile slipping. "But yes." His gaze locked with hers. "If you told me you wanted to have sex, we'd be having sex just as fast as I could get you somewhere alone. But make no mistake—there won't be anything quick about it when we do and it won't be just me enjoying every touch of our bodies."

She pressed her fingertips to her suddenly pounding temple and contemplated what he said.

Part of her said, yes, yes, she did want to forget lunch. Another part kept reminding her that any involvement with Gabe beyond friendship was emotional suicide.

They rode in silence, but it didn't matter. Gabe didn't go far from the hospital, and when he stopped the car, Kami looked at him in surprise.

She wasn't sure what she'd expected, but certainly not a trip to the park.

"I thought we were going to lunch."

Grinning, he looked quite proud of himself. "We are."

"At World's Fair Park?" Not that she'd expected anything fancy, but they were at a park, not a restaurant. Whether it was nerves or hunger, her stomach gnawed at her and she wanted food.

She'd not had much of an appetite and had only eaten a few bites of her breakfast. No wonder she was starved.

"There's a couple of vendor trucks not far from here."

"Vendor trucks?" Well, she had said she didn't want anything heavy. She guessed hot dogs and hamburgers fit the bill. Still, eating at the park didn't quite jibe with their previous conversation. If he was trying to seduce her, surely he'd have chosen somewhere more impressive?

"You want me to take you somewhere else?" he offered as they got out of the car.

She shook her head. "Since I'm in jeans, a T-shirt, and tennis shoes, this is fine. I'm just surprised. I didn't think about you bringing me to a park for lunch."

"Never say I'm predictable." Stepping beside her, he closed her car door before she could. "It's Saturday. There's always something going on at Performance Lawn on the weekends. I thought we could walk along the waterfront, eat, and just hang out and enjoy being outdoors. No pressure."

"No pressure?" She eyed him suspiciously.

"I'll be on my best behavior. Scout's honor." But rather than hold up a scout's sign, his fingers made a space travel television show character's instead.

"I don't think Scout was his name," she mused.

"Probably not, but, either way, let's relax and enjoy the beautiful weather and the fact that we aren't at the hospital or having to sleep away a stressful night."

Tempting. And it fit with why she'd agreed to lunch to begin with. Gabe was her friend. She wanted to maintain that friendship. Maintain it? She cherished his friendship.

"Say yes, Kami." His tone was low, his smile full of temptation, his eyes mesmerizing. "Play with me this afternoon. I'll deliver you safely back to your car whenever you say the word, I promise."

The twinkle in his eyes, so familiar, so warm, eased some of the tension that had been bubbling just beneath the surface all morning.

"Okay," she agreed and meant it. An afternoon playing

in the park with Gabe. Wide open spaces. Lots of people around. Sounded safe enough.

Plus, the early spring sunshine and gentle breeze combination felt great. She'd always thought the park was beautiful and being outdoors really did feel awesome.

Already she could hear a great band playing, probably a local one, on the Performance Lawn and they were good. When she and Gabe reached the area, there was a small crowd spread out over the grass on blankets and some type of festival was going on.

A festival with food vendors.

Kami took a deep sniff of the afternoon air and her stomach rumbled in protest of how long it had been since she'd eaten. "Something smells good."

"I remember hearing about a Beer and Barbecue Festival this weekend. I think it was John from work telling me."

"Ah, now I know why you brought me here." She laughed. "Beer and barbecue."

"Not a beer and barbecue kind of girl?"

"Surely you know I'm a champagne and caviar kind of woman," she replied flippantly. She enjoyed a sip of celebratory champagne occasionally, but didn't recall having ever tried caviar. Wasn't really something on her bucket list to try, either. "But since we're here, I want to go find whatever smells so good and then find a place to sit and listen to the band while we eat. If that's okay with you?"

"Fine by me," he agreed, then, "Champagne and caviar, eh? I'll keep that in mind for future reference. For now, we'll make do with grabbing a bite of something here and listening to the band."

CHAPTER NINE

THE RELAXED ATMOSPHERE of the park and the gorgeous spring weather promised a perfect afternoon in spite of any lingering nerves Kami might have about their shared kiss.

At least, that had been Gabe's plan when he'd opted to go to the park. She'd been uptight from the moment she'd walked into the hospital and seen him. Not that he didn't understand, but rather than let her apprehension fester, he planned to knock it out of the ballpark. What better way to get her to relax than to take her to the park, surrounded by people, sunshine, and an overall air of well-being and happiness?

From a vendor he bought a small orange-and-white throw blanket emblazoned with the University of Tennessee's logo. From another, he got drinks and barbecue. Kami carried the blanket and spread it out on the grassy knoll, sat, then took the food and drinks from him while he joined her on the blanket.

They ate, chatted, then lay back on the blanket to listen to the band and soak up some vitamin D.

Gabe reached for Kami's hand, filled with pleasure when she didn't pull it free, but laced her fingers with his. It wasn't much, but holding her hand felt pivotal.

Her warm, small yet capable hand clasped within his made his insides smile much brighter than the brilliant sunshine.

Yep, a perfect afternoon.

Which was why it made no sense for him to go and ruin it, but he opened his mouth and risked doing so anyway.

"The code the other night," he began.

Kami turned her head to look at him and he considered stopping, but pushed on anyway, because he needed to tell her. Perhaps it made no sense, but the thought that he'd kept that from her nagged at him and wouldn't let up.

"The man reminded me of my father."

Kami's eyes widened. "Oh, I'm sorry. That couldn't have been easy." She squeezed his fingers. "I've never heard you mention either of your parents before."

"Yeah, neither one of us talk about them much, do we?"

Kami's nose crinkled. "There's a reason for that on my part, but let's not talk about mine. Tell me about your parents."

"My mom is great, always showered me with love and attention, and you'd probably say she spoiled me rotten."

Smiling and looking a little wistful, Kami tsked. "The woman has a lot to answer for."

Gabe smiled. "She tried her best."

"And your dad?"

Gabe's lungs locked down, refusing to budge to pull in much-needed air. "He died."

"Oh, Gabe, I'm sorry. I didn't know."

"How could you? Like you said, I never talk about him."

"How long ago did he die?"

"I was eight."

Kami rolled onto her side to stare at him. "That's young."

He nodded.

"How did he die?"

"Heart attack."

"So working a code on a man who reminded you of your father…" Her eyes watered. "Oh, Gabe."

"I don't want your sympathy," he rushed out. "I just wanted you to know."

She stared at him a moment, then surprised him by lifting their interlocked hands to her mouth and pressing a soft kiss against his. "I'm glad you told me."

Feeling awkward and more exposed than he'd felt in years, Gabe nodded, then rolled back over to stare up at the sky. Next to him, Kami did the same.

He wasn't sure how long they lay listening to the music, lost in their own thoughts—probably about another thirty minutes—but when the band took a break, Kami sat up and stretched.

"I feel lazy, like I could doze off," she admitted, smiling sheepishly down at him. "I need to move or I might."

"You didn't sleep well last night?"

"I slept great," she countered.

Glad she wasn't dwelling on their earlier conversation, he laughed. "So much for thinking you might have lain awake thinking about me."

"I slept like a log." Although her cheeks were a little rosy, she didn't look repentant and fortunately her shoulders didn't tighten back up with tension.

He didn't like Kami tense. Not when their relationship had always been the opposite, when being together had always made the world a better place no matter what was going on around them.

"I'm never going to get a big ego while you're around, am I?" He picked up their trash.

"You don't need me to inflate your ego." Kami dusted off stray bits of grass and foliage and folded the throw blanket.

"A little ego boosting now and again wouldn't hurt, though."

Laughing, Kami followed him toward the trash bins. "I'll keep that in mind."

"You do that." After he'd tossed their trash, he brushed his hands over his jeans. "Want to walk the waterfront? We can drop the blanket off at the car."

"Sure."

They put the blanket in his car, then strolled along the waterfront.

At one point, they stopped to stare out at the water. Then Kami turned and looked up at the Sunsphere.

"She's beautiful, isn't she?"

Yes, she was, but he didn't mean the big gold structure she referred to.

Still looking at the woman rather than the twenty-six-story-high Sunsphere, Gabe shrugged. "It's made up of real gold, so I guess it would appeal."

She furrowed her brows. "What's that supposed to mean?"

He shrugged. "Women like jewelry, and since the Sun-sphere's glass panels contain twenty-four-karat gold dust, you'd be more prone to appreciate it."

Giving him a look of pity, Kami shook her head. "That, my friend, might be the most sexist thing I've ever heard you say, and that's saying something."

He gave a *who, me?* look. "I meant no harm."

She held up her ringless fingers and wiggled them. "You shouldn't lump all women into the same category."

"Especially not present company," he added, grinning.

"Exactly." Because she did not want to be lumped in with all the women he'd known. What all that meant, she wasn't sure, just that she knew she didn't want to be like the others.

"I'm not like other women," she said, to be sure there was no doubt.

"Amen."

Obviously surprised at his affirmation, she cut her gaze back to him. "What's that supposed to mean?"

"You're different."

Her eyes narrowed. "As in good different or as in weird different?"

"Definitely weird different," he assured her, grinning, but inside feeling a bit sober at just how true saying she was different was. He'd never told any woman about his father, had never wanted to. And, as vulnerable as it left him feeling, he was glad he'd told her.

Kami playfully slapped his arm. "Tell me why I'm here with you, again."

"Because you like me."

"Lord only knows why."

That she didn't deny his claim reverberated through him. Finally.

Smiling, Gabe gestured toward the golden globe in the sky. "You want to go up?"

She glanced up at the iconic gold ball that had been built for a World's Fair decades before. "Seriously, you'd want to do that?"

"It's one of the first things I did when I moved to Knoxville. Amazing views of the city and the mountains."

"I've never gone up," she mused, staring up at the Sunsphere with a bit of longing on her face.

"You've never gone to the observation deck?"

"I was supposed to once, on a school field trip…" She paused, stared up at the golden globe with a glimmer of sadness in her eyes. "…but I ended up not being able to go."

"That settles it." He grabbed hold of her hand and was once again grateful that she didn't pull free. "We're going up."

Gabe was right. The views from the Sunsphere were spectacular. So was the man beside her.

When she let herself forget everything she knew about Gabe and allowed herself to glory in being the recipient of his attention and smile, it was easy to smile back, to give in to the chemistry between them.

When that little nagging voice reared its ugly head and reminded her of all the women Gabe had been through just during the time she'd known him, nervous energy boiled in her belly. They needed to establish that they were never going to be more than just friends, but she kept putting off the conversation.

She probably should've done that when he'd held her hand while lying on the blanket.

She'd been so relaxed, had been enjoying the music, the sunshine, the peacefulness of the afternoon so much that she hadn't pulled her hand away when he'd taken it.

Gabe's hand holding hers should have wrecked her peaceful feeling, but to her surprise, despite the electricity in his fingertips, it hadn't. Lying on that blanket next to him, eyes closed, the sun warming her face, lacing her hand with his had felt natural. Like just another part of what felt like a perfect afternoon, a happy afternoon.

Because she was happy.

Hanging out with Gabe at a city park made her happy.

That he'd shared with her what had happened to his father made her happy, too. He'd been too hesitant, his voice too raw, for her to believe that it was something he'd talked about much in the past. That he'd shared that with her made the afternoon all the more special.

"Just think, if you bought my date, you and I could explore those mountains."

So much for her peaceful, happy feeling.

She cleared her throat. "You promised you weren't going to ask me to bid on you again."

"I didn't ask you to bid on me. I was just making an observation. While on the observation deck." He winked and gestured to where they were.

She rolled her eyes. "Ha ha. You're so clever."

He grinned. "It's about time you noticed."

Ignoring his comment, she didn't point out that she'd noticed a lot of things about him, and, instead, smiled. "Are these panels really made of gold?"

He chuckled. "That got your attention, eh?"

Apparently when Gabe had previously visited the Sunsphere, he'd done his research because he launched into the history of when the iconic structure had been built and why.

"You sound more like a tour guide than a doctor," she teased, impressed at his knowledge of the architectural wonder and the World's Fair that had prompted it.

"A man of many talents."

"So I'm learning."

"You've barely begun," he assured, wagging his brows.

She rolled her eyes. Again. "There's that ego."

"Waiting for you to pop it."

She shook her head. "Not this time."

"What? No denials about my talents?"

"Like you said," she conceded, "I barely know what your talents are, so denying them seems a bit foolish."

He studied her a moment, then, eyes twinkling, said, "We need to remedy that."

His gaze dropped to her lips and any lingering sensations of peace dissipated into awareness. Awareness of the very maleness of the man holding her hand, of how he was looking at her, of how her insides trembled at the brevity of his touch, of his words.

Stop this, Kami. Stop flirting with him. You're supposed to tell him that you can only be friends, nothing more. That's why you came to lunch. Not to have a mini-date.

Mini-date? This afternoon was better than her last dozen dates. More than that.

"How do you suggest we do that?" That wasn't what she was supposed to say. Nor was she supposed to be staring back at his mouth, at those wonderful lips that had caressed hers not even twenty-four hours ago.

"You need a crash course in my many talents."

She suspected the course would be fabulous, full of pleasure and good times. It was the crash that worried her. "Sounds dangerous."

"Don't like to live dangerously, Kam?"

"Nope. I'm a safety first kind of girl." Although, if that were true they wouldn't be having this conversation, nor would she still be staring at his mouth and wondering if it had felt as good against hers as she remembered.

"I can appreciate that about you."

"Good thing, because I don't plan to change for any man." She'd watched her mother do that to no avail whenever a new man popped into her life. No, thank you.

"That why your previous relationships haven't worked out?"

"Why's that?"

His gaze lifted to hers. "Your unwillingness to change?"

"Are you saying you change to make relationships work?" she challenged, not believing he did.

He considered her question. "That's a good question. My initial response would be yes, but the truth is, probably not."

Interesting that he'd given such a thoughtful answer.

"A person shouldn't change to make a relationship work." Which was why she needed to point out that she had no desire to join the ranks of his has-beens. No way would she and Gabe ever work. He was a pro with women at his command and she was an amateur with really high checklist standards. They were a recipe for disaster.

"Sure they should."

Surprised at his comment, she frowned. "You just admitted you hadn't changed for past relationships."

"You're right. I did." Holding her gaze, he took a deep breath and said, "Which is why those relationships are in the past. For a relationship to work, both parties have to care enough about the other to give and take, to change. Otherwise, the relationship is doomed before it's started."

That was a good lead in to why a relationship between them would never work. And why they should stop this before they irreparably damaged their friendship.

Yet, she didn't. Instead, she turned back to stare out at the mountains just beyond the city limits and let her mind wonder. *What if?*

She'd had such a great time with him today. Thrilled at the tingles his hand holding hers shot through her entire being.

What if they *could* have a relationship and still be friends afterward?

"Safe and sound, as promised," Gabe reminded her as he pulled into the empty parking place next to Kami's sedan.

"Thank you for a lovely afternoon."

"You're welcome. We'll have to do it again sometime." The sooner the better as far as Gabe was concerned. He'd truly enjoyed the day.

Silence hit them and then Kami reached for the car door handle.

"I'd like to see you again, Kami." Surely she knew that, but he didn't want there to be any doubt.

Grinning, she pointed a finger. "Lucky for you, you get to work with me three to four nights a week."

There she went popping his bubble again.

"Not what I meant."

Although her hand toyed with the door handle, she didn't make a run for it. "I enjoy our friendship."

So did he.

"You'd enjoy dating me more," he promised. He'd make sure of it.

Her lower lip disappeared into her mouth. "I—I don't know."

"I'm attracted to you and want us to explore what's happening between us."

She stared at where her fingers perched on the door handle. "Which is what exactly?"

"Something worth taking our time to figure out."

"I really don't think I need to be here for this," Kami insisted as she got out of Gabe's car the following afternoon and stared at the faded white-framed house where Beverly Smith and her husband lived.

Debbie was a fast worker. She'd arranged a meeting and insisted on Kami and Gabe attending as well. Or maybe she'd just requested Gabe and he'd embellished to say Kami had to be there, too. She'd tried to plead out, but he'd insisted that if he had to spend the afternoon with Debbie, then so did she.

"That's because you're heartless and have no qualms

about throwing me to the wolves." Gabe came around to her side of the SUV and led her across the paved driveway.

"So dramatic. You really went into the wrong profession, Gabe. You'd have been great on prime-time television." Pausing on her way up the porch steps, she feigned a light-bulb moment. "Hey, I bet Debbie could introduce you to a few of her friends. You could be the latest and greatest thing since sliced bread."

"And deprive all our emergency-room patients of my tender, loving care?" He clicked his tongue. "No, thank you. Besides, you'd miss me."

"You have a point," Kami conceded, knocking on Beverly's front door. She gave Gabe a nervous look. "I hope this works out for Beverly. I can't imagine everything she and her family are going through right now. I'm going to feel terrible if it doesn't or adds to their stress."

"If Beverly and her husband don't want their story to be an episode of Debbie's show, then all they have to do is say no." Gabe touched her arm in what was meant to be a reassuring gesture.

Only his fingers against her bare arm added to the swirling in her belly.

She arched one brow. "Just like all you have to do is tell Debbie no?"

He chuckled. "Good point. Maybe we should bar the door and not let Debbie anywhere near the Smiths." Then his expression grew more serious. "But, really, whatever they decide is what they decide. Debbie can't force them to do anything they don't want to do."

"I know." She did know but felt protective, as if she'd be responsible since it was through her that the opportunity had presented itself.

The front door opened and a tired-looking twenty-five-year-old nurse and her husband of the same age stood on the other side.

* * *

"I wasn't sure if you'd both be here," Kami admitted to her friend, as they joined the couple on their sofa.

"My parents are with Lindsey while we're here," Beverly said, her face filled with guilt. "I wanted to meet at the hospital, but because of the show Debbie wants to do, she insisted upon meeting at the house. Leaving the hospital was hard, but…but Gregg says that we need to do this." She gave a little shrug. "I know he's right."

Lifting her hand to press a kiss there, her husband nodded. "If nothing else, you needed a few minutes away from the hospital, a shower in your own bathroom, a minute alone with your husband."

The two exchanged looks and, despite their horrid current circumstances, Kami felt a stab of envy.

That was how a relationship should be, she thought. Not the way her mother's relationships had been. Not the way her own relationships had been. But the deep abiding love that shone in the couple's eyes as they looked at each other, even while they dealt with great financial and emotional burdens with their new baby's health needs.

Debbie and her producer arrived moments later, along with a cameraman, who sat in a chair awaiting further instructions with his camera ready to go at a moment's notice.

Debbie asked Gabe's opinion several times and she threw out comments left and right to her producer, but, other than a few smiles and polite pleasantries, she didn't have much to say to Kami.

Truly, Kami was unneeded. Other than answering a few questions about the event, she didn't say a word.

Jerry was pleasant enough, but, again, he only had eyes for his show's star.

Motioning to the cameraman, Debbie led the Smiths through a series of questions about their relationship, Beverly's pregnancy, when they first found out about Lindsey's heart problems, and what her status was now.

The cameraman moved about, getting different angles.

Her hand locked with her husband's, Beverly's shoulders slumped as she looked at the television producer. Her voice quavered as she said, "Do you know how difficult it is to pray for a heart for your baby, so your child can live, when it means someone else's baby has to die to give that heart?"

Kami's eyes watered at the implications of what her co-worker said, at how heavy Beverly's heart ached for what her baby and family was going through, but also for what another family would have to go through for the Smiths to get their miracle.

Within minutes, Jerry presented the Smiths with a contract giving the television station the rights to the footage shot that day, permission to film their upcoming big moments, to have behind-the-scenes shots, and to completely renovate their home any way Debbie saw fit.

Neither of the Smiths looked nervous or hesitant.

No problem—Kami was nervous enough for them. "Are you sure?"

Without batting an eyelash, the Smiths both nodded.

"We talked about this before everyone arrived. Our biggest hope is that this will raise awareness of the need for organ donation. If us signing these—" Beverly gestured to the papers "—helps achieve that, helps one person sign their donor card, then it's worth sharing our story."

Her heart full of admiration for her coworker, Kami watched as the Smiths signed the contract.

Debbie made arrangements to meet with the couple at the hospital to film them with Lindsey. Then she, the Smiths, Jerry, and the cameraman went through the house.

Which left Kami and Gabe sitting in the living room. Alone.

Gabe's gaze met hers.

"They can always say no, you said," Kami mock whispered, but with a smile on her face and her eyes a bit watery.

"You think they should have?"

She shook her head. "How could I when their reasons for saying yes are so powerful?"

Gabe nodded. "If Debbie's cameraman is worth his paycheck, he got Beverly on film and they'll use that. If I wasn't already an organ donor, I would be after the emotion Beverly just poured into this room."

Feeling much better about the whole ordeal than when they'd arrived, she nodded. Maybe the story would help the Smiths and other families, too.

"You ready to leave?"

"Before we got here," she admitted, but was glad she'd come, was glad that she'd gotten to hug her friend, witness the love the couple shared, and was even more glad that she and Mindy had initiated the fund-raiser.

He grinned. "Me, too."

"Yeah, yeah. I saw you making googly eyes at Debbie," she teased.

"Any googly eyes I was making were meant for you, not her."

"Um…right." She was saved from having to comment further as the others rejoined them in the living room.

Kami hugged Beverly again, making her promise to call if there was anything she could do to help, even if it was just running errands or picking up something to bring up to the NICU as this was one of the few times Beverly had left the hospital since Lindsey's birth.

Within minutes, Kami was back in Gabe's car.

"You hungry?" he asked.

She was about to say no, but her belly growled, making any denial seem petty.

"Champagne and caviar?"

She smiled that he remembered her quip from the day before. "You planning to ply me with expensive food and drink?"

"Would it work?"

She shook her head.

"I didn't think so." He grinned. "How about we hit my favorite steak house instead? No caviar on the menu, but they have a wide variety of options and I've never been disappointed."

"Sounds good."

The steak house was good. Gabe ordered a cedar plank salmon and Kami ordered a shrimp pasta. Both were delicious.

"Only a few more weekends until the fund-raiser," Gabe mused. "Everything ready?"

Kami shrugged. "As ready as we can be. There are still some last-minute donations coming in, which is great. The more that come in, the better."

"Anything I can do to help?"

She gave him a pointed look. "Don't forget to show up the night of the fund-raiser."

He laughed. "As if I could."

Kami set her fork down next to her plate. "You know, I don't understand why you're so worried about Debbie. She's beautiful, talented, and successful. A guy could do a lot worse."

From across the table, he arched a brow. "Are you trying to sell me on my ex? I may not let you order dessert for such treachery."

Kami laughed. "You mean, like you trying to sell me on the new, improved Baxter?"

"Definitely not trying to sell you on him. Just trying to make sure you weren't interested in getting back together regardless of how buff he becomes."

She shook her head. "His physique had nothing to do with why he and I weren't working."

Eyeing her, he leaned back in his chair. "What were the reasons? Besides the fact that he wasn't me, of course."

"Of course," she agreed with a great deal of sarcasm, trying to decide if she really wanted to go there with Gabe, whose kiss made her feel everything Baxter's had lacked. "Let's just say our chemistry wasn't right."

Gabe studied her for a moment. Then to Kami's surprise, rather than push for her to elaborate, he accepted her answer.

"I'm glad."

"Because?"

"If you'd had the right chemistry with him, you wouldn't be here with me."

"This isn't a date," she pointed out.

"It doesn't make my comment any less true. If you and Baxter were still together, you wouldn't be with me regardless of how we labeled the meal."

She conceded his point. If she'd had the chemistry with Baxter that she felt with Gabe, she'd not have wanted to be with anyone but Baxter, would have wanted to spend all her spare moments, all her meals, with him. That wasn't the case.

Baxter had been ideal on paper, but in reality, not so much so. What he'd been was safe.

Gabe… Gabe was not safe, but that didn't seem to stop her silly mind from wondering *what if?* What if she gave in to the chemistry and told him she wanted him?

No matter what happened between them, friendship or something more, she would not make a fool of herself over him.

If, and that was a big if, something did happen between them, she'd not get attached and she'd be the one to walk away. She'd keep control.

She wouldn't chase him or hold on to unrequited feelings the way women tended to do where he was concerned.

She knew better.

Not that she planned on anything happening, but still…

Forcing herself not to stare at his mouth, she swallowed.

"Now, about dessert," she said, picking up the menu and studying it. "I'm more of a cake than a pie person, so if you're planning to share, I hope that's okay."

CHAPTER TEN

GABE HADN'T MEANT to share dessert with Kami, but watching her eat the sweets was more enjoyable than eating the carrot cake he'd ordered would have been. Not that she didn't let him have a bite here and there.

"This is really good."

"Better than your Death by Chocolate?"

Looking ecstatic, she nodded. "This could be Killed by Carrots."

Gabe laughed. "I don't think that's going to catch on."

"Probably not," she admitted, her lips wrapping around the fork, her eyes closing as she slowly pulled the fork out.

When she opened her eyes, realized he was watching her and that what she was doing was affecting him, she winced. "Sorry. I keep forgetting."

"Forgetting?"

"Nothing."

"You really think I'm going to let you get away with that?"

She shrugged. "You can only make me tell what I'm willing to."

He thought on her comment a moment. "The only thing you're willing to tell me is nothing?"

"Maybe."

"I never took you for a tease, Kami."

"Yeah, yeah. I've been teasing you for months. It's what you and I do. What we've always done. It's safe and fun and, despite your momentary lapses, it's probably all there should be between us."

Elated at her "probably," Gabe studied her, trying to decipher if she was serious or testing him, wanting him to correct her.

"My momentary lapses? Are you saying you didn't have a lapse when you kissed me back?"

"Oh, I had a lapse, all right. A big one."

"Meaning you regret having kissed me back?"

As if she was trying to keep them from spilling her secrets, her lips pressed tightly together.

Gabe smiled. He couldn't help himself. She couldn't admit that she'd enjoyed their kiss, but she couldn't lie and say she regretted it, either.

Whatever her reasons were for not wanting to move into a more physical relationship, Kami wasn't immune to the chemistry between them. Not by a long shot.

"Okay, you refuse to tell me if you regret kissing me. I can live with that. But what I really want to know," he mused, picking up his fork and feeding her a piece of his carrot cake, "is when are you going to let me kiss you again?"

Kami choked on the cake. Coughing, she cleared her throat, took the glass of water Gabe offered, then coughed some more.

"Not exactly the reaction I was going for," he said wryly, his lips twitching.

"I imagine not." She took another drink of water and this time the cool liquid went down correctly. "Don't do that."

"Don't do what?"

"Say things that catch me off guard."

Gabe laughed. "That caught you off guard? You who always have a fast comeback for anything I say?"

"Yeah, well, I didn't just then."

"Apparently."

She put her water glass down and pushed what was left of both cakes toward him. "I'm finished. You eat the rest."

Gabe motioned for the waitress, asked for a box and the check.

"I can pay for mine."

"You could, but you're not," he corrected. When she went to argue, he reminded her, "It's my turn. You paid last time."

"Actually, Jerry paid last time."

"I imagine the television station reimbursed him." Gabe got the check from the waitress and paid while Kami boxed up her leftovers.

When they exited the restaurant, the sky was streaked with yellow, orange, and red hues as the sun made its final splash of the day.

"Wow. Beautiful sunset," Kami exclaimed as they made their way toward the car.

"It is. Seems a shame to call an end to such a great evening. You want to go downtown and throw back a few?"

She started to ask him to bring her home. He could see it on her face. But then she took on a determined look.

"Sure. Let's throw back a few," she surprised him by saying. Her eyes glittered with challenge. "Why not?"

Gabe hadn't thought she'd agree, but then, Kami had been surprising him from the moment they'd met. Everything about her kept him on his toes. He drove them downtown to a place he knew, then paid for a parking spot.

He took her hand and they walked to the club, found two vacant seats at the bar, then ordered drinks.

An hour later, they were both laughing at anything and everything.

Gabe wasn't drunk, but he was feeling good. Too good. Not because of alcohol, but because of the woman smiling and laughing with him.

Kami went to order another round, but Gabe shook his head. "No more for me. I've got to drive us home. You go ahead, though."

Her mouth made an O, and then she changed the order to one.

"You doing okay, still?"

Smiling, she nodded. "Since I never do this, surprisingly, yes. What about you? You come here often?"

He glanced around the club. "I've been here a few times."

"With Debbie?"

He frowned. "No."

"Some other woman?"

"Be careful, Kam," he teased, watching her closely. "You almost sound jealous."

She glanced away. "I'm not," she quickly denied, her voice not feisty. "I know you've been with lots of women. That's why you kiss like the devil."

"The devil, huh?" He laughed. "Since I think you're giving me a compliment, thank you."

"You're welcome." She half turned on her bar stool to watch as a dance instructor called for more to join in the fun. A country song was playing and there were a bunch of regulars line dancing and a few watching the instructor and doing their best to keep up. "I never could line dance. No rhythm and two left feet."

"I thought line dancing was for people who had two left feet and no rhythm?" he ragged.

She turned, stared him straight in the eyes, and challenged, "I suppose you're an expert?"

She was beautiful, Gabe thought. Absolutely beautiful. Her eyes sparkled, her chin jutted forward, and her lips parted just so. It was all he could do not to lean forward, cup her face, and take her sassy mouth for another "devilish" kiss.

"I've been known to scoot my boots a time or two," he said with an exaggerated drawl.

Leaning on her bar stool, she peered down, her gaze dropping to his shoes. "Too bad you aren't wearing boots. I'd make you put your feet where your mouth is."

Gabe's lips twitched. "Not having boots has never stopped me before."

Her brow arched. "Is that a backwoods way of asking me to dance?"

Grinning, he slid off his bar stool and held out his hand. "You want to dance, Kam? I promise not to step on your toes any fewer than a dozen times."

He wanted her in his arms, wanted to embrace every moment because life was short—just look at how young his father had died. It should be lived to its fullest. Still, he'd settle for whatever she'd give him until she realized they belonged together.

Like what his parents had. That was what he wanted, what he'd been searching for and never found. Looking into Kami's eyes, his chest inflating, Gabe couldn't help but smile as he thought, *Until now.*

Placing her hand in his, she laughed. "Oh, this is going to be good. Especially since if you're stepping on people's toes while line dancing, you're way worse than me."

Gabe wasn't way worse than Kami. Not that Kami had expected him to be. He was one of those guys who excelled at everything, so of course he line danced with ease, quickly picking up the routine for whatever tune played if it wasn't one he knew.

Kami, on the other hand, decided she was just going to go with it and not worry about her two left feet. She probably mis-stepped more than she grapevined or ball-changed, but she was having fun and was keeping time, mostly, with the other dancers.

Then again, it might be the alcohol making her think she wasn't doing too badly.

Either way, she was laughing, spinning, and having fun. With Gabe.

In a completely different way than they'd ever spent time together before. She liked it.

A lot.

When the dance instructor announced she was taking a break, a slow number came on.

Kami started to head back toward where she and Gabe

had been sitting at the bar, but he grabbed her hand and pulled her toward him.

"Not so fast, my little do-si-do. This might be my favorite song."

Putting her arms around his neck, she fell into rhythm with him. "Might be?"

He grinned. "Ask me when the music is finished."

"Deal." Kami rested her head against Gabe's chest, marveling at his heartbeat against her cheek, at his arms around her, his hands at her waist.

Why had she been fighting this? Pushing him away? This felt so good, so right.

Unbidden, she giggled.

"What's so funny?"

She smiled at him. "I feel like I'm in high school dancing with the cutest guy in school."

His eyes crinkled at the corners. "How'd you know I was the cutest guy in school?"

Kami laughed. "Just a hunch."

"I wasn't really, you know."

"Weren't what, the cutest guy in school?" She leaned her head back to look up at him. "I don't believe you."

"I wasn't," he admitted. "Tommy Smithson had all the girls after him. The rest of us guys were just there to collect his leftovers."

"Tommy must be amazing," she cooed, her fingers toying with the soft hair at his nape. "When's your class reunion? I want to meet him."

Gabe shook his head. "You think I'd risk introducing you to Tommy? No way. I'm already struggling to convince you to be more than my friend. You meet Tommy and I'm not even in the ballpark anymore."

"He's an athlete? No worries. I'm worse at sports than I am at dancing. Not my thing."

"For whatever it's worth, I think you're a wonderful dancer."

Her heart skipped a few beats at his compliment.

"Ha," she countered, her insides feeling warm and mushy. "You must have drunk more than you realized."

"Nope, but it might be that you fit into my arms so perfectly that I don't notice anything else. Not sure I'd care if you stomped my toes so long as I get to hold you."

She couldn't argue. She did fit into his arms perfectly.

At least, from her perspective it felt perfect. Just to be sure, she snuggled closer and laid her head back against his chest.

Yep, pretty perfect.

Gabe moved to the slow music, Kami in his arms, her head nestled beneath his chin, and decided that this really was his favorite song.

But then the next one came on and the next, and as long as the music kept playing and he got to keep holding Kami, he'd keep on loving the songs.

Because he knew when the music stopped, he'd take her home, and he'd leave.

Not that he'd want to leave.

What he wanted was to make love to the sassy woman in his arms.

But he wouldn't.

Not tonight.

Not when she'd been drinking and might have regrets. As much as he wanted her, he didn't want her to think this was just physical, didn't want her to think he'd taken advantage of the first opportunity her guard was down.

He wanted more than just sex. Lots more.

So, he'd hold her, breathe in the sweet scent she attributed to soap, water, and lotion but that he was convinced was some aphrodisiac blend all her own, and he'd enjoy the moment.

In the moment, he was holding Kami.

And she was holding him back.

The line-dance instructor came back out and announced she'd be doing her last set of instructions for the night.

Full of enthusiasm, Kami jumped back in. Despite her fairly frequent incorrect moves, she seemed to be having a great time, which made Gabe happy.

Over the moon. Giddy drunk. But not nearly as giddy drunk as when he drove her home and walked her to her apartment and she kissed him.

He'd meant to just tell her good-night, but before he could say a thing, she'd stood on her tiptoes, wrapped her arms around him, and pressed her lips to his.

Fully, wholly, no holding back, hands in his hair, body grinding against his, enthusiastically kissed him.

His libido skyrocketed.

His willpower went to hell.

"Kami," he groaned, wondering how he was going to untangle himself when all he wanted was to lose himself in her arms and tell her all his crazy thoughts. "I have to stop."

"Why?" she breathed as she traced her mouth over his throat and spread her fingers over his back, holding him tightly to her. "I don't want you to stop."

"You're drunk."

"Not that drunk."

"Drunk enough."

Her hands slid down his back, pulled his shirt from his pants, and slid beneath the material.

Goose bumps prickled his skin.

Kami's fingers on his bare back undid him. His groin hardened. His jeans constricted to the point of pain.

Having to pull away from Kami caused pain, but he managed, instantly feeling defeat at the loss of contact.

"No," she told him, her green gaze locked with his and fire sparking to life. "You can't stop. Not now. Not when I want you."

Gabe groaned, then took a deep breath and cupped her face. "You have no idea what hearing you say you want me does to my insides."

"Apparently not what's happening to my insides," she complained. She moved against him, as if to show him.

"Worse."

"Impossible." She glared at him. "You're going to leave, aren't you?"

He nodded. "It's the right thing to do."

She let out a long sigh.

He was trying to do the right thing, but Kami wasn't making it easy. Not with her take-me eyes and pouty, kiss-me lips and with how she couldn't stand still, but instead swayed ever so slightly as if dancing to a song of seduction.

Gabe swallowed, fought for willpower. "What is it you think I should do right now, Kami?"

She stared at him a moment, then closed her eyes. "I think you should get back in your car and drive home. Alone. Without me. To a cold, lonely bed, knowing I would have rocked your world."

Knowing he was doing the right thing, Gabe leaned forward, kissed her forehead, then finished unlocking her apartment door and opening it for her to step inside. "For the record, you rock my world every single day."

With that, he picked her up, set her inside the apartment, reached around to make sure the lock would catch, then pulled the door closed.

With him locked on the outside of her apartment because, heaven help him, he was already questioning his decision to leave.

CHAPTER ELEVEN

"Go to breakfast with me?"

Having almost reached her car in the employee parking lot, Kami spun toward Gabe, not bothering to hide her surprise that he'd followed her out of the hospital and obviously jogged to catch her.

She'd seen him several times throughout the long night, had worked next to him, had talked to him in regard to patients, but she'd fought humiliation and felt the tension.

Not just on her part.

So his breakfast invitation truly did take her by complete surprise.

When she didn't immediately answer, he continued. "Your pick on where we go."

She bit the inside of her lower lip, then acquiesced. "Sure."

Why not? How much more could she embarrass herself than she had the other night?

"I tried calling yesterday. The day before, too," he said after they were settled in his car.

"I didn't feel like talking," she admitted, checking to make sure her seat belt was secure.

"What about now? You feel like talking about what happened the other night?"

"Nothing happened the other night," she reminded him, crossing her arms. Why had she agreed to this?

He shot a quick glance her way. "I wasn't sure how much

you remembered. If perhaps that was why you weren't answering my calls."

"If you're implying something happened that I don't recall, I'm not buying it." She'd know if something more had happened between them. It hadn't.

"Sorry, that's not what I meant." He raked his fingers through his hair. "You're not upset with me because I left, are you?"

She wasn't. Much.

"I wanted to stay," he continued, staring straight ahead at the road. "But I didn't want you to have regrets, but now I think you do anyway."

She cut her gaze toward him, took in his profile, the tense way he gripped the steering wheel. Gabe didn't want her upset. He was trying to make things right between them.

She leaned back against the headrest and inhaled deeply. They were friends. Nothing had happened. This awkwardness was ridiculous.

She sighed. "I'm sorry I didn't answer your call or text. I needed some space."

"Understood." He glanced her way, then back at the road. "You still feel that way?"

"That I want space between us?" She shook her head, then admitted the truth. "I value our friendship, Gabe. I missed talking with you last night the way we usually do at work. I don't want to lose that. That's what scares me about what's happening between us."

"Me, too. I should have been more persistent in calling, should have pulled you aside last night to clear the air, but I didn't want to put you on the spot or beg forgiveness at the hospital."

Beg forgiveness? Realization dawned. "You thought I was mad at you? That's why you were standoffish last night?"

His brow arched. "Weren't you?"

Only that he'd left her when she'd wanted him to stay.

"I was more upset with myself than you. I acted very

out of character on several counts. But it's okay, Gabe. I understand."

He slowed the car at a traffic light, looked her way. "Unbelievable. You thought I left because I didn't want to have sex with you, didn't you?"

His eyes were so blue, so intense, it was like looking up into the sky and losing one's self.

"I think you want to have sex with lots of women," she admitted, then sank her teeth into the soft flesh of her lower lip.

"You make me sound like I've no scruples and have sex with anyone."

"Don't you?"

"No." His answer was immediate and brooked no argument, almost as if he was offended that she'd thought he might.

"If you want to have sex with lots of women, it's not my business."

"I want to make it your business, Kam." He glanced to make sure the red light hadn't changed back to green.

The light changed and Gabe accelerated the car, driving in silence until he pulled into a restaurant parking lot and into an empty space near the entrance.

He didn't kill the engine, just turned to her and waited for her to say something.

She'd known the conversation wasn't over. She'd been able to feel the wheels turning inside his head as he drove them. She'd even known what he was going to say when he spoke next, so she'd prepared her answer in her mind.

She took a deep breath. "Despite what you might think from my behavior the other night, sex is a big deal to me."

"Sex is a big deal to me, too."

"No, it isn't," she countered. "You're casual about sex. I'm not."

"You're making assumptions about me that aren't true."

She turned in the seat, stared straight into his eyes, which shouldn't even be real they were so blue. "You've never had casual sex, Gabe?"

He didn't flinch but Kami read the truth on his face even before he said, "I didn't say that."

She reached for the passenger door handle so she could get out of his car. She'd gone from tense to her belly being in a tight wad to where she wasn't even sure she could eat. She should have asked him to take her back to her car.

"Sex between us wouldn't be casual, Kami. If you believe that, then you're fooling yourself and denying us both something that would be amazing."

"What's amazing is my friendship with you to begin with and why I want to hang on to that relationship when you're determined we completely destroy it."

"Is that what you believe would happen if we had sex? That we can't be friends and lovers? That's the real reason you won't have sex with me? Because of our friendship?"

"At the moment, I'm not sure we can be friends," she threw back.

"Then what's stopping you from closing your car door and asking me to drive us to my place right this very moment?"

Hand still on the handle, she glared at him. "What? So you can reject me again? I don't think so."

"Is that what this is about? I left because I didn't want to take advantage of you. Rather than see the truth, that I left because I care about you and want things to be right when we take that step, instead, all you see is that I left."

Kami's heart pounded in her chest. Her hands shook as she dropped them back into her lap.

"Take me home, Gabe."

"Fine." His movements full of frustration, he restarted the engine and backed out of the parking spot.

He drove in silence, pulling in at her apartment complex. When she went to get out, he gripped the steering wheel and leaned forward.

"I'm sorry, Kam."

"Me, too." She gave a resigned sigh, then a little shrug. "Because even though I asked you to take me home, well, my car is still at the hospital and, short of walking to work tonight, I'm going to need a lift back there."

"Oh! You're here!"

Startled by the woman stepping into the apartment, Kami glanced up from the worn sofa where she'd fallen asleep while petting Bubbles. The cat had apparently dozed off, too, and, yawning, stretched.

"Someone has to take care of your cat," Kami reminded her, sitting up on the sofa and staring at her, obviously shocked to see her mother.

"Hey, babe, where do you want me to put these?" A long-haired free-spirited man came into the apartment behind her mother carrying some grocery bags.

Ah, so that was why she was so startled at Kami being at her apartment. Eugenia had company.

Kami's mother glanced the man's way, then blushed. "In the kitchen is fine, Don."

Her mother didn't bother to introduce them. Why bother? None ever stuck around long.

The man nodded in her direction, then carried the bags to the small kitchen that was open to the living area and began unpacking the bags.

Don. Hadn't the guy her mother left with been named Sammy? Maybe Kami had misunderstood her. Then again, probably not.

"Hello, my Bubbles, did you miss Mommy?" her mother crooned to the cat as she picked her up and kissed her nose. The cat actually licked her mother's nose, so maybe the cat had missed her after all. "Mommy missed you, but it looks like Kami has taken care of you."

Had her mother thought she wouldn't? *She* wasn't the irresponsible one.

"You didn't mention you were going to be gone for so

long," Kami said, watching as her mother continued to love on the feline.

It was more of a greeting than Kami had ever gotten, so maybe her mother really did care about the cat, just wasn't responsible enough to actually take care of the poor girl.

"I didn't know I was going to be," her mother admitted, then gave Kami a semi-annoyed look. "Was it that big a deal to stop by and feed Bubbles? I can find someone else next time if you're too busy to help your own mother with something as simple as feeding her cat."

Ugh. How had her mother turned things to make her feel guilty?

Kami sighed. "It was no problem."

"I didn't think so."

Don came back into the living area, stood quietly in the doorway and gave Kami's mother an expectant look.

Eugenia gave a nervous giggle, then said to Kami, "Then I guess you can be on your way since I'm back. Bye."

Kami's jaw dropped. Maybe not literally, but figuratively, it definitely fell. Just like that, her mother was kicking her out of her apartment. No *thank you*. No questions about Bubbles. No explanation of where she'd been, what she'd been doing, why she'd been gone longer than expected.

Then again, why was Kami surprised? Her mother had been pushing her aside for whatever man was in her life for years.

Kami worked her three on, had Friday and Saturday night off, then worked Sunday, Monday, Tuesday, and Wednesday nights.

She and Gabe hadn't found a happy medium.

They hadn't found a happy anything.

Because she wasn't happy at the way they were walking on eggshells, talking to each other without eye contact, and talking without saying anything at all beyond work.

"Bay two's CT scan shows a non-obstructing renal calculus in the right kidney."

Glancing up from where she stripped the bedding off in the next bay, Kami met the eyes of the man toward whom all her thoughts were directed.

"I'm going to print off some scripts," he continued, not meeting her gaze, "then discharge with instructions to see Urology tomorrow."

"Okay."

He stood watching her a moment, then left. Kami quickly made up the bed with fresh sheets, wiped the countertops down with an antibacterial cleanser, then went to get the scripts and discharge orders from Gabe.

"Thanks," he said as he handed the scripts to her, their fingers touching. Her breath caught. His gaze jerked to hers as if he'd felt the jolt that shot through her at the contact.

Kami hesitated a few moments, wanting to say more, wanting him to say more, then berated herself for her idiocy.

She discharged the patient, then went back to do her nurse's note. Gabe still sat at the station, leaned back in a chair, with his eyes closed and a strained expression on his face.

Her heart squeezed. "You okay?"

He opened his eyes, nodded.

Again, she wanted to say more, but didn't know what. Maybe with time the tension between them would ease. Hopefully.

"I hate this."

Had he read her mind or what?

"Me, too," she admitted, sinking into the chair next to his.

Glancing around to make sure no one was close enough to overhear their conversation, he leaned close. "I miss you, Kami. I miss everything about you."

She bit her lower lip.

"I don't know what else to say. You know how I feel, what I want, that I don't like where things are between us. I'm trying to give you time and space to figure out we're worth taking a chance on." His gaze was intense. "I don't want to push you into something you don't want, but I don't understand why you refuse to give us a chance."

Oh, how easy it would be to give in, to tell him how much she wanted him. To tell him how she dreamed of his kisses, of knowing what it felt like to wrap her legs around his waist and...

Stop it, Kami, she ordered herself. *Just stop it.*

"You and I want different things out of life."

Seeming to understand her turmoil, he still refused to back down. "Are you so sure about that? Because I'm not."

She found herself wanting to believe, wanting to forget a lifetime of lessons and just give in to her heart's desires.

"Need I remind you that you're the one who left me?"

"No, you've reminded me often enough." He held her gaze. "Invite me again, Kam, because I assure you I won't make that mistake a second time."

CHAPTER TWELVE

GABE'S CHALLENGE HAUNTED Kami for the remainder of her shift.

Even now as she gave report to the day-shift nurse taking her place, his voice echoed through her mind.

Inviting Gabe into her bed wouldn't change what would ultimately happen.

She couldn't fall into the same pit her mother willingly leaped into time and again. She was smarter than that.

Only, maybe she wasn't.

Because before she left the hospital, she yielded to her need to see Gabe and found him alone in the dictation room. When he looked up and her gaze met his, she saw the question in his eyes.

She didn't look away.

Couldn't look away.

She stared into his beautiful blue eyes and let herself be mesmerized, knowing she was about to change everything between them.

Who was she kidding? Everything was already changed between them. She might have been denying it, but they'd been in a relationship for weeks.

She was tired of denying that truth. Reality was, she was a woman. A woman with needs and wants and hopes and desires.

A woman who wanted Gabe more than she'd ever wanted anyone.

Scary, but also exciting.

Cocking her hip to the side, she gave what she hoped would pass for a seductive look.

"You're invited. Don't make the mistake of disappointing me a second time."

Gabe had been waiting for this moment for weeks. Longer. Now that he was here, in Kami's bedroom, he wasn't going to rush.

At least, he was going to do his best not to rush.

What he really wanted was to rip off her scrubs and taste every inch of her.

But part of him was enjoying letting her set the tone of what was happening.

Another part of him was still stunned that he was here, that Kami had invited him to her apartment, that she was taking this step. With him.

He wasn't a fool. He knew what being with her meant.

Finally, Kami realized how much she meant to him, was embracing what was between them.

Anticipation building, he'd followed her home from the hospital, parked next to her car, stood next to her while she unlocked her door, then followed her to her bedroom.

Calm, controlled, as if his insides weren't shaking in eagerness of finally making love to her.

Now he waited to see what was next with this lovely woman who monopolized his every thought.

Similar to his own bedroom designed for daytime sleeping, her window shades were drawn, leaving the room dark despite the morning sunshine.

Rather than raise the heavy shade, she flipped on a lamp, casting a low light around the room.

Pillows. Lots and lots of pillows registered first.

Then yellow. A pale yellow, the color of moonlight. And grays.

There was only one photo in the room and he didn't catch

sight of who it was because the moment his gaze landed on it on the bedside table, she turned the frame face down.

"This wasn't preplanned, so I don't have protection." She shrugged a little self-consciously. "I am on the pill, though. I just kept taking it even after Baxter and I broke things off."

Gabe didn't like the thought of her with Baxter or any other man, but the past didn't matter. What mattered was that she was here, with him, and that she was finally accepting that they had a future together.

"I have protection."

She nodded, as if she'd thought he might.

Rather than say anything more, she lifted her hair from her nape. At first Gabe just stared, then realized she was waiting for him to undress her.

With hands that trembled from the significance of what was happening, he slowly pulled up her scrub top and the T-shirt beneath it, revealing her creamy flesh as he lifted the material over her head.

He intentionally kept his fingers from touching her skin, but did his best to take it slow, to savor every second of this moment he'd wanted for so long. One touch and he would be a goner.

He was already a goner.

Unable to resist, he slid his fingers inside her waistband and pulled down her scrub bottoms, placing a soft kiss on each thigh as he did so.

Her flesh goose bumped and her fingers went into his hair.

His knees almost buckled.

Yet he still had to pause, look up at her and ask, "You're sure this is what you want?"

"If you leave me now, I'll never forgive you." Kami wanted this.

Wanted him.

If he changed his mind, she really might curl up and cry.

She wanted her phenomenal sex experience even when

she knew she'd pay the price later. She'd decided the price was worth what she'd get in return: Gabe. For however long they lasted, Gabe would be hers. Her friend and her lover.

"I'm not going anywhere," he assured her.

Kami trembled as his fingertips brushed over her skin. Wearing only her bra and matching panties, she stepped out of her scrub pants, waiting on his next touch.

She wasn't disappointed.

Gabe kissed her knees. Soft, delicate kisses. Then he stood and kissed her neck as his palms trailed down her shoulders, her arms.

Taking her hand, he stepped back and took her in. His eyes deepened to a dark blue as his gaze skimmed over her from head to toe.

"Mercy."

A smile spread across her face. She didn't have to ask if he liked what he saw. She saw it on his face, felt it in his touch, in his kiss, as he possessed her mouth in a blistering kiss. Gabe really did want her as much as she wanted him.

She wanted to touch him, to see him; her hands found their way to his waistband and tugged his shirt free, but he stopped her by taking her hands into his.

"No." She pulled her hands free.

Surprise darkened his eyes.

"You aren't going to deny me touching you back," she told him, not willing to be a passive participant in what was happening. "I get to touch, too."

Rather than argue, he took her hands and placed them back at his waistband and helped her undress him. "I'm all yours."

She wished.

Which scared her.

But now wasn't the time for such thoughts. Now was time for enjoying the here and now because what was happening would be fleeting.

She planned to enjoy it.

Every touch of her hands over his body. Every touch of his hands over hers.

His lips, his mouth tasting.

Hers replying in kind.

"Gabe," she moaned as he pushed her back on the bed and tossed a half-dozen pillows to the floor.

He stared down at her as he donned protection, then joined her on the bed, his body poised over hers.

His eyes were dark, turbulent. "I've wanted this for so long."

"Me, too," she admitted, knowing the time for denials had long passed. "I want you, Gabe." She gripped his shoulders, lifted her hips to push against him, ready for everything his eyes, his body, promised. "I want you now."

"Kami," he groaned, shifting his hips to join their bodies.

She kept her eyes locked with his as he stretched her body to accommodate him, as his hips rocked against hers, creating a rhythm that melted her insides into a hot, quivery mess.

Until she exploded beneath him and had to hold on to keep from shattering into a million pieces.

Then he did it all over again.

Blown away, Kami stared at the ceiling, tracing patterns in the tiles as she caught her breath.

Ha. She'd never catch her breath. Not after what she'd just experienced.

She'd never be the same.

Not her body, her mind, or her heart.

She turned to look at Gabe, to see if he was as affected as she was. Instead, her gaze landed on the face-down photograph.

A photo of her and her mother that had been taken at her nursing school pinning.

A day on which she'd felt empowered because she'd checked off another important step in her life. Graduate from college with honors.

Her next big life goal had been to get her dream job. Most nights, she believed she'd checked that one off, too.

Up next was buy a house—a goal she'd been saving for from her very first paycheck.

Because, as much as she loved her, she didn't want to be like her mother.

She didn't want to get so caught up in a man to the exclusion of all else and make bad decision after bad decision.

Taking her hand into his, Gabe gave her a little squeeze, drawing her attention to where he lay next to her.

"You have to go."

Okay, so her voice had sounded strained, but surely that could be chalked up to the vigorous activities she'd just engaged in.

With Gabe.

Sex with Gabe was a marathon. A marathon with orgasms around every bend. Who knew? Who knew her body could have such a meltdown of pleasure? Could shatter into a million pieces and yet still be whole?

She'd had sex with Baxter, with Kent. Pleasant enough, but no meltdowns. How did one live without meltdowns once one had experienced them?

How was she going to live without Gabe now that she'd experienced him?

"You want me to leave?" He rolled onto his side and stared at her. Confusion shone in his blue eyes. "Why?"

"Because *I* can't. *I* live here."

"I'm not leaving you, Kam. Not after what we just shared."

"This is my apartment," she reminded him, surprised that he wasn't leaping at the out she'd given him.

"You're overthinking, going back into that shell you hide behind. What we just shared was amazing. I know you felt it, too. So, again, I ask, why are you telling me to go?"

Kami closed her eyes. "Because you will leave, Gabe. It's what you do. What men do."

She waited, waited for him to say whatever he was going

to say, but only silence met her ears. Slowly, she opened her eyes, looked into his.

His brows furrowed. "You dumped Baxter. I know you did. He told me himself one day at the gym."

He'd talked to Baxter about her at the gym?

"And that Kent guy, too," he continued. "I don't know about the men in your life beyond that, but I do know that the two guys you've dated since I've known you didn't leave you. You left them."

"What does that have to do with this?"

"Because this is about you. Not me. You're the one who always leaves in your relationships. The one telling me to leave now. Why is that?"

What he said hit her hard.

"What?" She scooted up in the bed and glared at him. "You want me to wait a couple of months? Wait until you get bored, then you'll leave? Is that it? You have to be the one to make that call?"

He stared at her as if she'd grown two heads, then calmly reminded her, "A very smart woman once pointed out to me that if she ever gave me a chance it wouldn't be me who left. Perhaps she's forgotten that, but I haven't."

How dared he quote her to herself?

"Yeah, well, she was bluffing because you were so full of yourself and needed to be taken down a peg or two."

He studied her. "Is that what this is about?"

"No," she denied, shaking her head and feeling very exposed. She flipped the comforter up, covering her vital parts, yet still felt vulnerable. Reaching over, she grabbed one of the few throw pillows still on the bed and hugged it to her.

"Then what?" he pushed.

Why couldn't he have just said okay and left? Why did he have to question everything? Make her question everything?

She didn't want to admit the truth.

She didn't like the truth, didn't like how naked she felt.

"I don't want to be like all the others, Gabe. Nor do I want to admit any of this to you." She hugged the pillow tighter to her chest. "If you leave me and I care, it makes me…weak."

He scooted up beside her, took her hand in his, and studied their interlocking fingers. "You're the strongest woman I know."

Fighting the emotions threatening to overwhelm her, she shook her head. "I'm not strong."

"Because you're with me?"

She didn't answer.

"Kam, I don't want to leave you. Not now or this afternoon or even tonight. But at some point, I will go home. What I don't want to happen is for you to question how I feel. Nothing has changed."

She scowled at him.

"Okay, so some things have changed. Obviously. But not how I feel about you."

"Which is what?"

She waited for him to answer, curious as to what he'd say. Would he feed her a bunch of crock?

"I care about you."

His voice was too sincere to be crock and she heard herself admit, "I care about you, too."

He lifted her hand, kissed it. "That's a pretty good start, I'd say."

Her insides trembled at what was happening between them. "A good start to what?"

"That's what time will tell us. For now, I'm not leaving because I plan to sleep with you in my arms and make love to you again this afternoon."

"You're quiet this morning."

Turning to look at Gabe in the driver seat of his car, Kami forced a smile. What could she say? Over the past twenty-four hours, the man had made her smile. A lot.

"You were there," she reminded him. "The ER was swamped last night."

Looking unfazed, he nodded. "It did get a bit crazy for a

while. So crazy, in fact, that I failed to execute my plan to woo you into the supply room for a kiss or two."

Kami's eyes widened. She wouldn't have put up much resistance had he done any wooing. "There's always tonight."

He laughed. "Want to swing by and get breakfast before we go to your place? I don't think either one of us took time for a break and I can't have you weak from starvation."

She was hungry.

"Breakfast sounds great." An idea hit her. "Pancakes, please. Wherever you got those the morning you first showed at my place."

The corner of his mouth twitched. "Whipped cream and cherries?"

"That's the one."

"You going to show me?"

Although Gabe had no doubt that Kami knew exactly what he referred to, she played innocent. If you could call her toying with the long-stemmed cherry innocent.

"Show you what?"

"I think it's time."

She sighed, put the cherry in her mouth, then, a few seconds later, pulled a de-cherried knotted stem from between her lips.

Gabe grinned. "Such a talented tongue."

"You should know."

Oh, he knew.

"You might need to show me again."

She glanced down at the remaining cherry on her plate. "If you insist."

Eyes locked with hers, he laughed. "I didn't mean tying knots. Although that might be an interesting twist."

Her eyes widened. "Oh."

"Yeah, oh."

She pushed her plate away. "Think we can get an order of these to go?"

* * *

Gabe brushed stray hairs away from Kami's face. "I'm crazy about you."

Wondering where his comment had come from, Kami smiled up at him. "You are pretty crazy," she teased, turning her head to where her lips brushed against his fingers so she could press a kiss there. "For the record, I'm rather fond of you, too."

She'd expected him to grin or to say something silly back. He didn't, just stared down at her with a look in his eyes she couldn't quite read.

The longer he stared, the more unease filled her and she found herself babbling just to be saying something.

"I have an appointment with a Realtor next week." Now, why had she told him that?

"You moving?"

"Maybe." She shrugged. "I've been saving for a while so I could put a down payment on my own place and I've finally reached my minimum-down-payment goal. I'm not in a rush, but I don't want to miss it when the right place comes along. I'm meeting with the Realtor so she knows exactly what I'm looking for and can be on the lookout."

Propping himself on his elbow, Gabe regarded her. "What is it you're looking for, Kami?"

"In my dream world or what I'll most likely end up with?" She gave a little laugh. "I dream of a place of my own, not too far from the hospital, but far enough out that I can have a decent-sized yard. A yard with trees," she added. She'd never lived in a house with trees before. Just apartment complexes with a few decorative trees in front occasionally. "And I think I'd like a pet."

His brows rose. "A pet?"

She nodded. "I've never had a pet."

"Never?"

She shook her head. "We moved a lot while I was growing up. Most of the places we lived didn't allow pets, so it was easier not to have one, even when we lived at the few places where we could."

Odd that her mother had Bubbles now. Kami remembered many a time begging her mother to keep some stray she'd found and brought home. Her mother hadn't once even considered letting her, demanding Kami get rid of the animal and not dare bring it into their home.

"What about you? Did you have pets growing up?"

"A few. Dogs mostly, but a few cats along the way, too. My mother liked a full house."

"Sounds heavenly."

"It wasn't really. Mainly, she just liked a lot of things to keep her distracted from thinking about my father."

"She must have missed him a great deal."

Gabe sucked in a deep breath and waited so long to answer that Kami didn't think he was going to. Then he said, "She did. We both did. For years I had nightmares about him dying."

"Oh, Gabe."

"I watched him die, Kam." Gabe wondered why he was still talking, why he was admitting the horrible truth to her. "I watched him take that last breath and didn't do a thing."

"You were eight years old. What were you supposed to do?"

"Logically, I know you're right, but it took me a long time to accept that."

She hugged him. "I'm sorry, Gabe."

"It was a long time ago." So long ago, he wondered why he'd been thinking of his father so much over the past few weeks. Why he'd had to tell her that day at the park. Then again, after working the code the other day, no wonder thoughts of his father had haunted him.

"At least you were old enough to remember him."

What would she think if he admitted that he'd likely be better off if he'd been young enough not to recall? Gabe closed his eyes. No, not true. Because prior to the heart attack that had claimed his father's life, Gabe's memories of the man he'd helplessly watched die had all been good.

"What about you?" He changed the subject. "You talk about your mother, but never a word about dear old dad."

Kami snorted. "My father was just some guy who came in and out of my mother's life. Not anyone special or amazing. Just another in a long string of failed relationships."

"That's sad. Tell me she found happiness eventually."

"Oh, she finds happiness a lot. He just never sticks around."

Gabe rolled over, took Kami's hand into his, and stared up at the ceiling. "Guess that's why you're so adamant that men don't stick around even when you have no personal basis for thinking that way."

Kami pulled her hand free. "No personal basis for thinking that way? Did you not just hear everything I said? Every man who came into my mother's life used her, then left. That's a pretty strong personal basis for thinking that men don't stick around."

"Not all men are like that, Kami."

"I didn't say they were."

"I'm not like that."

Kami didn't comment. Next to her, Gabe sighed, then, after a brief silence, lifted her hand and pressed a kiss to her fingertips. "Good luck with the Realtor next week. If you want someone to go with you to look at houses, I'm your guy."

"Unless she just has something perfect, I won't start looking until after the fund-raiser."

"Makes sense." He closed his eyes; his breathing evened.

"Guess we'd better get a little shut-eye before having to be back at the hospital tonight." She leaned over, kissed his cheek. "Sweet dreams, Gabe."

"Unfortunately, I'm going to have to take a pass this morning," Kami told Gabe at shift change a few mornings later.

Gabe glanced up from the computer where he made notes regarding a patient, his expression concerned. "What's up?"

"My mother."

His eyes darkened. "Something wrong?"

Kami shrugged. Where did she begin to explain about her mother's frantic phone call? A call during which her mother had been crying so profusely she'd barely been able to understand her pleas for Kami to come to her apartment.

"Let me finish here and I'll go with you."

Kami shook her head. The last thing she wanted was for Gabe to meet her mother. Especially as her mother was already so upset. Kami hadn't asked over the phone, but past experience told her what the problem would be.

"Sorry, but now isn't the time for you to meet my mother." She gave a look she hoped conveyed she'd much rather spend the morning with him and didn't reveal that she didn't expect him to ever meet her mother. Her heart squeezed and she fought back the panic that rose in her chest, reminding herself that it was the call from her mother making her antsy, not Gabe. She forced a smile. "I'd say to call me when you wake up, but, truth is, who knows what time I'll even get to go to sleep?"

"Then you call me when you wake up. We'll go somewhere for dinner."

Leaning against the doorjamb of the small physician's area, she eyed him and smiled for real. "Sounds perfect."

When she got to her mother's, Kami found her mom was a bumbling mess, as was the apartment. How someone could accumulate so much trash in the short amount of time since Kami had cleaned the apartment, she couldn't fathom. The place was a wreck, stank of the stench of the cat litter box and old food.

Ugh.

"Where's Don?" she guessed. Although was it really a guess when she had years of experience of seeing her mother all to pieces over whichever guy had just walked out on her?

"Gone."

Kami sighed and stared at the woman who'd raised her; the woman who fell in love at the drop of a hat and left herself vulnerable to any Tom, Dick, or Harry. Or in this case, Don.

How was it her mother continued to put herself out there after all these years? Didn't she ever learn to protect her heart?

"He didn't deserve you," she offered, trying to comfort her mother. How did one comfort a woman who'd been through more men than stars in the sky? When none of them had ever stuck around and most had taken everything they could and then some from the pitiful woman hunched over on the sofa with her cat cradled in her arms?

Why did her mother keep diving into relationships with her heart wide open?

Amid another big tearful bout, her mother cried, "That doesn't stop me from giving my heart."

Frustrated at her mother's reaction to the man leaving when surely she'd expected it, Kami reminded her, "Mom, you hardly dated Don for any time at all."

"What does time have to do with anything? I loved him."

Hardly any time at all. That's how long you have been "dating" Gabe. What if it was her who'd been dumped? Would she feel any different than her mom?

Of course she would. Unlike her mother, she knew Gabe would leave. For some reason, her mother believed Don, and all the others, was actually going to stick around.

Kami sighed, moved closer. "I'm sorry. It's just that he didn't seem so different from any of the others."

Her mother blew her nose. "Maybe not to you."

True. To her, he hadn't.

"To me, he was the one."

"You think that with every man you date."

Her mother looked up at her with sad eyes. "Is it so wrong to believe that I'm lovable? That this man is finally the one who will love me back and won't do me wrong? Just because you've never been in love and don't know how it feels, don't you judge me."

Kami opened her mouth to correct her mother, to say she had been in love, that she *was* in love, then, stunned, bit her tongue, instead.

Shaken to her very core, she tried to comfort her mother the best she could.

Finally, her mother drifted off to sleep. Unable to walk away from the messy apartment, Kami emptied the litter box, picked up the trash, then sat in the chair opposite the sofa where her mother slept.

Bubbles jumped up into Kami's lap for some attention, purring in pleasure when she got it.

"I don't love him," Kami told the cat. "Well, as a friend, but I'm not in love with him."

Bubbles ignored her and circled back around for another head-to-tip-of-tail stroke.

"But if I'm not careful that's what's going to happen."

Her gaze focused on her pitiful mother, who had nothing in life because she'd given away what little she had to useless men.

For the rest of the morning, Kami's insides felt rattled.

That would be her. Someday soon. How much longer until Gabe lost interest? Until he moved on to someone new and left her brokenhearted like her mother?

Kami slept a little but was restless and finally got up to run errands and catch up on her laundry, all the while battling the demons in her head.

That night, when Gabe called, she apologized for not calling, begged off dinner, stating she'd not slept much and really just wanted to go to bed and catch up on her sleep.

When he called first thing the following morning, she declined breakfast under the guise that she'd fallen behind with her cleaning.

To keep her mind occupied, she pulled everything from her closet and began sorting through the items, culling out things she never wore and straightening favorites.

The knock at her apartment door startled her, but the person on the other side of the door wasn't really a surprise.

"Gabe," she said as she opened the door and stared at the smiling man. "What are you doing here?"

"Two sets of hands are better than one."

She eyed him suspiciously. "You're going to help me sort my closet?"

He gave a suspicious look of his own. "If that's what you're doing."

"See for yourself." Grateful she'd dug out a ton of stuff, she led him to her bedroom.

He eyed the stack of clothes on her bed, then turned to her with a dubious look. "Maybe I can give a thumbs up or thumbs down while you try those on."

Kami suppressed a laugh. "Sorry. You're too late. That's the bye-bye stack I'm donating to charity."

"Want me to load them into your car?"

She shrugged. "I can do it later."

"Or I could do it now and you wouldn't have to."

He had a point. "Fine."

While Gabe loaded the stack into her car, she stored the keep items back into her closet, and was waiting in the living room when he came back into the apartment.

"What next?"

She shook her head. "Nothing. I'll finish up later."

"I didn't mean to interfere with what you were doing. I wanted to help."

"You did. Thank you for carrying the load to my car."

He studied her a moment. "Everything okay?"

"Fine."

Not looking convinced, he eyed her. "That's what you said on the phone, too. So why don't I believe you?"

She shrugged but had to glance away.

He sighed. "You're never going to trust me, are you?"

She lifted her gaze to his. "What do you mean?"

"No matter how long we're together, you're always going

to be waiting for me to leave just like all those guys did to your mom."

She shrugged. "It's what men do."

Staring at her for a long moment, he nodded. "I can't deny that it's what I've done in the past."

"And what you'll do in the future."

He didn't deny her claim, just sank onto the sofa and looked defeated.

"I knew something wasn't right when you canceled dinner. I thought something had happened at your mother's, so I stayed away last night. But it's just this same old thing, isn't it? You not trusting in me, in us."

She didn't answer. Something had happened at her mother's but she wasn't telling him that.

"Kami, the past couple of weeks have been wonderful."

They had.

"But, even after everything we've shared, you don't trust me any more than you did that first morning."

Going on the defensive, Kami lifted her chin. "Don't pretend you plan to stick around, Gabe. We both know that isn't your style."

He studied her. "Is that what you want me to say? That I'm never going to leave you? Would you believe me if I did tell you?"

Pain shot through her at what she saw in his eyes. This was it. What she'd been dreading.

She shook her head in denial.

"I didn't think so." He raked his fingers through his hair. "I care about you, Kami. If you haven't figured that out by now, then you're never going to."

Was this how he did it? Tried to convince women that it was their fault that he was leaving?

Heart breaking, she crossed her arms.

Face gaunt, he added, "I came here because I wanted to be with you. Too bad you can't believe that."

He got up and walked out of her apartment, quietly closing the door behind him.

CHAPTER THIRTEEN

"I HEARD A dirty rumor that you and Gabe had broken up."

Kami shrugged without looking at her best friend. She was at the hospital to work, not gossip about her nonexistent love life.

"This is the part where you tell me I shouldn't believe dirty rumors," her friend persisted.

"That particular rumor is true."

Mindy slapped her hand against her forehead. "What happened?"

"Nothing."

"Couples don't break up over nothing." Mindy frowned. "Did you have a fight?"

"Not really." How could she explain to Mindy what she didn't want to acknowledge? What was easier to ignore? "It was just time for us to end."

"Kami, you and Gabe are perfect together. Why would things ever end?"

"Because that's what he does."

Mindy looked taken aback. "He broke things off with you?"

"Yes. No. I think so." She thought back over their conversation for the millionth time. "He left. He hasn't called or texted." She shrugged and kept her voice monotone. "So, yeah, he broke things off."

"You don't sound too upset."

Was that what her friend thought? Tears didn't change

anything. She would not cry at work. Would not break down. Would not carry on as her mother did.

She refused.

"I knew before we started that we weren't going to last."

"Because you wouldn't let it."

Mindy's staunch defense of Gabe irritated Kami.

"Why do you always take his side? You're supposed to be my friend."

Mindy put her hands on her hips. "I am. Which is why I'm pointing out that you refused to give this relationship a chance."

"Where have you been? I gave this relationship all I had to give."

"Not your heart."

"I gave him all I had to give," she repeated. "It's not my fault that all I had wasn't enough."

She spun to walk away and almost collided with Gabe. A red-faced Gabe.

"We need to talk."

"I can't. We're at work."

Gabe glanced at Mindy.

"I'll come get you if I need either of you," Mindy assured them.

His grasp on her arm firm, but not painful, Gabe marched Kami to the tiny dictation room and shut the door behind them.

"All you had wasn't enough? Seriously? That's what you think?"

"You shouldn't have been eavesdropping on my conversation."

"You shouldn't have been talking about me if you didn't want me to overhear."

"This is ridiculous. We have nothing to say to each other."

"Wrong." He put his hand on the door, preventing her from being able to open it. "We have a lot to say to each other. Perhaps this isn't the best place to say it, but hell if

I'm going to just let you walk away without explaining your comment."

"I don't have to explain myself to you. I owe you nothing and you can't make me stay."

Her words hit their target and seemed to deflate him. His hand fell away from the door.

"You're right. I can't keep you here."

Kami reached for the door.

"But you're wrong, Kami."

She hesitated.

"All you had was enough. The problem was—*is*," he corrected, "that you never gave all you had. Not even close. Maybe it was me who wasn't enough."

The rest of the night passed in a blur. They had a couple of wrecks come in, several upper respiratory infections, an overdose, and a chest pain.

Kami worked side by side with Gabe, pretending that there was nothing between them.

Pretending that her heart wasn't breaking.

Pretending she hadn't lost something, *someone*, special.

"Oh, Kami! We got the call."

At Beverly's breathy, nervous tone, Kami didn't have to ask which call that was. A heart had been located for Lindsey.

Even as excitement filled her for her friend, she felt a stab of pain for the family who'd donated the heart.

"When?"

"The transplant team is prepping her for surgery now. I'm so scared and can't believe this is happening," her co-worker gushed over the phone line. "Gregg and I wanted you to know that she's going into surgery."

Kami glanced at her fitness watch. She'd had a half-dozen things on her to-do list for the day, most of them picking up donations for the fund-raiser, but none of them mattered in light of what was happening in the Smiths' lives. She could pick up the items later.

"I'll be there."

"The surgery is going to take hours and hours. I don't expect you to sit here with us. I just wanted you to know Lindsey is getting a new heart. You did so much for my family and we love you."

Kami's chest squeezed. "I want to be there. See you soon."

Gabe winced when the first person he saw in the transplant family waiting room was Kami.

He should have known she'd be here.

Of course she would.

If Beverly had called him, she'd certainly called Kami.

He'd been out with friends on the lake when the call had come and, after they'd returned from their water-skiing trip, he'd showered, then headed to the hospital.

Several hours had passed, but Lindsey was still in surgery and would be for some time.

Kami averted her gaze.

Anger and frustration filled Gabe. Anger that she'd not given them a fair shot.

If she couldn't freely care for him, they were just wasting their time.

Ignoring Kami, he went to Beverly, hugged her, then shook Gregg's hand. He chatted with them for several minutes, then joined the others in the waiting game.

As luck would have it, the only empty chair in the small, crowded private waiting area was next to Kami.

He'd almost rather stand than take it, but to do so for who knew how long was ridiculous.

With a nod of acknowledgment her way, he sat and pulled out his phone, skimming through his text messages.

Five, then ten, then fifteen awkward minutes went by, during which he was acutely aware of how near she was, of how much he missed her.

But she'd made her choice. Her choice wasn't to open

herself up to him, wasn't to give them a chance, to trust in what was between them.

Maybe he didn't even blame her. Lord knew he had enough issues of his own without digging into hers.

On the Friday night before the fund-raiser event, volunteers had worked hard finishing the baskets and organizing the donated items. As he'd promised, Gabe came, helped, and made several of them laugh when he finally got his ribbon to curl just right after several failed attempts.

Not that Kami laughed.

Or even looked his way, but he refused to let that dampen his spirit.

Over a week had passed since Lindsey's heart transplant. The first few days were the most critical, but Lindsey had gotten through them with flying colors. She still had a long road ahead, but the tiny baby was holding her own.

When they'd finished the last basket and had each auction item to be listed, labeled, and numbered, Kami thanked them all for their dedication to their friend and her family.

"Well, I don't know about everyone else, but I'm parched. Anyone up for drinks?"

Kami's gaze narrowed and he realized how she might take his comment. Too bad. He wasn't going to walk on eggshells just because she'd bailed on their relationship.

"Unwinding for a while before the big event sounds perfect." Mindy spoke up. "Hope that's okay with you, Kami, since you rode here with me. We won't stay late, I promise."

Kami looked as if she wanted to argue, but when all the other volunteers said they were going, she just nodded.

Gabe and Kami ended up next to each other in a large round booth with their friends bookending them on each side.

No one commented on the sitting order, but Gabe doubted it had been accidental. Although few of their friends had commented on their personal relationship, or recent lack thereof, they all knew something had transpired between him and Kami; knew and were obviously playing match-maker by trying to throw them together.

Good luck with that.

Kami ordered water and Gabe ended up doing the same.

She didn't speak directly to him, but conversation was going on all around them.

The chatter was loud, fun and varied from the fund-raiser to an upcoming marathon several of them were running. There were lots of laughs.

Except nothing felt right.

Not to Gabe.

He needed to forget her and move on. Fine, he could do that. He would do that.

He turned and started talking to Eddie, the paramedic who'd volunteered with them, asking if he'd caught any of the Stanley Cup playoff game the night before.

Fortunately he had and they launched into a discussion regarding their winner predictions.

Saturday morning, the day of the fund-raiser dawned bright and early. Kami leaped out of bed and rushed about, getting her day started. It was going to be a long day, but a good one.

At least, she hoped so. What they had raised from selling raffle tickets and dinner tickets would more than pay for the few expenses for the event and would be a nice addition to the Smiths' funds. Hopefully, before the night was over the coffer would be overflowing and they wouldn't have to worry about how to pay the bills for months to come so they could focus on Lindsey.

Kami, Gabe, and a handful of other volunteers moved the baskets and donated items from the hospital conference room to the convention center where the event was being held.

When they got there, Mindy and other volunteers were setting up the tables.

"Here, let me get that for you," Gabe offered when Kami went for a particularly heavy basket.

"Thanks." She stepped aside and let him effortlessly grab the basket and head into the building.

She watched him go and was filled with such frustration she wanted to scream. Frustration at him. At herself. At the whole world.

Frustration that had interfered with her sleep and had her edgy as she'd dreamed of stomping his toes under the table and demanding he talk with her the night before. He'd totally humiliated her, turning his back to her and publicly shunning her in front of their friends.

Then today, he showed up and was all nice. What was with him, anyway?

Not that it mattered. It was just as well that he'd turned his back. Maybe their friends would take a hint and quit with the cupid.

When the fund-raiser was over and she didn't have that worry hanging over her, she'd go back to feeling like her old self. Not this uptight, frustrated, on-edge woman who couldn't stop overanalyzing everything that happened.

Sighing, she grabbed a lighter basket and followed him inside the hotel.

"Where do you want me to put this one?" he asked when she walked up beside where he stood in front of one of the display tables.

"All the items are numbered. We're going to auction them in numerical order to make it easier for the emcee and the recorders to keep up with what's what during the auction." She realized she hadn't really answered his question and he was still holding the basket.

"Here." She pointed to the right area on the display table. "It goes here."

Gabe set the basket in the appropriate spot, then turned back toward her. "Everything looks fantastic. You've done an amazing job."

"Mindy and the other volunteers have done most of the decorations and taken care of the food. I was in charge of

donations and we won't really know until tonight how that
went."

He gestured to the numerous items on display. "I'd say
you did good."

"For the Smiths' sake, I sure hope so."

"Are they coming tonight?"

Look at them making small talk. Kami's heart hurt from
the brevity of it. This was her friend whom she'd teased
and laughed with on so many occasions, her lover who had
wowed her time and again. Now carrying on a simple conversation that was nothing but a farce.

Not able to bring herself to look him in the eyes, she answered, "As long as there are no changes with Lindsey at
the hospital, they plan to. She's doing great, but everything
hinges on her, of course."

"Kami, where does this artwork go?" one of the volunteers asked, joining where they stood by the table.

"Somewhere around here is a display stand for that piece.
We're going to put it at the end of one of the tables. It's the
first item up for auction."

Gabe stuck his hands in his jeans pockets and shrugged.
"Guess I'd better get back outside. There's still several
things to be carried inside."

"I…uh… I'm going to help position the painting," Kami
said needlessly since he hadn't waited on her response. He'd
just walked away.

When they'd finished arranging everything on the tables
and had double-checked to make sure everything was lined
up numerically, Kami and her volunteers joined in on setting up the guest tables and their decorations.

When mid-afternoon rolled around, Kami glanced at her
fitness watch and gave Gabe a pointed look.

"Don't you need to head home to shower? We need you
looking good so you'll bring top dollar."

"You make him sound like a piece of prized meat,"
Mindy accused, having overheard Kami's comment.

"What about you?" he asked. "Won't you and Mindy need to be heading out to clean up, as well?"

"I'm heading out in the next five," Mindy said, then winced. "Except the band's not arrived yet to set up their equipment and I promised I'd wait around so they could."

"I'll wait until they get here," Kami offered. "I'm planning to stay until the rescue squad arrives anyway. They had some last-minute donations to be auctioned off tonight and I'll need to get them labeled and on the recorder's list."

Mindy offered to stay, but Kami declined. "Go," she ordered Mindy. "Just get back as soon as you can in case I'm still here."

Her friend gave her a quick hug and promised to do just that.

Kami turned to Gabe, who was still standing next to her. He looked so good her heart hurt.

"You should go, too," she told him, keeping her voice light. "It's going to be time to get started before you know it."

He hesitated, then nodded. "You're right. The night of the big auction."

"I really do appreciate all you've done."

His gaze met hers. He raked his fingers through his hair, took a step toward her. "Kami, I..."

She wasn't sure what he'd planned to say as at that moment a long-haired kid twirling a drumstick came walking into the ballroom and asked if this was the Smith party.

She stared up at Gabe, wondering what he'd been going to say, wondering what, if anything, words could change.

"Looks like the band is here." Not what he'd been going to say, but whatever had been on the tip of his tongue was gone. She could see it in the way his expression had hardened.

"Looks like it." She waved at the guy who'd been joined by a few others. "Over this way."

When she finished showing them where to set up, she glanced around the room and noted that Gabe had left.

Good. He had to be back soon.

So that he could be auctioned off to the highest bidder, because she'd asked him to.

Not just because of that, she assured herself. He wanted to help the Smiths.

She understood. She wanted this night to be all it could be, for as much money to be raised as possible to help the sweet family.

She'd hoped to make it home in time from the setup to leisurely get ready for the big event.

No such luck.

Still, she got a quick shower, styled her hair, and put on more makeup than she usually wore, so she figured she was doing well.

When she got to the convention center and saw Gabe already there, looking like a zillion dollars in his tuxedo, her breath caught. Right or wrong considering the state of their relationship, she wanted Gabe to think she looked good, too. For him to look at her and feel the same *vavoom* her lungs had undergone when she'd caught sight of him.

Was that why she'd donned a splashy short dress that showed off her legs? She'd be on her feet too long for heels, but her comfy sparkly slip-ons weren't bad. Either way, she was showing leg.

Gabe had said he liked her legs.

Only, when he turned her way, caught her watching him, his gaze didn't drop to her legs. His pale blue eyes locked with hers for a brief moment, and then he averted his gaze.

Because he was no longer interested in her legs. Or anything about her.

Kami couldn't avoid Gabe all night, and it wasn't long before she got drawn into a conversation with the volunteer running the sound system.

The volunteer he'd been talking to gushed for a few minutes, then was called over to double-check the equipment.

Which left Kami alone with Gabe.

He glanced around the room. "Everything looks great."

Ah, there went the small talk.

She responded with more small talk. "There have been dozens of volunteers. Everyone has worked hard."

"True, but without you and Mindy putting it together, I doubt tonight would be happening, so, again, great job."

"Sometimes it just takes someone getting a project started to have lots of volunteers jumping in. Certainly, this is one of those cases where we've been blessed by so many helping out from the hospital and from the community." A blonde in a flashy red dress stepped into Kami's periphery. "Speaking of volunteers from the community…"

Gabe turned, frowned a little. "Let me brace myself."

"I don't know why you say such things. She seems nice."

"She is."

Kami started to say more, but instead smiled as the television hostess descended upon them.

"Everything looks perfect," Debbie praised. "My cameraman and I are going to do a few commentary pieces as everyone arrives."

Kami nodded. "We really appreciate all you're doing to help the Smiths."

"When we run the piece on tonight's news, there should be more money raised via the online donation page. Especially with the shots we have of that adorable baby girl." Debbie gave a heartfelt sigh. "Seriously ill babies pull on people's heartstrings and make for great stories."

Kami would take the woman's word for it on the great story part as she didn't find anything great about her coworker's baby having been born with a defective heart. Thank goodness a match had been found, the transplant had been a success so far, and Lindsey was getting stronger every day.

"If you'll excuse me, I need to make sure everything is going smoothly with the food preparation." Kami was pretty sure she had made the woman's night by leaving her and Gabe alone.

Good. More power to them. Kami didn't care.

Much.

Fortunately, everything was going smoothly. The volunteers from the rescue squad and the fire department were ready to serve the five hundred guests who'd bought meal tickets.

"Do you feel as crazy as I do?" Mindy gushed as she came up and hugged Kami.

"Crazier. Thanks for letting me sneak away long enough to get cleaned up."

"Cleaned up? Girl, you did more than that." Mindy gave her an up and down. "You look great."

Kami's cheeks heated at her friend's praise. "Thank you. I feel a lot more presentable than when I headed out of here earlier, for sure."

A feminine laugh rang across the room. Both Kami and Mindy turned toward where Debbie chatted with Gabe.

"Please tell me you're all dolled up for him."

"I wouldn't hold your breath."

Mindy eyed Debbie with Gabe, and her nose crinkled. "Surely, you aren't going to let her win him."

Kami fought to keep an I-don't-care expression. "It's an auction for a single day's date. What he does beyond that is up to him."

She eyed how the hostess brushed an imaginary speck off Gabe's tuxedo jacket. An excuse to touch him, no doubt.

She'd touched him, had her arms around those shoulders while he held her close when they'd danced, when they'd kissed, when they'd made love.

Mindy sighed. "Just seems such a shame for you to let this opportunity pass you by."

"What opportunity is that?"

"To win Gabe back."

"As if I'd buy a date to try to win him back," Kami scoffed. Buying a man was even worse than the things her mother did.

"Your loss." Looking disappointed, Mindy shrugged. "Maybe you'll get lucky and Debbie won't win him back, but I think you're a fool to risk it. That woman has talons she's dying to hook into him."

Kami's gaze cut to the couple. Despite his woe-is-me antics, Gabe didn't appear to be in any hurry to get away from his beautiful ex.

Quite the opposite.

No, she wasn't jealous. Kami rubbed her pounding temple. She wasn't jealous. Only...she averted her gaze from the couple and met Mindy's curious eyes. Rather than launch into another spiel about why she should bid on Gabe, Mindy just gave her a look of pity.

"What?"

Her friend sighed. "Whatever your reasons are for not hanging on to that man, I hope you don't live to regret that decision."

Glancing back toward where Debbie smiled up at Gabe, Kami agreed. Yeah, she hoped she didn't live to regret that decision, too, but for her long-term sanity and heart, she'd made the right choice.

Not that she'd really made the choice. He'd been the one to leave her apartment. He'd been the one to stop calling and texting. He'd been the one to step out of her life.

Why her friend acted as if it were all Kami's fault was beyond her. He'd left. Just as she'd always known he would. She'd let him, but he'd been the one to leave. End of story.

The dinner went off without a hitch and the band played while everyone ate. Both the food and the meal were a hit.

After the meal finished, the auctioneer relieved the band, taking command of the stage.

Time for the auction.

Prior to the date packages being auctioned off, the baskets and donations were being auctioned. One after another, prizes were sold.

Kami won a basket full of body, hair, and bath products donated by a local hair salon and felt quite proud of herself.

"Practicing?" a male voice whispered close to her ear.

Turning toward Gabe, she caught a whiff of his spicy

scent and fought inhaling and holding the scent of him inside her forever.

Her heart sped up at his nearness, at how his whisper in her ear toyed with her equilibrium. *He left you, remember?* her heart whispered. *Sure, you kind of pushed, but he left.*

Pulling herself together, she smiled. "You wish."

"I like that your sass is back."

She cut her gaze toward him, thinking a more handsome man had never lived. "It never left."

His dark brow rose. "Just wasn't pointed my way?" He scanned the room, spotted the television crew at a table near the front of the venue. "Pretty sure Debbie plans on picking out china with me in the near future."

"Poor Gabe. It's so hard to be you and have to fight off beautiful women."

Rather than smile back or make a quip, he turned, searched her eyes a moment, then said, "The only beautiful woman I'm interested in won't give me the time of day."

Kami's heart thundered in her chest. He shouldn't say such things, but her silly body responded full throttle that he had. Unbidden, her eyes closed. She wasn't sure she could deal with him making such comments, not when her heart ached so.

"Kami?"

Opening her eyes, she flashed her teeth at him in a semblance of a smile and glanced down at her fitness band. "It's almost eight."

Looking as if he'd seen more on her face than she'd have liked, he asked, "You going to bid?"

"Only in your dreams."

He studied her a moment, then softly said, "You'd be surprised what you do in my dreams."

Kami wanted to ask, wanted to know what he dreamed of her doing, but what would be the point? She was not going to act on anything Gabe said.

Been there, done that, and had a lost friendship and tearstained pillow to prove it.

CHAPTER FOURTEEN

THE NIGHT'S TAKE was going to be awesome even before
Gabe's date came up for bid. Kami had been keeping a mental tally of what the different items and dates were going
for and the Smiths must have been relieved.

She glanced toward the couple sitting at the front of the
room. Despite the stress of the past few months, her friend
was smiling and enjoying her evening with her husband.

That Lindsey was doing so well so quickly after her heart
transplant went a long way in causing those smiles.

The emcee who was doubling as their auctioneer introduced the last package to be auctioned before Gabe's.

Gabe was next.

Kami's stomach knotted and she suddenly wished he'd
never agreed to the auction, that she'd never asked him to
take part in it.

Which was silly.

Several of the others had gone for four figures. His date
would raise a nice amount for the Smiths.

She needed to shove aside her selfish thoughts. They'd
had their time. He never went back to the same woman after
he'd left her. He had left Kami. Sure, he'd given some spiel
about her not opening herself up to him, not trusting him,
but he'd been the one to walk.

She had opened herself up to him. She had. Only...

Her blood doing a jittery dance through her veins, Kami
shook her head to clear her thoughts.

"Please tell me you're shaking your head in protest of what is about to happen."

Kami looked at Mindy. "What's that?"

"You blowing what might be your last chance with Gabe."

"He left me. That was our last chance."

"Seriously? Is that pride speaking, Kami? Because I don't understand how you could just let him leave without putting up a fight to hang on to him."

"Isn't that what started all of this? Him asking me to bid on him tonight to keep one of his exes from trying to hang on?"

"Are you really so blind?" Mindy asked, shaking her head. "Did you ever stop to think that it's not Debbie buying his date that ever concerned him? That it's wanting you to buy his date that's important to him? That all of this has been about you from the very beginning? Not his ex or any other woman."

No, Kami hadn't considered that. Nor did she believe it.

Gabe hadn't teased her about buying his date package because he'd been interested in her and wanted her to bid on him. He hadn't.

The current auction ended and the emcee told the crowd about Gabe's Gatlinburg Getaway.

The bid started at a thousand dollars and quickly rose five hundred dollars at a time as Debbie immediately countered every bid anyone else made.

The others being auctioned off had smiled and flirted with the crowd, encouraging more bidders. Kami had thought Gabe would work the stage, too, but he wasn't. Then again, Gabe didn't need to do anything but stand and smile at the crowd.

It was good to be Gabe. To have women wanting you to the point of them thinking nothing of emptying their wallets for the opportunity to spend time with you.

Then again, she supposed it was the way of the world. Men emptied their wallets to impress women by taking them to fancy restaurants and driving fancier cars. Women emptied their wallets to buy the latest fashions and to try to preserve their youth.

Her mother had emptied her already rather pitiful wallet anytime a new guy came along, that was for sure. Even if it meant not being able to pay the rent or buy groceries.

How many times had they been kicked out of their home because they couldn't pay the rent—all down to her mother's foolish heart?

"Bid," Mindy stage-whispered.

Kami frowned. "Mind your own business."

"You're my best friend. Your happiness is my business. Fight for him. Let him know he matters, that your relationship matters, and that you want to date him."

"You have this all wrong, you know," she corrected her friend, her gaze going back and forth between the current bidders. "He doesn't really want to date me. He just wants…" Kami paused. What did Gabe want? To have sex with her again? Why? He could have sex anytime he wanted it. The room full of rabid wallet-wielding women was testament to that.

Mindy gave her a *duh* look. "Then why aren't you bidding?"

Kami's eyes widened. "You want me to have sex with him, knowing it won't last? That he's left me once and will leave me again? Knowing if I do this, he'll only end up hurting me? How is it that we're friends when you give such bad advice?"

Her heart was pounding so loudly it must be drowning out the emcee. She had life goals, and getting used by a man, even a man as fabulous as Gabe, wasn't on the list.

Only, what if he really had left because of her? Because she'd constantly been waiting for the ax to fall? What if she'd pushed him into doing exactly what she'd feared most?

She had done that.

"Bid, Kami. Do it now."

"Are you crazy? Or just deaf? The bid is way out of my budget." Financially and emotionally.

"He's worth it and you know it," Mindy prompted. "Bid now before it's too late. Blame me, if you must, but *bid*."

The stage lighting prevented Gabe from seeing where the bids were coming from, but it didn't matter. Debbie wasn't going to let anyone else win him. Even if a miracle happened and Kami had considered bidding, the bid was too high.

Who would have thought a day with him would go for so much?

Especially when he couldn't get the woman he'd wanted to spend that day with to admit she wanted him, to open her heart and trust in what was between them.

He'd thought… Never mind what he'd thought, what he'd wanted. It no longer mattered.

Kami wasn't willing to risk anything for their relationship. Instead, she'd kept up her defenses and in the end that had suffocated what was happening between them.

Perhaps he shouldn't have expected more. What made him think he deserved more in life? That he should get to have what few attained?

Love.

It was what his parents had had prior to his father's death. What he'd wanted with Kami, but that kind of relationship took two working at it.

"Going once," the auctioneer said, working the crowd. "Going twice… Wait—we have a new bidder!"

Gabe couldn't see where the new bid had come from, but his belly did a flip-flop because he instinctively knew who the bidder was.

The crazy thumping in his chest told him.

Kami had just bid on his date package. Why would she do that? Guilt? Pity?

He didn't want either.

Well, hell, this was unexpected and left him not quite sure what to think.

* * *

"Yes!" Mindy squealed in Kami's ear and did a happy dance next to her. "Yes. Yes. Yes."

Kami ignored her friend's antics and kept her gaze trained on Gabe.

Because if she looked away she might wonder why she'd just raised her number and bid on his Gatlinburg Getaway.

She'd just bid a lot of money. So much, her stomach hurt.

Of course Debbie immediately countered her bid, looking around the room to try to spot who her new competition was. She looked bored, annoyed, but resilient. She planned to take Gabe's date package home.

She planned to take Gabe home.

"You in?"

Swallowing the lump in her throat, Kami nodded to the auction volunteer who'd taken her initial bid and was waiting on her answer.

The man called her bid and the auctioneer ate it up that there was a new battle on.

Ha. Not much of a battle, she thought, as Debbie seemed to grow tired of the back-and-forth and raised the bid by a whopping four-figure amount.

Kami bit into her lower lip. What was she doing? Why?

"I'll toss in a few hundred," Mindy offered. "Bid again. Don't lose Gabe. This is important. You know it is."

Kami hadn't really seen this auction as winning or losing Gabe.

But suddenly it did feel that way.

That if she didn't win this bid she'd be losing him forever. That she'd never get another chance to show him he was important to her, that he mattered, that she regretted letting him walk away.

She had to risk this, had to put herself out there and bid. She didn't have time to analyze or to figure it out. The auctioneer was calling for another bid.

She couldn't.

But she had to.

Kami nodded to the volunteer and he called out to the auctioneer.

Again, Debbie turned to search the crowd and countered Kami's bid by going up another four figures.

Kami gulped. This was getting serious.

Getting?

It had been serious for a while now. They were talking figures that equaled long periods of work time for her to earn. *Long* periods.

Which was why raising her number and saying the exact amount in her house down-payment fund would be absolutely crazy.

Her down payment that she'd been building for years in order to buy the house which was the next big item on her life list.

Her down payment that would give her the security of knowing she owned her home and that she'd never be homeless again.

Her down payment that proved she wasn't like her mother, that she didn't throw away everything she had on a man.

If she bid on Gabe, she'd literally be throwing away everything she had on a man.

But the bid was for a good cause, right? She remembered the emotion in Beverly's voice when she'd talked about why they'd agreed to the television bit.

What was making a down payment on a house compared to helping pay for the medical expenses of a precious baby?

Or bidding on the only man to ever make your belly do somersaults because you didn't want him to go on a date with his ex?

Or anyone else.

Ever.

Just you.

Or bidding because you had to prove to him that you did trust in him, in what was happening between you. What had happened between you.

Bidding on Gabe and emptying her savings would be something her mother would do.

It would be stupid in so many ways.

It would be the antithesis of everything Kami had always held important.

So her next move made no sense.

She raised her number and kept it held high as she quoted the amount in her down-payment fund.

"What?" Mindy gasped from beside her, reaching out to take hold of her arm, trying to pull it back down.

The bid taker repeated the amount to be sure he'd heard her correctly.

Number still held high despite Mindy's tugging on her arm, Kami nodded and repeated the amount.

Looking impressed, the bid taker called out her new bid to the emcee.

This time Debbie's gaze collided with Kami's and she stared at her for what felt like an eternity but could only have been a few seconds.

Myriad emotions shot toward her like daggers meant to knock her off her feet, no doubt.

No matter. Not Debbie, nor any other woman, could have Gabe without a fight. Without Kami telling him, showing him, how much he meant to her. If he couldn't forgive her stupidity, then she only had herself to blame.

But until she'd tried, she wouldn't give up.

Hand high with her number on display, Kami held her breath, waiting to see what the television hostess would do. Gabe had said she didn't like to lose.

One penny higher bid and she'd have Gabe.

His date package, at any rate. Because even if the woman bid higher, Kami had gone all in. All she had for Gabe—her heart and very being, her dreams, her future.

As they eyeballed each other, Kami was positive the woman knew she'd put all her cards on the table.

When the emcee pushed for a higher bid, the television

hostess surprised the entire room, especially Kami, by shaking her head and saying, "I'm done. He's hers."

"Sold! To the pretty woman in the blue dress," the emcee announced, eliciting a loud round of applause from everyone in the room save three people.

Debbie, Kami, and Gabe.

She'd just bought a day in Gatlinburg. With Gabe.

By using her house-deposit fund.

By proving that she was her mother's daughter and the acorn didn't fall far from the tree no matter how many times she'd sworn she'd never be like her mother.

She'd lost her mind.

But maybe, just maybe, she hadn't lost Gabe, a small voice whispered.

Gabe watched as a shell-shocked Kami was pushed toward the stage by well-wishers giving her high fives and hugs. The emcee held out his hand and escorted her up the couple of steps onto the stage.

"Little lady," the emcee said into his microphone, "make sure this fella gives you your money's worth."

"Oh, I intend to," she assured him, garnering a few laughs from the crowd, as the emcee escorted her over to where Gabe stood.

Trying to make sense of the fact that Kami had just bid on him—had won his bid—Gabe bent, kissed her cheek, then clasped her hand.

She didn't look directly at him, just nervously faced the crowd and gave a thumbs-up with her free hand. The event photographer moved around them, snapping pictures.

Gabe felt dazed, and not from the flashes of light.

The emcee called for all ten couples to come back onto the stage for photos.

While they were waiting for the others to join them on stage, Gabe took advantage of the moment to lean down and ask, "What changed your mind?"

"I… You're my friend. I couldn't not rescue you."

"Pricey rescue."

Not meeting his eyes, she nodded. "Guess I'll be staying in my apartment longer than I once thought."

What?

"You used your house savings to bid on me?" Gabe must have misunderstood.

Only he hadn't. Then again, hadn't he thought earlier that the bid had already escalated far beyond Kami's price range, even if she'd wanted to bid? Never in a million years would he have guessed she would use her savings. For him.

Her face was pale, but she nodded, confirming what he'd guessed.

"Why?" When she didn't look at him, he touched her face, turning her toward him. "Tell me why, Kami."

"We're being watched," she reminded him through clenched teeth. "Smile, Gabe."

She was right. He'd forgotten where they were, that they were literally on stage being photographed at an event that was important to the Smiths.

He smiled as several photos were taken, then escorted Kami off the stage. As soon as they were out of the spotlight, he turned her to him.

"Why, Kami?"

One blue-spaghetti-strap-covered shoulder lifted. "It was for a good cause."

He'd wanted her to bid on him, had secretly craved her taking that step and admitting she wasn't ready for them to end, that she didn't want him with another woman, not even for a second or for charity. But he hadn't meant for it to cost her so much.

It had cost her so much.

It had cost her everything. He knew how important buying a house was to her, how long she'd been working toward that goal. Why would she throw her deposit fund away on him?

The only possible reason hit Gabe and he stared down at her in wonder.

No way could he let her give up her savings. "I'll pay for your bid."

Not quite meeting his gaze, she shook her head. "I placed the bid. Not you. Besides, I wanted to help Beverly and her family."

Gabe considered her a moment, trying to decipher if helping their coworker had actually been what had motivated her outrageous bid rather than how he'd taken her bid.

"Don't look now," she warned, "but we're about to be accosted. Will she hurt me?"

"You were the one saying how nice she was," he reminded her, squeezing her hand.

"That was before I snatched you away from her. Now I'm just plain scared."

Both Kami and Gabe had pasted-on smiles as they greeted Debbie and Jerry.

"I knew it," Jerry announced, sticking his hand out toward Gabe. "Congrats."

Staring at Kami, Gabe fought with the realization that she hadn't pulled her hand away from his even after they'd been out of the limelight, that she'd given up something she'd worked hard for to win him, something she held dear that gave her a sense of security. She'd gone out on a limb, for him.

Whether she'd realized it or not, Kami had made a monumental decision regarding their relationship.

Mainly, that they had one at all, and that it was worth sacrificing for, fighting for, changing for, that it was worth trusting in.

Which left him feeling exactly what?

Kami stared at the television producer, a bit baffled. She'd won Gabe's date package. Nothing more. Surely the man's enthusiastic pumping of Gabe's hand was overkill?

"I knew there was no point in raising my bid once I realized you were the new bidder," Debbie admitted while the men were distracted.

"I couldn't have gone any higher," Kami confessed, although she wasn't sure why she was making her confession.

"I knew you were all in," Debbie admitted, "that I could win if I raised the bid."

Kami regarded the woman. "Why didn't you?"

"Because once you were all in there was no way I could win what I was really after." The woman shrugged, gave a self-derisive smile, then surprised Kami with a hug. "Congrats. May you hold on to him longer than I did. Something tells me you will."

"I, uh… Okay. Thanks," Kami blustered, wondering if she should check herself for knife wounds or maybe even claw marks. Was Debbie really so nice that she'd just conceded and congratulated Kami on her win?

The next hour passed in a blur. A blur where Gabe didn't leave her side as the emcee brought the event to a close and a loud round of applause went up at the large amount that had been raised by the event.

"Need me to stay to help clean up this place?"

In a bit of shell shock at everything that had happened and not knowing exactly what would happen next, what she needed to do next to make sure Gabe knew how she felt, Kami shook her head at his offer. "No, a group from the medical floor agreed to break down the decorations and pack them in boxes to be donated. The hotel will do any cleanup beyond that."

His expression unreadable, he asked, "Any reason you have to stay?"

Kami's gaze cut to where Mindy was giving instructions to the volunteers on what to put where and what to trash.

She caught her friend's eye, read Mindy's expression, which seemed to say, *Get out of here now 'cause I have this and I'm so happy for you.*

Kami's stomach twisted. Her friend might be happy for her, but Kami wasn't sure exactly what she'd gotten herself into.

Just what did buying Gabe's date package mean? Other

than that she was financially broke and wouldn't be buying a home anytime in the next few years?

Could he forgive her for how she'd refused to trust in him? Refused to let her guard down?

Not that it had mattered. She'd fallen for him the same as if she'd dived in headfirst with all the enthusiasm her mother did time and again.

Fighting the nervous flutter in her belly, she forced a smile. "I can leave anytime you're ready."

Gabe regarded her for long moments. "Does that mean you're leaving with me?"

Why didn't he smile or say something to let her know where his thoughts were? Where his heart was?

Kami mentally took a deep breath, assured herself that she was not making the biggest mistake of her life, but she was all in now, so what did it matter?

Only everything. He meant everything.

Sure, she'd be fine if he walked away. She wouldn't wallow, or go into some deep pit of despair. She'd work and keep moving toward achieving her life goals, would save up another down payment.

But nothing would shine quite as bright without Gabe to share her life with.

She looked straight into his blue eyes and knew that she wasn't going down without a fight.

"Yes, I'm leaving with you. You're mine, remember? Bought and paid for."

Gabe's eyes darkened and one corner of his mouth slid upward. "Is this part of getting your money's worth?"

Finally, a smile.

That smile was priceless.

"Only if it's what you want, too. Like I've told you from the beginning, your only obligation to the winner is your date in Gatlinburg. Beyond that is up to you." Kami took his hand, clasped their fingers, and hoped her eyes told him everything she was feeling. Then she realized that hoping wasn't enough. She needed to tell him. "But, just so you know, I will spend every day between now and our 'date' making sure you know how important you are to me and that I don't intend to let you walk away from me ever again without doing everything I can to convince you to stay."

"Is that so?" His eyes danced with mischief as he reached out and caressed the side of her face.

"Everything in my arsenal," she assured him, turning her head to kiss the inside of his palm. "And I'm not above playing dirty if I have to."

Gabe's smile made everything else in the ballroom fade away, everything but him and the way he was looking at her, the way his hand cupped her face. He stared into her eyes with more emotion than she'd ever had directed her way.

Her heart squeezed in her chest, racing and slowing down in the same beat, making her head spin.

"As intrigued as I am by the thought of you playing dirty, I have to ask—what if I want a lot more than a date in Gatlinburg?"

Reaching up, she wrapped her arms around his neck. "Good, because otherwise I might have to ask for a refund."

"I've missed you, Kam."

Kami's cheek pressed against Gabe's chest as she listened to the beating of his heart. "Not as much as I've missed you."

"You going to tell me what happened tonight?"

Toying with the light spattering of hair on his chest, she considered his question.

Her gaze went to the photo on her nightstand. The photo she'd stuck inside a drawer after that first morning with Gabe and hadn't pulled out until after he'd walked out on her. Somehow, looking at the photo had been a balm to her achy heart, a reminder that Gabe had only done what she'd expected him to do.

What she'd pushed him to do.

"I decided I wanted to be more like her."

Gabe turned and looked at the photo. "Your mother? You look a lot like her."

Kami nodded. "I've spent my whole life doing everything I can not to be anything like her. It almost cost me you."

"What's so bad that you didn't want to be like her?"

"She loves with all her heart and that makes her an easy target to be taken advantage of."

"She's been taken advantage of a lot, I assume?"

"Time and again. My whole life I've been waiting for her to finally learn, to finally realize, and not jump into love heart first. She never has. I thought that made her weak, foolish."

"Doesn't it?"

She rose up, propped herself on her elbow, and stared at him. "I thought so. Until I bid my entire house down payment at a charity auction."

"Let me at least halve the bid with you, Kam. Don't get me wrong. I appreciate what you did, what it meant, how it made me feel to know you'd do that for me, but I don't want being with me to cost you your dream."

She shook her head. "It didn't. That money bought me exactly what I need most. You."

He cupped her face, his thumb caressing her cheek. "Not just a Gatlinburg date?"

"As many dates as you'll have me."

He grinned. "Before this is all said and done, you're going to think you got a bargain."

She leaned down, kissed his lips. "I already do."

He wrapped his arms around her and hugged her close. "I'm never going to leave you."

"I know," she whispered back, knowing in her heart he spoke the truth. "Nor would I let you. Not ever again. Not now that you're bought and paid for."

He laughed. "I love you, Kam."

Her heart filled with joy, because Gabe wasn't just spouting off words. He meant what he was saying.

She knew because she recognized what she saw in his eyes, what she felt in his touch. It was what was in her own.

"I love you, too, Gabe."

EPILOGUE

"OKAY, GABE, YOU'RE freaking me out a little," Kami admitted, adjusting the blindfold he'd insisted upon putting on her prior to leaving her apartment.

"Oh, ye of little faith. Bear with me for a few more minutes."

"Yeah, yeah. Easy for you to say. You aren't the one being hauled around town blindfolded."

"You trust me, don't you?"

"With all my heart." She did. She and Gabe had been inseparable for the past six months and she was looking forward to their first Christmas together as a couple in just a few days.

"Good answer," he praised from the driver's seat of his car.

Not that she could see him thanks to the heavy blindfold.

"Honest answer. Are we there yet?" she asked, wondering where he was taking her. A show maybe? Or perhaps he'd rented them a cabin in Gatlinburg for the holidays? They'd had so much fun in the idealistic little town on their "date."

He'd certainly given her her money's worth a million times over. Every time she looked into his eyes and saw the love there, she thanked her lucky stars that he was hers.

"Has the car stopped moving?" he teased.

"No."

"Then we aren't there yet."

"Is this like a Christmas surprise?" she asked, hoping he'd give her a clue where they were going and why he was being so secretive about it.

"I'm not going to tell you, so it's pointless to try guessing."

Kami sat back in her seat and quietly contemplated the wonderful man she was so desperately in love with.

How could she ever have doubted him?

He'd loved her so fully, filled her heart so completely, she couldn't imagine not having his love or giving him hers.

"Hey, the car stopped moving," she said, realizing that he'd turned the engine off. "Does that mean I can take this off?" she asked, reaching for the blindfold.

"Not yet…" He pushed her hands away from the thick material. "…but soon. No peeking."

He got out of the car, then came around and opened her car door. A swoosh of cold winter air filled the car.

"Brr. I hope we're going somewhere warm," she told him as she took his hand and got out of the car. Letting him guide her, she took a few steps away from the car, then stood while he shut the door.

She wrapped her arms around herself, pulling her coat tight. "Gabe, I'm freezing."

She felt him move in front of her, undo the blindfold and remove it from her face. He stood right in front of her, his body inches from hers.

A goofy grin was on his face. A goofy grin that was full of excitement.

"What are you up to?" she asked, staring into his gorgeous blue eyes. She went to lean in for a kiss, but he stopped her by pulling back.

Her gaze went past him.

"Gabe?" She looked back at him. If anything, his grin had widened.

"Where are we?"

He gave an address.

"I mean, why are we here? Who lives here?"

"What do you think?"

She looked at the house beyond him. It was a beautiful home surrounded by trees and a big yard. "It's gorgeous, but... Gabe?"

"Do you want to go inside and get out of the cold?"

"Um...sure."

When they got to the front door, Gabe pulled a key from his coat pocket and unlocked the door.

"Whose house is this?" she asked again, stepping inside. Then she realized there was no furniture. "Gabe?"

"Come on. Let's look around." He grabbed her hand, guiding her through the house.

Kami took in the gorgeous staircase, the large open-plan living room with lots of windows, the oversized kitchen with granite countertops and solid wooden cabinets, the master suite bedroom-bath combo, three other bedrooms, and then back into the living area.

"Wow, it's a beautiful house, Gabe." Her gaze went past him to a package on the fireplace mantel. A package that hadn't been there earlier. Had it?

He turned, saw what she was looking at, and, grinning, picked up the present and handed it to her.

"This is for you."

"That's not fair. It's still a couple of days until Christmas and I didn't bring your present."

"You are my present. Christmas and every other day of the year."

Leaning forward, she plopped a kiss onto his lips. "Thank you." She glanced down at the box she held. "I can wait until Christmas if you want me to."

"Open the present, Kam."

She laughed. "Well, if you insist..."

Carefully tearing off the paper, she eyed the velvet box inside. The small square velvet box.

Her breath caught and she lifted her gaze to Gabe's. Joy shone there. Joy and excitement and anticipation and perhaps a bit of nervousness, too.

Hands trembling, she lifted the lid, then swallowed at the diamond ring glittering back at her.

Before she could say anything, Gabe took her hand and dropped to one knee.

"Gabe…" Her voice broke as she said his name.

"Marry me, Kam."

Not quite believing what was happening, she nodded. "Yes." Tears streamed down her face. "Yes. Oh, yes."

Smiling, he took the ring out of the box, took her hand and slid the diamond onto the third finger of her left hand.

Kissing her finger, he stood, then kissed her with so much love she thought she might faint from the enormity of it.

"The house is ours if you want it. I told the Realtor what I thought you'd want, what your likes and dislikes were, what the things you once told me you wanted in a home were. I've been looking for weeks. When I walked into this one, it felt like you, like coming home."

Kami stared at him in amazement at the lengths he'd gone to.

"I've talked to your mother. As soon as they're old enough, you get first pick of Bubbles's kittens."

Kami's eyes widened further. "She's going to let me have Sunshine?"

"The runty little yellow kitten you love all over every time we visit?"

Kami nodded.

"I think she's hoping you'll take that one. House, pet, me," he ticked off items, then grinned. "I'm hoping kids are somewhere on that list of yours, because this house is way too big for just the two of us, and someday, if we have a son, I'd like to name him after my dad."

Kids with Gabe. Only in her wildest dreams would she have ever dreamed any of this possible once upon a time.

"A son named after your father sounds perfect. I love you," she whispered.

"I know." One corner of his mouth hiked up. "Any

woman who uses her life savings just to spend a day with me must be in love."

"Yeah, well, you make sure I get my money's worth," she teased, wrapping her arms around his neck and smiling at him with her heart in her eyes.

"Every single day for the rest of my life."

And he did.

* * * * *

FUGITIVE BRIDE

PAULA GRAVES

For Melissa, whose cheerleading
got me to the end of this book.

Chapter One

The afternoon was perfect for a wedding, currently sunny and mild, with no hint of rain in the forecast until after the ceremony. Staring out the bride's room window at the blooming dogwood trees that lined the church lawn, Tara Bentley had the urge to check her to-do list to see if "achieve a perfect day" was somewhere on the page.

Everything she had so meticulously planned had fallen into place with ease. Her dress fit perfectly. The white tulip bouquet brought out the delicate floral pattern of the lace in her veil. Her wavy hair had, for once, cooperated when the hairdresser straightened it and twisted it into a sleek chignon low at the back of her head, where the snowy veil provided a striking contrast. And she was ten minutes ahead of schedule, which gave Tara a few moments to simply breathe and think about what came next.

Robert. He came next. Robert James Mallory III, successful lawyer and all-around Mr. Perfect. Literally.

Two years ago, as her midtwenties suddenly became her almost-thirties, Tara had written out her list of perfect traits for a potential mate. It hadn't been a particularly long list—she might be hyperorganized and prone to overpreparing, but she wasn't a robot. People weren't ever really perfect, so her list included only things that would be deal breakers.

Things like honesty. Hard work. Respect for her mind. Ambition. And, okay, a few bonus wishes, like a man who was good-looking, fit and amusing.

Three dates with Robert Mallory, and Tara knew she'd met the man who ticked off every item on her checklist. Now she was less than an hour from marrying him.

"I'm so happy," she told the green-eyed woman who stared back at her in the full-length mirror by the vanity table.

Her reflection looked skeptical.

Dang it.

She turned away from the mirror and sat on the small vanity bench, taking care not to wrinkle her wedding dress. Without planning it, she snaked out her hand and snagged the cell phone lying next to her makeup bag. She gave the lock screen a quick swipe and hit the first number on her speed dial.

A familiar, growly voice answered on the second ring, his soft drawl as warm as a fuzzy blanket on a cold Kentucky night. "Shouldn't you be practicing your vows?"

"Owen, am I making a mistake?"

Owen Stiles was quiet for a second. When he spoke again, the lightness of his earlier tone had disappeared. "What's happened?"

The serious tone of his voice made her stomach hurt. What was she doing, dragging poor Owen into her self-doubts? As if he hadn't already suffered half a lifetime of being her sounding board and shoulder to cry on.

"Nothing. Forget I said anything. See you soon." She ended the call and set the phone on the vanity table again.

A few seconds later, the phone trilled, sliding sideways on the table with the vibration. Tara didn't even look at the display. She knew who it was. She picked up the phone. "Owen, I told you it's nothing."

"If you're wondering if you made a mistake, it's not nothing. Are you in the bride's room?"

"Owen—"

His rumbly voice deepened. "I'll be there in two minutes."

"Owen, don't." Her voice rose in frustration. "Please. Just stay where you are. Everything is fine."

There was a long pause before he spoke again. "Are you sure?"

"Positive. Today is absolutely perfect. Beautiful weather, the sanctuary is gorgeous, my dress fits perfectly and I'm marrying the most perfect man in the world. Nothing can possibly be wrong on a day like this." She stared at the bride in the vanity-table mirror, defiance glaring from her green eyes.

"If you're sure." Owen didn't sound convinced.

"I'll see you at the altar." She hung up the phone again and set it in front of her, her hand flattened against the display.

"Nothing will go wrong," she said to the woman in the mirror.

The bride stared back at her, unconvinced.

It was just cold feet. Everybody got cold feet, right?

This was where having a mom around would have come in handy. Orphanhood sucked. Her mom had died when she was small, and her father had never remarried before his death three years ago. Not that Dale Bentley would have been much help on a day like today. "Suck it up, soldier," she muttered aloud, mimicking her father's gravelly growl. "Make a decision and stick to it."

Man, she missed the old sergeant. He'd have known what to make of Robert. He'd have known whether or not Tara really loved the man or if she loved the idea of him instead.

That was the sticking point, wasn't it? She just wasn't sure she loved the man she was less than an hour away from marrying.

She pushed to her feet. What in the world was she doing getting married if she wasn't sure she loved the man? Had she lost her mind? Was she so addicted to her stupid lists that she trusted them over her own heart?

She had to tell Robert what she was feeling. Talk to him, let him try to talk her out of it. Then she'd know, wouldn't she?

You already know, Tara. Listen to your gut.

Maybe she already knew, but either way, she had to tell Robert. And now, before it was too late.

She was halfway to the door when a knock sounded from the other side. She crossed to the door and leaned her ear close. "Yes?"

The voice from the other side was male and unfamiliar. "Ms. Bentley? There's a package outside we need you to sign for."

"A package?" Sent here, to the church? That was strange. "I'm not expecting anything."

"I don't know, ma'am. It's just for you and it requires a signature. You want me to tell them to send it back?"

"No," she said quickly, curiosity overcoming her impatience. Maybe a distraction was just what she needed to get her head out of her navel for a few minutes. Robert would still be on the other end of the church with his groomsmen, so it wasn't like he'd accidentally get a peek at her dress before the wedding, right?

Assuming there was even going to be a wedding...

Stop it. Just go see what the package is. One thing at a time.

She opened the door to a tall, broad-shouldered man wearing a blue polo shirt and khaki pants. "Hi," she said, feeling a little sheepish as he took in her seed pearl–studded dress and tulle veil. "It's my wedding day."

"I see that." He nodded toward the door down the hall that led to the church's parking lot. "Out here."

She followed him down the hall and out the door, taking care as she crossed the threshold not to let the skirt of her dress get caught in the door closing behind her. Once her dress cleared the door, she started to turn her attention back to the deliveryman, but something dropped over her face suddenly, obscuring her view.

Instinctively sucking in a quick breath, she got a lungful of something sweet and cloying. Her lungs seemed to seize up in response, making it hard to take another breath. Fighting panic, she tried to lift her hands to push the offending material off her face. But thick, strong arms roped around her body, holding her arms in place. Her head began to swim, her throat closing off as she struggled for oxygen. She seemed to float into the air, which was impossible. Wasn't it? She wasn't floating. People didn't float.

Somewhere close by, she thought she heard a voice shouting her name. It sounded familiar, but her suddenly fuzzy brain couldn't make sense of what she was hearing. Then she heard a swift thump and the voice went silent.

There was a metallic clank and suddenly she wasn't floating anymore. She landed with a painful thud onto a hard, cold surface, unable to make sense of what was happening to her. The sweet, slightly medicinal smell permeated everything, seeping into her brain as if it were a sponge soaking up all those heady fumes.

Another thud shook the floor beneath her, and something solid and warm settled against her back. She struggled against the encroaching darkness, one lingering part of her acutely aware that something terribly wrong was happening to her. Today was supposed to be her wedding day, even if she'd decided it was a wedding she didn't want.

She should be looking for Robert to tell him what she'd decided. She had to let people know the wedding was off. She had to call the florists to take away the beautiful roses and tulips that festooned the sanctuary. She supposed she could let the reception go on as planned, feed everyone as an apology for her attack of cold feet.

She had too much to do to be sinking deeper and deeper into the darkness now spreading through her fuzzy brain. But within seconds, she could no longer remember what those things were.

Slowly, inexorably, darkness fell.

OWEN STILES WOKE to darkness and movement. He tried to lift his hands to the hard ache at the back of his head, but his arms wouldn't move. He was bound, he realized, animal panic rising in his throat. He forced it down, trying to remember what he'd learned at Campbell Cove Academy.

First, ascertain where you are and what the danger is.

The where was easy enough. He was in the white van that had been parked outside the church when he went looking for Tara.

He hadn't liked the way she'd sounded on the phone. And if he was brutally honest with himself, there was a part of him that had been nearly giddy with hope that she was going to call off the wedding.

He wasn't proud of feeling that way. His love for Tara was unconditional. Her happiness meant everything to him.

But he couldn't deny that he wanted her to be happy with him, not some blow-dried, Armani-wearing Harvard Law graduate with a chiseled jaw and a cushy job with a top Louisville law firm.

Ignoring her command to stay put, he'd turned the corner of the hallway that led to the bride's room just in time to see a wedge of tulle and lace disappear through the exit door about twenty yards away.

Hurrying out after her, he'd been just in time to see a large man throw a pillowcase over Tara's head and haul her into a white panel van parked in front of the door. He'd called her name, shock overcoming good sense, and earned a punch that had knocked him into the side of the van. At least, that was the last thing he could remember.

Okay, so he'd ascertained where he was. And the fact that he was trussed up inside the moving van made the danger fairly clear, although he couldn't see anyone lurking around, ready to knock him out again, so he supposed that was a plus.

The back of the van seemed to be closed off from the driver's cab area by a metal panel. That fact posed a problem—he couldn't see how many people were in the front of the van, so he couldn't be sure exactly what he was up against. However, he had seen only two men wrestling with Tara, and they'd both been big guys. He wasn't sure there was room in the van's cab to accommodate more people.

So there were probably two bad guys to deal with. And thanks to the closed-off cab, he could move around unobserved, which would give him a better chance of working out a way to escape.

He felt warmth behind him. Tara?

With a grimace of pain, he rolled over and peered through the gloom. A bundle of silk, lace and tulle lay on the floor of the van beside him. The pillowcase over her head was still there, and he caught a whiff of a faintly sweet, medicinal odor coming from where she lay.

He wriggled closer, ignoring the pounding ache in his head, until his face lay close to the pillowcase. The odor was much stronger suddenly, giving off fumes that made him feel light-headed.

Ether, he thought. The pillowcase was soaked with ether.

Those idiots! Ether could be deadly if used without care, and they weren't even monitoring her condition.

He jerked at the bindings that held his arms behind his back to no avail. They'd apparently duct-taped his hands together. They weren't going to come apart easily. But he had to get the pillowcase off Tara's head.

Wriggling closer, he gripped the top of the pillowcase with his teeth. The smell of ether nearly overwhelmed him, but he held his breath and tugged upward. Inch by harrowing inch, he dragged the ether-soaked pillowcase from Tara's head until he finally pulled it free.

He spat the taste of ether out of his mouth. Then, his heart in his throat, he leaned over to make sure Tara was still breathing. A few terrifying seconds passed before he felt her breath on his cheek. Shaking with relief, he pressed a kiss to her forehead. "That's my girl. Stay with me, sweetheart."

As he waited for her to come around, Owen started working on the tape that bound his wrists together. His eyes had finally adjusted to the darkness inside the van, giving him a better look at their immediate surroundings.

The interior of the cargo van was empty except for Owen and Tara. Also, what he'd mistaken for a closed panel between them and the front cab wasn't technically closed. There was a large mesh window in the panel that should have given him a look at the occupants of the cab. But their captors had covered the mesh opening with what looked like cardboard, not only blocking out any light coming through the front windows but also keeping them from hearing whatever conversation might be going on between their captors.

The upside to that, Owen thought, was that their captors probably couldn't hear much of what was going on in the back of the van, either.

He looked around for any sharp edges he could use to tear the tape around his wrists. The covering over the wheel well was bolted to the floor of the van, but the bolts were old and worn, not providing much of a cutting edge. Still, he scooted over to the nearest bolt and gave it a try.

The van must have left Mercerville Highway, he realized a few minutes later when the swaying of the vehicle increased, forcing him to plant his feet on the cargo hold's ridged floor to keep from toppling over with each turn. But he couldn't stop Tara from rolling across the floor. A moment later, her head knocked into his hip with a soft thud.

"Ow," she muttered, her voice thick and slurred.

"Oh, sweetheart, there you are," he said softly, twisting so that his bound hands could reach the side of her face. He brushed away the grit on her cheek with his fingers. "Tara, can you hear me?"

Her head lifted, her hair and the torn remains of her tulle veil obscuring part of her face. "Owen?"

"Yeah, it's me. Careful," he added when she tried to sit up and nearly fell over.

She managed to steady herself in a sitting position and shoved her hair and the veil away from her face with clumsy hands. They, too, were secured by duct tape, he saw, though her captors had bound her hands in front of her rather than behind her. She seemed to belatedly notice the bindings and stared at her wrists. "What's happening?"

"We've been abducted," he said, though he wasn't sure *abduction* was the right term. Neither of them was exactly rolling in dough, so he didn't imagine they'd been taken for ransom purposes. Tara's fiancé was successful but not what anyone would term wealthy. Not yet, anyway.

So why *had* the men grabbed her?

"That's insane," she muttered, still pawing at her veil, which sat askew on her head. "Why am I so woozy?"

"They put a pillowcase over your head." He waved his hand at the offending piece of material lying against the front of the cargo hold. "I think it was soaked with ether."

"Ether?" Tara finally pulled her veil free and threw it on the floor beside her. The van took another turn, forcing Owen to brace himself against the side of the cargo hold. Tara was unprepared, however, and went sprawling against his side, her nose bumping into his shoulder.

"Ow." She righted herself, rubbing her nose. She finally noticed Owen's bound hands, her eyes widening. "You're tied up, too."

"Think you can get the tape off me? Then I'll return the favor." He twisted around until his back was facing her.

"My fingers aren't working so well," she warned him as she started fumbling with the tape. She wasn't lying; it took a full minute before she was able to find the end of the tape on his bindings and start to slowly unwrap his wrists. But she finally ripped away the last of the tape, making the flesh on his wrists sting.

He stretched his aching arms, grimacing at the pain.

"What time is it?" Tara asked.

He pressed the button on his watch that lit up the dial. "Just a little after four."

"Oh."

He turned to look at Tara. "You were supposed to get married at four."

She nodded. "I was supposed to."

He reached for her, taking her bound hands in his. "We'll get you back there, Tara. We'll get out of this and get to a phone so you can call Robert and tell him what happened. And then we'll get you back to the church and you'll get married just the way you planned—"

"I was going to call it off."

He went still. "What?"

In the low light he couldn't make out much about her features, but the tone of her voice was somewhere between sad and embarrassed. "I was going to call it off. Right before that guy knocked on the door and told me there was a package outside."

"That's how they got you outside to the van?"

"Yeah." She wriggled her bound hands at him. "Get this off me, please?"

He pulled the tape from her wrists, taking care with the last few inches to spare her as much of the sting as possible. When she was free, he rolled up the tape from both of their bindings and shoved it in his pocket. It might come in handy if they could get themselves out of this van alive.

Freed from her restraints, Tara curled into a knot beside him, wrapping her arms around her knees. The puffy skirt of her wedding dress ballooned around her, almost glowing in the low light, making her look like a piece of popcorn.

Owen had the clarity of mind not to speak that thought aloud.

He put his arm around her, trying not to read too much into the way she snuggled closer to him. They were in the middle of an abduction. Of course she was seeking a little comfort from the guy who'd been her best friend since middle school.

"What do they want?"

"I don't know," he admitted. "I don't suppose Robert is secretly a multimillionaire with a hefty trust fund?"

"Not that he's ever told me." She made a soft mewling noise. "I am so woozy. They used ether?"

"That's what it smelled like to me."

She cocked her head toward him. "Exactly how do you know what ether smells like?"

"I took a history of medicine course in college, when I was still considering a medical degree."

"And they let you sniff ether?"

Tara's skeptical tone made him smile. She was sounding more like her old self, which meant the effects of the ether were wearing off. "Not on purpose."

He glanced to the far side of the van's cargo hold, where he'd thrown the ether-soaked pillowcase. In this confined area, the fumes it emitted might still be affecting them, he realized.

"We need to find a way to wrap up that pillowcase so that we limit the fumes it's putting out in this van," he told Tara. "I wish I had a garbage bag or something."

"Don't suppose you carry one of those around in your back pocket?"

"Not in a rented tux, no," he answered with a grin, feeling a little less grim about their chances of survival now that his smart-ass Tara was back. He shrugged off his jacket. "I can wrap it in this."

"The rental place isn't going to like that," Tara warned.

"Not sure it's enough, though."

"Well, I have about twenty yards of silk, lace and tulle you can use." Holding his shoulder, she levered herself to her feet and started to tug at the seams of her skirt until the fabric tore free. In the darkness of the van's enclosed interior, Owen couldn't make out much besides a cloud of faint brightness in the gloom floating away from her body. Tara gathered the fabric into a ball and presented it to him. "Will this do?"

He crossed carefully to the corner of the cargo hold, feeling a distinct unsteadiness he attributed to the moving van, although he should be a lot more worried about the blow he'd taken to the head. He'd been unconscious long enough for their captors to shove him inside the van and tie him up. He might have a concussion. Or worse.

But for now, he was conscious. His head didn't hurt too badly. And he had a job to do.

He wrapped up the pillowcase inside the layers of silk, tulle and lace, and pushed it back into the corner. Already, the distinctively sweet scent of the ether was almost gone.

Gingerly, he edged his way back to where Tara perched on the wheel well cover. "That should take care of—"

The van gave a hard lurch, sending him toppling over. He landed hard on his side, pain shooting through his rib cage and hip.

"Owen!" Tara grabbed his arms and helped him to a sitting position. "Are you all right?"

He rubbed his side, reassuring himself that nothing was broken. "I'm okay—" He broke off, aware that something had changed suddenly.

The engine. He no longer heard the engine noise, or felt the vibration beneath them.

The van had come to a stop.

Chapter Two

Most of the haziness left in her brain from the ether disappeared in a snap when Tara heard the van's engine shut off.

"We've stopped." She looked up at Owen, wishing he wasn't just a shadowy silhouette in the gloom. Sometimes just the sight of him, so controlled and serious, could make her feel as if everything in the world would be okay. At least she could hear his voice, that low Kentucky drawl that had always steadied her like a rock, even in the midst of the craziness life had a habit of throwing her way. "What are they going to do to us now?"

"I don't know. Maybe nothing." He didn't sound confident.

She reached across the narrow space between them and grabbed his hands. "We need a plan."

"We don't have anything to fight with, Tara."

"Yes, we do." She squeezed his hands and pushed to her feet, heading for the corner where he'd buried the pillowcase inside the remains of her skirt. She grabbed the whole bundle and brought it to where Owen waited.

She saw the faintest glimmer in his eyes when he looked at her, just a hint of light in the darkness. "You are brilliant, sweetheart."

"There were two of them. One who came to get me, telling me there was a package waiting for me, and one standing by the van. I think he was the one who put the pillowcase over my head." She kept her voice low, in case their voices carried outside the van. "They think we're still tied up. At least, we'd better hope they do."

"It'll still take two of them to get us out, so we won't have an advantage. Except surprise."

She grabbed his hand and gave it a squeeze. "Surprise can go a long way. So, first one through the door gets the ether pillowcase over his head."

"And we shove him back onto the second guy while he's off guard."

She looked at Owen, wishing she could see him more clearly. "Think this has a chance of working?"

"No clue, but it's all we've got. So let's make it work." He reached across and gripped her hands briefly. Then he unwrapped the pillowcase from the dress skirt.

The sickly sweet odor of the ether made Tara's stomach twist, but with a little effort she controlled her nerves. She had one job—to fight with every ounce of strength and will she had to get out of this dangerous spot.

At least she wasn't alone. Owen was with her, and if there was one thing in her life she knew completely, it was that Owen would do everything he could to keep her safe. He'd been doing that for her since high school.

The back door of the van rattled, and Tara's heart skipped a beat. She sneaked a quick look at Owen and found him staring at the door, his focus complete.

He'd undergone training at Campbell Cove Academy, which was part of the security company where he now worked, but Tara hadn't really given much thought to what that training entailed. After all, Owen was a computer geek. Computer geeks didn't have much need for ninja skills, did they?

He'd been teased as a child because his skills and talents lent themselves to academic pursuits instead of sports. Even his own father had undermined Owen, calling him weak and inept because he wouldn't try out for the football team in high school.

Tara wished some of those people could see Owen right now, ready to take on two possibly armed men in order to protect her.

The door to the van opened, and light invaded the back of the van, blinding Tara for a long panicky moment, until a rush of movement from Owen's side of the door spurred her into motion. Her vision adjusted in time for her to see Owen jamming the pillowcase over a man's head and giving him a push backward. The man fell over like a bowling pin, toppling the other man who stood right behind him.

Owen grabbed Tara's hand. "Jump!" he yelled as he jerked her with him out the back door of the van.

She saw the two men on the ground struggling to right themselves. It wouldn't be long before they did, she realized. The thought spurred her to run faster. Thank God she'd opted for low-heeled pumps for her wedding, she thought as she ran across the blacktop road and into the woods on the other side, her hand still firmly clasped in Owen's.

The pumps proved themselves more problematic once they hit the softer ground of the woods. Behind her, the men they'd just escaped started shouting for them to stop, punctuating their calls with a couple of gunshots that made Tara's blood turn to ice. But, as far as she could tell, none of the shots got anywhere near them.

"Come on," Owen urged, pulling her with him as he zigzagged though the woods. It took a couple of minutes to realize there was a method to his seemingly mad dash through the trees. They were moving from tree to tree, finding cover from their pursuers.

What was left of her wedding dress was a liability, she realized with dismay. The white fabric stood out in the dark woods like a beacon. At least Owen's tux was black. He blended into the trees much better than she could hope to do.

"You go without me," she said as they took temporary cover behind the wide trunk of an oak tree. "I'm the one they're after. I stick out like a hooker in a church in this dress. You could find help and send the police after the van. You could tell Robert what happened."

Owen looked at her as if she'd lost her mind. "I am not leaving you," he growled.

The sudden urge to wrap her arms around his neck and kiss him caught her off guard. She'd set aside those nascent feelings of attraction to Owen a long time ago, valuing his loyal friendship far more than she valued any sort of sexual attraction she might feel toward him. To have it come back now, in this awful situation, was confounding.

"Now!" Owen growled, and he tugged her with him through the underbrush to their next bit of cover.

Behind them, the sound of their pursuers was close enough to spur their forward movement. But the men following them weren't any closer, Tara realized. So far, she and Owen seemed to be staying ahead of the danger pursuing them.

But what would happen if they ran out of woods?

A brisk breeze had picked up as they ran, rustling the leaves overhead. Thank heaven for spring growth; two months ago, these woods would have been winter bare and couldn't have provided them with nearly enough cover. But even here in the Kentucky mountains, the woods couldn't go on forever, which could be a good thing or a bad thing. If they managed to find a well-populated town around the next copse, they'd be safe.

But if they ran into a clearing with neither cover nor the safety of numbers to protect them...

"How long do you think they'll keep chasing us?" she asked breathlessly as they crouched behind another tree.

"I don't know," Owen admitted. "I don't suppose you know why they grabbed you. Did they give you any indication?"

"No, it's like I told you—one of the men came to get me and the other put the pillowcase over my head before I could even get a good look at his face. Although he definitely asked for me by name. Ms. Bentley." She risked a peek around the side of the tree providing them with cover. "I don't see them anymore."

"I don't think we should move anytime soon. They may be hunkered down, waiting to flush us out."

Tara frowned. "How long are we talking?"

"I don't know. A couple of hours?"

She grimaced. "I suppose it's a bad time to mention that I desperately need to pee."

Owen gave a soft huff of laughter. "Can you hold it awhile?"

"Do I have any choice?"

"No."

"Well, there you go."

Owen gave her a look that made her insides melt a little. She might have decided years ago that she'd rather be his friend forever than risk losing him by taking their relationship to a more sexual place, but that didn't mean she wasn't aware that he found her just as attractive as she found him.

And right now he was looking at her as if he wanted to strip her naked and slake his thirst for her up against the rough trunk of this big oak tree.

Oh, God, Tara, you're hiding from crazy kidnappers and you choose now to conjure up that visual?

"I think I know where we are," Owen murmured a few minutes later.

Moving only her eyes, Tara scanned the woods around them, seeing only trees, trees and more trees. "How on earth is that possible?" she whispered.

"Because while you went to cheerleading camp, I went to Boy Scout camp."

"And what, got a badge in telling one gol dang leafy tree from another?" Staying still was starting to get to her already. She wasn't the kind of woman who stayed still. Ever. And the urge to look behind them to see if their captors were sneaking up on them was almost more than she could bear.

"No," Owen said with more patience than she deserved. "It's because I stayed in a rickety little cabin with five other boys about two hundred yards to our east."

She slanted a look at him. "How can you possibly know that?"

"See that big tree right ahead? The one with the large moon-shaped scar on the trunk about five feet up?"

She peered through the trees. "No."

"Well, trust me, it's there. And that moon shape is there because Billy Turley and I carved it in the trunk on a dare. Our camp counselor didn't buy that we were trying out our trailblazing skills like Daniel Boone before us."

There had never been a time in her life when she'd felt less like smiling, but the image conjured up by Owen's words made her lips curve despite herself. She and Owen had met around the time they were both in sixth grade. In fact, she could remember Owen taking that trip to the woods because she'd been over-the-moon excited about being invited to cheerleading camp, since only girls who went to the camp in middle school ever made the varsity squad in high school.

Oh, for the days when life was so simple that her biggest worry was crash-landing a herkie jump in front of twenty other judgmental preteen girls.

"I know you're about ready to squirm out of your skin," Owen said quietly, slipping his hand into hers, "but I have a plan."

She curled her fingers around his. "Okay. What is it?"

"As soon as I'm pretty sure our kidnappers have retreated, we'll head for the cabin."

She looked up at him, narrowing her eyes. "The one you stayed in twenty years ago when you were eleven?"

"I think it's still there."

"Maybe, but in what kind of condition?"

His lips flattened with exasperation. She felt his grip on her hand loosen. "Must you always be so negative?"

She tightened her fingers around his again. "Yes. But sorry."

He gave her fingers a light squeeze. "I suppose it's part of your charm."

"Sweet talker," she muttered.

"So we're agreed? We head for the cabin?"

"If it's still there." She looked up. "Sorry. Negativity."

"If it's still there," he agreed. "And we'd better hope it is."

The dark tone of his growly voice made her stomach turn a flip. "Why's that?"

"You know how the wind has picked up?"

"Yeah?"

"I think the rain may be getting here a little earlier than expected tonight."

Owen was right. Within a few minutes, the brisk wind began to carry needles of rain from which the spring growth overhead provided only partial shelter. Owen tried to tuck Tara under his coat, but the rain became relentless as daylight waned, darkness falling prematurely because of the lowering sky.

Tara wiped the beading water from her watch face. Nearly six. The wedding would have long been over by now, if she'd gone through with it. Robert must be going crazy, wondering what happened to her. Her car would still be in the parking lot, her purse in the bride's room. The only thing missing was the bride and her puffy white dress.

Would everyone realize something had gone very wrong? Or would they assume that Tara had succumbed to cold feet and bolted without letting anyone know?

Was Robert thinking he'd just made a narrow escape from a lifetime with a lunatic?

Stop it, Tara. This is not your fault.

Owen was right. She was way too negative. She added it to her mental list of things she needed to work on, right behind cellulite on her thighs and—oh, yeah—running away from dangerous, crazy kidnappers.

"You're thinking, aren't you?" Owen asked. "I always worry when you're thinking."

"I'm thinking I haven't heard anything from the kidnappers back there recently. I'm also thinking that there may be ants crawling up my legs. And I'm thinking if I have to hide behind this tree for a minute longer, getting soaked to the skin, I'm going to run crazy through the trees, screaming *I give up! Come get me!* at the top of my lungs."

Owen turned toward her, cupping her face between his hands. His fingers were cool, but the look in his eyes was scalding hot. "I know you're scared. I know wisecracking and complaining is how you show it. And you're right. We haven't heard those guys recently. I don't think they were eager to spend the rest of their day hunting you down in the woods when they know who you are and can take a chance on grabbing you another time."

She stared up at him. "You really think they'll try this again?"

"You said they asked for you by name."

"But why? I'm not rich. Robert's not even rich, not really. Not enough to warrant a risky daylight abduction."

"I know. But even if you can't think of a reason, they clearly had one." He dropped his hands to his sides. "It's time to make a run for it. You ready?"

"Born ready." She flashed him a cheeky grin, even if she felt like crying. It earned her one of Owen's deliciously sexy smiles in return, and he touched her face again. His fingers were cold, but heat seemed to radiate through her from his touch.

He grabbed her hand and started running, pulling her behind him.

Even though she'd convinced herself that their captors had given up and made their escape, every muscle in Tara's body tensed as she zigzagged behind Owen, her heart in her throat. Every twig that snapped beneath her feet sounded as thunderous as a gunshot, even through the masking hiss of the falling rain.

Two hundred yards to the cabin, Owen had said. Surely they'd run two hundred yards by now. That was two football fields, wasn't it?

Owen jerked sideways suddenly, nearly flinging her off her feet. He grabbed her around the waist as she started to slide across the muddy ground and kept her upright. "There," he said, satisfaction coloring his voice.

Tara followed his gaze and saw what looked to be a ramshackle wooden porch peeking out from the overgrowth about twenty yards away.

"You have got to be kidding me," she muttered.

His lips pressed to a thin line. "Shelter is shelter, Tara."

He let go of her hand and started toward the wooden structure with a brisk, determined stride.

She stood watching him for a moment, feeling terrible. The man had saved her life, and she'd been nothing but a whining ingrate.

Lighting flashed overhead, followed quickly by a bone-rattling boom of thunder that shook her out of her misery and sent her dashing through the muddy undergrowth as fast as her ruined pumps would carry her. She skidded to a stop at the edge of the porch and stared at what Owen had called a cabin.

It was tiny. She didn't have any idea how Owen and his fellow Boy Scouts had managed to squeeze themselves inside the place. The three shallow steps leading up to the porch looked rickety and dangerous, though apparently they'd managed to hold Owen's weight, for he was already on the porch, peering inside the darkened doorway of the small structure.

"I remember it as being bigger," he said quietly.

"You were eleven." She made herself risk the steps. They were sturdier than they looked, though the rain had left them slick. At least the stair railing didn't wiggle too much as she climbed to the porch and joined Owen in the doorway.

Years had clearly passed since any Boy Scouts had darkened the door of this cabin. What she could see in the gloom looked damp and dilapidated. The musty smell of age and disuse filled Tara's lungs as she took a shaky breath. "The roof leaks, doesn't it?"

Owen took a step inside. Almost immediately, he jerked back, bumping into Tara. She had to grab him around the waist to keep from falling.

Something small and gray scuttled out the door past

them, scampered off the porch and disappeared into the undergrowth.

"Possum," Owen said.

Tara grimaced. "So that's what I'm smelling."

He whipped around to look at her. "I'm sorry I've disappointed you. Again."

She grabbed his hand. "You saved me. I wouldn't have gotten out of there without you."

He gave her hand a little squeeze before letting go. "If it weren't for you, I'd have never gotten loose from that duct tape."

And he'd never have been in trouble if she hadn't called him to share her doubts about the wedding. Which maybe she wouldn't be having if she didn't still find Owen so darn attractive.

They could play this game forever, going all the way back to sixth grade when she saved Owen from a bully and he'd helped her pass math.

They were darn near symbiotic at this point.

"You're thinking again," Owen murmured.

"I am," she said. "I'm thinking if we're planning on hunkering down here until the rain passes, I'd like to make sure there's no possum surprises waiting for me in there. Any chance we could find a candle or two in this godforsaken place?"

"Maybe." Owen entered the dark cabin. A moment later, she heard more than saw him scrabbling around in a drawer. "Ha." He reached into the pocket of his tuxedo pants and pulled out something. A second later, a small light flickered in the darkness.

"You had a lighter in your pants pocket?"

"I wanted to be sure your candle lighting at the wedding went off without a hitch." He shot her a sheepish grin. "I take my man-of-honor duties seriously."

Her insides melted, and she crossed to where he stood, wrapping her arms around his waist and pressing her face to his chest. "You're the best man of honor ever."

He rubbed his free hand down her arm. "Oh, Tara, you're freezing. You really need to get out of those wet clothes."

"And into what?" she asked, her voice coming out softer and sultrier than she'd intended.

He stared back at her, wordless, his eyes smoldering as strongly as the flickering candle in his hand. The moment stretched between them, electric and fraught with danger.

And forbidden desires…

A loud thud sounded outside the door, and in a flash, Owen extinguished the candle and pulled Tara behind him.

There was another thud. Slow. Deliberate.

Someone was outside the cabin.

Chapter Three

Owen tucked Tara more fully behind him, squaring his shoulders in an attempt to look larger than he was. What he wouldn't give to have the pecs and deltoids of Mike Strong, who'd instructed him in hand-to-hand combat during his first grueling weeks of probationary training at Campbell Cove Security Services. Strong had insisted that Owen's lean, wiry build didn't mean he couldn't hold his own in a fight, but until today, he'd never had a reason to test that theory.

And given how badly his attempt to save Tara outside the church had gone, he wasn't confident that Strong would be proven right this time, either.

He could hear his father's voice, a mean whisper in his ear. "You're weak, Owen. Life ain't kind to the weak."

Grimly shutting out that voice, he searched the shadowy interior of the cabin for something he could use as a weapon, but the place had been stripped mostly bare a long time ago, from the looks of it. There was a rickety camp bed left in one corner, and the mattress of another lying on the floor nearby, but that was all. What he wouldn't give for one of those cheap little bow and arrow sets he and the other Scouts had learned to use that summer twenty years ago.

Not that he'd remember how to use it.

The footsteps on the porch moved closer, the steps careful. Deliberate. There was an oddly light touch to the sounds that didn't remind him much of the hulking men who'd shoved him into the side of the van earlier that day. These footfalls sounded almost—

A face peered around the edge of the door. Small, pale, freckled and terrified.

A kid, no more than ten or eleven. He froze there, his face framed by the bright red hood of his rain slicker. A second later, a second face appeared next to the boy's, smaller. More feminine. She had big, dark eyes and frizzy curls framing her face beneath her pink rain hood.

Owen took a step toward them. "Hello—"

The boy opened his mouth and screamed, triggering an answering shriek in the girl. They sped off into the rainy woods, their terrified wails turning to hysterical giggles of pure adrenaline rush before they faded from earshot.

Owen felt Tara's forehead press hard against his back. "Kids?"

"That could have been us twenty years ago." Owen turned to look at her. "Sneaking around Old Man Ridley's cabin, trying to catch him red-handed at murder."

Tension seeped slowly out of her expression, a faint smile taking its place. "Remember that summer he almost caught us?"

"One of the top ten most terrifying moments of my life." He laughed softly.

"Do you think those kids will come back with grown-ups next time?"

He shook his head. "Are you kidding? They'd probably be grounded for life just for sneaking around this old cabin." He pulled out the lighter and relit the candle he'd extinguished. "Come on, let's see what kind of shelter we can make of this place."

The place was grimy and drafty, but the tin roof seemed to have weathered the years without springing leaks, which had kept the interior dry and mostly free of mildew. The cot mattresses were a disaster, but Owen uncovered an old military footlocker half hidden by the remains of one of the cots. Inside, he found a couple of camp blankets kept well preserved within the airtight trunk. They smelled of the cedar blocks someone had placed inside the trunk to ward off moths.

"Here, wrap up in this." He unfolded the top blanket and wrapped it around Tara's shoulders, not missing the shivers rattling through her. "I wish we could risk starting a fire in that fireplace," he said with a nod toward the river stone fireplace against the near wall. "But the chimney's probably blocked by now, and besides, we don't want to risk smoke alerting anyone to where we are. Not yet."

She stepped closer to him, curling into him like a kitten seeking heat. "Just hold me for a minute, okay? They say body heat is the best heat."

Owen quelled the instant reaction of his body to hers, a talent he'd honed since their early teens, when Tara's femininity blossomed in time for his hormones to rev up to high gear. She'd put deliberate boundaries between them, first unspoken ones and then, later, when he'd wanted to push those barriers out of the way, spoken ones.

"I've never had a friend like you, Owen," she'd told him that night after the high school football game when he tried to kiss her in the car after he'd driven her home. "I need you to be Owen. My best friend. We can't risk changing that. Do you understand? Boyfriends are complicated. Relationships are volatile. I have enough of that in my life."

He couldn't argue with that. Motherless since just before they'd met, Tara had struggled to connect with her rough-edged, emotionally conservative father, who'd had to give up the military life he'd loved to take care of his daughter. Tara had felt as if he resented her for the end of his Marine Corps career, which had added to the existing friction between them right up until his death.

Owen had swallowed his desire and given Tara what she needed, as much as it had cost him to do so. But the desire had never gone away, married as it was to his enduring love for his best friend.

And at times like these, with her slender body pressed so intimately to his, what was left of her clothing clinging to her body and leaving little to his imagination, tamping down that desire was a Herculean task.

"Maybe the rain will stop soon," she mumbled against his collarbone, her breath hot against his neck.

"Maybe," he agreed. "Those children must live nearby, which is promising, because when this was a Boy Scout camp years ago, there were no houses in easy walking distance at all."

She burrowed deeper in his embrace. "I wonder how I'm going to explain walking around in the woods wearing a slip, half a wedding dress and my ruined silk pumps."

"Very carefully," he answered, making her chuckle. The sound rippled through him, sparking a shudder of pure male need.

"I don't think the rain is supposed to end before morning," she said with a soft sigh that heated his throat again. "We're going to need to find somewhere to sleep tonight. And I have to say, I'm not thrilled about sharing a cot where a possum was probably nesting."

"The blankets from that chest are pretty clean. We could cover the mattresses with those."

"Mattress," she corrected.

"Mattress?"

She looked up at him, her expression serious. "It's too cold in here for us to sleep apart. Right?"

He stared at her, his heart rattling in his chest like a snare drum. He swallowed hard and forced the words from his lips. "Right. Body heat is the best heat."

He was in so much trouble.

BAGLEY COUNTY SHERIFF'S DEPARTMENT investigator Archer Trask walked slowly around the small groom's room, taking in all the details of the crime scene. There was less blood than one might expect, to begin with. The victim had taken two bullets to the base of his skull—double tap, the big-city cops would call it. A sign of a professional hit.

But who the hell would target a groom on his wedding day?

"Vic's name is Robert Mallory. The third." The responding deputy flipped a page in his notepad. "Mallory Senior works in the Lexington DA's office, and he's already screaming for us to turn this over to the Kentucky State Police."

"Any witnesses?"

"No, but the bride is missing. So's her man of honor."

Trask slanted a look at the deputy. "You're kidding."

"Nobody's seen either of them since about an hour before the wedding."

"Bride's name?"

"Tara Bentley."

Didn't sound familiar. Neither did the groom's name. "Have you talked to the bride's parents?"

"She's an orphan, it seems." The deputy grimaced. "Her side of the aisle is a little sparse."

Trask rubbed his forehead, where a headache was starting to form. Why didn't he ever get a cut-and-dried case these days? "I want the groom's parents kept apart so I can question them separately. And any of the wedding party who might have seen anything. Do we have an estimated time of death yet?"

"Last time anyone saw him was around three, about an hour before the ceremony was supposed to start. Last time anyone saw the bride was round the same time."

Trask frowned. Missing bride, dead groom, professional-looking hit—nothing seemed to fit. "You said man of honor."

The deputy flipped back a page or two in his notepad. "Owen Stiles. Apparently the bride's best friend from childhood."

Stiles. The name sounded familiar. "What do we know about Stiles?"

"Not much. His mother is here for the wedding. She's the one who told us she couldn't find him. By the way, according to the man of honor's mother, their cars are still in the church parking lot."

Trask looked up at the deputy's words. "You're telling me the bride and her best friend took a flyer and left their cars behind?"

"Looks like. We've already checked the tags and they're registered to our missing persons."

Well, now, Archer thought. That was a surprising twist. "Let's get an APB out on both of them. Persons of interest in a murder for now. We need to check if either of them have another vehicle, too."

"I'll call it in." The deputy finished jotting notes and headed out of the room.

Trask looked down at the dead man lying facedown on the floor. Poor bastard, he thought. All dressed up and nowhere to go.

"Do you, Tara, take Robert as your lawfully wedded husband? To have and to hold from this day forward. For better or worse, in sickness and in health, forsaking all others…" The pastor's intonation rang in Tara's head, making it throb. She wanted to run, but her feet were stuck to the floor as if her shoes were nailed to it. She tried to tug her feet from the shoes, but they wouldn't budge.

Breathing became difficult behind the veil that had seemed to mold itself around her head and neck, tightening at her throat. She attempted to claw it away, but the more she pulled at the veil, the more it constricted her.

"Owen!" she cried, the sound muffled and puny. She knew he was here somewhere. Owen would never let anything bad happen to her.

"I'm here." His voice was a warm rumble in her ear, but she couldn't see him.

"Owen, please."

Arms wrapped around her from behind. Owen's arms, strong and bracing. The veil fell away and she could breathe again. Her feet pulled loose from the floor and she turned to face her rescuer.

Owen gazed at her, his face so familiar, so right, even in the shadows.

"You awake now?"

The shadows cleared, and she realized where she was. It was the old Boy Scouts camp cabin in the woods. Night had passed, and with it the rain. Misty sunlight was peeking through the trees outside and slanting into the cabin through the dusty windows.

And she was wrapped up tightly in Owen's arms on the mattress they shared.

"Yes," she answered.

"You were dreaming. Must have been a bad one."

She forced a smile, the frightening remnants of her nightmare lingering. "Just a stress dream. You know, late for class."

"You called out to me."

She eased away from his embrace and sat up. "Probably wanted you to do my algebra homework for me."

He sat up, too. The blanket spilled down to his waist, revealing his lean torso. She rarely saw him shirtless, and it came as a revelation. Owen might not be bulked up like a bodybuilder, but his shoulders were broad, his stomach flat and his chest well-toned. He'd talked often about Campbell Cove Security's training facilities, which were apparently part of the company's connected training academy, but she'd been so wrapped up in her wedding plans she hadn't listened as closely as she should have.

"Did you hear it, too?" he asked in a half whisper, and she realized he'd been talking to her while she was ogling his body.

She lowered her voice to match his. "Hear what?"

"Voices. I think I'm hearing voices outside. Listen."

Tara listened. He was right. The voices were faint, but they were there. "A woman and a man," she whispered. "Can't make out what they're saying."

"Maybe one of those kids did tell their parents about seeing us last night." Owen rose, grabbing his shirt from where it lay on the floor nearby and slipping it on as he crossed to the cabin's front window. Tara noticed that grime had smudged the snowy-white fabric.

"Can you see anyone?" she whispered.

He nodded. "They look normal."

"By normal, I assume you mean nonhomicidal."

He turned to flash her a quick grin. "Exactly."

"Maybe we should go out and meet them. It'll look less suspicious."

"Good idea." He glanced her way. "Wrap the blanket around your bottom half. It'll be hard to explain half a wedding dress."

Smart, she thought, and grabbed the blanket that had been covering them to wrap around her. She joined him at the door. "Ready?"

He took her hand. "Let's not tell them what really happened. Too hard to explain. I'm just going to say we're newlyweds whose car broke down in the storm."

"Okay." She twined her fingers with him and followed him onto the porch, surprising the couple approaching the cabin through the underbrush.

"Oh!" the woman exclaimed as they came to a quick halt. "I reckon y'all are real after all."

"You must be the parents of one of the kids we scared last night," Owen said with an engaging smile. "Sorry about that."

The woman, a plump brunette with a friendly smile, waved off his apology. "Don't you worry about that. Those young 'uns had no business bein' out here in the middle of a rainstorm. But we figured we should at least come out here and make sure you weren't in some kind of trouble."

The man grimaced at the cabin. "Y'all had to sleep here last night?"

"Sadly, yes," Owen said. "Our car broke down late yesterday afternoon, and then the rain hit, so we had to settle for what shelter we could find. And then, to our complete horror, we discovered we'd both left our cell phones at the church. So we couldn't even call for a tow."

The woman took in their appearances—the beaded bodice of Tara's torn dress, Owen's grimy white tuxedo shirt and black pants—and jumped to the obvious conclusion. "You're newlyweds, aren't you? Bless your hearts—this is where you spent your wedding night?"

Owen laughed, pulling Tara closer. "It'll be quite the story to tell on our golden anniversary, won't it? I don't suppose we could borrow a phone to call for help?"

"Of course you could." The woman dug in the pocket of her jeans and provided a cell phone. "Here you go."

"Thank you so much." Owen took the phone and went back inside the cabin to make the call, leaving Tara to talk to the friendly couple.

"Do you live close?" Tara asked.

"Half a mile. Kind of hard to see the place through all the trees. If it was winter, you'd probably have seen us and not had to spend the night here," the husband said. "I'm Frank Tyler, by the way. This is my wife, Elaine."

"Tara B—Stiles. Tara Stiles, and my husband's name is Owen." Tara smiled, even though her stomach was starting to ache from the tension of lying to this nice couple. But Owen was right. As crazy as the "newlyweds with car trouble" story was, the truth was so much more problematic.

Owen came back out to the porch, a smile pasted on his face. But Tara knew him well enough to know that his smile was covering deep anxiety. It glittered in his eyes, tense and jittery. He handed the phone back to Elaine Tyler. "Thank you so much. I've called someone for a tow, so we're set."

"Glad we could help. You know, we could drive you to where your car is parked."

"Not necessary. I've arranged for someone to meet us on Old Camp Road. Easy walk from here to there. You should get back to your family." Owen shook Frank Tyler's hand, then Elaine's. "Thank you again."

"Yes, thank you so much," Tara added, smiling brightly to hide her growing worry. Who had Owen called and what had he heard?

When the Tylers were out of earshot, Tara moved closer to Owen. "What's wrong?"

He caught her hand, his expression pained. "Tara, I don't know how to break this to you. Robert's dead."

She stared at Owen, not comprehending. "What?"

"He's dead. Shot, from what my boss told me."

She covered her mouth with one shaky hand, not certain what she was feeling. Her fiancé was dead. The man she'd been close to marrying. Even if she had become convinced he wasn't the man for her, it didn't mean she hadn't cared deeply for him.

And now he was gone? Just like that?

It was crazy. It had to be wrong.

"This has to be a mistake," she said, her legs suddenly feeling like jelly.

Owen led her to the steps and eased her into a sitting position on the top step. Ignoring the uncomfortable dampness of the wood, she turned to look at Owen as he settled down beside her and wrapped one strong arm around her shoulder. "I'm so sorry, sweetheart."

She leaned her head against his shoulder. "There's more, isn't there?"

He leaned his head against hers. "Yes."

She sighed. "Just get it over with."

"Robert was murdered at the church around the time you and I were taken by the kidnappers. Nobody knew where we went, so—"

"So now we're the prime suspects," she finished for him.

Chapter Four

"How long do you think it'll take your boss to get here?"

Owen looked away from the empty road, taking in the lines of tension in Tara's weary face. "He should be here soon. It's not that far from the office to here."

He didn't know how to comfort her when his own nerves were stretched to the breaking point. How had they gone from kidnap victims to murder suspects in the span of a few hours? And how could they ever prove their story? The only evidence left was a wad of duct tape still hidden in his tux pants, which was hardly dispositive. Any ether left in Tara's system would be long gone by now, and any ether that might have been deposited on her hair and clothing would have been washed away by the rain.

"What are we going to do, Owen?" Tara looked tiny, wrapped up as she was in the drab camp blanket. "What did your boss say we should do? Turn ourselves in?"

"He just told me to sit tight and let him figure it out." Owen didn't like admitting that he didn't have a clue what they should do, either, but he'd never been a suspect in a murder before.

"Do you trust him?"

How to answer that question? Owen technically had three bosses—Alexander Quinn, Rebecca Cameron and Maddox Heller, the three former government employees who now ran Campbell Cove Security Services. Cameron, a former diplomat, and Heller, a former marine, seemed nice enough, but Owen's department, Cybersecurity, was mainly under the hawkeyed control of Quinn, a former spy with an epic reputation for getting things done no matter the cost.

Owen didn't know if it was ever wise to trust someone like Quinn, who saw even his employees as expendable if it meant securing the safety of the country he'd spent decades serving. But Owen had no doubt that Quinn was dedicated to the cause of justice. And if he and Tara ended up in jail for something they didn't do, how would justice be served?

"I think he'll want the right person to go to jail for what happened to Robert," he said finally.

Tara's narrow-eyed gaze told him she hadn't been mollified by his answer. "Well, he'd better get here soon, because it won't take long for those nice people we met this morning to find out about Robert's murder on the morning news and start to wonder about that half-dressed bride and groom they saw hiding in the woods."

She was right. Owen checked his watch. Where the hell was Quinn? "I wish I had my phone."

"Is that him?" Tara nodded toward a small, dark dot at the far end of the narrow two-lane road. It grew bigger as it came near, resolving into a dark blue SUV. It stopped about forty yards down the road, and a sandy-haired man got out.

Not Quinn but Maddox Heller. Owen didn't know whether to be worried or relieved.

Heller motioned for them to come to him. Grimacing, Owen started walking. The rain had tightened the leather of his dress shoes, which were pinching his feet. Tara didn't look any happier about the walk, wobbling a little in her grimy pumps and taking care not to step on the hem of her blanket wrap.

"Sorry," Maddox said when they reached the SUV. "I wanted to be sure you weren't being used as bait for an ambush."

Tara pulled herself into the front seat and sighed deeply. "Twenty-four hours ago, my life was so simple."

Heller gave her a sympathetic look. "I'm sorry about your fiancé. Are you warm enough? Let me turn up the heater."

Owen sat on the bench seat behind them, closing his hand over Tara's shoulder. He felt her skin ripple beneath his touch, but when he started to pull his hand away, she caught it and held it in place.

"For now, I'm taking you to a safe house. We'll get you some clothes and something to eat, and you can try to get some sleep. I can't imagine you slept well in a cold cabin."

"What about the police?" Tara asked.

"Quinn wants to look into that issue before we decide what to do. For now, he wants you to just stay put."

Easy enough, Owen thought. He wanted nothing more than a hot meal, some warm, dry clothes and to sleep for a week.

"Do you know how Robert was killed?" Tara asked as Maddox reversed the SUV and headed back the way he'd come. "Owen said he was shot, but when? How?"

"The details are sketchy. We have some friends in the local sheriff's department, but they're hunkered down at the moment, as you can imagine, just dealing with the press and with your fiancé's family."

Tara rubbed her forehead. "I didn't even think about his poor parents. Who would do something like that? And why?"

Owen squeezed her shoulder. "We're going to find out. I promise."

She looked at him over her shoulder. "You can't promise that."

"I promise to do everything I can to figure this out and
keep you safe."

She smiled wanly. "I know you'll try."

The drive to the safe house took about twenty minutes,
taking them out of the woods and down a long country
road dotted here and there with farms and pastureland
where horses grazed placidly in the morning sun. Halfway there, Maddox Heller turned on the radio and tuned
in to a local news station, which was covering Robert's
murder with almost salacious excitement.

They learned nothing new, however, and Tara bluntly
asked Heller to turn it off.

The safe house was a small, neat farmhouse nestled near
the end of a two-lane road sheltered on either side by apple
trees. There were no other houses on the road, no doubt by
design. Even the house itself was sheltered on three sides
by sprawling oak trees that hid most of the property from
view unless someone was driving by on purpose.

"It's fairly rustic," Heller warned as he led them up the
flagstone walkway to the river stone porch. "But you'll
have what you need, and the property is protected by a
state-of-the-art security system."

"Will there be anyone protecting us?" Tara asked. "I
mean, if those guys who grabbed us try to find us again."

Heller glanced at Owen. "Owen's trained for the basics.
The security system should do the rest, and we'll have an
agent check on you regularly until Quinn decides how to
proceed. You shouldn't be here long."

Tara glanced Owen's way. He wasn't sure if she was
looking for reassurance or expressing skepticism. He
smiled back at her, hoping it would suffice as a response
either way.

Heller showed them how to set and disarm the security system. "You can set your own codes if that makes you feel more secure, or you can leave the code as is. We have an override code in case there's trouble, but only Cameron, Quinn and I know that code, so you should be very safe."

He led them deeper into the house. It was rustic, as Heller had warned, but everything looked to be in good working shape. There was wood in the bin next to the fireplace, and the kitchen appliances proved to be up-to-date. "We stocked the fridge and freezer, so you'd have enough to eat for a few days if things don't resolve sooner," Heller told them as they left the kitchen and entered the hallway that led to a couple of large bedrooms near the back of the house. He guided Tara to the room on the right. "There are several sizes of clothing you can choose from in there. We took up a collection from all the women we could reach on quick notice. Hopefully, you'll find a few things that work. Let me know if you don't." He nodded toward the other room. "I grabbed some of the stuff you had stashed at work, and got a few of the taller guys to lend you some clothes," he told Owen.

Heller followed Owen into the room and closed the door behind them. "You okay? Quinn said you had a knock on the head. Did you lose consciousness?"

"Briefly," Owen answered. "I'm fine."

"I could have Eric come take a look at you, although Quinn wants to keep as few people as possible in the loop on this, at least until he can get a better idea what's going on."

"I haven't had any symptoms. My head doesn't even hurt where I hit it, except a little tenderness in the skin."

Heller took a look at the lump on the side of Owen's head, frowning. "Don't take chances. Head injuries aren't anything to mess around with."

"I'm fine."

"What about Tara? Any lingering effects from the ether exposure?"

"Not that I can tell. I'll keep an eye on her."

Heller opened the top drawer of the tall chest next to the bedroom door and withdrew a lockbox. He set it on the bed and opened it with a key he pulled from his jeans pocket. Inside, nestled in foam padding fitted snugly to it, lay a Smith & Wesson M&P .380. "There's ammo in the drawer. Quinn said you'd been trained to use one of these."

Owen stared at the pistol, trying not to feel queasy. "I have, but—"

"No buts. You're trained to use it. Which means you also know when not to use it. Trust your training. And your own good sense." Heller handed Owen the key. "Quinn sent over a team from your department to set up a computer. You should be able to access the office server through an untraceable remote access program. I'm told you're the one who created the system, so I'm sure you know how to make it work."

Owen managed a weak smile, his gaze wandering back to the open pistol case. "Computers I can do."

Heller clapped his hand over Owen's shoulder. "You can handle all of it. Remember your training. Let it do the work for you."

Owen walked Heller to the front door. "Any idea when we can expect to hear something from you or Quinn or whoever?"

"Soon. I can't be more specific until Quinn's finished his investigation." Heller's smile carved dimples in his tanned cheeks, making him look a decade younger. "We're on your side, Stiles. Try to relax. We'll be in touch."

Owen blew out a long breath after he closed the door behind Heller, his heart pounding in his chest. What the hell had he and Tara stumbled into? And how was he supposed to protect her when he was shaking in his boots?

"There's a gun on your bed."

Tara's voice made him jump. He turned to look at her. "Heller left it for me, in case we need it."

Her eyes narrowed. "Do you know how to use it?"

"Yes."

She looked tired and scared, her arms wrapped protectively around herself. Still in the tattered remains of her wedding dress, she looked small and vulnerable, two words he'd never before associated with Tara. The Tara he knew was fierce and invincible. Seeing her so uncertain, so fragile, made his stomach ache.

"You need a shower and some sleep." He crossed to where she stood, rubbing his hands lightly up and down her arms. "Come on, let's see if we can find the bathroom."

She flung her arms around him suddenly, pressing her face to his chest. Her arms tightened around his waist, her grip fierce. "Thank you."

He wrapped his arms around her, wishing he could ease the tremble he felt in her limbs. "For what?"

"You came to find me, even when I told you not to worry." She looked up at him. "You always do."

"Always will," he promised.

Her gaze seemed to be searching his face for something. He wasn't sure what. Reassurance? Reliability?

Tell me what you want, Tara, and I'll give it to you.

"You're right about one thing. I need a shower and about a week of sleep," Tara said, pulling away from his embrace.

He needed a shower, too, but he felt suddenly wide awake, as if the reality of their dilemma had flooded his veins with adrenaline. He needed to figure out why Robert had been murdered and how it related to Tara's kidnapping.

Tara had disappeared into her room, and the sound of

running water coming from behind the closed door meant there must be a bathroom connected to her room. His bedroom didn't have an en suite bathroom, but the large bathroom just down the hall was more than convenient.

He took a quick shower, changed into a pair of jeans and a thick sweatshirt, and settled down at the desk nestled in the corner of his bedroom, where one of his colleagues in the computer security section had provided a high-tech setup.

Everything was up and running, so he connected to the Campbell Cove Security system and quickly found the files on Robert Mallory's murder. The details were sketchy, but the agent Quinn had assigned to compile information, Steve Bartlett, had pulled together a timeline of the murder, including the details Owen had provided to Quinn over the phone.

The coroner would narrow down the time of death, but witness testimony suggested that he'd been killed between two thirty, when his father had talked to him briefly as the groom was dressing, and around three thirty, when the best man had stopped in the groom's dressing room for a last minute pep talk and found his body.

Tara had been abducted about ten minutes after three, which gave her only a partial alibi for the murder, unless the coroner could nail down a more precise time of death for Robert. Had her abduction been part of the murder plot? But why grab her? Why not just shoot her the way Robert had been shot?

Owen rubbed his gritty eyes. Adrenaline might be keeping his brain awake, but his body was aching with exhaustion. He needed rest. To give his brain a break so he'd be focused and clearheaded enough to make sense of the tangled threads that might—or might not—connect the abduction and the murder.

The only thing Owen was sure about was his own involvement. He wouldn't have been anywhere near Tara and her kidnappers if she hadn't made that phone call to him. He had been in the church vestibule with the bridesmaids and would have remained there until Tara arrived for the start of the ceremony.

He had been collateral damage. Tara had been the target.

But why?

"I couldn't sleep."

His keyed-up nerves jumped at the sound of Tara's voice behind him. He swiveled his chair to look at her and felt an immediate jolt to his libido.

Her dark hair, still damp from the shower, fell in tousled waves over her shoulders. She'd found a long-sleeved T-shirt that fit snugly over her curves. It was thin enough for him to see that she wasn't wearing a bra.

He forced his gaze down to the slim fit of the gray yoga pants that revealed the rest of her curves, the well-toned thighs and shapely calves. She was always worrying that she was a little too curvy, but he thought she was perfect. Soft and sleek in all the right places.

"I couldn't sleep, either." He had a lot of practice suppressing his desire for her. He put it to use now, ignoring the stirring sensation in his jeans and concentrating on the fleeting expressions crossing Tara's face.

She had never been one to wear her feelings on her sleeve, and over the years she'd gotten pretty good at hiding her thoughts, even from him. He wasn't sure now if he could read her emotions, but she couldn't hide the sadness shadowing her green eyes.

He crossed to where she stood and waited. If she wanted his comfort, she'd take it.

She caught one of his hands in hers, a fleeting brush of

her fingers across his. Then she dropped her hand back to her side. "I wonder if the story has made the local news," she murmured, wandering toward the hallway.

He followed her into the front room, where she sat on the sofa, picked up the remote on the coffee table and turned on the TV. He settled beside her as she started flipping channels, looking for a local news station.

He hated to tell her the story might already have made the national cable news channels by now. It was sensational enough to draw the attention of news directors looking for stories to fill their twenty-four-hour formats.

He was right. She settled on one of the cable news stations, her attention arrested by a photograph of her own face filling the screen. "Fugitive Bride" was the graphic that filled the bottom of the screen in big, blocky letters.

"Oh, lovely," she muttered.

Unfortunately, the cable station didn't have any extra information about Robert Mallory's murder, though there was plenty of innuendo about the bride's untimely disappearance. The newsreader skirted the edge of libel. Barely.

As the news host moved on to a different story, Tara turned off the TV and lowered her head to her hands. "Robert's parents must be distraught."

"I'm sure they are."

"They must believe I killed him. It's what everyone believes, right?"

"No, of course not. No one who knows you believes that."

"Not that many people know me. Do they?"

He wanted to contradict her, but what she said was true. Tara had never made it easy for people to get to know her. Even Owen, who'd been her closest friend since childhood, knew there were pieces of herself she didn't share with him and probably never would.

She was good at her job as an analyst for a global security think tank based in Brody, Virginia, just across the state line. But how many of her colleagues there really knew her? They knew her qualifications, her educational background, her experience in security analysis gained working for a defense contractor for several years right out of college.

But did they know what she liked to do when she was home alone? Did they know she was a sucker for kittens, dark chocolate and flannel pajamas? Did they know that she made lists she wouldn't throw away until she'd marked off everything written there?

Did they know there was no way in hell she'd ever have killed Robert Mallory?

"Why would someone kill Robert and kidnap you?" he asked aloud.

"I don't know."

"It seems weird, doesn't it? Kidnapping you might have made sense if they were looking for ransom. I know you said Robert wasn't rich enough for kidnapping for ransom to make sense, but his parents are. So I could see the kidnappers pressuring Robert to pay up for your release, if they knew he could ask his parents for money."

"But instead, Robert was murdered. By the same people?"

"Obviously not the same people as our kidnappers, but maybe someone they were working with?"

"But why?" Tara asked. "If kidnapping me was to collect a ransom, why on earth did they kill Robert?"

"I don't know," Owen admitted, turning to face her. He took her hands in his, squeezing them firmly. "But I promise you this—we're going to figure this out. And we're going to make sure nothing like this happens to you again."

She gave him a look somewhere between love and pity before she released his hands and rose from the sofa. She crossed to the window and gazed out at the sun-bleached lawn that stretched from the side of the house to the sheltering oaks encroaching on the farm yard.

She looked terribly, tragically alone. And not for the first time in his life, Owen wondered if she'd ever really let anyone inside her circle of one.

THE WARRANT IN HAND gave Archer Trask and his team the right to search Tara Jane Bentley's small bungalow for any firearm she might own. As she was already a person of interest in a murder, he did not have to announce his presence before forcing entry, since doing so might give her time to flee if she was inside the home. But when he opened the front door, all optimistic notions of finding Tara Bentley hiding out at home went out the window.

The place had been trashed, top to bottom, and from the faintly sour smell in the kitchen, where the refrigerator contents lay in a spilled or broken mess across the tile floor, it hadn't happened in the past few hours.

Next to him, one of the deputies uttered a succinct profanity.

Trask got on his radio and ordered a crime scene unit to meet him at Tara Bentley's house. He didn't know if this destruction had anything to do with what had happened to Robert Mallory, but someone had tossed this place, clearly looking for something.

But what? What secrets was Ms. Bentley keeping? And did those secrets have anything to do with Mallory's death?

He stepped gingerly back through the living room at the front of the house, pausing as a framed photograph lying on the floor caught his eye. The glass was cracked, but the photo remained intact. Dark-haired Tara Bentley, grinning at the camera, leaning head-to-head with a dark-haired man with sharp blue eyes. His smile was a little less exuberant than hers, but he was clearly happy to be with her.

"Owen Stiles," Trask murmured.

"Sir?" a passing deputy asked.

"Stiles," he repeated, showing the man the photograph. "Bentley's partner in crime."

"You think the bride killed the groom and ran off with the best man?"

"Not the best man. The man of honor. He was standing up for the bride, not the groom." Trask put the photograph back on the floor where he'd found it and walked out the front door, motioning for the other deputies to follow him. They crossed back to their vehicles to wait for the crime scene unit to arrive.

Leaning against the front panel of his unmarked sedan, Trask pulled out his phone and dialed a number. A deep-voiced man with a distinctive drawl answered on the second ring. "Heller."

"Mr. Heller, it's Archer Trask. We met back in December when I was looking into the threats against Charlie Winters."

Heller's voice was wary. "I remember."

"I need to talk to you about one of your employees, Owen Stiles. I can be there later today, if you can see me?"

There was a brief pause. "Of course. Three o'clock?"

"I'll be there." He pocketed his phone and looked around the neat property, trying to picture Tara Bentley there. The place was small but well maintained. He suspected the house would have been the same if someone hadn't trashed it.

"What were they looking for, Tara?" he murmured aloud. *And where are you now?*

Chapter Five

The blank notepad on the desk in front of her seemed to be taunting her. With a grimace, Tara picked up her pen and wrote a single word across the top of the pad: *Why?*

Why had those two men kidnapped her? Why had someone killed Robert? Were the two events connected?

Surely they had to be. It would be too much of a coincidence if they weren't.

She wrote those two questions beneath the header. Below that, she wrote another word: *What?*

What had the kidnappers wanted from her? What had they been planning to do with her? Ask for a ransom? Trade her for someone else, like a hostage exchange? If so, for whom?

A quiet knock on the bedroom door set her nerves rattling. "Come in," she called, turning to watch Owen enter her bedroom.

"I thought you were going to take a nap," he said.

"I tried," she lied. She hadn't tried, because the questions swirling through her head wouldn't let her rest.

The look Owen sent her way suggested he knew she was lying, but he didn't call her on it. Instead, he sat on the edge of the bed and leaned toward the desk beside it. "Making lists?"

"It's what I do."

His lips curved in a half smile, carving distinguished lines in his handsome face. He really had no idea how beautiful a man he was, but she knew. He'd been something of a late bloomer, growing into his lanky frame and thin, serious face. By the time adulthood had fulfilled the nascent promise of good looks that had only occasionally flashed into view during his awkward adolescence, his quiet nature and tendency toward shyness had already left an indelible mark on his personality.

He was brilliant at his work as a computer wizard, possibly because of his tendency to hide behind the computer screen, where he was the king of his own little world. His circle of close friends was even smaller than Tara's, and hers wasn't exactly expansive. In fact, Robert Mallory had been the first person she'd let get close to her in years. And now that he was gone, she was feeling a crushing amount of guilt at having led him on when she was beginning to admit to herself that she'd never really loved him the way she'd claimed to.

Owen picked up the notepad. "You think your kidnapping and Robert's murder are connected?"

"Do you think it's likely they're not?"

He thought for a moment before replying. "No. But damned if I can figure out what the connection might be."

Tara rubbed her gritty eyes. "That's where I am. I have no idea why anyone would have abducted me. Ransom is the usual reason, but if that was the motive, why on earth would someone kill the only person with the potential to supply the money?"

Owen's gaze narrowed. "These are the thoughts keeping you from sleep?"

She frowned. "You think that's strange?"

"I think you're avoiding what's really driving your unease."

Here we go, she thought. Owen was going to psycho-analyze her again. As usual. She leaned back in her chair and folded her arms across her chest. "I suppose you're going to tell me what I'm avoiding?"

His lips pressed into a thin line of annoyance, as she'd known they would. But his irritation didn't deter him. "Your fiancé was murdered today. You were kidnapped, rather roughly, if those bruises on your arms are any in-dication. But rather than deal with the fear and grief you must be feeling, you're making lists." He picked up the notepad and flipped it onto the bed beside him. "This is what you always do."

"And this is what you always do," she snapped, snatch-ing the notepad from the bed and putting it back on the desk in front of her. "You think you know what I'm feel-ing and when I tell you you're wrong, you tell me I'm sub-limating my emotions or something."

"Because you are."

"Says you."

"Yes," he said.

Infuriating man! She turned back to the desk and picked up her pen, determined to shut out him and his unsolic-ited opinions.

"I'm sorry," he said a moment later, after she'd struggled without any luck to come up with another entry for her list. "I've known you so long, I tend to think I know ev-erything you're thinking or feeling, but obviously, I don't. So why don't you tell me about your list?"

Even though she suspected his apology was just a back-door attempt to get back to his psychoanalysis of her emo-tional state, she hated when she and Owen were at odds, so she handed him the list she'd made. "Like I said, I think my kidnapping and Robert's murder have to be connected. But I don't know how."

He read over her jotted notes. "Good questions," he noted with a faint quirk of his lips. "I'll tell you what sticks out to me, if you like."

She waved her hand at him. "Please."

"What *did* they want from you? If you're right, and Robert's murder was connected to your kidnapping, then I don't think ransom could be the motive for your kidnapping."

"Agreed."

"So what would they have accomplished by kidnapping you?"

"I don't know."

"You don't have money. You're not a romantic rival someone needs to get out of the way—if Robert had some obsessive stalker, she'd have kidnapped you by herself, not hired two thugs to take you, and she probably wouldn't have killed Robert, at least not this early in the game."

"Your mind works in some really scary ways," Tara muttered.

His smile was a little wider that time. "It's part of my charm."

"Okay, so no ransom, no crazy jealous chick."

"You do have one thing that someone might want," Owen said after a brief pause. "Your work."

She frowned. "But how many people really know what I do? Most of my friends think I'm a systems analyst, and frankly, they don't know or care what that is anyway."

"But you're a systems analyst for one of the top security and intelligence think tanks in the country—the world, in fact. And more to the point, you have a pretty astounding security clearance level for a civilian contractor. I'm your best friend in the world, and even I don't know exactly what it is you and your company are planning these days, except that it must be pretty damn big if you couldn't take a couple of weeks off for a honeymoon."

Owen was right. The project she was working on these days was huge and considered top secret in her company. Only a few people she worked with knew what her part of the job entailed, and that was on purpose, since she had been tasked with planning a supersecret security symposium that would be drawing some of the highest-ranking security and intelligence officers from friendly—and even a few not-so-friendly—nations across the globe. Not even her fiancé, Robert, knew the full scope of what she was doing these days, though he'd been insatiably curious.

She frowned, a terrible thought occurring to her. "What if Robert was killed in an attempt to find out what I was doing for my company?"

"You mean they tried to get information from him and something went wrong?"

She swallowed with difficulty. "Or they realized he didn't know anything and wasn't any use to them, so…"

"They killed him," Owen finished for her. "I suppose it's possible, if your job is really what's behind what happened today."

She rubbed her neck, where tension was building into coiling snakes of pain. "I'm so tired I can't think, but I can't seem to turn my brain off."

Owen reached out and caught her hand. "I'll give you a neck rub. That'll help, won't it?"

She met his gaze, seeing no guile there. Owen wasn't like most other men. His offers of kindness had no ulterior motives. That was one of the reasons she trusted him in a way she'd never trusted anyone else in her life, not even Robert. To Owen, a neck rub was just a neck rub.

She turned her chair until her back was in front of him. The elastic band holding her ponytail had slipped a little, so she reached up and tightened it, giving him a clear view of her neck.

A moment passed before his hands touched her neck. They were neither hot nor cold, just pleasantly warm against her flesh. He eased his way into the massage, first with light strokes that sent minute shivers rippling down her spine. But soon, his fingers pressed deeper into her muscles, eliciting a flood of pleasure-pain that sent tremors rumbling low in her belly.

A neck rub might just be a neck rub for Owen, she realized, but it had never been, and never would be, just a neck rub for her.

He wasn't anywhere near the perfect man of her wish list. He was too much the introvert, too prone to shutting out the world and burrowing into his own head when he got interested in a project. He lacked the driving ambition that might have made him the next Steve Jobs or Elon Musk. His occasional social awkwardness, which seemed to hit him at the worst possible moments, was such a contrast to the sort of social charm and ease that Robert Mallory had checked off her must-have list.

And yet he was deliciously sexy in the way that a really smart, really decent man could be. He had a wicked sense of humor and a delight in all things absurd that always seemed to be able to bring her out of even the worst mood, on those days when the weight of her world seemed insupportable. His intensely blue eyes could mesmerize her when he was talking about something he was passionate about, whether it was some intricacy of computer science she couldn't understand or his love of baseball, an obsession they shared.

And his hands. He had the best hands, long-fingered and strong, with a deft dexterity that could turn a simple neck rub into pure seduction.

"Are you being nice to me now to make up for pissing me off earlier?" She kept her tone intentionally light, struggling against his spell.

His low voice hummed against her skin. "Is it working?"

Spectacularly, she thought. "If I say yes, you might not try as hard."

"Nonsense. I always strive to do my best."

If he were anyone but Owen, she'd be seriously contemplating sex right about now, she realized. But he was Owen, and Owen was off-limits, so she eased away from his touch. "That was just what I needed. I think maybe I can get a little sleep now."

As she'd known he would, Owen stepped away from the bed. "You do that. I'll try to get some sleep myself and then if you're awake in a few hours, we'll see about something for supper."

Impulsively, she caught his hand as he turned to go and pulled him into a tight hug. His arms enfolded her, strong to her unexpectedly weak.

"It's going to be all right," he murmured against her temple. "We'll figure all this out, I promise."

She let go and covered her emotion with a soft laugh. "We've had our share of figuring our way out of trouble, haven't we?"

He gave her ponytail a light tug. "Tara and Owen, the terrors of Mercerville."

"That was mostly me," she said wryly.

He smiled. "True."

She watched him leave the room and close the door behind him, feeling suddenly, terribly alone.

MADDOX HELLER WAS not alone in his office when Archer Trask arrived for their meeting. He took in the three people sitting in the small office space with unexpected trepidation, for he wasn't a man easily intimidated. But Heller had called in the other two chief officers of Campbell Cove Security, the enigmatic Alexander Quinn, a former CIA agent and a man who seemed to grow inexplicably more mysterious with each revelation about his past; and the elegant and beautiful Rebecca Cameron, a woman who Archer Trask knew primarily by her reputation as an accomplished diplomat and a brilliant historian. It was she who rose to greet him, extending her graceful, long-fingered hand for a shake.

"I hope you don't mind if Alexander and I join the meeting," she said with a friendly smile that brought sparkles to her dark eyes and carved handsome curves in her otherwise ageless face. She smelled good, Trask thought, her scent delicate but intoxicating. She was probably his elder by at least five or six years, but she had a youthful grace that made him feel ancient next to her.

"Saves you the trouble of questioning us separately," Maddox drawled, flashing a quicksilver smile that Trask didn't quite buy.

More like prevents me from separating you in the effort to catch you in a discrepancy, he thought. He took the seat Maddox offered, situated in front of their chairs, subtly surrounded by them.

As if he were the one being questioned.

"How long has Owen Stiles worked for your company?" he asked before someone could interrupt to offer him coffee or some other distraction.

"Almost a year now," Quinn answered. "He was one of our earliest hires and has worked out very well."

"He's in your IT department?" Trask asked, knowing it was a leading question. He already knew Stiles worked in Cybersecurity, although even his best intel hadn't managed to uncover exactly what cybersecurity meant to a company like Campbell Cove Security. Was he an analyst? Or was he a white hat hacker of some sort?

Or perhaps both?

"He's in Cybersecurity," Quinn answered blandly. "He analyzes security threats in both government and civilian networks and comes up with solutions to close the gaps that terrorists try to exploit."

Quinn came across as open and honest on the surface, but Trask didn't buy it. The only problem was, he wasn't sure Quinn was actually lying. He might be telling the truth, or he might be leaving out something important. Trask honestly couldn't tell.

"Do you have any idea where he is now?"

"No," Quinn answered. "We've been trying to find him, as you can imagine. He's vital to our work here, and his disappearance is troubling."

Trask narrowed his eyes, looking past Quinn to Rebecca Cameron. Her expression was as placid as the surface of a lake on a still day, reflecting her surroundings more than revealing anything beneath the surface. As for Maddox Heller, he simply shot Trask a look that was somewhere between a smile and a smirk, as if he knew exactly how frustrating this interview was turning out to be.

Clearly, they had circled the wagons around their employee, and nothing Trask asked in this particular interview would cause them to break ranks. So he changed direction.

"Do you know Tara Bentley?"

He spotted a slight flicker in Heller's expression before he pasted on that smirky smile again. "She asked Owen to be her man of honor in her wedding, so I know they're good friends."

"I believe they grew up together," Quinn offered blandly.

"Since middle school, didn't Owen say?" Cameron offered. "Sweet, to have stayed friends so many years, don't you think?"

"Have any of you met her?"

"Briefly, I think. She's come by to take him to lunch a couple of times, hasn't she?" Cameron smiled at her co-workers.

"But other than that, you know nothing about her?"

There wasn't even the briefest of pauses before Alexander Quinn answered, "No. Nothing at all."

OWEN HAD GONE to his bedroom with good intentions, but moments after he'd stretched out on the bed, the call of his computer overcame his weariness. Planting himself in front of the computer array, he considered his options.

Something had been bothering him since Maddox Heller rescued him and Tara from the road near the old Boy Scout camp. At the time, he'd been too wet, tired and hungry to ask any questions, but now that he was dry and warm, with a light lunch still filling his belly, he'd had time to realize something wasn't quite right about the situation.

For one thing, Maddox Heller had asked almost nothing about what had happened to them. He'd taken Owen's terse explanation over the phone at face value, asking no questions of any import. He'd simply accepted that Tara and Owen must be telling the truth, no matter how strange the circumstances of their abduction and despite the utter dearth of proof of their story.

Yes, he'd been their employee for a year now, but he knew that if one of the people working under him in the Cybersecurity section at Campbell Cove Security had come to him with such a strange story, he'd have asked a few more questions himself.

So why hadn't Heller?

He bypassed the normal remote desktop access to his work computer and instead decided to exploit a back door he'd created to anonymously monitor any computer activity company-wide. But to his astonishment, he found that his back door was blocked.

What the hell? Had Quinn ordered his full network access to be revoked? Why? Did he suspect Owen of something nefarious after all?

Maybe that was why Heller hadn't asked any extra questions. Maybe they were trying to contain Owen and Tara, keeping them under control in the secluded little safe house until they could finish an investigation.

He kept digging, trying other potential network access points until he managed to get back into the system through another narrow gap in security. It wouldn't take long for someone to notice the network intrusion, so he had to work fast before he was detected.

He went right to the most likely source of information—Alexander Quinn. If anything worth knowing about was going on at Campbell Cove Security, Alexander Quinn would know about it.

He was running out of time, fast, when he stumbled across a file about five levels deep in his user directory. It was hidden among Quinn's download files, though the file itself seemed to have been created in the directory rather than downloaded.

What caught Owen's eye was the file name: Jane0216.

Jane was Tara's middle name. And February 16 was her birthday.

Acutely aware of the ticking clock, Owen quickly copied the file to his personal cloud server account and backed out of the network. He was pretty sure his intrusion hadn't been detected; he'd seen no signs of anyone trying to block him out. He made a mental note to shore up the security for the network entry point as soon as he could. And he was going to do a little digging around when he got a chance to see how the cybersecurity team at Campbell Cove Security had blocked him out of his usual entry point.

But first he wanted a look at that mysterious file.

It was password protected, of course. But one of the courses Owen taught at Campbell Cove Academy was on password cracking for law enforcement. In fact, Owen had written a program for password cracking, using a set of queries that helped create a list of likely passwords based on an individual's unique set of personal connections and statistics. Of course, Quinn posed a particular problem, since both his past and present were shrouded in mystery. Owen was too smart to use the usual password prompts, but with a little creative thinking, combined with his knowledge of Quinn's past exploits, he managed to sniff out the password in a couple of hours.

"'DaresSalaamNairobi_080798,'" he read aloud with a satisfied smile. The boss had made a mistake after all, using a seminal moment in his history as a CIA agent to create his password. Quinn had once told Owen that it was August 7, 1998, not September 11, 2001, that had been the real start of Osama bin Laden's war against the United States. "He and Zawahiri killed over two hundred people in those attacks on our embassies in Tanzania and Kenya, including friends of mine. But it happened halfway around the world, so people just didn't pay attention, even though the intelligence community was practically screaming for them to wake up."

Holding his breath, Owen opened the file.

It was a background check on Tara Bentley, he saw. Detailed and intrusive, chronicling her life back to childhood. It appeared to cover all the details Owen knew about Tara and a few he didn't.

"What on earth is that?"

Tara's voice, shockingly close behind him, made him jump. He whirled around in his desk chair to look at her and found her staring at the computer screen, her eyes wide with horror.

"You have a file on me?" she asked, her pained gaze meeting his.

"Not me," he said, reaching out to take her hand, overwhelmed by the need to connect with her before she withdrew from him completely. "This isn't my file. I found it on the Campbell Cove Security network. Specifically, on my boss's computer."

"Maddox Heller?" she asked, her expression still a vivid picture of dismay. She felt violated, Owen knew, and he didn't blame her.

"No. Alexander Quinn."

"The CIA guy?" She looked confused. "Why would he be keeping a dossier on me?"

"That," Owen said, "is what we're going to find out."

Chapter Six

Weekends weren't technically days off at Campbell Cove Security. Most of the security experts who worked for the company had signed on knowing they were on call 24/7. But Alexander Quinn wasn't a heartless beast, despite his reputation. He knew several of his agents were married and many had children, and he had already seen the murky world he and his fellow agents navigated rip apart too many marriages and families. After the meeting with Archer Trask, he'd sent Heller home to his pretty wife and adorable children, and even Becky Cameron had wandered off to do whatever it was she did on her time off.

His part of the building was very quiet, though he knew there were a few classes going on in the academy section and some of the unmarried employees actually preferred to work weekends and take their days off during the week. Now and then he heard the faint tap of footsteps down a distant hall or the muffled shout coming from the academy wing, but he seemed to have the executive office area to himself.

Which was why the sound of a ding on the computer behind him sent a frisson of alarm racing through his nervous system.

He turned to look at the computer and found a query box blinking back at him.

"Why do you have a file on Tara Bentley?"

His eyes narrowing, he tapped an answer on his keyboard. "Because she's important to you."

There was a long pause before another message popped onto the screen.

"Do you know why she was kidnapped?"

How to answer that question? In truth, while Quinn had some ideas what might be behind the woman's abduction, he didn't know anything for sure. Her work at the Security Strategies Foundation was, in part, classified, requiring a certain level of security clearance.

Technically, based on his own company's contract with the US government, Quinn's clearance was sufficient to access that level of information, but there were protocols of information sharing that would take time to work through. And unless the government deemed the situation to be a national security risk, Security Solutions could always refuse to share the information.

"I have ideas," he finally typed.

After another significant pause, another message appeared on screen. "You didn't supply us with phones. Why?"

Quinn didn't suppose Owen would buy the idea that he'd just forgotten about phones. So he told the truth. "I didn't want the two of you to try to contact anyone on the outside."

Owen's next message was blunt. "Because you haven't decided what to do with us?"

Exactly. But Owen had a point. Talking to him on the computer, without the benefit of hearing the tone of his voice, was less than informative.

"I'm coming to see you in person," he typed. "I will explain everything and we can talk strategies. I'll be there in an hour. Now get off my computer."

He waited for a reply, but no more dialogue boxes appeared on his computer screen. He finally turned back to his desk and picked up his cell phone.

Becky Cameron answered on the second ring. "Not a good time."

"I'm going to go see our guests. Don't suppose you'd like to join us?"

There was a protracted pause, then a sigh. "Actually, I'd love to. But I can't. I'm in the middle of something and can't get away. But I'm very curious to hear your thoughts about the situation. Maybe we could meet tomorrow evening? I was thinking about driving into Whitesburg to try that new Greek restaurant that just opened."

Quinn raised an eyebrow. Becky was an old friend, one of his closest, in fact, but she was almost militantly protective of her private life. He supposed she might see the dinner invitation as just a way to combine work with her need for food, but driving all the way to Whitesburg seemed a little more personal than that.

"I can meet you there," he said, more curious than he liked to admit. "Seven?"

"Perfect. I'll see you there and you can catch me up."

She had to know they couldn't talk about Owen Stiles and Tara Bentley in public that way. So what was she up to?

Despite his reputation for embracing all things enigmatic, Quinn really didn't like a mystery, especially when it involved one of his closest colleagues.

"Do you trust him?" Tara managed not to nibble her thumbnail as she waited for Owen's reply. She'd spent most of her teen years trying to break her nail-biting habit and she'd be danged if she started doing it again now. She might be hiding from both kidnappers and the law, but that was no excuse for bad grooming.

"I don't know."

Owen was cleaning the kitchen counters, even though they were virtually spotless. It was his version of nail biting, she supposed, though he generally fine-tuned his computer rather than cleaned the house when he was puzzling over a troubling problem. She supposed the new computer system was too state-of-the-art to provide him quite enough distraction for their current dilemma.

"That's not reassuring," she said.

He stopped wiping the counter long enough to offer her a halfhearted grin. "I know."

"He used to be with the CIA. Which could be a good thing or a very bad thing."

"The problem with Quinn, in my admittedly limited experience, is that he's a big-picture guy. He's going to look out for the country first, his company next and then individuals fall in line behind those two things. Which is why I began to suspect Quinn may think what happened to us is connected to something bigger."

Such as the symposium she was supposed to be planning. The event so important that she and Robert had planned to postpone their honeymoon until late summer so she could get things done.

Tara perched on the bar stool in front of the counter Owen had resumed cleaning, taking care not to leave fingerprints on the nice, shiny surface. "There's something I've been doing at work that has been my entire focus for months now. Nobody else knows all the details except for me and the company's operating officers. Now I'm no longer there to do the job. What does that do to the equation?"

"You tell me." Owen stopped wiping and draped the towel over the edge of the sink. "If something happens to you, who takes over your job?"

"It would have to be one of the three partners. They were very careful to keep all the information about my project secret, with good reason."

Curiosity gleamed in his bright blue eyes, but he didn't ask her anything about her project. "So that's why you postponed the honeymoon."

"Yes."

"Could someone outside the company know what you were planning?" he asked.

"Yes, of course. It involves other people outside the company, and any of them could have experienced an intelligence leak. But that's one reason why the details of the project were so closely guarded. Even if someone found out what was going on, they wouldn't have the vital details to work with because those details won't be settled until about a week before it comes together."

"So it's an event."

"Owen, I can't tell you anything else. I'm sorry."

He smiled. "Understood. But if it's an event, then perhaps someone wants to sabotage it in some way. Would that be a possibility?"

She didn't reply, but Owen's expression suggested he'd read the answer in her face.

"Maybe that was the point of the abduction," he suggested. "To get the information out of you under duress. Or am I being too dramatic here?"

"It's possible," she admitted. "Without going into details, it's very possible that someone would like to get his hands on the information I have. I'm a more vulnerable target than any of the directors of the company would be, and nobody else has the information."

At the time the directors had approached her to run the project, she was over-the-moon delighted about the responsibility, knowing it meant the company valued her organizational and analytical skills as well as her reliability and discretion. While she'd consulted with the directors regularly, they'd allowed her to take the reins as far as planning the logistics of the symposium was concerned. She'd been the point person with all the countries and dignitaries invited, the face of their very prestigious think tank.

But now she was beginning to realize the steep price that such a high-profile position of authority could exact. The job had quite possibly made her a target.

She might still be a target, she realized. Her disappearance and the mystery surrounding Robert's murder would likely cause her bosses to shore up their already tight security. The kidnappers would have a difficult time getting through their defenses.

But she was still largely defenseless. If Owen hadn't come to her aid, she probably wouldn't have been able to escape the kidnappers. But even that situation had been nothing more than pure luck. The kidnappers had underestimated their resourcefulness, and they hadn't prepared for Owen's surprise arrival. They'd also been sloppy, binding her hands in front of her instead of behind her. She doubted they'd be that careless a second time.

While she'd been pondering her vulnerability, Owen had put up the cleaning supplies and washed his hands in the sink. He turned to her now, drying his hands on a paper towel, his eyes narrowed. It was his "I wonder what you're thinking" expression, and she realized that she was far more tempted right now to tell him everything about her secret project than she'd ever been with Robert.

She supposed that was the difference between a whirlwind romance and twenty years of enduring and unbreakable friendship. That fact only made her more certain than ever that she'd made the right choice when she began feeling attracted to Owen. Boyfriends were unpredictable and, in her experience, undependable.

Owen was her rock. It was a mistake to sleep with your rock.

Wasn't it?

A sharp rap on the door rattled her nerves. Owen tossed the paper towel in the waste bin and headed for the front door. Tara trailed behind him, her heart pounding with anxiety.

Owen checked the security lens. "It's Quinn. You ready?"

Tara took a couple of deep, bracing breaths and nodded. "Ready."

Owen opened the door to a broad-shouldered man with sandy hair and intelligent eyes the color of dried moss. He wore a neatly groomed beard a couple of shades darker than his hair and liberally sprinkled with silver. He looked to be in his midforties, but in his eyes Tara saw an old soul, a man whose life had been one struggle after another. The weight of the world was reflected not in lines on his face but in the shadowy depths of those hazel-green eyes.

He was dangerous, Tara realized with a flutter of alarm. But he also seemed like someone who'd be invaluable in a fight, as long as you were on the same side.

He was not an enemy she wanted to make.

"You must be Tara Bentley." Quinn shook hands with a firm, brisk grip. "I've heard a good deal about you."

"You've mean you've snooped around my life and uncovered a great deal about me," Tara corrected, her voice edged with tart disapproval.

"Fair enough." Quinn nodded toward the sofa. "Shall we sit and talk?"

TARA SAT IN the armchair, leaving Quinn and Owen to share the sofa. It put her at a slightly elevated angle, which made her feel more in control of the situation. "Do you know why we were kidnapped?"

Quinn's lips quirked slightly. It wasn't quite a smile, but there was a hint of humor in his eyes. "I believe it might have something to do with your work at Security Solutions."

"And why was Robert killed?"

"I don't know." His voice softened. "My condolences on your loss."

"Thank you."

"What do you know about my job?" Tara asked.

"I contacted your company directors and explained my concerns about my cybersecurity director disappearing along with their top analyst. We had an illuminating discussion about the work you've been doing."

"Why would they tell you anything illuminating?" Tara asked, wary of being tricked into revealing more than she should.

"Because I have a security clearance as high as theirs. I'm a security contractor for the government. I know things that few federal employees know about the government's security apparatus."

"Do I need to go take a walk so you can speak freely?" Owen asked, starting to rise.

"No," Quinn said. "Your own security clearance is high enough for you to hear what Ms. Bentley and I have to say."

"You first," Tara said as Owen sat again.

The quirk returned to Quinn's lips, a little broader this time. Definitely his version of a smile, Tara thought. He inclined his head slightly toward Tara before he spoke. "Your bosses didn't give me the details of the project, of course, for the sake of situational security. But I know that you're planning a global symposium on new terror tactics and strategies for preventing them from succeeding.

You've invited over seventy nations to participate. I don't know where or even when the meeting will take place, but I know it's going to happen on US soil, and someone very much wants to know the details."

"Which is why they kidnapped Tara," Owen murmured.

"Yes." Quinn looked at Tara, his expression hard to read. "You are the most wanted woman in a lot of terror-sponsoring countries. Any number of groups, foreign and domestic, would love to get their hands on the information you know. Your bosses at Security Solutions don't know why or how you disappeared, so obviously they're deeply worried. It's not just the local authorities who are looking for you."

"I have to turn myself in, then," Tara said.

Quinn cleared his throat before he spoke. "That does seem to be the best course of action."

"I didn't kill Robert."

"I know that. And there's no evidence to connect you to his murder. I think at this point, you're primarily wanted for questioning, just to clear up why you disappeared and where you've been."

"We can't provide any evidence of what happened to us," Owen warned. "All we have is our word."

"And you're not a disinterested witness," Quinn agreed. "But neither of you has any reason to kill Robert. Since no marriage had taken place, there's no profit motive for Ms. Bentley. There's not a whiff of conflict between the two of you, according to interviews with Robert's family and your friends. It's not like you and Owen are secret lovers who killed your fiancé so you could run away together."

Tara glanced at Owen. "No."

There was a flicker of something in Quinn's eyes as he looked from her to Owen. "Is there anything I need to know about the events of yesterday that either of you haven't already told me?"

"There is one thing," Tara said, "although nobody knows about it but Owen and me. I was planning to call off the wedding right before I was abducted."

"I see."

"Owen didn't know beforehand," she added. "I didn't tell him until after we escaped."

"I suspected," Owen said. "She called me and—"

"The less I know about that, the better," Quinn interrupted. "If you don't have a lawyer, Campbell Cove Security can provide one."

"Thank you. That would be helpful," Tara said. "How will this work?"

"I think, because of the threats against your life, we shouldn't schedule the time to turn yourself in. You, Owen and the lawyer will show up unannounced at the Bagley County Sheriff's Department and ask for Deputy Archer Trask, the investigator in charge of the Robert Mallory homicide investigation. The element of surprise will be your best safeguard against a repeat of yesterday's abduction attempt."

Tara glanced at Owen. He met her gaze with an almost imperceptible nod. She looked at Quinn again. "Okay. That sounds good."

"Tomorrow morning would be best. Get a good night's sleep, take time to shower, shave and dress in your Sunday best. You're the victims, not the perpetrators. You need to be confident and at ease. I'll return in the morning with your lawyer, we'll go over the case and then we'll drive you to town."

"Sounds like a plan," Owen said with a faint smile.

Quinn flashed that half quirk of a smile toward Owen. "You did well, under difficult circumstances. We will get you both through the rest of this."

"Thank you."

She and Owen walked with Quinn to the door. He turned in the open doorway, his features dark and indistinct against the bright afternoon sun. "We'll do everything in our power to protect you, Ms. Bentley. Know that."

"Thank you. I appreciate it." She watched, her heart thudding heavily in her chest, as if his words had been a warning instead of a promise.

She was a target. She'd known the possibility existed, but until Quinn had said the words aloud, the notion had been just that. A notion, something possible but not certain.

Now the cloud of threat hanging over her head felt heavy with foreboding, as if she were trapped without any hope of escape.

The touch of Owen's hands on her shoulders made her jump. She turned to look at him and felt the full intensity of his blue-eyed gaze.

"We will get through this. Tomorrow, we'll turn ourselves in and the police will protect you."

"What if they can't? It's a small county in a small state. They're not prepared or trained to provide protection from determined terrorists."

"Then Quinn will put agents in place to watch your back." The visit from his boss had apparently shored up Owen's defenses. He sounded strong and confident, and the firmness of his grip on her shoulders seemed to transfer that sense of strength into her, so that by the time he let her go and nodded for her to precede him into the hallway, she felt steadier herself.

Maybe everything really would be okay.

OWEN STOOD OUTSIDE the groom's room, trying to gather his courage to go inside. On the other side of the door stood the man who was about to take Tara away from him, and he was supposed to be wishing him good luck.

How could he do it? How could he shake Robert's hand and tell him to take care of the woman Owen loved more than anyone else in the world? How was he supposed to be okay with any of this?

Do it because Tara needs you to. Do it because it's the only way you'll be able to stay in her life.

His heart pounded wildly. His palms were damp with sweat. Though he'd met Robert dozens of times since he first started dating Tara, the man had remained little more than an acquaintance. There had always been a wary distance between them, as if Robert understood that Owen would never really be all right with his presence in Tara's life. And Robert would never truly be comfortable with how important Owen was to Tara, either.

But if they both wanted to stay in her life, they were going to have to create some sort of truce, however wary and fragile it might be.

He took a deep breath and reached for the door.

But a scraping noise from within the room stopped him midstep. The world around him seemed to disintegrate, and he was suddenly lying on his back, darkness pressing in one him, heavy and cold. It took a moment to realize he was in an unfamiliar bed in an unfamiliar place.

The safe house. He'd been dreaming. Groping for the small digital clock on the bedside table, he squinted to see the time. Only a little after eight, he saw with surprise.

As he rubbed his eyes, he heard another faint scrape of metal on metal. It seemed to be coming from the front of the house.

Tara? Maybe she hadn't been able to sleep.

But when he rose from the bed, he grabbed the unloaded Smith & Wesson .380 from the locked box he'd stashed in the bedside table drawer. He'd put the ammo in the dresser across the room, the way he'd been trained—don't keep the ammo with the gun. The rule had always seemed reasonable to him, as it would make it hard for an intruder to load the gun and use it against him. But now that he was trying to go out and face a potential threat, the extra step seemed to slow him down.

He had to protect Tara, even if it meant carrying a gun and facing the unknown.

Heart pounding wildly, he opened the bedroom door.

Chapter Seven

A furtive sound roused Tara from slumber. She sat upright in bed, her pulse roaring in her ears. Straining to hear past the whoosh of blood through her veins, she tried to remember what, exactly, she'd heard. Was it a scrape? A tap? It hadn't been as loud as a knock.

It's an old house, she told herself. Old houses made noise. A lot.

Then she heard the noise again. It was a scrape, like metal against metal. It came not from her room but from somewhere down the hall.

Someone trying to enter the front door?

Suddenly, Owen seemed an impossible distance away, even though his bedroom was just across the hall. She didn't think the sound was coming from there, but with her door closed, it was impossible to know for certain.

Owen had the gun. She hoped to goodness he really did know how to use it.

She eased her bedroom door open, holding her breath at the soft creak of the hinges. In the distance, thunder rumbled, and for a moment Tara wondered if it had been the gathering storm that had wakened her so suddenly. But it had barely been audible at all, certainly not loud enough to stir her from a dead sleep. And the noise she'd heard earlier definitely hadn't been thunder.

She slipped out into the hallway, the wood floors smooth and cool beneath her feet. The temperature had fallen along with the night, and she shivered as she crept across to Owen's room.

As she reached for the door handle, it twisted in her hand, startling her. She jerked back, stumbling over her own feet.

In the murky gloom, she felt as if she were tumbling backward into an abyss, the world turned upside down.

Then arms wrapped around her, stilling her fall. Owen's arms, his familiar scent unmistakable. He pulled her tightly to his bare chest, his own heart galloping beneath her ear as he held her close.

The moment seemed to stretch into infinity, as all her senses converged into an exquisite flood of desire. His skin was hot silk beneath her hands as she clutched his arms. He smelled like soap and Owen, a clean, masculine essence that had always made her feel safe and happy, even when the world around her was going crazy. The bristle of his crisp chest hair rasped against her breasts beneath the thin fabric of her tank top, bringing her nipples to hard, sensitive peaks.

She forced herself to shut down all those sensations, the way she'd been doing since she turned fifteen and began to realize that the gangly boy next door was becoming an attractive young man.

"Did you hear the noise?" Owen whispered, his voice barely breath against her hair.

She nodded.

He eased her away from him, and in the flash of lightning that strobed through the window at the end of the hall, she saw the gleam of gunmetal in his hand as he slipped down the hall toward the front of the house.

She stayed close behind him, unwilling to allow him to

confront whatever danger lurked ahead alone. She might not have been trained for danger the way he had been, but she was fit, she was resourceful and if she'd let herself admit it, she was also angry as all get-out.

She might not have loved Robert the way a wife should, but he was a good man. A sweet man. He hadn't deserved to die, and the thought that he'd taken a bullet because someone was after her made her want to break things. Starting with the killer's head.

Owen paused in the doorway to the living room, and Tara had to stumble to a sharp halt to keep from barreling into him. Reaching behind him, he caught her hand briefly, gave it a squeeze, then entered the larger room.

The scraping noise came again, louder this time. It was coming from outside the house.

"Stay here," Owen whispered urgently. "I need to know you're not in the line of fire."

Her instincts told her to ignore his command, but she made herself stay still, pressing her back against the living room wall as he edged closer to the front door and took a quick look through the peephole in the door.

He backed away, glancing back at her. He shook his head.

Outside, the wind had picked up again, moaning in the eaves. The first patter of rain on the metal roof overhead was loud enough to set Tara's nerves jangling. Owen crossed quietly to where she stood, rubbing her upper arms gently. "I'm pretty sure it's the wind rattling something outside. Maybe a loose gutter or a window screen. I don't see anyone lurking around."

"They wouldn't be out in the open, would they?"

"Probably not." He glanced back toward the door.

She followed his gaze. It was an ordinary wooden door, but somehow, in the dark, with her heart racing and her skin tingling, it seemed more like an ominous portal to a dangerous realm. "Someone could be trying to lure us outside."

"Or we could be letting our imaginations run away with us, the same way we used to do sneaking around Old Man Ridley's cabin twenty years ago," he countered. "I really do think it's just the wind."

She let out a huff of nervous laughter. "You're probably right."

"The only way to figure that out is to go outside and try to find the source of the sound. Do you want me to do that?"

Part of her wanted to say yes, just so she'd know one way or the other. But it was cold and rainy, and even if there were a threat outside, which she was starting to doubt, they were safer inside than outside.

"No," she said. "I think you're right. It's just the wind rattling something outside. I'm sorry for being such a scaredy-cat."

"You want to try going back to bed and ignoring all the creaks and scrapes outside?"

"Could we maybe light a fire here in the living room and camp out on the sofa instead?"

His lips curved. "We could do that. Let me grab a shirt and a blanket."

"I'll pop some popcorn," she said, starting to finally feel a little more relaxed.

Owen had a way of making everything a little easier to bear.

OWEN WOKE IN STAGES, first vaguely aware of light on the other side of his closed eyelids, then of a warm body tucked firmly against his side. Tara, he thought, his eyes still closed. He could smell the scent of shampoo in her hair and the elusive essence of the woman herself. The soft warmth of her body against his felt perfect and necessary, as if it were an extension of himself he couldn't bear to live without.

He opened his eyes to morning sunlight angling through the east-facing front windows of the farmhouse. He'd left his watch in the bedroom, but that much light had to mean the day was well under way.

Giving Tara a gentle nudge, he said, "Wake up, sleepyhead."

She grumbled and burrowed deeper into the cocoon formed by his side and the sofa.

"It's probably after eight. Quinn and the lawyer will be here soon."

She gave a muffled groan against his side and added a soft curse for emphasis. "I was having the best dream," she complained, lifting her head and looking at him through strands of her hair.

Even makeup-free, with her normally tidy brown hair mussed and tangled, and her morning breath not quite as sweet as the rest of her, she was still the most desirable woman he'd ever known. His morning erection became almost painfully hard.

She shook her hair away from her face and stared at him, too closely curled against his body to have missed his physical response to her nearness. He waited for her to make a joke and roll off the sofa to make her escape to the bedroom, but she didn't move, her eyes darkening as exquisite tension lengthened between them.

"I don't know what I'd do if I didn't have you," she whispered.

This was the point where he would crack a joke and make his escape, but he was pinned between her and the sofa. And even if he weren't, he didn't think he'd have been capable of moving away from her luscious heat, especially when she reached out with one slim hand and touched his jaw.

He couldn't find his voice. Didn't want to risk saying anything that would ruin this moment. It felt as if he were standing on the edge of a cliff, ready to jump into a beautiful void. What lay below might be a crystalline sea, cool and cleansing, with a whole universe of wonders and pleasures lying just beneath the surface. Or he might find himself dashed on sharp rocks to lie bleeding and dying for his gamble.

What was it going to be?

From somewhere in the back of the house, two alarm clocks went off with a loud, discordant blare.

Tara and Owen both laughed, snapping the tension of the moment. "We'd better get moving," she suggested, rolling off the sofa and straightening her tank top and shorts.

He pushed to his feet, shifting his own shorts to hide the worst of his erection. "How about scrambled eggs for breakfast?"

"We need something a little more decadent," she said, pausing in the doorway of her bedroom. "I'll make French toast."

Not exactly the sort of decadence he'd been thinking about when he woke up in her arms, but he could make do.

By the time he got out of the shower, he could smell eggs cooking from down the hallway. He laid out one of the suits he'd found in the closet, hoping it would fit, but went to the kitchen in fresh boxer shorts under a shin-length black silk robe.

"Are you worried about today?" she asked as she flipped a couple of the egg-crusted pieces of bread onto a plate and handed it to him.

"A little." He set the plate on the small breakfast nook

table and retrieved the bottle of syrup from the refrigerator. "I know we didn't do anything wrong, but we don't have any real proof of our story."

She brought her own plate of French toast to the table and sat across from him. "I have half a wedding dress."

"Which could have been torn in any number of ways." He handed her the syrup bottle. "But you really didn't have any motive to kill Robert."

"What if they think you did?"

He paused with his fork halfway to his mouth. Syrup dribbled on the table and he put down the fork and grabbed a napkin. "Because you and I are so close?"

"Best friends forever." She managed a weak smile. "You know people have always mistaken us as a couple. Ever since high school."

Their closeness had broken up more than one of his romantic relationships over the years. Not without reason. "But we've only ever been friends."

"Because we choose to be only friends. But we both know there's an attraction between us that we could build on if we ever chose it. Robert knew it. He just realized that I wasn't ever going to risk my friendship with you that way, so he didn't feel threatened." A cloud drifted over her expression. "He was remarkably understanding."

Owen wasn't sure that understanding would have lasted. Or that he could have allowed the status quo between him and Tara to continue once she was married.

Which, he supposed, *makes me a viable suspect in Robert's murder.*

THE LAWYER ALEXANDER QUINN provided was younger than Tara had expected. Anthony Giattina was tall, broad shouldered and sandy haired. He spoke with a mild southern accent and there was a sparkle in his brown eyes as he shook hands with her and Owen after Alexander Quinn's introduction.

"Call me Tony," he said. "I think we can get this handled with a minimum of fuss."

"Has Mr. Quinn told you what happened?"

"I told him I wanted to talk to each of you first. So I know the basics from news reports—your fiancé was murdered and you disappeared." His eyes softened. "My condolences."

"Thank you."

"We need to get on the road," Quinn interrupted. "You'll ride with Tony so you can talk in private. I'll follow." He nodded toward the two vehicles in the driveway and started walking toward them. He got behind the wheel of a large black SUV while Tony Giattina led them to a sleek silver Mercedes sedan parked behind Quinn's vehicle.

Owen waved Tara to the front seat and settled in the back behind her.

"So, from the beginning," Tony said after they were on the road. "Did either of you witness anything connected to Robert Mallory's murder?"

"No," Tara answered. "I didn't."

"I didn't, either," Owen said.

Tony's gaze flicked toward the backseat. "You sound uncertain."

"I saw him briefly when I arrived at the church," Owen said in a careful tone that made Tara turn to look at him, as well. "I was planning to talk to him before the wedding. Wish him well, that sort of thing. But I got the call from Tara before I could enter the groom's room."

"The call from Tara?" Tony asked.

"I was having cold feet," Tara confessed. "I called Owen because I wasn't sure I was doing the right thing, and he's always been my best sounding board."

"And what did the two of you decide?"

"I had no part in it," Owen said. "She told me nothing was wrong and hung up before I could ask her more questions. That's why I was on the way to the bride's room when I spotted what I now know was Tara going out to the parking lot."

"Runaway bride?" Tony arched one sandy eyebrow in Tara's direction.

"No. A man knocked on the bride's room door, and when I answered he told me there was a delivery outside for me."

"And you went with him?"

"I thought it might be a misdirected wedding gift."

"And was there a delivery?"

"No. As soon as I got outside, someone put an ether-soaked pillowcase over my head and threw me into a panel van."

There was a long moment of silence as Tony digested what she'd told him. He finally cleared his throat and spoke. "Go on."

She was beginning to lose him, she realized. Of course she was. She and Owen had both realized early on that their story sounded like pure fantasy.

"I think it was at that point that I happened upon the scene," Owen said before she could speak. "I saw two men pushing Tara into the van. I ran to try to stop them, but one of them punched me and I slammed headfirst into the van. I lost consciousness at that point and didn't come to until sometime later, inside the van. My hands were bound behind my back with duct tape."

"I see," Tony said in a tone that suggested he didn't see at all. "For how long were you in the van?"

"I'm not sure. It might have been an hour or more. We ended up about twenty minutes away from the church, though, so I think maybe the men driving the van took a twisty route, maybe to be sure nobody had seen them and taken chase."

"You think."

"I can't be sure. We weren't able to hear them plotting their next move or anything like that." Owen's voice took on a sharp edge. "Look, I can tell you're skeptical of what we're saying. Maybe you're not the lawyer we need."

"You're going to have to sell your story to people a lot more skeptical than I. And I never said I don't believe you."

Tara glanced at Owen. He met her gaze with a furrowed brow.

"How did you manage to get free?"

"I got the pillowcase off Tara's head. They'd left it on when they threw her in the van, so I guess they were hoping it would keep her sedated for the trip." Owen's voice darkened. "The idiots could have killed her."

"When I woke, I was a little disoriented from the ether. My hands were tied in front of me," she said.

"Their mistake," Owen murmured, his voice warm. "They didn't anticipate both of us waking up and working together, I think."

"Do you have any idea who took you or why?"

"We're not sure," Tara said quickly. "We're both wondering if it was connected to Robert's murder."

Tony slanted a look toward her. "You're taking his death well."

She looked down at her hands, which were twisting around each other in her lap. She stilled their movement. "I don't think it's real to me yet. I didn't see his body. Maybe if I did…"

"The police will be wondering why you're so composed."

She looked up sharply at the lawyer. "Do you want me to pretend to be hysterical?"

"No, of course not."

"I cared about Robert. I loved him. I can't even wrap my brain around the idea that he's gone."

"You said you were having cold feet."

She glanced at Owen. He was looking down at his own hands, his expression pensive.

"I was going to call off the wedding."

"Why?"

"Because I realized that I wasn't in love with him. Not the way I should have been if I were going to marry him."

"Did he know that?"

"No. The kidnapper grabbed me first."

"I see." Tony tapped his thumbs on the steering wheel. "Why do you suppose the kidnappers took Owen into the van rather than killing him and leaving him in the parking lot?"

"I have no idea," she answered.

"I suppose a body in the parking lot would have raised an alert sooner than the kidnappers planned," Owen added.

"A body in the groom's room raised the alert quickly enough."

"Hidden behind a door, not out in the open in a church parking lot," Owen pointed out.

"I wonder if they were planning to use you as leverage against me," Tara murmured.

Owen looked at her, his gaze intense.

"Leverage to do what?" Tony asked, sounding curious.

"Whatever they kidnapped me for. Anyone who knows anything about me knows about my friendship with Owen. We've been nearly inseparable since sixth grade. We went to the same schools, including college. On purpose. Maybe they realized they could use him against me, to force me to do whatever it was they wanted from me."

"And you really have no idea what that could be?" Tony sounded unconvinced.

"It's all a mystery to me," Tara answered.

Tony fell silent after that, though Tara suspected the mind behind those brown eyes was hard at work, figuring out all the legal angles of their dilemma.

She hoped it would be enough.

Within a couple of minutes, they were entering Mercerville, the Bagley County seat. The sheriff's department was located in the east wing of the city hall building, with its own entrance and parking area. Tony pulled the Mercedes into an empty visitor parking spot and cut the engine.

"I'm going to call the lead investigator on the case now. I want him to meet us at the door. I don't want to just walk in unannounced."

"Quinn said we shouldn't give them any notice we were coming."

"You want to be sure you meet with the lead investigator. That requires a courtesy call ahead of time to be sure he's here. We don't want to be handed off to someone down the food chain." He made the call. From what Tara could glean from his end of the call, the lead investigator was in and would meet them at the door.

Tony ended the call and turned to face them both. "Don't offer any information they haven't asked for. Nothing. Understood? If a question confuses you, let me know and we'll stop the interviews to confer. If I think the questioning is treading on dangerous territory for you, I'll step in. Agreed?"

"Yes," Owen said.

"Agreed." Tara looked at Owen. He met her gaze with a half smile that didn't erase the anxious expression in his eyes. She felt a flutter of guilt for her part in putting Owen in this position. If she hadn't been so stupid as to leave the safety of the church with a stranger—

Movement outside the car caught her eye. Turning her head, she spotted a man in the tan uniform of a Bagley County sheriff's deputy. He was tall and broad shouldered, with a slight paunch and a slightly hitching gait that seemed familiar. As he reached the sheriff's department entrance, he turned his head toward the parking lot.

She sucked in a sharp breath.

Owen put his hand on her shoulder. "What is it?"

"That deputy." She nodded toward the front of the building, where the deputy had just pulled open the door.

"What about him?" Tony asked.

"That's the man who lured me out to the van."

Chapter Eight

Owen had seen only a flash of square jaw and a long, straight nose as the deputy disappeared through the glass door of the sheriff's department, but it was enough to send adrenaline racing through his system. The skin at the back of his neck prickled and his muscles bunched in preparation. Fight or flight, he thought, remembering the lessons of his threat response classes at Campbell Cove Academy.

Flight, his instinct commanded. He was outgunned and on the defensive here.

"Let's get out of here," he growled to Tony.

"What? Are you insane?" Tony turned to stare at him. "You came here to turn yourself in to the authorities. If you leave now, you're just going to make things worse."

"Owen's right." Tara's voice was deep and intense. "If that man is a cop, they will never believe us over him. You know how it works."

"You can't know that—"

Owen snapped open his seat belt and tried to unlock the back door of the car, but the child-safety locks were engaged. "Unlock the door," he demanded.

Tony shook his head. "I'm telling you as your lawyer, this is insane."

"You're fired." Tara reached across the console and grabbed the key fob dangling from the ignition. Before

Tony Giattina could stop her, she pressed one of the buttons and the lock beside Owen made an audible click. He opened the door and exited the car.

Cool spring air filled his lungs, dispelling the faint feeling of claustrophobia he'd experienced while trapped inside the backseat. Tara was already out the passenger door, turning to him with wide eyes.

"What now?"

Owen looked back at the black SUV that had followed them to the sheriff's department. Quinn was already stepping out of the vehicle, his gaze sharp, as if he could sense the rise in tension. If anyone knew the danger they were in, it was Quinn, Owen realized. His wily boss understood that, sometimes, playing by the rules could get you killed.

Grabbing Tara's hand, he started resolutely toward the SUV.

Quinn's eyes narrowed at their approach. When Owen was close enough, Quinn muttered, "Hit me."

Owen's steps faltered. "What?"

"Hit me," Quinn said, taking a step forward. "I can't help you openly, but you can't go in there."

"How do you know…"

Quinn tapped the earpiece barely visible in his ear. "Hit me, damn it."

Without another second's hesitation, Owen let go of Tara's hand and punched Quinn as hard as he dared. His boss sprawled backward into the front panel of the SUV, his keys falling to the ground beside him.

As Owen bent to pick them up, Quinn murmured, "Not the safe house. It's compromised now. There's a stash of cash in the glove box. Use it and try to get in touch when you can." Shaking his head in a show of grogginess, he dragged himself clear of the SUV's wheels.

Tony Giattina was out of the Mercedes, his phone to

his ear. Probably calling in the escape attempt, Owen realized, which meant they had only seconds before half the sheriff's department would be pouring through the doors into the parking lot.

"Let's go," he growled as he opened the front door of the SUV. Tara climbed into the passenger seat and turned to look at him, her expression terrified.

"Maybe I was wrong," she said, sounding far less confident than she had seemed a few moments earlier.

"You weren't," he assured her, putting the SUV in Reverse. He cut off a car approaching from the left, earning an angry horn blow, and headed east on Old Cumberland Road. He could take a few twisty back roads over Murlow Mountain and reach the Virginia border in less than an hour.

But what then?

"They'll have an APB out on this car in no time," Tara muttered, fastening her seat belt. "They'll scan our license plate and we'll be done for."

She was right. He had to switch the plates with another vehicle. Preferably another black SUV, but any vehicle would do, at least for a while.

Meanwhile, he stuck to the twisty mountain roads that wound their way slowly but steadily eastward toward the state line. He'd traveled with his brother in Virginia a couple of years earlier and had learned, to his surprise, that travelers could overnight in their vehicles at rest stops. That would give them accommodations for tonight, at least, until they could figure out what to do next.

But first, he needed to find a big shopping center where they could pick up supplies.

"Is anyone following us?" Tara twisted around in her seat, nibbling her thumbnail as she peered at the road behind them.

"I don't see anyone, but I'm not exactly an expert at tailing. Or being tailed."

Tara looked at him. "Do you have a plan?"

"Yes, but I'm not sure you're going to be thrilled about it."

"Better spill, then."

"Did you know that it's legal to overnight at public rest areas in Virginia?"

"Please tell me that's a non sequitur."

"I'm going to stick to back roads for another hour or so. Then I'm going to drive down to Abingdon. I think there's probably some sort of shopping center there where we can pick up some supplies—food, blankets, water."

"Those had better be thick blankets," Tara muttered.

"I'm not sure what to do about the license plates, though."

"You'd think, with your boss being a former super-spy, he'd have extra license plates stashed in the trunk or something."

Owen slanted a quick look at her. "Do you think?"

"I don't know. He's your boss."

Even after a year, Owen knew very little about two of his three bosses. Maddox Heller was an open book, gar-rulous and friendly. His pretty wife and his two cute kids visited often, and the previous summer, Heller had invited everyone in the company out to their house on Mercer Lake for a Labor Day cookout.

But Rebecca Cameron was a very private person, de-spite her friendly, good-natured disposition. And Alexan-der Quinn was a positive enigma.

However, if there was one thing Owen knew about his inscrutable boss, it was that the man always seemed pre-pared for any eventuality. Including the possibility of hav-ing to go on the run at a moment's notice.

There were very few turnoffs on the curvy mountain

road they were traveling, but within a few minutes, Owen spotted a dirt road on the right and slowed to turn, hoping he wasn't driving them into a dead-end trap.

"What are you doing?" Tara asked.

"I'm going to find out if Alexander Quinn is as wily as he seems."

Almost as soon as they took the turn, the dirt road hooked sharply to the right. Owen eased into the turn and the SUV was immediately swallowed by the woods, which hid not only the road from their view but, more important, hid them from the view of the road.

He pulled to a stop and cut the engine. "If you wanted to stash something secret in this SUV, where would you start?"

"The glove compartment is too obvious," Tara said.

"Quinn did tell me there was stash of cash in there."

Tara opened the glove box. Inside was a wallet, weather-beaten and fat. She pulled it out and opened the wallet. "Lots of receipts," she said as she riffled through the papers inside. "And a ten-dollar bill. I don't know your boss well, but if this is what he thinks qualifies as a stash of cash…"

Owen unbuckled his seat belt and leaned over to look. The distracting scent of Tara's skin almost made him forget what he was looking for, but he managed to gather his wits enough to search the glove compartment. Besides the wallet, there was only the car registration, a card providing proof of insurance, and a thick vehicle manual.

But Quinn had clearly told him there was a stash of cash in the glove compartment. Was this some sort of trap? A test?

He sat back a moment, thinking hard. Assuming Quinn had been playing things straight, why would he have said there was cash in the glove box if there wasn't?

Narrowing his eyes, he leaned over and looked into the

glove compartment again. There could be no cash hiding
in the registration paper or the insurance card. But what
about the manual?

"What are you doing?" Tara asked, leaning forward
until her head was right next to Owen's in front of the
open compartment.

Owen turned to look at her, his breath catching at her
closeness. Her green eyes seemed large and luminous as
her eyebrows rose in two delicate arches.

He forced his gaze back to the glove compartment and
pulled out the manual. Easing back to his own side of the
SUV, he opened the manual.

There was a fifty-dollar bill slipped between the first
two pages.

He flipped through the book, a smile curving his mouth.
Nearly every page sandwiched money. Dozens of tens,
about that many twenties, several fifties and even a handful
of hundreds. Nearly five thousand dollars in cash, Owen
realized after adding up the sums in his head.

"Does he usually carry that much money in his vehicle?" Tara asked when Owen told her the sum.

"I have no idea." He handed her the manual full of
money. "Leave it in there for now. I'm going to see what
else I can find in this SUV."

"I'll check up here in the cab," Tara said as he opened
the driver's door. "You see if there are any underfloor
compartments."

Fifteen minutes later, they had uncovered a set of Tennessee license plates, another fifty dollars in change hidden in various places around the SUV, a Louisville Slugger
baseball bat, a small smartphone with a prepaid phone card
taped to its back, a duffel bag full of clothing and survival
supplies and a dozen MREs—military-issued meals that
could be prepared without cooking utensils or even a fire.

"He likes to cover all his bases," Tara said, looking at their bounty.

"I'll switch out the license plate and put the Kentucky one in the compartment where I found the Tennessee plates," Owen said. "Then I'm going to see if there are any minutes left on that phone."

"Do you think that's a good idea?"

"It's a burner phone. Quinn said to get in touch when we could. I think this is how we're supposed to do it."

Tara shook her head. "Not this soon. The police might be keeping an eye on him. Let's wait a day or two before we call him."

Owen gave her a considering look. "Okay. You're right."

"Don't sound so shocked." She shot him a quick grin. "Go change the tags and I'll see if I can find any more treasures."

Owen took a screwdriver from the small toolbox inside Quinn's survival kit and switched out the Kentucky plates for the Tennessee ones.

"What now?" Tara asked.

"I'm a little tempted to see where this road leads," Owen admitted, peering through the trees to the twisting dirt road ahead.

"You've got to be kidding me."

"I doubt anyone would think to look for us here."

"Where exactly is here?" She leaned forward, as if doing so might somehow reveal more of the road than was currently visible.

"I have no idea."

She shook her head. "I liked your idea of sleeping in the car at a rest area better. At least rest areas have bathrooms and vending machines."

"We have MREs, plus some protein bars and several bottles of water in the survival kit."

"Unless there's a relatively clean bathroom stashed in that kit, my opinion stands."

He sighed. "You used to be more adventurous."

"And you used to be less reckless. When did you change?"

When I realized playing things carefully was getting me nowhere, he thought. *When you met Robert and threw yourself headfirst into a romance with him because he ticked off all the items on your wish list.*

"If you want to go to Virginia and find a rest stop, that's what we'll do. But let's wait here until dark. It'll be easier to escape attention in the dark."

She sighed. "You have a point."

"Don't sound so shocked," he said with a grin.

His echo of her earlier words was enough to earn him a small laugh. "I know I shouldn't be happy you got sucked into my mess, but I'm really glad you're with me. I'm not sure what I would have done if you hadn't been there in that van when I regained consciousness."

He reached across the space between them and brushed a stray twig of hair away from her cheek. "You'd have done what you always do. You'd have come out on top."

Her smile faltered. "I don't feel as if I've come out on top."

"We're not through fighting yet, are we?" He should drop his hand away from her face instead of letting his fingertips linger against her cheek. But with Tara showing no signs of unease, he couldn't bring himself to pull away. He liked the way her skin felt, soft and warm, almost humming with vibrant life.

"I suppose this is a bad time to mention I could use a bathroom break." Tara gave him an apologetic look.

He checked his watch. "Don't suppose you could wait another four hours or so?"

She shook her head.

So much for waiting until after dark to hit the road. "Well, can you wait another hour? I was planning to drive to Abingdon anyway so we could pick up some supplies. We should be there in an hour or so."

"Yeah, I can wait that long."

"If we can find a thrift store, we could stock up on some clothing without making a big dent in our resources," he suggested.

"Good idea. It would be nice to have something that actually fits again." She tugged uncomfortably at her too-tight T-shirt.

He forced his gaze away from her breasts. "I might be able to pick up a laptop computer at a reasonable price, too."

She glanced at him. "Is that a necessity? Five thousand dollars isn't going to last long if we make big purchases."

"I need to be able to stay up on what's happening in the outside world while we're hunkered down."

"Won't you need an internet connection to do that?"

"Yes, but there are ways to do that without being entirely on the grid." He got the SUV turned around on the narrow road and headed for the main road again, hoping the stop hadn't allowed their pursuers to catch up with them. At least they were no longer wearing the Kentucky tags the police would be looking for.

"Do you think we should come up with disguises?" he asked aloud.

"Such as?"

"You could cut your hair. Dye it another color. I could keep growing this beard and buy some gamer glasses—"

"Gamer glasses?"

"Tinted-lens glasses gamers wear to cut down on screen glare. Good for computer users, too. I can probably find some if I can track down a computer store or gamer's store in Abingdon."

"You should buy the hair dye. I'll buy the glasses. In case anyone's paying attention."

"Good thinking." He had reached the main road and he pulled over to a stop, sparing her a quick look before he got back on the blacktop. "So, we find a shopping center. I'll go with you to the computer store to pick out what I need, but you can pay for it. Then we do the opposite when we pick up your hair dye. You pick, I pay."

She flashed a wry grin. "As long as the first place we stop has a bathroom."

"YOU'RE TELLING ME you don't have any sort of security system in your vehicle?" Archer Trask gave Quinn a look of disbelief. "In your line of work?"

"Rather like the doctor who ignores his yearly checkup." Quinn shrugged. "I'm afraid it's a failing many of us have—focusing more on our clients' security needs rather than our own."

Trask didn't appear to believe him, but Quinn didn't care. Trask could prove nothing, and Quinn had access to enough legal help to keep the Bagley County Sheriff's Department from doing any harm.

Meanwhile, he needed to get back to his office and convene a task force to dig deeper into the Tara Bentley case. First line of attack—find out the name of the deputy who'd helped kidnap her and Owen. If he'd been able to get a decent look at the guy himself, he knew Giattina, who'd been parked closer, must have, also. As soon as Quinn finished this pointless interview with Trask, he planned to find Giattina and compare notes. He'd already warned Tony against sharing information with the police that Owen and Tara had revealed while he was acting as their lawyer. Attorney-client privilege was something Tony took seriously, so Quinn doubted he'd have revealed anything about the suspicious deputy to the investigators interrogating him.

Trask gave Quinn a copy of his statement to sign. "We have your license plate number and the description of your vehicle. We'll find Owen Stiles and Tara Bentley sooner or later." Trask frowned. "If you should hear from them, I'm sure you'll warn them that their decision to flee hardly makes them look innocent."

Quinn signed the statement. "Of course. Am I free to go?"

"You'll let us know if you hear anything from the fugitives?"

"Of course," Quinn lied.

He caught up with Tony Giattina outside, where the lawyer waited by his Mercedes, talking on the phone. His dark eyes met Quinn's, and he said something into the phone, then put it in his pocket. "Would you like to tell me why you're aiding and abetting fugitives?"

Quinn nodded toward the Mercedes. With a sigh, Tony unlocked the car and joined Quinn inside.

"You knew what was going on," Tony said with a grimace. "Is my car bugged?"

Quinn reached under the dashboard and pulled out a small listening device. "I'm sorry. I needed to hear what they had to say to you."

"You breached attorney-client privilege."

"I'm not an attorney."

"No," Tony said with a grimace. "You're a damned spy."

"Former."

"Former, my shiny red—"

"They're in trouble. And I believed them when they told you they recognized one of the Bagley County Sheriff's Department deputies as one of the men who kidnapped them."

"You think the cops were in on what happened to them?"

"Not the whole bunch of them, no. But at least one. And possibly more."

"So why didn't they stick around and identify the guy instead of punching your lights out and running for the hills?"

"Because who would believe them?" Quinn waved at the listening device sitting on the console between them. "You didn't believe them, and you're their lawyer."

Tony fell silent a moment. "What do you expect from me?"

"Your silence. They told you about the kidnapper as part of your attorney-client relationship. It remains privileged until such time as they give you permission to reveal it."

"You don't want me to tell what I know? If you and my clients are right, there's a kidnapper working as a Bagley County deputy, and you want that information kept silent?"

"I do."

Tony shook his head. "That makes no damn sense."

Quinn reached for the listening device and slipped it into his pocket. "What do you think would happen if we told what we know? Let's say Trask believes us. He'd track down the deputy you saw, get your identification of the man and start questioning him. Which would be a disaster."

"Why would it be a disaster?"

"Because I've come to believe the people behind Tara Bentley's kidnapping are up to something far more dangerous than a simple abduction. And if we tip our hand, we may not find out what their plan is until it's much too late."

Chapter Nine

"Wow. Is that you?"

Tara looked up at the sound of Owen's voice, but it took a moment to realize that the gangly hipster in the saggy gray beanie shuffling toward her was her best friend. The cap looked ancient and well used, and it went well with the rest of his slouchy attire, from the baggy faded jeans to the oversize navy hoodie with the name of an obscure eighties' metal band on the front. The sleek design of his amber-lensed glasses should have looked out of sync with the rest of his slacker aesthetic, but somehow the glasses seemed perfectly at home perched on his long, thin nose.

"I almost didn't recognize you," she said as he set a large shopping bag from an electronics store on the hood of the SUV.

"Likewise." He waved his hand toward her hair. "I like the purple."

She patted her now-short hair self-consciously. The budget hair salon in the Abingdon shopping center had done a decent job giving her a spiky gamine cut, but the spray-on color she'd added was way outside her normal comfort zone.

"We need to hit the road, but I had an idea for the SUV." Owen pulled a small bag from inside his jacket and reached inside, withdrawing a small stack of bumper stickers. "Start sticking them on the back of the SUV."

The stickers, she saw, embraced every social justice issue known to man, including some that contradicted each other.

"It would be better if this were a Volkswagen Beetle," she muttered when he rejoined her at the back of the SUV after he'd stashed his new computer inside.

"You make do with what you have," Owen said with a shrug. "The main thing is, it doesn't look like the SUV that left Kentucky this morning."

She tugged at the ends of her hair. "And we don't look like the people who left Kentucky this morning."

"Exactly." He cocked his head. "Don't suppose you could get your nose pierced?"

She gave his arm a light slap. "No."

"Maybe your belly button?"

"Get in the car."

From Abingdon, they took I-81 north, heading for the next rest stop. Spotting a sign for a sub shop at one of the interstate exits just south of the rest area, Owen pulled off the highway to grab a couple of sandwiches for their dinner.

By the time they finally reached the rest stop, the afternoon had started fading into twilight. Owen found a parking place a few spaces away from the nearest car and parked.

"Home, sweet home," he murmured.

"Let's take a restroom break," Tara suggested. "Give me a couple of dollars and I'll buy some drinks to go with our dinner."

The bathrooms were blessedly clean and human traffic at the rest stop was just busy enough for Owen and Tara to be able to blend in without any trouble. She bought the drinks and, while she was there, picked up a few of the brochures for south Virginia campgrounds and attractions.

She showed Owen one of the brochures over dinner. "It's a campground about two hours east of here. We pay a small fee for a campsite. There's a communal restroom within walking distance, and a charging station for electronics. They even advertise free Wi-Fi."

Owen looked at the brochure, his brow furrowed. "There is a tent stashed in the back of the SUV..."

"We stay here tonight, and then tomorrow we can settle in there. Maybe you can put that computer you bought to use."

"How's the salmon?" Becky Cameron asked.

"Delicious." Quinn tried to remain expressionless, not sure he was ready to let his colleague know that her sudden desire to socialize was beginning to make him uneasy. He turned keeping people at arm's length into an art form. Becky knew that better than most, having worked with him off and on for more than fifteen years.

"Are you ever going to tell me about your adventure this morning?" she asked, delicately picking at her own pan-seared trout.

"Not much to tell."

She gestured with one long-fingered, graceful hand toward the bruise shadowing his jawline. "Owen Stiles packs a nice punch."

"We taught him well."

"You don't seem particularly incensed at the idea of having your vehicle stolen by a trusted employee."

"Life is full of surprises."

Becky smiled, showing a flash of straight white teeth. "Subject dropped."

"That's for the best," he agreed, glancing around the crowded restaurant. "For the here and now, at least."

She nodded, taking a dainty bite of the trout. "We can catch up at work in the morning."

A few minutes of thick silence stretched between them before Becky spoke again. "You're wondering why I invited you here when I know as well as you do that there are certain topics we can't discuss in public."

"The question did cross my mind."

Becky's smile was full of sympathy. "I don't mean to be so enigmatic. That's your bailiwick."

He managed a smile. "But you clearly brought me here for a reason."

"Socializing isn't reason enough?"

He quirked one eyebrow, making her smile.

"Right," she said, the smile fading. "I wanted to talk to you about something not connected to work. And I was afraid if I tried to approach you at the office, I would lose my nerve."

Now he was intrigued. "I can't imagine you ever losing your nerve, Becky. About anything."

"It's about Mitch."

Suddenly, the half filet of salmon he'd eaten felt like a lump of lead in his stomach. He laid down his fork and took a drink of water to cover his sudden discomfort. "Has something changed?"

"Maybe." A furrow creased her brow. "There's some indication that he might not have died in the helicopter crash in Tablis."

Quinn froze in the act of straightening his napkin across his lap. "I saw the crash myself. We searched the area thoroughly for over a week. Men under my watch died trying to recover all the bodies. But it was the rainy season, and the current in the river where they crashed was brutally swift. Several bodies washed downriver and were never recovered."

"I saw film of the crash. I know how unlikely it is that he survived."

Quinn reached across the table and covered her hand with his. "I know you want to believe there's a chance he survived."

"I don't know what I want to believe, Quinn. It's been nearly ten years. If he survived, why didn't he try to reach someone? I know it's grasping at straws. It's just—what if he's out there? Maybe he doesn't remember what happened or who he is. Maybe he just needs to see a familiar face to trigger the rest of his memories."

He gave her hand another squeeze before letting go. "I don't think it works that way. But if you want me to put out some feelers with some of my old contacts in Kaziristan—"

"I'd appreciate it," she said with a grateful smile. She looked down at her plate. "I don't know about you, but I think my appetite is gone."

"You want to get out of here? Maybe we could head back to the office and talk about the subject we were supposed to talk about?"

She nodded. "You go ahead. I'll get the check and meet you there."

"I can wait," he said, feeling an unexpected protectiveness of her. He'd never thought of Becky as someone who needed anyone or anything. Even her relationship with Mitch Talbot, a marine colonel she'd met when she was stationed at the US embassy in Tablis, Kaziristan, had seemed lopsided. She was the diplomat, a woman of culture, education and power, while he was a gruff leatherneck more at home in fatigues leading his men into combat.

But clearly, she'd loved him deeply if she was willing to

put her reputation and her connections on the line to find him ten years after his presumed death. Was she setting herself up for a fresh new heartbreak?

She was obviously going to look for the man, whether Quinn helped her or not. And even though the thought of trying to dig up those old bones made him positively queasy, it was the least he owed her.

After all, he was the man who'd sent Mitch Talbot to his death.

MORNING WAS JUST a hint of pink promise in the eastern sky when Owen woke from a restless sleep. At bedtime the night before, he and Tara had tried to sleep on the narrow bench seats, but after the second time Tara tumbled off the seat into the floorboard, they decided it made more sense to fold down the seats and use the now-flat cargo area to deploy the sleeping bags stashed among other survival gear in the underfloor storage area of the SUV. Given the dropping temperature outside, they decided to zip the two bags into one spacious double bag. Curling up back to back, they'd fallen asleep in relative warmth, if not comfort.

At some point during the night, however, they'd ended up face-to-face, their limbs entangled beneath the down-filled cover of the sleeping bags.

For a heady moment, Owen wanted nothing more than to stay right where he was for the rest of his life, his skin against hers, her warmth enfolding him with a sense of sublime rightness he had never felt with anyone but her.

It would be so much easier if he could have found that feeling of completion with another woman. He'd tried more than once over the years to move on, to seek a relationship, a life, where Tara Bentley wasn't the most important part of it. It had taken a long time for him to come to terms with the fact that as long as Tara was in his life, she would always be the most important part of it.

Which meant the only way to move on with his life would be to let her go completely.

He gently extricated himself from her sleeping embrace. She made a soft groaning noise that echoed inside his own chest, but he forced himself to keep moving rather than return to the warmth of her body. Trying not to wake her, he unzipped his side of the sleeping back, wincing at the rush of cold outside its down-filled insulation. He grabbed his jacket from the front seat and added it to the sweatshirt and jeans he'd worn last night for warmth before he opened the door and stepped out into the chilly morning air.

Across the rest area parking lot, a handful of other travelers were up and moving, taking advantage of the bathrooms and vending machines. One machine seemed to dispense hot coffee, he noticed, swirls of steam rising from cups held by weary travelers exiting the building.

He pulled up the collar of his jacket and tugged the ratty beanie over his head, grimacing at the need for disguise. It was too dark for the glasses, so he left them in his jacket pocket as he slouched his way across to the rest area center.

After a quick bathroom break, the siren song of coffee drew him to the vending machine. He bought a couple of cups and tucked them to his chest under one arm while he studied the vending machine selections. Sweet or salty? Tara wasn't much of a breakfast person, but they couldn't be sure when they'd be able to eat again, so she needed something with some protein. A bag of peanuts and a pack of cheese crackers would have to do.

He didn't immediately notice a new arrival at the rest area center, so it was with a flutter of shock that he turned away from the vending machine to find a Virginia State Police officer standing only a couple of yards away.

He froze at first, his heart beating a tattoo against his ribs. Coffee sloshed in the cups pressed against his chest, almost spilling down his shirt.

Turning as slowly as he dared, he settled the cups and edged toward the side of the room, where a few travelers were looking through the brochure racks advertising local tourist stops.

He glanced back toward the policeman. He seemed to be looking for something.

Or someone?

Owen edged toward the door with his purchases, hoping he wouldn't do something stupid like trip over his own feet and draw attention toward himself. Tara was asleep in the SUV, with no idea how close they were to being discovered.

One foot in front of the other...

"Excuse me, sir? Have you seen this woman?" The voice, so close, made him jerk with surprise. Some of the coffee spilled onto the pavement in front of the rest-area door.

Slowly, he turned to face the policeman. The man was holding a printed flyer with a woman's photograph on it. Owen nearly melted with relief when he realized the woman on the flyer wasn't Tara.

"I'm sorry, no," he said, faking a midwestern accent. "Just driving through."

"If you see anything, give us a call." The policeman started to hand Owen a card, then belatedly realized his hands were full. He slipped the card into the pocket of Owen's jacket. "Have a safe trip."

"Thanks." Owen gave a nod and headed quickly across the parking lot to the SUV.

Tara was awake when he opened the door. He set the coffee and snacks on the floorboard and glanced over his shoulder. The policeman had remained outside the rest area center, talking to travelers as they entered and exited the place.

Following his gaze, Tara asked with alarm, "Is that a cop?"

"He seems to be looking for a missing woman. I nearly had a heart attack when he stopped me to ask if I'd seen her."

"Do you think he recognized you?"

"He didn't seem to." He looked at Tara. "Stop staring at him. He'll think we're up to something."

"We *are* up to something. Sort of." Tara forced her gaze away from the policeman, letting it settle on Owen's vending-machine bounty. "Coffee. Thank goodness."

"You need to eat something, too. I bought you some peanuts for protein."

"Yes, Mom." She tore open the packet of peanuts. "Want some?"

Owen's appetite was gone. Even the coffee, which he'd been craving just a little while ago, seemed entirely unappetizing. "Go ahead. I'll worry about getting us ready to get back on the road."

They'd filled the gas tank back in Abingdon, so they were good for several more miles before they'd have to worry about stopping for fuel. The tires looked fine, and all of the SUV's gauges were reading in the normal range. He settled in the driver's seat, his nerves finally steady enough for him to sit still without fidgeting.

"I think enough time has passed now that we can leave without looking as if we're running away," he said, glancing over his shoulder at Tara.

She licked salt off her fingertips and looked back at him. "Even though that's what we're doing."

"You have a better idea?"

She shook her head. "Let's get out of here."

"You can stay in the back and get a little more sleep if you want."

"No, I'm wide awake. Hold on and I'll come up front." She exited the back door and climbed into the front, first putting Owen's cooling cup of coffee in the console's cup holder. "You should drink that before it gets cold."

He looked at it and shook his head. "You can have it if you want."

She climbed into the passenger seat and buckled in, then picked up the cup. "If you insist."

They fell silent until they were well clear of the rest area and moving east on I-81. As they passed through the scenic town of Rural Retreat, Tara set down her empty coffee cup and turned in her seat to look at him.

"Maybe we should call your boss," she suggested.

"I'm not sure it's safe."

"Is it that? Or is it that you don't want to ask for help."

He angled a quick look at her. She gazed back at him, a knowing look in her eyes that made him feel completely exposed.

"I know you don't like asking for help," she added, her tone gentler. "I know why."

"I'm not afraid to call Quinn if we need him."

"But you're afraid if you call him now, he'll see you as weak. Just like your father used to accuse you of being."

He pressed his lips to a thin line, annoyed. "Not every decision I make in my life is influenced by what my father said to me when I was fifteen."

"Then call Quinn. He told you to get in touch, right?"

"Yes, but—"

"No buts." She pulled the cell phone from the caddy at the front of the console, where it had been charging all night. "Call him."

"I'm driving."

"I'll dial. Just tell me the number."

With a sigh, he gave her the number of Quinn's business cell phone. "It's still awfully early," he warned.

"Didn't you once tell me you think Quinn never sleeps?" She put the phone on speaker and dialed the number.

Quinn answered on the first ring, "Don't tell me anything about where you are. Just tell me if you're all right."

"We're fine," Owen answered, surprised at the relief that flooded him at the sound of his boss's voice. He wasn't close to Quinn at all, having barely spoken to the man more than a dozen times since he took the job at Campbell Cove Security. But just knowing he had someone besides Tara out there, trying to watch his back, was enough to bolster his sagging spirits. "We've disguised ourselves and the vehicle, so we're trying to find somewhere to hunker down until we can formulate a plan for our next steps."

"I think your next steps should include trying to figure out who wants the information Tara has in her head that they can't find anywhere else."

"That's where you could give us some help," Tara interjected. "I know what information they're looking for, but I'm not in the know about which groups might be looking for that information. Do you have a dossier on the groups most likely to be trying to make a big show of force at the symposium?"

"That's going to be a lot of dossiers," he warned.

"What about the deputy we saw? Maybe if we could get an ID on him, we could dig deeper and figure out who he associates with," Owen suggested.

"On it. The Bagley County Sheriff's Department inconveniently doesn't have a website, but Archer Trask has cooperated with us on a previous case he was investigating, so I'm going to see if I can exploit that relationship to get information without raising his suspicions."

"You're going to try to outcop a cop?" Tara asked skeptically.

"We have our ways." There was a hint of amusement in Quinn's voice. "I'll handle that end of things. Meanwhile, you need to stay off the grid as much as you can. You found the cash and all the supplies?"

"We did," Owen answered.

"You're a scary man, Alexander Quinn," Tara added.

"I like to be prepared," he said. "Call again in four hours. If everything is good, tell me that it's not. If you're in trouble, say everything is okay. Understood?"

Owen exchanged glances with Tara. Both her eyebrows were near her hairline, but she said, "Understood."

Quinn ended the call without another word, and she put the phone back in the console holder.

"So," she said, "where exactly do we plan to hunker down?"

"I think we need to find that campsite I was telling you about. And fast."

The sooner they were off the road, the less likely it was that someone would spot their SUV and start wondering if it might be the missing vehicle from Kentucky with the two fugitives inside.

Chapter Ten

"I can't believe you bought marshmallows."

Tara looked up from the shopping bag she was unpacking to find Owen holding a bag of the puffy white sweets. "I don't go camping without marshmallows. Or hot dogs," she added, pulling a pack of wieners from the shopping bag.

Owen sighed, but she saw the hint of a smile cross his face. "I hope you got mustard, too."

She waggled the mustard bottle at him. "And ketchup for me."

He made a face. "I appreciate the fact that you're trying to make this a fun experience—"

"I'm trying to get through this without losing my sanity," she corrected, her voice rising with a rush of emotion. "If I treat this like one of our nights out camping at Kingdom Come State Park, maybe I can get through this thing without being institutionalized."

Silence fell between them for a long, tense moment before Owen finally spoke. "I'm sorry."

She shook her head. "You have nothing to be sorry for. You're in this mess, too, and it's all because of me."

"No, I meant I'm sorry about Robert. I haven't really said that to you. I know you loved him, even if you didn't love him enough to go through with the wedding. And you haven't really had a moment to yourself to just grieve."

"I don't have time to grieve. I have to figure out this whole mess. It's about me and what I know. It's my responsibility."

He stood up from where he crouched by the fire pit he was building and crossed to where she stood by the SUV. He cupped her face between his hands, and emotion surged in her chest, making her feel as if she were about to explode. She tamped down the feelings roiling through her and forced herself to meet his soft-eyed gaze.

"You don't have to do this alone. Any of it."

Blinking back tears she didn't want to spill, she managed a smile. "I know you're on my side. You always are."

Something flickered in his gaze, an emotion she couldn't quite read, and he dropped his hands from her face and stepped a couple of feet away. "I'll put the hot dogs in the cooler." He picked up the pack of wieners and walked back to the campsite.

Even though he was only a few feet away from her, she suddenly felt as if she were alone, cut off from anything and anyone important to her. It was a hollow, terrible feeling.

She shook off the sensation. She wasn't alone. She hadn't been alone since the sixth grade, when Owen Stiles had literally stumbled into her life, dropping his lunch tray at her feet and soiling her favorite pair of Chuck Taylors. Once she got past the desire to strangle him, she'd found a friend who'd never, ever failed her.

He wouldn't fail her now. If there was anything in her life that was constant and permanent, it was Owen Stiles. His friendship was everything to her, which was why she'd fight anyone and anything, including her own libido, to keep him in her life.

While she was picking up camping supplies at a store in the nearby town of Weatherly, Owen had been busy setting up camp. The tent he'd found stored in the SUV now stood next to the campfire. It was larger than she'd expected, but still cozy enough that they should be able to stay warm in the night.

"Did you find any nightcrawlers?" he asked as she crossed with the rest of the supplies to where he crouched by the fire pit.

"Of course. No grocery store this close to a campground would be caught dead without a bait shop section." She sat cross-legged on the ground next to him and dug in her grocery bag until she retrieved two small plastic bowls full of dirt. There were little pinprick holes in the plastic lid of the containers. "Here. Have some worms."

"There's a curve of the river that runs near here, according to the online map." He pulled the cell phone from his pocket and waggled it at her, a smile flirting with his lips. "I don't know how Daniel Boone made it across the wilderness without Google."

A gust of wind lifted Tara's short locks and rustled the grocery bag. She looked up through the trees to discover that the sunny sky that had greeted them earlier that morning was gone, swallowed by slate-colored clouds scudding along with the wind.

"I don't think we're going to get to have marshmallows or hot dogs tonight," she said with a heavy sigh. "I bought a few cans of soup, though. I think we could probably heat one up using the camp stove before the rain hits."

"You're being a good sport about this," Owen commented as he gathered up the supplies he'd laid out on the ground by their would-be campfire. "I know how you like your creature comforts."

"It's not like this is your mess, Owen. You didn't drag me into this. It's the other way around."

"I dragged myself into it."

"Trying to help me."

"You'd have done the same." He finished stowing away the equipment in the waterproof duffel and stuffed it into the tent, leaving out only the portable camp stove and a small saucepan. He looked up at the sky. "We probably have another fifteen minutes before the bottom falls out of the sky, so what kind of soup do we have there?"

She pulled out three cans. "Chicken noodle, vegetable and beef, and chicken-corn chowder."

"The chowder sounds good. Filling."

She put the other two cans back in the shopping bag and pulled the tab ring on the can of chowder. It opened with a quiet snick. "Hope there aren't any bears nearby."

"Me, too." Owen added the butane canister to the camp stove and turned the knob until it clicked and a flame appeared at the center of the burner. "Oh, look, it works."

"You weren't sure it would?" Tara asked.

"I hoped it would." He set the saucepan on the burner and reached out for the can of soup.

Tara handed it to him and crouched beside him. "I didn't think to buy any paper bowls."

"There are plastic bowls and eating utensils in the duffel bag."

She retrieved them and sat down beside Owen in front of the stove. "I still think your boss is some sort of madman, but at least he's a madman who knows how to prepare for any eventuality."

"I imagine he learned about being prepared the hard way. I've heard some stories—all told in hushed tones, of course—about some of his adventures during his time in the CIA."

"Do you believe them?"

"Most of them, yeah. You don't get the kind of reputation Quinn has if you spent your years in the CIA behind some cushy desk in an embassy."

The advent of the clouds overhead had driven out most of the warmth of the day, and there was a definite damp chill in the increasing wind. Tara edged closer to Owen, glad for his body heat and the warmth drifting toward her from the camp stove. The soup was already starting to burble in the pan.

"Maybe we should eat inside the tent," she suggested. "I think it's going to rain any minute."

He looked up at the sky. "Good idea. Here, hand me the bowls and I'll spoon this up. Then you can take the food inside and I'll clean up out here."

Tara took the bowls of soup Owen handed to her and ducked inside the tent. Their sleeping bags covered most of the tent floor; as they had the night before, they'd zipped the bags together in order to take advantage of each other's body heat. With the sudden dip in the temperature, Tara had a feeling it was going to be a damp, chilly night.

Owen appeared through the flap of the tent, carrying the extinguished stove and the cleaned-up cooking pot. He left the stove just inside the tent to cool but stowed away the cooking pot, then took his food from Tara. He nodded at her untouched bowl. "Eat up before it gets cold."

She took a bite of the hearty chowder. It was pretty good for canned soup. "I don't suppose Quinn has sent you the dossiers we asked for."

Owen pulled the burner phone from his pocket. "To be honest, I haven't checked. I was keeping the phone off to conserve the battery, since I don't want to risk putting any sort of drain on the SUV's engine until we're on the road again."

They had agreed not to camp too close to the campground amenities, wanting to avoid interaction with other campers. The restrooms were only a hundred yards away, hidden by the woods, but the office was another hundred yards away, which meant the charging stations available to campers were also that far away.

"I'm getting a Wi-Fi signal from the campground. It's not the strongest, but it's better than nothing."

"Think it'll be strong enough for a file to download?"

"There's an email trying to download. It's slow going, but I'll bet it's from Quinn. Nobody else would have the email for this phone." He stuck the phone back in his pocket. "Let's finish eating. I'll check again when we're finished. Maybe it'll have downloaded by then."

Tara suddenly felt anything but hungry, but she forced herself to eat. If they were going to be running for their lives over the next few days, she needed her strength. Food wasn't a luxury. It was a necessity.

She managed to remain patient until her bowl was empty. She set it aside and looked up at Owen. "Can you check the email again?"

He gave her a sympathetic look and pulled out his phone. "Looks as if it's finished. Let's see what we've got."

She scooted closer so she could see the phone screen. The file attached to the email appeared to be a portable document file. Owen clicked the pdf file and a summary page appeared. Tara scanned the words, which informed them that the following files contained background details on the employees of Security Solutions. According to Quinn's notes, he was also trying to come up with potential connections between the sheriff's department and Security Solutions along with trying to connect members of the sheriff's department to any of the known terror groups who had both the motive and the means to stage a significant terror event on American soil.

"What do you expect to find in these dossiers?" Owen asked.

"Connections," she answered. "I'm thinking it would have to be someone who's in a position to take any of the information I might have supplied to the kidnappers and do something with it."

"Who might that be?"

"Well, obviously, my bosses, but since they already have the information I have, they wouldn't need to bother with a kidnapping."

"Do you have an assistant?"

"Yes, but Karen wouldn't be next in line for the job if I suddenly disappear."

"But could she use the information you have if she could get her hands on it?"

Tara thought about it. "Theoretically, anyone could. But it's likely that by now, my bosses have already changed all the details of the event. Either postponed it or moved venues."

"So maybe you're not in danger anymore."

The same thought had just occurred to her. "Maybe. But why do I still feel as if I'm in danger?"

"I think maybe because Alexander Quinn thinks you still are, and if he does, he must have a reason." Owen set aside his empty soup bowl and pulled the burner phone out of his pocket. "Let's find out why."

"Will he answer?" she asked as he dialed the number.

"He'd better."

Tara scooted closer so she could hear the other end of the call. The phone rang twice before a drawling voice answered, "Roy's Auto Repair."

"I'm calling about my green Cutlass GT," Owen said, arching his eyebrows at Tara.

"I'll check, sir." After a brief pause, the voice on the

other line continued. "Still checking, but Roy told me to ask how you're doing today."

"Just lousy," Owen answered.

"Sorry to hear that." The voice on the other end of the line suddenly sounded like Quinn. "Thought I said I'd call you."

"You did. But we have a question."

"Shoot."

"Why exactly do you think Tara is still in danger, when you have to know her bosses have already changed the details of the project?"

SHEFFIELD TAVERN WAS less a bar and more a restaurant that happened to serve liquor at a bar in the back. On this Monday afternoon, the bar crowd was laid-back and sparse, though it would probably pick up later in the evening.

Archer Trask had agreed to meet Maddox Heller for an early dinner at the tavern more out of curiosity than any real desire to deal with the Campbell Cove Security agent, given the way his previous day had gone. But the chance that Heller might provide some needed information about what, exactly, had sent Tara Bentley and Owen Stiles on the run again was worth putting up with bar food and average beer.

To his surprise, Heller brought his wife, Iris, a tall, slim woman with wavy black hair and coffee-brown eyes. She smiled at Trask, extending her hand as Heller introduced them.

As Trask shook Iris's hand, he felt an odd tingle in his hand, almost as if static electricity had sparked between them. But if Iris noticed, she didn't show it.

Trask took a seat across the table from Heller and his pretty wife, looking curiously from one to the other. "I'm wondering why you asked me to meet you here."

"Alexander Quinn requested that I contact you about something that's arisen in the Robert Mallory murder case," Heller said. "He's on other business, or he'd have asked to speak with you himself."

Something about this meeting didn't quite feel right, but Trask decided to play along as if he weren't suspicious. "Not sure there's much point talking to y'all, considering you weren't there."

"Actually, there is." Heller bent down and picked up the worn leather satchel he'd brought with him to the tavern. He unbuckled the latch and flipped the satchel cover open. "You see, my wife, among her many other talents, is an artist. And we've begun to use her talent in some of our cases where we work with witnesses—"

"She's a sketch artist, you mean," Trask interrupted, beginning to lose his patience. His day had been long already, and the rest of the week stretched out in front of him like a series of endless frustrations and dead ends. "But unless she saw who shot Robert Mallory, I don't see how she can help us."

"Has anyone told you what Tara Bentley says happened to her the day of her wedding?"

Trask tried not to show his sudden spark of interest, but he couldn't help sitting up a little straighter. "No. I assume she and her partner in crime told their lawyer something about their disappearance, but he invoked the lawyer-client privilege thing, so we're still in the dark. Damn inconvenient, that. Kind of makes it hard to do my job, you know?"

"She was kidnapped," Heller said bluntly. "Two men in a white cargo van. Owen Stiles happened upon them in the middle of it and was knocked out and thrown into the van, as well."

Trask stared at him in disbelief. "You've got to be kidding me."

"Yeah, that was about the reaction Owen and Tara were expecting," Heller drawled, looking so disappointed that Trask started feeling a little guilty for his instant reaction.

Then he got angry about feeling guilty. "It's a ridiculous story. Did they happen to tell you why someone would kidnap a bride on her wedding day when, oh, by the way, the groom ended up facedown in his own blood in the groom's room?"

"They don't know why. That's part of the problem."

"How did they get away?"

"Their captors miscalculated when they bound Tara's hands. They bound them in front of her with duct tape rather than behind her, and she was able to undo the tape around Owen's hands. He freed her, and that gave them time to prepare for a blitz attack on their captors when they stopped and opened the doors to transfer them wherever they were planning to take them."

"What then?" Trask asked, glancing at Heller's wife to see how she was reacting to the story Heller was telling. She had a placid look in her eyes, tinged by a hint of jaded knowing that suggested she'd seen and heard far stranger things in her life.

"They were able to get away, although the kidnappers pursued them in the woods for a while. Finally, the kidnappers retreated, and Tara and Owen found an old abandoned cabin for shelter from the rain that night."

"What then?"

"They got in touch with us, and we got them a lawyer. You know the rest." Heller's expression was completely neutral, which in his case was a tell. There was a little more to the story about how Bentley and Stiles got from point A to point B, but Heller wasn't going to share. Trask supposed in the long run, it wasn't that big a deal. What he really wanted to know was why they changed their minds about turning themselves in.

"They decided against turning themselves in while they were right outside the police department," Trask said. "Why?"

"Because yesterday morning, when they showed up to turn themselves in, they spotted one of the men who kidnapped them entering the sheriff's department, dressed in a deputy's uniform. Alexander Quinn saw the man, too, and he described him in detail to Iris. She made this sketch." Heller pulled a sheet of paper out of his satchel and laid it on the table in front of Trask.

Trask looked at the sketch. It was extremely well drawn, full of details and nuance. He recognized the face immediately.

"You know him, don't you?" Heller asked, his tone urgent.

Trask looked up at Heller, too stunned to hide his reaction. "Yes, I do."

"Who is he?"

Trask shoved the sketch back across the table, his stomach roiling. "This is bull. Just like the story Bentley and Stiles shoveled your way."

"Who is the man in the sketch?" Heller persisted.

"Maddox," Iris said in a warning tone, clutching his arm.

Something passed between Heller and his wife, and the man's bulldog demeanor softened. When he spoke again, his voice was gentle with a hint of sympathetic understanding. "You obviously recognize the man. Even if the story Tara and Owen told is bull, like you think, there must be a reason they chose this man as the scapegoat. Who is he?"

"He's my brother," Trask growled, his stomach starting to ache. "All right? He's my brother."

Chapter Eleven

The long pause on the other end of the line only convinced
Owen that he and Tara were right. Quinn had his own
agenda, as always. He and Tara might be valuable pawns
in this particular chess game, but pawns they were, nev-
ertheless.

"It doesn't matter whether or not her bosses have
changed the details of the project," Quinn said finally.
"What matters is letting your opponent continue to believe you're better armed than he is."

"What does that even mean?" Owen asked, trying not
to lose his temper. Getting angry wouldn't get him any
closer to uncovering Quinn's motives.

Tara put her hand on Owen's arm. "It means Mr. Quinn
wants the people who kidnapped me to think there's a reason I'm not rushing back to civilization with my story."

"There is a reason. One of the guys who kidnapped us
is working for the cops."

"They'll be wondering what information we're trying to
protect by keeping you hidden," Quinn explained. "They'll
want to know what that information might be, and they'll
take risks to find out."

"But how does that help us if we don't know who they
are?" Tara asked.

"We know who one of them is," Quinn corrected after

a brief pause. "I just got a message from Maddox Heller. I don't believe you know this, but his wife is working for us as a freelance sketch artist. I gave her the description of the deputy you say kidnapped the two of you."

"You saw him?" Tara asked.

"Yes."

"Unbelievable," Owen muttered. "I barely got a glimpse of him myself. How did you get a good enough look to give anyone a description?"

"Close observation is what I do. It's what I've done for decades now." Quinn's tone was abrupt. "The point is, Heller showed Archer Trask the sketch Iris made, and now we have an ID on the man who kidnapped you."

"Who is he?" Owen asked.

"He's Virgil Trask. Archer Trask's older brother."

"Trask identified him?" Tara looked at Owen, her eyes wide.

"Reluctantly, according to Heller. I haven't briefed him yet. He left a text for me on my other phone."

"Unbelievable," Tara muttered. "The kidnapper is the brother of the cop trying to bring us in."

"This could end up working in our favor," Quinn said. "Their relationship is going to force Trask to either play this investigation strictly by the book or risk being accused of a cover-up. He knows it, and he knows we know it, too."

"But is he going to take seriously the possibility that his brother is involved with a terrorist plot?" Owen asked.

"It doesn't matter. He knows *we're* taking it seriously, and we have the clout to make waves if he doesn't at least explore the possibility."

Tara shook her head. "What if he takes himself off the case? Won't that be the protocol if his brother is now a suspect?"

"If it were a large department, yes. But the Bagley

County Sheriff's Department has only three investigators, and one of those is on maternity leave. The other one is Virgil Trask."

"Great. He's an investigator, too?"

"We're on top of this." Quinn's tone was firm and, if Owen was reading him correctly, impatient. "I'll call back before ten. You continue lying low." He ended the call abruptly.

"Your boss is a sweetheart, isn't he?" Tara's tone was bone dry.

Owen looked at the phone display. The battery was getting low. He dug in Quinn's duffel for one of the portable chargers Quinn had packed. As he plugged in the phone to charge, he looked up at Tara, waving the portable charger in front of him. "This is why we need to trust him. He's always prepared. He's always a step ahead of whatever problem he faces."

"You make him sound like a superhero."

"No, just a man who's seen the worst the world has to offer and knows what it takes to face it." Owen pushed the phone aside and shifted position until he was face-to-face with Tara, their knees touching. The sense of déjà vu made him smile. "Remember the last time we shared a tent like this?"

The tension lines in Tara's face relaxed. A smile played on her lips. "The summer before we started high school. We sat just like this in the tent and swore we'd be friends forever."

He smiled back at her. "High school should have posed a problem for us. You, the cute little cheerleader with all the popular boys in love with you, and me, the socially awkward computer geek…"

She reached across the space between them and took his hand. "You, the brilliant, funny, kindhearted friend who never, ever let me down."

He twined his fingers through hers, his pulse picking up speed until he could hear it thundering in his ears, nearly eclipsing the steady syncopation of rain on top of the tent. "Then why do you think I'll let you down if things change between us?"

She stared at him in shock, as if he'd just reached across the space between them and slapped her. She pulled her hand back from his. "You know how I feel about this."

"I know you're afraid of things changing between us."

"You should be, too." She had turned away from him and now sat with her shoulders hunched. "I don't know what I'd do without you."

"You wouldn't be without me. Don't you see that? You'd just be with me in a different way. A deeper way."

She shot a glare at him over her shoulder. "You don't know that's how it would go. What if we discovered we weren't good together that way?" She shook her head fiercely. "I can't risk that."

Owen didn't push her. It would be useless when she had so clearly closed her mind to the idea that they could have something more than just friendship.

He pulled his jacket on like armor, protecting himself against both the dropping temperature outside and the distinct chill that had grown inside the tent with his tentative attempt to address the ongoing sexual tension between them.

But he didn't know how much longer he could keep denying what he felt for her. Maybe she was happy living this half life, but he was all too quickly reaching the point where something had to give.

ARCHER TRASK POURED himself two fingers of Maker's Mark bourbon and stared at the amber liquor with an ache in his soul. It would be one thing if he could just laugh off the allegation against Virgil with full assurance, but he couldn't really do that, could he? Virgil might be wearing a badge now, but he'd spent most of his youth caught up in one mess or another.

Their father's money had spared him the worst consequences of his reckless spirit, but even after Virgil left behind his teenage years, there had been whispers of questionable behavior, hadn't there? Complaints from prisoners of rough treatment. A tendency to rub some of his fellow deputies the wrong way.

But getting involved in a kidnapping?

Archer swirled the bourbon around in the tumbler, his mouth feeling suddenly parched. Just a sip wouldn't hurt. A sip and the burn of the whiskey to drive away the chill that seemed to seep right through to his bones.

But as one of the sheriff's department's three investigators, he was always on call, especially with Tammy Sloan out on maternity leave. He couldn't afford to show up on a call with liquor on his breath.

He pushed the glass away and picked up his cell phone. Virgil's number wasn't exactly first on his speed dial. In fact, as brothers, they weren't much alike at all. Trask had always chalked that fact up to having different mothers— his father's first wife had died suddenly of an aneurysm when Virgil was a small boy. Maybe that loss so early in his life had led to his wild ways when he reached adolescence. Or maybe Virgil had just been one of those people who could only learn by making his own mistakes.

Trask pushed the number for his brother and waited for Virgil to answer. Three rings later, Virgil's gravelly voice rumbled across the line. "What's up, Archie?"

Trask gritted his teeth at the nickname. "Just haven't talked to you in a while. We always seem to miss each other at work."

"You can thank Tammy Sloan for that. Squeezing out another kid and leaving us to pick up her slack."

"What are you working on these days?"

"Car theft ring over in Campbell Cove, mostly. You've got that rich kid's murder, don't you?"

"Yeah. Wonder why you didn't catch that call? You're senior in rank."

"I was off that weekend. Out of town."

"Yeah? Where'd you go?"

"Camping up near Kingdom Come. Me and Ty Miller. Thought we'd see if we could pull a few rainbow trout out of Looney Creek, but we got skunked."

"Rainbows won't be stocked in Looney Creek for another month."

"Reckon that's why we got skunked." Virgil laughed. "Why the sudden interest in my itinerary?"

"Just wondering why you weren't the one called to the church. It's turning out to be a real puzzle."

"So I hear. Grapevine says the girl and her boy on the side nearly turned themselves in to you yesterday morning but something spooked them away. Any idea what?"

"No," Trask lied, his stomach aching. "Not a clue."

"If you need a little help, let me know. This car theft ring ain't going anywhere anytime soon, and I could spare some time for my little brother."

"I'll keep that in mind." Trask realized he was gripping his phone so hard his fingers were starting to hurt. He loosened his grip and added, "We should meet up for lunch soon. Catch up with each other."

"Sounds like a real good idea. I'll call you tomorrow and we'll set up a time. Listen, I hate to rush you off the phone, but I've got some catch-up paperwork to do—"

"Understood. Talk to you tomorrow." Trask hung up

the phone and stared at the glimmering amber liquid in the tumbler still sitting in front of him.

Just one sip wouldn't hurt, would it?

He shoved himself up from the table and grabbed the tumbler. At the sink, he poured the glass of whiskey down the drain. The fumes rising from the drain smelled vaguely of charred oak and caramel.

He wasn't sure what his brother had been doing the day of Robert Mallory's murder, but he was pretty sure Virgil was lying about going camping with Ty Miller up near Kingdom Come State Park.

The question was, why was he lying? To give himself an alibi for something? Or to give an alibi to Ty Miller, his longtime best friend and former partner in crime?

One way or another, Trask had to find out where Virgil had really been the day of the Mallory murder.

No matter where the investigation took him.

IT WAS CHILDISH to blame her mother for dying. Only a foolish little girl would sit at the end of her mother's bed and curse under her breath at a woman who hadn't planned to drive in front of a truck with brake trouble. And Tara couldn't afford to be a foolish little girl anymore. She was the woman of the house now, or at least as much a woman as a girl of nearly eleven could be.

She was starting a new school this year, and Mama was supposed to go with her to sixth grade orientation. Daddy would be useless, grumbling his way through whatever presentation the teachers had planned, muttering things like "shouldn't be coddling young'uns this way" and "when I was this age, I was working in the fields all day, school or no school."

Now orientation was going to be horrible. And it was all Mama's fault for going away.

She pushed off her mama's bed and crossed to the window, looking out across their lawn at the house across the street. A new family was moving in, her father had told her. The Stiles family. Daddy had been in the Marine Corps with Captain Stiles, and he said the man was a good enough sort *for a gol dang officer.*

He hadn't actually said gol dang, but Mama had taught her she shouldn't cuss or use the Lord's name in vain, and even though she was really, really mad at Mama right now for going away just before sixth grade started, she still lived by Mama's rules.

A boy came out of the house across the road. A tall, skinny boy with dark hair that flopped across his forehead and braces on his teeth that glittered in the sunlight as he said something to his father as he passed.

The old man answered in a voice loud enough for Tara to hear it all the way across the road, though she couldn't make out the words. Whatever the man had said, it made the boy look down at his feet until the man had entered the front door with the boy he was carrying and closed the door behind him.

Then the boy's head came up and for a moment, Tara was certain he was looking straight at her.

She felt an odd twist in the center of her chest and stepped back from the window, not sure what she had just felt.

TARA WOKE SUDDENLY to darkness and a bone-biting cold that made her huddle closer to the warm body pressed close to her own. Owen, she thought, because of course it would be Owen. It had always been Owen, ever since she'd first laid eyes on him the day of her mother's funeral.

The unchanging constant in her life.

He made a grumbling noise in his sleep, and his arm

snaked around her body, spooning her closer. A humming sensation vibrated through her to her core, spreading heat and longing in equal measures. Oh, she thought, how easy it would be to let go and just allow this tension between them to build and swell to fruition.

She had a feeling it would be amazing, because Owen himself was amazing, a man of both strength and gentleness. She'd seen his passion—in his work, in his hobbies, and yes, even his passion for her, which flickered now and then like blue fire behind his eyes when he couldn't control it.

Keeping things platonic between them was difficult but necessary. Because Tara had lost enough in her life. She wasn't a coward, and she knew how to take calculated risks in order to achieve rewards.

But she could not lose Owen. She couldn't. Things between them had to remain constant or she didn't know what she would do.

Even when her body yearned for him, the way it was doing now. When it softened helplessly in response to the hardness of his erection pressing against the small of her back.

His hand moved slowly up her body, tracing the contours of her rib cage before settling against the swell of her breast. One fingertip found the tightening peak of her nipple through her T-shirt and flicked it lightly, making her moan in response.

Was he awake? His breathing sounded even, if quickened. Maybe he was seducing her in his sleep, giving sway to the urges they both kept so tightly reined in during their waking hours.

If he was asleep, it didn't really count, did it?

His fingers curled over the top of her breast, cupping her with gentle firmness. He caressed her slowly, robbing her of breath, before he slid his hand down her stomach. His fingers dipped beneath the waistband of her jeans and played across the point of her hip bones before moving farther down.

Closer. Closer.

He jerked his hand away suddenly, a gasp of air escaping his lips and stirring her hair. He rolled away from her, robbing her of his heat.

His breath was ragged now, ragged and uneven, a sure sign that he was no longer asleep.

"Tara?" he whispered.

She stayed still, her body still thrumming with hot need that would never be satisfied. That, she understood with aching sadness, was the cost of keeping her relationship with Owen the same as it had ever been.

But she could spare him the embarrassment of knowing she'd been awake for his dream seduction. Spare him knowing how very much she'd wanted him to keep touching her, to keep driving her closer and closer to the brink of ecstasy.

Behind her, Owen blew out a soft breath and sat up, being careful not to jostle her as he rose to his feet and headed outside the tent.

As soon as she was certain he was out of earshot, she rolled onto her back and stared up at the top of the tent, her heart still pounding wildly in her ears. She felt flushed and unsatisfied, and the urge to finish what Owen had started burned through her.

But she'd earned this frustration. She was the one who'd decided that it was too risky to test the sexual waters between them.

She would just have to live with the consequences.

Chapter Twelve

That had been close. Too close.

Owen let the water in the sink grow icy cold and splashed it on his face and neck, despite the chill bumps already scattered across his flesh from the walk through the woods this cold March morning. Another early riser, an older man brushing his teeth at the next sink over in the camp's communal men's room, glanced at Owen with curiosity but kept his comments to himself.

Owen could remember only a few tantalizing fragments from his dream, but the very real memory of Tara's hot flesh beneath his exploring fingers remained vibrant in his mind.

Thank God she'd still been asleep. Thank God he'd awakened before he'd allowed himself any further liberties with her.

He soaped up his hands and rinsed them, as if he could somehow wash away the sensation of her skin on his fingertips, but the feeling remained, on his skin and in his head.

He should feel ashamed. Dirty, even. But all he felt was a ravenous need to finish what he'd started in his dream.

He tried to gather his wits, get himself under control before he returned to the tent. But the man staring back at him in the mirror looked fevered and hungry, his blue eyes dark with the memory of touching Tara the way he'd longed to touch her forever.

He closed his eyes and bent his head, feeling tired. Tired of pretending he didn't feel what he most certainly did. Weary of denying himself the very natural desire he felt for Tara.

If he were going to be around her, he'd have to find a way to rein in that desire for good. He just didn't know if that was possible, which left one other option.

He could leave her life for good. Put her behind him, cut himself off from the constant temptation she posed and try to live without her.

As terrible as the idea of excising Tara from his life seemed to him right now, the thought of a lifetime of pretending he didn't want her as much as he loved her was even worse. It was a lie to behave as if he was okay with being nothing more than her friend.

He wasn't okay with it. He couldn't keep doing it.

The bearded man at the next sink had apparently watched the spectacle long enough. "Are you okay?" he asked.

Owen lifted his chin with determination. "I will be," he said.

He felt the other man's gaze follow him out of the bathroom. Outside, frigid air blasted him, reigniting a flood of goose bumps down his arms and back. Only belatedly did he realize that he shouldn't have drawn attention to himself the way he had. Even now his face might be plastered across TV screens throughout Kentucky and nearby states. How long before someone realized the scruffy-faced, bleary-eyed man in the hipster beanie they'd seen in the campground bathroom was the fugitive from Bagley County?

He didn't know whether to hope Tara was still asleep or

awake when he got back to the tent, but when he ducked back into the tent to find her up and snugly dressed in a down jacket she'd bought back in Abingdon, he found he was relieved. The extra clothing she wore seemed like armor donned specifically to cool his ardor, which made him wonder if she'd been awake for at least part of his unconscious seduction.

But the smile she flashed his way was pleasant and unclouded by any sort of doubt, so he decided she couldn't know what he'd almost done.

"I'm starving," she announced. "I was thinking, we should probably use up the eggs and bacon in the cooler, don't you think? Before the ice melts and they start to spoil? And I bought a little bottle of syrup back in Abingdon in case I got the chance to make my famous French toast. What do you think? French toast and fried bacon?"

He forced a smile. "Who could say no to French toast and bacon?"

"I'll go get the stuff from the cooler. Can you get the camp stove started?" She passed him in the opening of the tent, her arm brushing his. Even with the added layers of clothing they both wore, Owen could swear he felt the same tingle in the skin on his arm he'd felt in his fingertips when he woke that morning with his hand under her shirt.

He lowered his head until his chin hit his chest. How was he going to keep up appearances with her? Already, he was one raw nerve, acutely aware of her constant nearness.

It had to be because they were forced together by these circumstances, stuck in a situation where neither of them could go far from the other for any length of time. Back home, he could escape to his own apartment, indulge his fantasies about her and, on occasion, indulge his body's demands as well, without Tara having to know about any of those feelings or urges.

But there was nowhere to escape to now, no way to channel his desires without Tara knowing what was going on. He was stuck between the blissful heaven of being close to her and the burning hell of not being able to do a damn thing about it.

He forced himself out of the tent and went about the business of firing up the camp stove, glad for the distraction. But it lasted only as long as it took Tara to return from where they'd parked the SUV with the styrene cooler they'd picked up during their shopping trip. He felt her before he heard her footsteps crunching through the undergrowth. Her presence skittered up his spine like the phantom touch of fingers.

"I thought I'd bring the cooler to us so we didn't have to keep going back and forth to the SUV," she said as she set it beside him. "The ice has barely melted at all. I guess the cold snap helped slow the melting. I think we're good with the perishables for another day or so."

"Good," he said, mostly because he could think of no more cogent response. He backed away and let her take over at the camp stove, turning his back to the sight of her while pretending to take in the rain-washed beauty of the sunrise just visible through the trees to the east of them.

"I wish we'd thought to buy a radio," Tara said over the thumping of her spoon whipping the eggs into a batter. "I'd like to know what the news folks are saying about us after this weekend."

"Probably better not to know," Owen murmured. "I'm sure Quinn will keep us up with the latest news."

"I don't know," Tara muttered. "He's not exactly been a font of information to this point."

"He called when he said he would last night."

"And told us blasting nada."

He couldn't stop a smile. Tara had a thing about making

up her own versions of profanities in order to avoid cursing. She'd told him once that her mother loathed swearing, even though she indulged her leatherneck husband's proclivity toward salty language. Tara didn't talk much about her mother at all, but he'd gotten the feeling that her attempts to temper her own language were a result of her mother's influence.

"Maybe there's nothing to tell yet," he said.

"It has to have hit the news by now, at least in Kentucky. Robert's family is very influential in Lexington."

"I'm sure it's been on the news."

"Which means whatever photos of us they could find are being plastered all over local Kentucky news stations. And maybe Virginia ones as well, if they've figured out we were headed for here."

She was right. But what else could they do at this point? They'd already changed their appearances. His beard was growing in thick enough to change the way he looked, and the beanie and glasses made him even harder to recognize. Tara was almost unrecognizable with her new spiky haircut and ever-changing streaks of spray-on color in her hair.

He knew a few ways to go completely off the grid. Change their names, assume new identities with documents that would pass all but the most in-depth scrutiny. But that would be the act of someone who'd lost all hope of justice prevailing.

Had they really reached that point?

"Maybe we should have turned ourselves in to that Virginia state policeman I almost ran into back at the rest area," he said.

"They'd just send us back to the Bagley County Sheriff's Department and we'd be right back where we started." Tara rubbed her eyes, smearing the remains of her heavy mascara and eyeliner.

Without thought, he reached across the narrow space between them and ran his thumb under her right eye to wipe away the worst of the smears.

Instantly, heat flared between them, searing in its intensity.

She trembled beneath his touch, her eyes darkening with unmistakable signs of desire. He'd seen such a reaction in her before but never this strong, this undeniable.

And in that instant, he knew. "You were awake."

She licked her lips. "Yes."

"Why didn't you stop me? Why didn't you wake me up?"

She looked away, closing her eyes. "Because I didn't want you to stop."

He touched her again, tipping her chin up to make her look at him. Her eyes fluttered open and again he was struck by the potency of desire he read in her gaze. "Tara…"

She drew away from him, shaking her head. "We can't, Owen. You know why we can't."

"Because you're afraid that it'll all go wrong and you'll lose me."

"I can't deal with losing you, Owen."

"Do you know what I was thinking about this morning? When I went to the restroom?"

She stared back at him mutely, the desire in her eyes replaced by apprehension.

"I was thinking that if things between us didn't change, I was going to leave Kentucky. Go to Texas or California or, hell, I don't know, maybe Idaho. Anywhere you weren't, so I could get you out of my system once and for all. Because I don't think I can live in this endless limbo, Tara. Maybe you're okay with our relationship staying as innocent and platonic as it was when we met in sixth grade. But I'm not."

She stared at him in horror. "You don't mean that."

"I do, Tara. I'm sorry. I know you want to keep things the way they are, but people change. Circumstances change. I love you. Desperately. In every way a person can love another person."

"I love you, too."

"Then you have to let me go."

She shook her head violently. "No." She rose to her knees, reaching across the space between them to cup his face between her palms. "I don't want to let you go. I can't. You're all I have anymore."

He saw her expression shift, as if she finally realized what she was asking of him and why. Her eyes narrowed with dismay, and she looked so stricken that he wanted nothing more than to put his arms around her and promise her everything would be okay.

But he couldn't do that anymore. He'd finally reached his breaking point.

He put his hands on hers, gently removing them from his face. "I can't be your safety net, Tara. I don't want to do it anymore. If you can't take a chance on us, then that's fine. I'll accept it and go so we can both finally move on."

Tears welled in her eyes, but she blinked them away, anger beginning to drive away the hurt he'd seen in her expression before. "You promised you'd never let me down."

"I know." He hadn't let go of her hands, he realized, as if holding them was as natural as breathing. He gave them a light squeeze before letting go. "I just don't believe the status quo is good for either of us anymore."

Anger blazed in her eyes now, giving off green sparks. "Is this an ultimatum? Sleep with me or I won't be your friend anymore?"

"That is totally unfair, Tara! You know that's not what I'm talking about here." He turned away from her, anger beginning to overtake his own pain.

"That's the only thing we don't have between us, don't you see?" She caught his arm, tugging him back around to look at her. "We have everything else. Friendship. Understanding. Loyalty."

"We don't have marriage together. Children together. We won't make a family together or grow old together. If you think you can find a man or I can find a woman who'll put up with what we do have together, you're wrong."

"Robert was going to."

"Tara, Robert was already trying to push me out of your lives."

She stared at him, shocked. "No, he wasn't."

"Not where you could see it, no."

She sat back on her heels. "Why didn't you tell me?"

"I didn't want to come between you that way."

"If I'd known what he was doing, there wouldn't have been an us to come between," she said fervently. "Robert knew what you are to me. I made it clear from the beginning. One of the reasons I thought we could work together was that he took your presence in my life so well."

"Please, don't do this." Owen sighed, hating himself for even bringing up Robert's issues with him. "I don't want you to remember him badly."

"My life is so upended right now and I honestly can't understand why." She raked her fingers through her spiky hair, looking faintly surprised to find it so short. "I mean, intellectually, I can understand that someone wants to get his hands on something I know, and I also get that it's information that's dangerous for someone with bad intentions to know. But like I said earlier, I'm sure what I know has already been changed by my company. I'm as out of the loop now as anyone else."

"Is there anything you knew that could still be dangerous if someone else knew it?" he asked, glad for the change of subject. Despite his declaration to Tara about cutting the cord between them, he wasn't any more eager to do so than she was.

"I honestly don't think so. Whoever's taking over my job now that I'm gone is probably far more in danger for what he or she knows than I am now."

Owen frowned. "You think your bosses would already have put someone in your position?"

"I'm sure they have. It's not a job that can go unfilled for long, especially with the upcoming symposium details having to be changed so close to the planned time of the event."

So there was now someone else who knew the details of the symposium, Owen thought. Who was in the job only because Tara was now unavailable.

"What would happen if you went back to Mercerville and managed to get yourself cleared of Robert's murder?" he asked. "Would you get your job back?"

"If my bosses were satisfied that all the charges against me were bogus, I'd say yes. We had a good relationship and I was good at the job."

"Even if they'd already replaced you?"

"I think so. It would be hard for someone to come in and learn my job in a few weeks, much less a few days. What I did, nobody else in the company duplicated."

"So how did they find someone to replace you?"

She seemed to give it some thought. "I guess they would have promoted my main assistant, although he wouldn't be able to pick up everything I was doing very quickly. It was a pretty complex system, with lots of security protocols in place. Plus, I had a more personal relationship with the people we were inviting to the symposium than anyone else in my section would have. That kind of interpersonal connection can be hard to maintain. Lots of personalities and egos involved."

Owen nodded. "Who is your primary assistant?"

"Chris Miller."

Owen pulled out his phone and typed in a text to Quinn.

"What are you doing?" Tara asked.

"Telling Quinn to do a deep background check on Chris Miller."

"You think Chris is involved in this mess?"

"I don't know," Owen admitted. "But we have to look at all the angles. Maybe the real reason Robert was killed was to make sure you couldn't go back to your job before the symposium began."

"Because I would be a suspect."

"We couldn't figure out why they kidnapped you. Maybe that's why."

"I thought they wanted to get the information out of me."

"Which would have been far messier than just making sure you were a suspect in a murder and unsuitable for classified work."

Tara cocked her head. "So by staying out here on the run, we're actually playing into the hands of the people who kidnapped me and maybe even killed Robert?"

"Maybe we are."

"So why is your boss making sure we stay where we are?"

That, Owen thought, was a good question. Alexander Quinn had a way of positioning his own allies as pawns in a bigger game. He would do everything possible to protect them, but sometimes collateral damage happened. An unfortunate but inescapable result of the high-stakes game Quinn and the people at Campbell Cove Security played.

"I guess maybe he's already figured out what's going on," Tara murmured, her eyes narrowed with thought. "Maybe Chris Miller is already on Quinn's radar."

Owen wouldn't be surprised if that were true. "But if he is, can he move fast enough to stop whatever plot is underfoot?"

"I don't know. It all depends on whether they moved the symposium back or up."

"What do you think they did?" Owen asked. "If you could read the minds of your company officers?"

"Up," she said after a moment more of thought. "If they moved the symposium up rather than back, it wouldn't leave bad actors much time to put their plot together."

"All the more reason to keep you on the run. Even if you went back now, you'd have to work through all the red tape and the explanations of why you fled in the first place. You wouldn't have time to get back to your job before the symposium took place."

Tara's lips twisted with irritation. "Damn."

Owen lifted his eyebrows at her curse.

One side of her mouth curled up in amusement at his reaction. "Sorry, but sometimes a profanity is the only word that'll do."

"So, what do you think we should do next?" he asked.

Her green-eyed gaze lifted to meet his, full of determination. "I think it's time to go home."

Chapter Thirteen

"So Ty Miller works evenings?" Archer Trask peered through his windshield, sunlight glaring off the back windshield of the vehicle in front of him. The rain that had soaked the area the previous night was long gone, replaced by blinding sunlight and rising temperatures.

"That's right," the receptionist on the other end of the line replied.

Ahead of him, the light turned green and traffic started to move. Trask put his phone in the hands-free holder. "What about Friday evening? Was he working Friday?"

"Let me check the schedule." There was a brief pause, and then she answered, "No, he was off Friday and Saturday."

"Is he working tonight?"

"Yes. He's scheduled to work every night through Friday of this week."

Trask grimaced. "Okay, thank you." He ended the call and stared at the road ahead, frustrated. So far, his brother's alibi seemed to be holding, although Trask hadn't gotten far. For one thing, he didn't want Virgil to know what he was doing, because his brother would certainly want to know why he was trying to establish his alibi.

And for another, he wasn't sure he should be giving any credence to the story Heller had told him in the first place.

It was a secondhand, maybe even thirdhand story from a pair of people who were currently on the run from the law. Some people, including his boss the sheriff, might not appreciate him spending time trying to prove his brother's innocence when there was an actual murder case on his plate.

The problem was, Trask was pretty sure Robert Mallory's murder was connected to whatever had happened to Tara Bentley the day of her wedding. He no longer thought she'd willingly left the church. But that left a lot of possibilities open, possibilities that didn't necessarily involve kidnapping.

Maybe Owen Stiles had spirited her away, not willing to watch her marry another man. Everyone seemed certain they were just friends, but Archer knew it was hard to keep sex out of the equation, friends or not. Tara Bentley was a healthy, attractive woman, and Owen Stiles was a healthy, reasonably good-looking man. The situation was ripe for sexual tension.

Had Stiles killed Mallory? Of the two fugitives, he seemed the more likely suspect. Jealousy, possessiveness, lust, obsession—all potential motives for murder.

But if he'd murdered Tara's fiancé, why was she still with Stiles? Was her friendship stronger than her love for and loyalty to the man she planned to marry? Or had she been the one whose feelings transcended friendship?

He rubbed his head as he reached the intersection with Old Cumberland Highway. If he turned left, he'd be heading back toward Mercerville and the sheriff's department, where three days' worth of paperwork awaited him. If he turned right, he'd end up in Cumberland, not far from Kingdom Come State Park.

He wondered if anyone in the area remembered seeing his brother and Ty Miller at the camping area outside the park the previous Friday.

When the light turned green and traffic started to move again, Trask signaled a right-hand turn.

"Are you going to tell Quinn what we're doing?" Tara looked up from stashing the last of the supplies in the duffel and stretched her back. "Because I don't think he's going to be happy that we're changing the plan he's working, whatever it is."

"Too bad. It's not his life. It's ours." With his usual precision, Owen folded the tent into a tidy square. He crossed to where she stood and slipped it inside the duffel before zipping it shut.

He stood close enough that she caught a whiff of the soap he'd used earlier when they risked heading into the more crowded camping area to use the campground's shower facilities. Not for the first time, she'd spent her shower time trying not to think of Owen naked under the spray of his own shower, water sluicing down his chest to catch briefly in the narrow line of hair that bisected his abdomen before dipping farther south.

But her imagination had seemed so much more potent, so much harder to deny, now that she'd actually felt his fingers against her flesh, moving with sexy determination, making her shiver with need.

Was this how it was for him, too? This trembling ache in her core when she looked at him, the way even his voice could send little flutters of awareness up and down her spine?

She was beginning to understand why he'd snapped earlier this morning. Wanting something you knew you could never have was painful. The pain didn't go away just because you were the one putting up all the obstacles, as she was coming to understand. Was it even worse when you were the person who wanted all the obstacles to disappear?

She had to clear her throat before she spoke. "It's probably better if we don't give him any forewarning."

"You do realize he knows exactly where we are, don't you?" Owen met her troubled gaze. "All of the Campbell Cove Security vehicles have GPS trackers on them."

"Even his personal vehicle?"

"Even his personal vehicle. While we were in the general camping area, I logged on to my computer and went through one of my back doors at the company to check the GPS monitoring. There we were, one stationary red dot on the map."

"So when we start heading back to Kentucky—"

"Quinn will know," Owen finished for her. He picked up the duffel and took a quick look around the campsite area to make sure they hadn't forgotten anything. They'd already packed all the other supplies, including the camp stove, into the back of the SUV. "But we should have a few hours of travel before he starts getting suspicious. Should we be planning our next moves during that time?"

"Probably should be," Tara agreed as she followed him through the undergrowth to the rocky path where the SUV was parked. "Except I'm not sure I know what those next moves should be."

"You don't think the first thing we should do is turn ourselves in?" He put the duffel in the back of the SUV and turned to look at Tara. "Isn't that the best way to get you reinstated at Security Solutions?"

"Theoretically, yes. But what if it doesn't work? What if we're locked away and nobody believes us? We need proof of our theory, and the only way to get that is to—"

"Don't say it."

"We have to break in to my office."

Owen shook his head. "Your office, which has probably had security doubled or tripled over the past few days? That office?"

"Yes. You're right, they've almost certainly hardened the security, but they're trying to keep terrorists out, not me."

"I'm not so sure about that."

"Okay, I guess it's possible they're trying to keep me out, as well. But either way, they're not trying to keep *you* out."

"Tara, I don't know anything about your company's security measures."

"You don't know yet. But you've spent the past few years as a white hat hacker, haven't you?"

"That's not what I call it."

"But it's what you are, right?" He gave a slight nod, and she pushed ahead, the idea making more sense the longer it percolated in her head. "With my knowledge of the company and its general protocols, and your knowledge of computer systems, I'm betting we can get inside the office building without being detected. Even at code red security, only certain areas of the building will be under twenty-four-hour surveillance."

"It seems to me that any part of the company where we might be able to discover anything helpful would be one of those areas of the building." Owen nodded toward the driver's door. "You want to drive or do you want me to?"

"You drove all the way here. I'll drive back. Maybe you could catch up on some sleep."

He looked skeptical as he climbed into the passenger seat.

While he buckled in, she addressed his previous protest. "You're right that the parts of the building where the most top secret material is kept will be under constant surveillance. But my office isn't one of those spaces. I went to the classified material when I needed it. I didn't take it out of its place of safekeeping."

"So your office won't be considered a high security risk area."

"Exactly."

"If that's so, how does getting into that area help us?"

"Because Chris Miller and I shared office space. Not right on top of each other, but in the same section. If I'm able to successfully get into my office undetected, I may be able to get into his office and see if there's anything incriminating to find."

"Do you expect there to be?" Owen asked curiously.

She considered the question carefully. "Honestly, I don't know. The only thing about Chris Miller that's ever given me pause is that he's a little too friendly."

Owen frowned at her. "Friendly how?"

She glanced at Owen. "Not that kind of friendly. I just mean, he doesn't have a suspicious bone in his body, which is weird for a guy who works in security. I've had to warn him about phishing emails, that kind of thing. He opened an email not too long ago and nearly let loose a virus in our system. I figured out what he'd done just in time to warn our IT guys and they stopped the program before it could open up any holes in our cybersecurity."

"How does he even keep his job? For that matter, why on earth would he be next in line for your job?"

She made a face. "Nepotism. Chris's uncle is the founder of our firm."

"Maybe he's the weak spot in your company's security without even knowing it," Owen suggested. "Someone could be using him. Manipulating him to get the information they want."

"More likely than not," she agreed. "Which is why I need to get into the office and see what he's been up to. It might help me find out if anyone has been trying to exploit his position to get secure information."

Owen remained silent for a long time while they headed southwest on I-81 to Abingdon. Only as they exited the interstate and began heading due west toward Kentucky did he speak again. "You realize if we get caught, it will make it nearly impossible to prove our innocence."

"I know. But it may be our only chance to find out what's really going on and who's behind it in time to stop whatever they're planning. That's reason enough to take the risk, don't you think?"

As Tara braked at a traffic light, Owen reached across the space between them and touched her face with the back of his hand. "Has anyone ever told you what a brave person you are?"

She stared back at him, a shiver running through her at his touch. For a moment, as their gazes locked and the air in the SUV's cab grew warm and thick, she found herself wondering if she'd made the wrong choice all those years ago when she felt the tug of attraction to Owen and ruthlessly subdued it. What if he was right? What if they could have everything? Their deep and enduring friendship and the heady promise of intense passion?

Wasn't that what everyone really wanted? To have it all?

The traffic light changed to green. Owen dropped his hand away from her cheek and nodded for her to drive on.

She headed west on Porterfield Highway, feeling chilled and unsettled.

WORKING FOR A small law enforcement agency had its benefits and its drawbacks. For the most part, Archer Trask liked the slower pace of his job at the Bagley County Sheriff's Department. There was enough petty crime to keep him busy most of the time, and in such a small place, he generally got to know the citizens he helped as people rather than impersonal names and case file numbers, the way he had done when he worked a couple of years in the Louisville Police Department before returning home to Bagley County.

But one of the drawbacks of working for a small agency was the glacial pace at which the wheels of information gathering turned. Which was why it had taken almost a day for a simple background information request about the security company where Ty Miller worked to make its way to his email inbox.

He had just spent a frustrating hour trying to track down anyone in the Cumberland area who might have seen his brother and Ty Miller up near Looney Creek on Friday, but the problem was, Kingdom Come State Park wouldn't open until the first of April, and most of the people who weren't park visitors had been too busy at their own places of work on Friday to notice if a couple of middle-aged men had wandered by with fly rods and tackle boxes that day.

In fact, he had begun to think he'd wasted a whole day chasing a false lead when his phone pinged with the email notification. He pulled over onto the shoulder and checked the message. It was from Don Robbins, the deputy he'd assigned to dig up background information on Cumberland Security Staffing.

He read through the list of companies that hired the staffing company to provide security personnel for their firms. There were a couple of shopping strip centers, a movie theater, a couple of mining companies and even a church or two that had showed up on the list of clients.

It was only on his second read through that Trask came across a familiar but unexpected name.

He stared at the email for a moment, then dialed a phone

number, unease wriggling in his stomach as he waited for an answer.

"Security Solutions," answered the female receptionist.

"This is Deputy Archer Trask. Is this Diane?"

"Yes, Deputy," she said, her tone warming as if she were pleased that he'd remembered her name. "How can I help you?"

"Diane, does your company still use Cumberland Security Staffing?"

There was a brief pause before she replied, "I'm not really supposed to answer that question."

"Could you put me through to someone who can?"

There was another pause. "I've been asked not to disturb any of the officers this afternoon." She lowered her voice. "Is it urgent for you to know this information right now?"

"Yes," he answered. It was urgent to him, at least.

"We do employ them. They provide our four night guards."

"Can you tell me the names of the guards?"

"I don't know if I can do that—"

"Okay, maybe you can tell me this. Is one of them named Ty Miller?"

After a long pause, Diane whispered, "Yes."

"Thank you, Diane. You've been very helpful."

He hung up the phone and stared at the narrow road stretching into the mountains ahead of him. So Ty Miller was a security guard at Security Solutions, the company where Tara Bentley worked. And according to Maddox Heller, Tara Bentley was kidnapped by two men outside the church where she was supposed to marry Robert Mallory, who had mysteriously turned up murdered in the groom's room.

Tara Bentley, who had told her lawyer that his brother Virgil was one of the men who'd kidnapped her.

His brother, Virgil, whose alibi for the day of Robert Mallory's murder and Tara Bentley's alleged kidnapping was Ty Miller. Who worked for the same company as Tara Bentley, albeit indirectly.

Trask rubbed his temples, his head aching with the sudden twists and turns his murder case had started to take. Worse than the complications was the fact that he didn't know what he was supposed to do next. Bring his brother, the deputy investigator, in for questioning? Interrogate Ty Miller about his whereabouts on Friday, even though he had less probable cause to question him than he had where Virgil was concerned?

He needed to find Tara Bentley and Owen Stiles. They were the only people who really knew, firsthand, what had happened to them the day of Robert Mallory's murder.

"Why are you back in Kentucky?" Quinn's voice was tight with annoyance over the cell phone speaker.

Owen glanced toward Tara. She gave a nod. "Tell him."

"How secure is this line?" Owen asked Quinn.

"About as secure as any cell phone can get. Someone would have to be listening for your transmissions specifically to find you. Or get very lucky."

"I'm not sure that's secure enough."

"Then perhaps we should meet," Quinn said.

"Where?"

"Where Maddox picked you up Saturday," Quinn answered. It was oblique enough a response that only Owen, Tara, Maddox Heller and Quinn would know where he meant.

"I can do that," Owen said. "In about an hour?"

"I'll see you there." Quinn hung up.

Tara glanced at Owen. "Do you think he'll try to talk us out of it?"

Owen thought about the question for a moment, then shook his head. "No. I think he'll devise some ingenious way for us to get away with it."

For the first time in many miles, Tara shook off her troubled expression and managed a smile. "I think maybe I'm starting to like Alexander Quinn."

"Don't go crazy, now," Owen joked, to cover his own anxieties starting to rise to the surface the closer they got to Bagley County. He wasn't as sure as Tara that breaking into her company office was a smart thing to do. The risks were high and the possibility of rewards was scanty in comparison.

Maybe he'd been right that Quinn would support their crazy scheme, but he wasn't sure he'd consider that good news.

Chapter Fourteen

So far, Ty Miller hadn't answered any of Trask's calls, and attempts to catch him at home had so far proved futile. However, a check with the receptionist at Cumberland Security Staffing had revealed that Miller would be working the night shift at Security Solutions tonight, starting at eleven.

In the meantime, Trask had been studying his file on Robert Mallory, trying to examine the case from a different angle. Mallory's death had seemed to be the main event, with Tara Bentley's disappearance a side story. But what if that assumption was wrong? What if Tara's disappearance were the focus of the crime, with Mallory's murder a peripheral event?

Had Mallory stumbled onto something that had led to his murder? Could he even have been complicit in whatever had led to his fiancée's kidnapping?

"Assuming she was kidnapped," he muttered as he checked the clock on his office wall. Only a little after five. Almost five more hours to go before he could head to the Security Solutions compound and wait to catch Ty Miller before he started work.

With a sigh, he returned his attention to the files. He preferred legwork to paperwork, but at least this particular bit of paperwork involved trying to pull together the scattered threads of a mystery.

Starting with Tara Bentley.

Who was Tara Jane Bentley? He knew the basics—the only daughter of former Gunnery Sergeant Dale Bentley and Susan Bentley, both now deceased. She was born in Campbell Cove, grew up there and only left town to attend the University of Virginia.

Trask paused, reaching for a second stack of papers. Hmm. Owen Stiles had also attended the University of Virginia. Coincidence? Unlikely.

He set aside questions of their unusually close friendship, since it would only lead him back to mundane motives for Robert Mallory's murder, and that road hadn't been leading him anywhere definitive.

For the past five years, Tara had worked at Security Solutions, a nonprofit think tank dedicated entirely to analyzing security threats both global and domestic and searching out strategies for prevention and even prediction of future events, helping security experts to stay ahead of the terrorist threat rather than reacting after an event took place.

Since joining as an analyst, she'd moved quickly up the company ladder to director of global relations, whatever that meant. Because the company was a nonprofit entity, she wasn't exactly rolling in dough, though his tiptoe through the company's public profile suggested she made a decent salary.

But he'd already examined the idea of a profit motive in Robert Mallory's murder, at least where Tara Bentley was concerned. Mallory's income had been generous, and would've grown considerably as he took over more and more of his father's law practice. He'd recently become a partner, and if Tara Bentley had gone through with marrying Mallory, she could have led a financially comfortable life indeed. But she wasn't going to see a penny of his money now, since he'd died before the wedding.

So what had really happened the day of the wedding that had left Mallory dead and Tara Bentley running for her life?

Could it have anything to do with his brother Virgil and his elusive alibi for the day in question?

Trask leaned back in his chair and rubbed his burning eyes, feeling further from the truth than ever.

"WE ALMOST WENT to this school," Tara commented as Alexander Quinn walked with her and Owen down the long corridors of Campbell Cove Security. "It closed about two years before our freshman year. Do you remember?"

"Vaguely," Owen said, looking around. "I guess I never really gave any thought to what this place was before it became Campbell Cove Security."

"It was scheduled to be demolished before I came in and bought up the property and the building." Quinn's tone was brisk, as if he was annoyed by the trip down memory lane.

Tara kept her mouth shut for the rest of the walk. When they reached the end of the corridor, instead of turning right or left, Quinn led them forward through a dark red door marked Exit.

Outside, twilight had fallen while they were in Quinn's office, updating him on everything they'd done since their last contact. Tara had been expecting a little more push-back from Quinn about their breaking-and-entering plan, but he'd been remarkably positive about the idea, with a couple of caveats.

"First, if something goes wrong, there can be no direct links back to my company," he said firmly. "So that means I can't send you any of my agents to help you out with your plan. Just Owen, and he's not going to be there in any company-related capacity."

"Understood," Tara said quickly.

"And second, if you do end up in trouble because of this, I'm not going to be able to help you the way I have so far. You'll be on your own completely. Can you deal with that?"

Despite the tightening sensation in the pit of her gut, Tara had nodded.

"We have to figure out what's really going on before we risk going to the police again," Owen added with more resolve than Tara felt. "There could be a terror plot already in motion, and this could be our chance to stop it cold."

"Which is exactly why I'm going along with this crazy plan," Quinn said with a smile. "And why I'm going to help you figure out all the angles so we can avoid any of the obvious pitfalls."

Among the obvious pitfalls, Tara had learned, were the exact security protocols followed by Security Solutions' night security team. Quinn refused to reveal just how he'd come by the information, but he was able to tell them when the security patrols would be in what part of the building. "It's not smart to stick to a set plan," he'd commented with disapproval, "but I guess that's the price of outsourcing your site security instead of building your own in-house staff."

Tara's guess about the company's security focus had been correct. Except for a single walk-through of the company's nonsecure office wing early in the shift, just after eleven o'clock, the security patrols would spend the rest of their eight-hour shift patrolling the secure areas. None of the guards had keys to the securest rooms, where the classified material was, Quinn told them. "You won't be able to get in there, either," he warned.

"We don't think we'll need to," Tara assured him.

Over the next couple of hours, they'd worked out a plan that even Quinn agreed might get them in and out of the building without detection. He admitted he'd already checked with Tara's bosses to see if they'd done anything about revoking her credentials. They hadn't, they'd admitted. They weren't ready to give up on her innocence, and blocking her credentials seemed too much like admitting she could have done something wrong.

"Foolish sentimentality" had been Quinn's succinct assessment, but at last it made it more likely she could get through inside her office building without triggering any alarms.

"They'll have evidence of an ingress," Quinn warned, "and they'll have the code number used to enter, if they decided to check the security system logs."

"If I don't trigger an alarm, they won't have any reason to check," Tara told him. "And even if they do, all they'll see is that someone entered the office building using the security code for my department. But everyone in the department uses the same code number to disarm the alarm."

Quinn's stony expression was as good as an eye roll. "Our nation's security is in good hands."

"Well, it'll work in our favor this time," Owen murmured.

They'd shared a pizza with Quinn while going over a quick checklist of things they wanted to accomplish and how they planned to go about it. There was a brief discussion about using night vision equipment to aid in their getting safely inside the security perimeter, but they all agreed that since both Tara and Owen lacked experience with night vision equipment, the goggles would be more of a detriment than an asset.

Finally, Quinn had handed over a couple of heavy backpacks and led them down the corridor to this exit into the encroaching woods behind Campbell Cove Security.

"We're being banished to the woods?" Tara murmured as she struggled to keep up with Owen's long strides behind Quinn.

"I have no idea," Owen admitted.

Ahead of them, Quinn strode confidently through the dark woods, avoiding obstacles in the underbrush as if he knew exactly where they were, even though the path beneath their feet was little more than a tangle of weeds and vines, anything but well traveled.

About a hundred yards into the thickening woods, they reached a small clearing of sorts. There were no trees in the small area, but kudzu vines took up the slack, nearly covering what looked like a small shack in the middle of the woods.

"It used to be one of the school's outbuildings," Quinn told them as they approached the kudzu-swallowed building. Only the door remained vine free, and even it would have been difficult to pick out at a cursory glance, painted with a mottled green camouflage pattern that nearly perfectly matched the surrounding kudzu. "We left the kudzu when we cleaned it up and put it to use. Cheaper than camo netting."

Inside, the place was remarkably clean. It was little more than a room with a couple of camp beds, a tiny kitchen area with a sink, a one-burner electric cooktop and a mini refrigerator. The door in the back of the building led to a small but usable half bath with a tiny shower and an even tinier sink.

"Please tell me this works," Tara said as she eyed the shower with near desperation.

"It all works. Electricity and plumbing should get you by until you have to leave for your rendezvous with Security Solutions," Quinn said. "I had someone park the SUV in the woods due north of here, just off the road into Mercerville. They've topped off your fuel tank and changed out the license plates again, just in case." He slanted them a wry look. "Got rid of the bumper stickers, too."

"Thought of everything," Tara murmured.

"You'll stay here until then. I thought you might both enjoy a hot shower and a hot meal. From this point forward, I expect no contact from either of you unless you achieve your ends. Agreed?"

Tara glanced at Owen. He gave a brief nod.

"Agreed," Tara said. Owen echoed her response.

"Clean up after yourselves and try not to knock off any of the kudzu." Quinn opened the door, quickly slipped out and closed it behind him.

The silence that fell afterward made Tara feel as if she were about to smother. The small outbuilding itself wasn't cold, nor was it overly warm, but it felt closed in, suddenly, after days of living outside or in an SUV.

"I'll be magnanimous and give you first dibs on the shower," Owen said. He had taken a seat on one of the camp beds and was digging through the backpack Quinn had supplied. He pulled out each piece and laid it on the bed, revealing a couple of changes of clothes, a pair of hiking boots and a handful of protein bars. Owen waved one of the protein bars at Tara as she sat on the bed opposite. "He meant what he said about cutting us loose, but at least he gave us a change of clothes and a couple of meals to get us through to the next hidey-hole."

"Yay?" Tara pulled out the clothes Quinn had provided for her. They looked as if they'd fit well enough, though she longed for her own closet and her own wardrobe.

What she wouldn't give to be in her cute little house in Mercerville, cuddled up in front of the fireplace.

With Owen, an unrepentant little voice whispered in her ear.

She grabbed the change of clothes and headed for the small bathroom. "I'll try not to use up all the hot water."

Easy enough, she thought as she turned the cold tap all the way on.

ARCHER TRASK EYED the clock as he closed up the file folders. Three hours to go, and he wasn't any closer to a theory about Robert Mallory's murder than he'd been when he started.

Unless he wanted to believe his brother and Ty Miller really had kidnapped Tara Bentley and killed her fiancé.

But what was the motive? Trask's brother was a pretty ordinary guy. Divorced, no kids, worked a tough job and spent his off time hunting, fishing and four-wheeling. About the average for a guy from Bagley County, Kentucky. He wasn't particularly religious or political, as far as Trask knew, which would seem to rule out those particular motives.

As far as Trask knew. Which was the problem, wasn't it? Even when they were younger, he and Virgil had never been close. Virgil was a decade older than Trask, and he'd never had much time for his younger half brother, too busy raising hell with his friends to do any brotherly things with his tagalong sibling.

After a while, Trask had stopped trying to be close to Virgil, which had seemed to be fine with him.

There was quite a lot about Virgil that he didn't know, wasn't there?

Really, if anyone knew Virgil at all, it was their father, Asa. He had always had a soft spot for Virgil, even during the worst of his delinquency. *We used to call it sowin' wild oats*, Asa would say when Trask's mother complained about Virgil's latest misdemeanor.

Trask had long suspected that Asa had never really gotten over his first wife. Marrying Trask's mother, Lena, had been a matter of expediency—he had a young boy who needed a mama, and he was a man who needed a warm body in his bed. Lena Lawrence had been a beauty in her youth, and she'd fallen hard for the older widower with a child.

Trask suspected she'd long ago given up on true love and was still married to the old man much for the same reason he'd married her in the first place—neither of them wanted to go through life alone.

He picked up his phone and dialed his parents' number. His mother answered, her voice warm, "Archer, how are you?"

With some embarrassment, he realized it had been at least two weeks since he talked to his mother. "I'm good," he said quickly, realizing she might be wondering if he was calling with bad news.

Of course, in a way he might be.

"I heard you're workin' that murder case at the church."

"Yeah. I can't really talk about it."

"Oh, I know. Your daddy's always tryin' to get Virgil to spill the beans about his cases, too, but Virgil tells him just enough to make him want to know more, then laughs and says it's police business and he can't spill the beans." Even though there was laughter in his mother's voice, Trask could tell she didn't like Virgil's form of teasing. "Makes your daddy crazy."

"Speaking of Virgil, have you seen much of him lately?"

"Some, here and there. He's been spendin' a lot of time with Ty Miller. You remember Ty, don't you?"

"Yeah, I remember Ty. What are they doing, hunting and fishing?"

"No, they just seem to hang out in Ty's garage with some of their friends, smokin' and talkin' if he's not on duty."

"Really?" That didn't sound much like Virgil, who'd never been much of a joiner. "Who's he hanging out with besides Ty?"

"Oh, I don't know. I think I saw one of the Hanks boys there a couple of weeks ago, and Chad Gordon. Jenny Pruitt mentioned to me at church Sunday that her boy, Dawson, was hanging out with Ty, too." His mother's voice darkened. "She sounded a little worried about it, to tell the truth."

"Why's that?"

"I don't rightly know. I told your daddy about it, but he said not to worry, Virgil's a deputy now and we don't have to mind his business anymore." Lena laughed. "Thank goodness for that. He was a handful."

"I suppose we both were."

"Oh, you had your moments," Lena said, "but I never had to worry about bailing you out of jail in the middle of the night. Listen, I know it's a little late, but I'm betting you're calling from work, aren't you? I have some leftover supper—we had fried chicken, green beans and mashed potatoes. Your favorite. You want to drop by on your way home?"

"That's real tempting," Trask said, meaning it. "But I've got to work for a few hours longer tonight. But I'll definitely take you up on the offer the next time you cook my favorites."

"Oh, okay, then."

The disappointment in her voice almost made him give up on his idea of confronting Ty Miller at work tonight.

What would it really accomplish? So far, even the accusation against Virgil was third hand. He had yet to speak to Tara or Owen Stiles, face-to-face or otherwise. Hell, the only reason Ty Miller was on his radar at all was that Virgil had unwittingly named him as his alibi.

But Archer needed to hear that alibi himself, read Ty Miller's face and decide whether or not he was lying for Virgil.

"I'm really sorry," he told his mother. "I'll drop by and see you just as soon as I get a minute of free time."

"I'll look forward to it," she said, her tone loving. He felt an ache of love for his mother throbbing deep in his chest. He didn't know if she was living the life she wanted, but she was the sort of person who made do with what she had and looked for the bright side of every situation.

She deserved a more thoughtful son than he had been lately.

"Love you, Mama. I'll talk to you soon."

"I love you, too, sweet boy. You be careful, all right?"

"Will do." He hung up the phone, his eyes going toward the clock.

A little after nine. Almost showtime.

THE COLD SHOWER had done nothing to calm the urgent throb of heat at her core or the itchy, unsettled feeling that she was walking into the heart of danger with so many important things left unspoken.

If they were right that Robert's murder was about keeping Tara on the run, then they might encounter someone armed and very dangerous at her office tonight. She, Owen and Quinn had gone to great lengths to tie up all the loose ends and make tonight's break-in go as smoothly and safely as possible, but even Quinn had acknowledged the risk.

She had no family to say goodbye to. Her friends were

mostly people Robert had known or a handful of women she'd gone to high school or college with and rarely talked to anymore now that their lives had gone in different directions.

Owen was her family, her circle of friends, her rock. And she had denied him the only thing he'd asked of her in all the years of their friendship.

He was a man. They were attracted to each other. She was asking a lot of him to deny those feelings while continuing to be her friend.

But she couldn't bear life without him. He was her true north.

The heat in her core spread up into her belly and breasts, sending a quiver down her spine as the door to the small bathroom opened and Owen stepped out, wearing only a pair of jeans and a towel around his neck. His hair was still damp from the shower, a trickle of water sliding down his chest to follow the dark line of hair that dipped beneath the waistband of his jeans.

Friends with benefits. Wasn't that what people called it these days? She knew there were other terms for it, vulgar terms, but what she felt with Owen wasn't vulgar or base. She loved him. She just wasn't ever going to risk being *in* love with him. That complicated everything beyond hope.

But being his best friend, who he happened to sleep with now and then—that was something she could handle, wasn't it?

Owen gave her an odd look as he swiped the towel down his chest a couple of times before he tossed it aside and met her in the middle of the small room. "Is something wrong?"

She nodded, trying to find her voice. But her mouth was dry and her heart was pounding, drowning out all her thoughts.

"What is it?" Owen asked, his voice dropping to a gravelly half whisper.

"I was wrong," she said, her own voice coming out raspy. "I was wrong about us."

His brow furrowed, but he waited for her to speak.

Instead of words, she chose action, rising to her tiptoes and curling her fingers through his damp hair. She moved closer, sliding her other hand up his chest, reveling in the crisp sensation of his chest hair beneath her palm.

Owen opened his mouth as if to speak, but she didn't let him get that far. With a sharp tug of her hand, she pulled his head down and covered his mouth with hers.

Chapter Fifteen

She tasted like honey and heat, her lips soft and her tongue insistent, parting Owen's lips and demanding entry. He was powerless against her, just as he'd always known he would be. Tara was his soft spot, his Achilles' heel. In the end, he could never deny her anything, and that was why he was still by her side, long after a sane man would have walked away to find greener pastures. Tara was his one and only, and for all his talk of walking away, he now understood he never would do so.

Her hands seemed to be everywhere—on his shoulders, his sides, the tips of his fingers and the skin just above his hip bones. He was on fire, an unquenchable heat that seemed to grow and spread wherever she touched him.

Finally, her fingers dipped to the zipper of his jeans, and while every inch of his flesh seemed to sing with joy, a mean little voice in the back of his head asked a question.

What is she really offering you?

As if she'd heard the sudden note of discord, Tara stilled her hand and pulled back to look at him, her eyes dark with desire. "What's the matter?"

He wanted to tell her nothing was wrong, to proceed with what she'd been doing. Everything would work out the way it was supposed to.

But he'd never been a guy who worried about the future

when the future came. He was the guy who had his week planned on a spreadsheet. He was that much like Tara, he supposed, or maybe all these years of friendship had made her control freak side rub off on him.

He had to know what she was really offering before he agreed to take it. For better or for worse.

"What are we doing here?" he asked softly.

She gave him a quirky half grin. "Been that long?"

"Been forever, but that doesn't really answer my question."

Her fingers fluttered lightly against his rib cage, sending shivers down his spine. "I'm seducing you."

"I thought you were against our pursuing a romantic relationship."

A small frown creased her forehead. "I'm not against a sexual relationship. I think we could handle that, don't you? Solves the sexual tension problem, but we don't muck up our friendship with other kinds of expectations."

His heart sinking, he pulled her hands away from his body. "Sweetheart, that won't solve anything."

"Why not? People do this all the time. Friends with benefits."

"That never ends well."

"We could make it end well." She rose to her tiptoes to kiss him again.

And he let her. Drank in the sweetness he found there, the passion and the promise of pleasure. Drank and drank, losing his will to resist. Maybe this could work, he told himself as he wrapped his arms around her waist and dragged her closer, flattening himself against her so he could feel all the soft curves and strong edges of her body. He had known her intimately for years, except for this part of her, the seductress with a wicked imagination and an unimaginably sweet touch.

But what happens when she's ready to start a relationship with someone else again? the mean little voice asked.

With a low growl of frustration and regret, he pushed her away.

"No, Owen, don't do this..."

"I have to," he said, sinking onto the edge of the nearest bed. "Someone has to be sensible about this."

"No, don't you see? We've been too sensible about this for too long. We should have known we could figure out a way to have what we both want. We always have." She sat beside him on the bed, too close. The scent of bath gel on her heated skin was intoxicating.

He caught her hands before she touched him again. "I don't want sex from you, Tara."

She looked confused. "But isn't that the problem?"

"No, sweetheart, it's not. Sex is just a part of what I really want."

Her eyes flickered with annoyance, so very Tara-like. She hated when someone contradicted one of her plans. And nine times out of ten, if he was the one thwarting her will, he'd have gone along with her just to see her beautiful smile when she got her way.

But this was too important a decision to give in to Tara just to see her smile. Their friendship was on the line. One way or another, something had to give, because he couldn't bear to be just her bed buddy and her best friend.

He wanted what she'd been so ready to offer Robert Mallory, even though Owen had known all along she'd never loved Robert enough to spend forever with him. He knew it because he knew, deep down, that he and Tara were supposed to be together.

But what he knew, or thought he knew, didn't matter at all if Tara didn't see it, too.

"I don't want to be your best friend forever or your

friend with benefits, because that will never be what you are to me." She started to speak, but he touched her lips with his fingertip, stilling them. "Tara, I love you. I have loved you since the time you pantsed Jason Stillwell for stealing my lunch money. That love has never faltered, even through your snotty cheerleader years and the time you decided that dating only frat boys at Virginia was the best way to reach your life goals."

She grimaced. "Don't remind me," she said against his fingertip. He dropped his hand and she flashed another quirky half smile at him. "I love you, too, Owen. You know that."

"I do. But do you love me enough to marry me?"

Her expression froze, and for a moment, she turned so pale that he thought she was going to pass out. But then her color came back, rising to fill her cheeks as if she'd pinched them.

"Marry you?"

"Yes. Rings, cake, children, forever and ever and ever."

"No. I can't marry you." She pulled away from him, pacing across the floor to stand near the kudzu-draped front window. She stared into the greenery, clearly seeing something else. "You know why I can't."

"Just because your parents' marriage was a mess doesn't mean yours will be. You were willing to marry Robert."

"Because he ticked off everything on my list," she said, her voice rising with distress. "It felt like a sign. This is the one."

"But he wasn't."

Her face fell. "No, he wasn't."

"Because I am."

She didn't look at him. Didn't speak.

With a sigh, Owen retrieved his watch from the small bench beside the table and checked the time. Getting close to eleven. In an hour, they should be just outside the Security Solutions compound, sneaking in through a small back gate that most employees knew nothing about. Even Tara hadn't realized the gate existed until Quinn showed her where to look on the property.

"We'll have to table this for now," he said. "Let's get dressed and packed up. We have a long walk to the SUV. If we wait too long after the guards do their check on the office buildings, we won't have as much time to look for evidence before we have to leave."

She turned away from the window, her expression composed. She walked past him to the other bed and sat on the edge to pull on a pair of thick socks. "Dress warmly," she said. "Judging by the air I felt coming through that window sash, it's getting really cold out."

He pulled on a long-sleeved black T-shirt and shrugged a thick black sweater over it. The jacket Quinn had supplied was also black, a medium-weight Windbreaker that should keep him warm enough as long as the clouds scudding overhead didn't start spitting out snow rather than rain.

The hike to the SUV was painstakingly slow in the dark, and the heavy silence that had fallen between him and Tara didn't help to make the forward slog any more enjoyable. He finally spotted the SUV's gleam through the trees about a hundred yards ahead and breathed a sigh of relief.

He handed over the SUV keys to Tara. "Your company. You drive."

She took them without a word or even a smile and climbed behind the steering wheel. He rounded the vehicle and got in the passenger seat, looking at Tara's grim profile as he buckled up. "I don't think we can accomplish this mission without talking to each other."

"I'm sorry. I just don't know what to say."

He shook his head. "There's nothing else to say about us, is there? You're not willing to risk our friendship for something more, and I've come to the conclusion tonight that I can't walk away from you, even if I know deep down it's what I should do. So we go on the way we always have."

She looked at him. "Can we?"

"I don't know what else we can do. Do you?"

She shook her head and faced front again. For a moment she didn't move at all, just sat still and silent, her gaze fixed on something outside the SUV. Then she released a soft breath and put the key in the ignition. The SUV's engine roared to life.

Moving forward in the deepening night, they fell back into silence again.

THERE. JUST WHEN Archer Trask was beginning to think the receptionist from the security staffing company was wrong, Ty Miller's black pickup truck turned into the driveway of the Security Solutions compound and parked near the gate.

Trask was reaching for his door handle when he realized that Miller wasn't alone.

Easing his hand away from the latch, Trask leaned over to open his glove compartment and retrieve the small set of binoculars he kept there. He lifted the lenses to his eyes and took a closer look at the passenger seat of Miller's truck.

His stomach twisted as he recognized his brother's craggy face.

Damn it, Virgil.

THERE WAS NO good place to park the SUV, but Tara pulled the vehicle as far off the road as she could, hoping the darkness and the trees that lined the access road would be enough to hide the vehicle from any curious eyes that might pass by at this late hour.

The only real perimeter to the Security Solutions compound was an aging chain-link fence about eight feet high. Razor wire twists had been added at some point in the recent past, but there wasn't any real security outside of the kiosk just inside the front gate, and even it wasn't manned after hours. Employees had a key card that would allow them to enter through the automated gate, and anyone else would have to wait until morning for the daytime crew to arrive.

Getting in without going through the front gate, however, would seem to require a climb over the tall fence and braving the vicious edges of the razor wire. But somehow Alexander Quinn had uncovered a utility gate near the back of the property that made it possible for public utility repairmen and also law enforcement to enter the property after hours if necessary. It was a convenience not known to many in the company, Tara was certain, because she'd never heard a thing about it, and she was placed fairly high in the company's hierarchy.

"I'd guess he learned of it from your bosses themselves," Owen opined when she remarked on Quinn's knowledge of the back gate. "Or maybe from some of his law enforcement contacts. Quinn always seems to know where to find information he needs and how to exploit it."

"You make him sound scary."

"Most of the time he is."

They located the gate after a frustrating search through overgrown weeds and grass outside the company grounds. A heavy chain had been looped through the gate latch, giving the outward look of a locked gate, but closer examination revealed there was no lock at the end of the chain.

All they had to do was unwind the chain to open the gate and enter.

"Now what?" Owen asked.

"We're about three hundred yards from the building, I'd estimate." Tara peered through the gloom, trying to get a sense of perspective. "There's a side entrance on the east wing of the building, where my office is located. It opens with a key card, but if for some reason you can't put your hands on a key card, it'll also open with a numerical code."

"Not very secure."

"Well, after the third time Clayton Garvey left his key card at home and had to go through the humiliation of fetching a guard to let him in, they changed the system."

"You'd think people who deal in security threats would be able to identify the ones in their own systems."

"Human nature." They were close enough now to see the building looming in the darkness like a sleeping steel-and-glass behemoth. "That's the door we're heading for."

They slowed down as they neared the entrance, taking care not to draw attention to themselves. Just because the security guards would now be focusing attention on the more secure parts of the building didn't mean she and Owen didn't have to take precautions as they entered and started moving around. There were cameras at the end of each corridor, and while these weren't controlled by motion sensors, she and Owen would still need to be quick in hopes of avoiding immediate detection.

The cameras record everything, which is why you need to wear the masks I've provided until you're out of range of the corridor cameras, Quinn had warned them. They stopped now, while still clear of the building's external security cameras, to slip on the knit masks Quinn had put in their backpacks.

"Ready?" Owen asked, making last-minute adjustments to his mask.

"Yes."

He motioned for her to lead the way.

UNTIL THE VERY last moment, Trask had planned to confront his brother before Virgil and Ty Miller ever set foot into the building. But then Virgil had stepped out of the truck wearing the same security company uniform that Ty wore, and Trask was suddenly uncertain about everything he'd believed he knew.

As he froze in place, his mind racing through all the possible implications, Ty and Virgil walked across the narrow space between the parking lot and the front entrance, disappearing inside the building.

The automatic gate was still slowly closing. Spurred into action, Trask jumped from his truck and raced through the gate with inches to spare. But when he tried the front door, he found it locked.

He hadn't noticed Virgil or Ty stop to punch in an alarm code after entering, so he might be able to pick the lock without setting off any sort of alarm.

Within a few moments, he felt the last of the pins in the lock open and he gave the door a tug. It swung silently outward and he slipped into the building.

Stopping to listen, he didn't immediately hear any other noises. Wherever Ty and Virgil had gone, they'd gone quickly. There was an elevator bank a few feet inside the foyer. Maybe they'd taken the elevator to another level?

He moved toward the bank of elevators, glad he'd worn soft-soled shoes. They made a tiny, almost imperceptible squeak on the polished floors, but at least he wasn't leaving echoing footsteps ringing behind him as he walked.

He looked at the elevator indicator lights. Hmm. All

of them seemed to read Ground Floor. Wherever Ty and Virgil had gone, it appeared they hadn't gone by elevator.

Wandering a little deeper into the building, he spotted his first security camera. It stood still, which might mean it was showing a static image on a security monitor somewhere. If so, his presence here would need some explaining. Somehow he didn't think his bosses at the sheriff's department would be satisfied with whatever he managed to come up with.

Too late to worry about that now. He backtracked until he found an office directory sign. There were two wings, it appeared. The one he was in was called Administrative Services and included a long list of offices and names. Tara Bentley's office was on this floor, he saw, in an area marked Analytical Security Services Unit.

He had no idea what that meant, he realized. Or what, really, Tara did for Security Solutions. It was all very vague in general, the way a lot of job descriptions at security companies could be.

Owen Stiles's position at Campbell Cove Security was only slightly less mysterious, and that was only because Trask had a better grip on what "cybersecurity" meant than "analytical security services."

Maybe this was his chance to find out a little more about who his mysterious fugitive bride really was.

He turned right and headed for Tara Bentley's office.

Chapter Sixteen

The corridors were mostly dark, except for a few lights near the tops of the walls that shone at half strength every ten yards or so. Tara kept an eye on the security cameras as she walked quickly up the hall. She and a couple of her coworkers had noticed that just before each camera made a sweep of the service area, it twitched twice in the opposite direction of its eventual sweep. Then it would move in a slow arc before going stationary again until its next sweep.

The one down the hall started to twitch twice to the left. Tara grabbed Owen's arm and pulled him through the nearest door.

"Is this it?" Owen whispered.

"No, it's a conference room."

"Then why did we come in here?"

She told him about the camera sweep observation.

"How long will the sweep last?" Owen asked.

"Should be over now." She risked a quick peek into the hall and saw the camera sitting still again. She grabbed Owen's hand and they hurried up the hall, pausing as they reached a corner.

She took a quick look around the corner. It was empty, and the camera at the end of the hall was still. "Let's go."

Owen followed her forward as she led him swiftly down the corridor and around another corner. They managed to reach the door to her office without the cameras moving again.

But to her surprise, the door to her office was locked.

"These doors aren't usually locked," she whispered, giving the knob a second, futile twist.

"Let me take a look. You keep an eye on the cameras."

"Move in as close to the door as you can. I don't think the camera's view reaches into this alcove." Tara flattened her back against the door and watched with curiosity as Owen pulled a small leather wallet from his pocket. He unfolded the flaps to reveal a series of narrow metal rods of various sizes, all small. It was a lock-picking kit, she realized with surprise as Owen selected two of the metal pieces from the wallet and tucked the rest of them back in his pocket.

He inserted both pieces into the lock, wiggled them around in ways that made no sense to her whatsoever. But within a couple of minutes, the door lock gave a slight click and Owen twisted the knob open.

He entered first, with caution. Tara followed closely behind him, her hand flattened against his spine. "My desk is over here on the right. Chris Miller's desk is here to the left."

Suddenly, the light came on in the room, almost blinding her with its unexpected intensity. She squinted, wondering if Owen had flicked on the light. She was about to tell him to turn the lights off again when he stopped dead still in front of her, his back rigidly straight.

She realized with a sinking heart that he hadn't been the one who'd turned on the lights.

A drawling voice greeted them, a twist of humor tinting his words. "Well. This is an unexpected turn of events."

She turned around to see the man who'd lured her out to the church parking lot standing in front of them, holding a big black pistol.

"HEY!"

The voice that rang through the corridor behind him stopped Trask short. He turned slowly to find himself looking at Ty Miller, no longer dressed in his drab olive security uniform but a pair of khaki pants and a dark blue blazer over a white golf shirt.

No, that wasn't right. This man was younger, though his hair color, his features, even his general build were the same as Ty Miller's. In the low lighting of the nighttime building, it had been easy to see what Trask was expecting to see.

He hadn't been expecting to see Ty's brother Chris, even though he was also an employee of Security Solutions. It was after midnight now. What the hell was he doing here at this hour?

"Archer," Chris said as he stepped closer. "What are you doing here?"

"Looking for your brother, actually."

Chris looked puzzled. "Is he working tonight? He told me he was off this week. Guess he must be covering someone else's shift."

"What are you doing here this late?"

"I have an analytical paper to present tomorrow to the officers about the sym—" Chris bit off the last word. "For something we're planning. Anyway, I realized I left some files here in my office that I need to return to the secure section before morning, so I came here to get it."

"Do you mind if I come with you? This place is a little creepy at night. Don't tell my boss I said that."

Chris grinned. "It's our secret. And you're right. It's creepy as hell."

They headed down a long corridor side by side. The oppressive silence continued to make Trask's skin crawl. Then, suddenly, he heard the quiet murmur of voices coming from somewhere down the hallway and faltered to a halt. Chris Miller stopped short, too, an odd expression on his face.

When Chris spoke, it was in a whisper. "Nobody's supposed to be in this wing at this hour. Security should already be on the other side of the complex."

Trask eased his hand beneath his jacket and closed his fingers over the butt of his service pistol. He kept his voice as low as Chris's. "One quick question. Did you know my brother was working security here these days?"

Chris gave Trask an odd look. "No, he's not."

"Maybe he just started."

"No." Chris's voice rose a notch. He tamped it back down to a hiss of breath. "If we'd hired new security people, I'd know. One of my jobs is to screen the personnel Security Staffing sends our way. I'd know."

Damn it. Trask swallowed the bile rising in his throat and nodded toward the continuing murmur of voices drifting up the hallway. "Let's go find out who's here."

"Ty, GET OUT HERE." The man in the drab olive uniform kept the muzzle of his pistol pointed directly at Owen's heart. Owen forced his gaze away from the muzzle and concentrated on taking in every detail of their captor's appearance.

Definitely the same man he'd seen trying to shove Tara into the panel van outside the church. Also definitely the same man who'd been entering the Bagley County Sheriff's Department in a deputy's uniform the morning they tried to turn themselves in.

"You're Virgil Trask," Tara said, her voice strong, though Owen heard the slightest tremble on the last word.

"And you're a real pain in the ass, lady. Not real good at stayin' put."

"What were you planning to do with me? What was the point of drugging me and dragging me away from the church?"

Virgil looked at her as if she'd lost her mind. "Do you think this is some sort of *Scooby Doo* episode? You think I'm going to stand here and waste time telling you all the details of my nefarious plot?"

"You can't just shove us out of here at gunpoint," Owen said. "Security cameras will catch it all."

Virgil shot him a withering look. "Who the hell do you think runs the security cameras around here?" He turned his head toward a door in the back of the room. "Ty, you comin' out here or not?"

A big broad-shouldered man emerged from the door, his arms full of files. "He left them here, just like he said, Virgil." The man Virgil Trask called Ty stumbled to a stop, dropping a couple of the file folders stacked in his arms as he spotted Owen and Tara. He muttered a soft profanity.

"Yeah," Virgil said with a grimace. "I was really hoping I wouldn't have to kill anyone just yet."

"Do it now, do it later," Owen said with a studied shrug. "It's what you have planned, isn't it? Killing a whole lot of people from a whole lot of countries who are wanting to clamp down on terror attacks across the globe? What I don't understand is why."

Virgil said nothing, but Ty Miller dropped the rest of the folders he held onto a desk nearby and took a belligerent step toward Owen. "You think those people are coming here to make us all safer? They're just looking at more ways to tie our hands behind our backs."

Virgil shot Ty a look of disgust. "Would you shut up, Ty? Let's just figure out a clean way to get rid of them and get back to what we're here for."

"Those files are from the classified section," Tara said,

taking a few steps toward the files Ty had just deposited. "Chris had them in his office?"

"Uncle Stephen let him take them out for some paper he's preparing to present to the directors. You know Chris, he doesn't get everything on the first read through."

Tara glanced at Owen, looking faintly horrified. "And he left them in his office?"

"Stop talking, Ty. I mean it." For a moment, Virgil's pistol swung toward his partner in crime. It was a tiny opening at best, but Owen had a feeling there wouldn't be another.

He launched himself toward Virgil, knocking him hard into the nearest desk. Virgil hit it with a loud grunt of pain, already swinging his pistol back around toward Owen.

But Owen had already jerked the backpack from his shoulders and held it in front of him, using it to shove the pistol wide as Virgil pulled the trigger. Big puffs of fabric and insulation flew from the backpack as both Owen and Virgil fell to the floor.

"Owen!" Tara screamed.

All the breath seemed to rush from Owen's lungs, and the world around him started to go black.

THE SOUND OF a gunshot was easy to mistake for other things. A vehicle backfiring, or even the crack of a baseball bat hitting a pitched ball.

But neither of those things could be found inside this building at nearly half past midnight. While Chris Miller froze in place, Trask's cop instincts sent him running toward the sound.

A woman's voice rose in a wail. "Owen!"

The sounds seemed to be coming from the office just down the hallway, the one marked Analytical Security Services Unit. Trask would bet what little money remained in his savings account that the woman's voice he just heard belonged to Tara Bentley.

He'd found his fugitives. He just hoped it wasn't too late.

As TARA STARTED across the room to where Owen had fallen, Ty Miller grabbed her arms and held her in place. She struggled against his hold, but he was as strong as a bull and his grip was already digging deep bruises in her flesh.

Still, she kept fighting, her heart racing with terror as she watched Owen go dreadfully still.

"Let me go!" She kicked back against Miller's legs, her boot apparently connecting with one of his kneecaps, for he let out a howl of pain and his grip on her arms loosened.

She tore out of his grasp and ran to Owen's side.

"Get back!" Virgil trained his pistol on her from his position on the floor, desperation tinting his deep voice. "Get back, or I'll shoot you, too."

She lifted her hands toward him. "Please, let me go to him."

Virgil shook his head. "Stay where you are."

"He's hurt!" She could see a dark, wet patch spreading on the side of Owen's jacket. "I have to stop the bleeding or he could die."

"He's going to die one way or another." Virgil nodded toward Ty, who grabbed Tara's arms and pulled her backward again.

"We need those files, Virgil," Ty said.

"I'll get them. You take the girl."

"What about him?" Ty asked.

Virgil looked down at Owen. "He'll bleed out sooner or later. Then we'll come back here to clean up."

Tara thought for a moment she saw Owen's hand twitch,

but after that he was completely still, and she guessed with despair that she'd seen only what she wanted to see.

He might already be dead, his heart stopped by Virgil Trask's bullet. He could be gone and there were so many things she still hadn't told him.

Like how much she loved him. How much the image of that forever love he'd talked about had burrowed its way into her soul that she understood now how impossible it would ever be to walk away from what he was offering.

Now, when it was too late, she finally got it.

Don't die on me, Stiles. Don't die on me before we have our shot at forever.

CHRIS MILLER HAD remained where he stood down the hall while Trask made his way to the closed door. Just as well, he'd probably be more of an obstacle than an aid.

Trask waited against the wall, trying to hear what was being said inside the room. He heard the low rumble of his brother's voice, and the broader country drawl of Ty Miller answering. They were talking about cleaning up after themselves. Something about files. The woman was begging them to let her go to someone. She'd cried out Owen's name, so maybe Stiles had taken that bullet he'd heard fired down the hall?

"Let me go!" Tara's voice rose again to a shriek.

"Get her out of here!" Virgil bellowed.

Trask flattened himself against the wall, waving down the hall for Chris Miller to get out of the way.

Chris scurried down the hall and rounded the corner, out of sight. Trask saw him reaching for his phone as he ran. Calling 9-1-1? Trask hoped so.

There was a hard thud against the door, followed by several more thumps.

Then splinters of wood flew from the door beside

his head in concert with another blast of gunfire. Trask ducked, his heart galloping in his chest.

"WHAT THE HELL, VIRGIL! You nearly hit me." Ty Miller released one of Tara's arms, giving her the chance to pull away. Her cheek stung where a splinter of wood from the gunshot had sliced through the skin, but she didn't think she'd been hit anywhere else.

She jerked free of Ty's grasp and turned to look at Virgil. But he wasn't standing there holding a gun as she expected. Instead, he was grappling on the floor with Owen, whose eyes were open and locked with Virgil's. His hand covered Virgil's on the pistol, and he shouted, "Get out of here, Tara!" without ever looking in her direction.

He was alive. The words sang through her whole body, sending a flood of sheer relief pouring through her like fizzy champagne bubbles. But reality crashed through the brief moment of jubilation. He was still wrapped in a death grip with a man who'd already shot him once. And another man was already moving toward them, ready to help his buddy overpower Owen.

She grabbed the chair that sat near the door and swung it at Ty Miller, catching the big man right in the small of his back. Something made a loud cracking noise, and it wasn't the solid steel chair she'd somehow managed to wield like a club. Ty howled with pain as he crashed to the floor, writhing in agony.

"Go, Tara! Go!" Owen shouted as he started to lose his grip on Virgil's arm.

"No!" she cried, picking up the chair again and heading to his rescue.

Ty Miller's hand clamped around her ankle, stopping her short. Losing her balance, she fell hard to the floor, the impact sending stars sparking through her brain for a moment. She pushed through the disorientation and kicked with her free leg, hitting Ty in the chin. He yelled out a stream of profanities but let go of her leg.

She scrambled up again and grabbed the chair, grunting as the full weight of the steel behemoth made itself known. Earlier, with adrenaline spiking her strength, it had felt almost featherlight, but the adrenaline was starting to drain away.

She gazed desperately at Owen, who had managed to grapple Virgil Trask toward the window.

Suddenly, the door behind her slammed open, and both Virgil and Owen froze to look at the newcomer. Tara turned as well and found herself looking at a dark-haired man holding a big gunmetal-gray pistol. He aimed the pistol's muzzle across the room at Virgil Trask.

"Put the gun down, Virgil. It's over."

Owen let go of Virgil and stumbled back, falling into a chair a few feet away. Tara ran to him, her heart in her throat.

"What are you doin' here, Archie?" The tone of Virgil's plaintive query was somewhere between anger and dismay.

"I'm here to put an end to all of this, Virgil. Put down the gun."

Virgil shook his head. "You don't know what this is, Archie. I caught your fugitives. He tried to kill me."

"That's a lie!" Tara shouted as she paused in the act of trying to find the source of the blood dripping on the floor beneath Owen. "These two men tried to kidnap me the day of my wedding. I think one of them killed my fiancé. They're after some secret information."

"I know," the man in the doorway said. "I'm Archer Trask. I'm the lead investigator on your fiancé's murder case."

"Come on, Archie! She's your top suspect, and I found her. I was going to bring her in."

"It's over. Just put down the gun."

"Archie, it's me."

Archer Trask stared at his brother sadly. "I know, Virgil."

Suddenly, Virgil's gun hand whipped up a couple of inches, and Tara shouted a warning.

It wasn't necessary. Gunfire blazed from Archer Trask's pistol at the same time Virgil pulled the trigger of his own weapon. The bullet Virgil fired went wide, hitting the doorframe behind his brother's head. His brother's bullet, however, hit Virgil in the chest.

For a minute, Virgil stared in disbelief at the bloom of red spreading across his shirt. Then he looked back at his brother, the stunned expression frozen on his face as he slid to the floor. His chin fell to his chest, and only the desk beside him and the wall behind him, now streaked with his blood, kept him from falling over.

Archer Trask walked slowly to his brother's side, gazing down at him with a look of pure grief. He nudged the pistol away from his brother's slack fingers with his toe, moving it out of reach. Then he crouched in front of Virgil and touched his fingertips to his brother's throat.

The look of sheer agony on his face told Tara what that trembling touch had revealed.

Archer sat back on his heels, tears leaking from his eyes. "Damn it, Virgil," he said.

Chapter Seventeen

"Do we have to do this now?" Tara looked at the grim face of Bagley County Sheriff Roy Atkins as he loomed over where she sat in one of the small interrogation rooms at the county hall complex. "I know Deputy Trask must have already told you everything that happened tonight. I just want to make sure Owen is okay."

"He's still in surgery."

Shock hit her like a fist blow. "Surgery? He's in surgery? Why is he in surgery? He was awake and talking, and the paramedics seemed to think he was okay—"

"He was shot in the side. They want to be sure he didn't sustain any life-threatening internal injuries, so they need to get the bullet out of him before it causes any worse problems."

"Surgery?" She pressed her hand to her mouth, terror twisting her insides. She had thought it was over. She just had to get through all the debriefings, convince the authorities that she had been running for her life, and then she and Owen could move forward with the life they should already have been living together.

This couldn't be happening. Not now.

Owen deserved the forever he wanted so desperately, and somehow she had to find a way to give it to him.

But she couldn't do it from here, halfway across the

county from where he lay on an operating table, fighting for his life.

A brisk duo of knocks on the door drew Sheriff Atkins's gaze in that direction. His look of mild irritation deepened when Tony Giattina walked confidently through the door and set his gleaming leather briefcase on the table between the sheriff and Tara.

"Don't say anything else, Tara," he said, looking at her with far more sympathy in his expression than had been there the last time she saw him. He was dressed in an expensive-looking suit and a crisp linen shirt that would have been more at home at a morning court appearance than a two in the morning visit to the county jail. "Sheriff, are you planning on holding my client overnight?"

For a moment, the sheriff looked as if he wanted to say yes. But finally, he shook his head. "Just don't leave our jurisdiction this time, Ms. Bentley."

"She wouldn't dream of it," Tony said blithely, offering Tara his hand. She took it and rose, following him out of the interrogation room.

Outside, the corridor was buzzing with more movement than she'd noticed when she was first brought in. A lot had happened, including the death of one of their own deputies. That he'd been the cause of his own death hadn't really sunk in at this point, and some of the deputies sent furious glares her way as she walked out of the building with her lawyer.

To no one's surprise, Alexander Quinn was waiting outside the sheriff's department. He nodded toward Tony before turning his attention to Tara. "Are you all right?"

"I need to see Owen. The sheriff said he's in surgery."

"He is. One of my colleagues is there with him, waiting for word. I'm here to take you to the hospital." He opened the passenger door of a dark blue SUV and helped her inside. As she buckled in, he climbed behind the wheel and reached for his own belt. "On the way, why don't you tell me everything that happened tonight?"

One way or another, she thought with resignation, she was going to have to undergo an interrogation after all.

THE LAST PEOPLE Archer Trask had expected to see sitting at the bar of the Sheffield Tavern were Maddox Heller and his pretty wife. He almost turned around and walked out when he saw the expressions of sympathy in their faces, but he braced himself against the unwanted kindness and walked over to where they sat.

The bar was nearly empty at this time of the morning. It would close in another hour, which would at least give him a polite reason to escape, he thought with bleak humor.

"We heard what happened," Heller said as Trask settled on the bar stool next to him. "I'm sorry."

"So am I," Trask said. He waved at the bartender. "Bourbon and branch. Light on the branch."

"We think we've finally figured out what your brother and Ty Miller were involved in," Heller said. He had a glass of what looked like water with a twist of lime and had drunk a little of it. Even the wife was nursing her glass of white wine, barely taking a sip at all as she looked from her husband's face to Trask's.

"I can guess at some of it," Trask said. "My mother told me Virgil had been spending a lot of time with Ty Miller and some of his friends. I had a chance to talk to Ty's brother, Chris, for a few minutes before the police and emergency services arrived. He said Ty had gotten involved with some group of preppers."

"They weren't just preppers. Preppers mostly just want to be left alone to prepare for whatever might come," Heller said. "Your brother and his friends were determined to make sure our country cut its ties with the rest of the world. Extreme isolationism, I guess you could call it."

Trask remembered a few of the more objectionable things he'd heard his brother say over the years. He could definitely see him falling on the side of "kick the foreign bastards out and don't let them back in."

"Quinn and his previous security company back in the mountains of Tennessee came across a very similar group of nihilists—the Blue Ridge Infantry. We think one of the men in this group of people had familial ties to some of the former members of the Blue Ridge Infantry."

"I've heard of them. They were in Virginia, too, and there were less organized groups here in Kentucky with sympathetic leanings."

"I think maybe Ty and your brother were in the process of trying to organize this Kentucky group into something more cohesive. Through Chris, they found out Security Solutions was planning a security event that involves several other countries. I think your brother and Ty must have realized that if they could create a big, deadly disruption of that event, their success would be a spectacular recruiting tool to pull off bigger and more influential attacks against the government they think has betrayed them. But they needed more information about the event to be successful."

"So they kidnapped Tara Bentley? Why? To get her to tell them what she knew?" Trask asked with a frown. "You think they were going to try to torture it out of her?"

"We thought that might be the case at first," Heller admitted. "But we couldn't quite make Robert Mallory's murder fit our theory."

The bartender arrived with the bourbon and water. Trask took a sip and grimaced. "Neither could I. It seemed to be completely out of the blue. No motive seemed to fit."

"They wanted Tara Bentley out of the way, and they

wanted the cops looking in a completely different direction," Heller said. "If they'd killed her, where would your investigation have taken you?"

"To her. Her connections. Her job," Trask answered. "But instead, it was her fiancé who died. And she was my prime person of interest instead of the victim. I didn't even look at her work as a possible reason for what happened until recently."

Heller nodded. "Your brother was a cop. He would have known the direction you'd look in."

"Leaving him and Ty free to look for the information they would never have gotten from Tara."

"They planned to stash her somewhere until they got what they wanted from her second-in-command."

"Ty's brother, Chris." Trask took another sip of the bourbon. It burned all the way down, leaving him feeling queasy and unsettled. He pushed the drink away. "They found some files tonight."

"We heard. Security Solutions has already sent people from their secure documents division to return them to a place of safekeeping."

"I don't think Chris was intentionally involved."

"We don't think so, either," Heller agreed. "He was just too careless for the job he was tasked to do."

Trask stood up, feeling stifled and claustrophobic in this place. He pulled a couple of bills from his wallet and put them on the bar next to his drink. "I gotta get out of here."

Heller and his wife followed him outside. "Trask," Heller said, stopping him in his tracks.

He turned to look at them. "I really need to be left alone."

It was the wife, Iris, who reached out and took his hand. As had happened the last time they met, he felt a strange zip of energy flow through him where her fingers touched his flesh. "I'm so sorry about your brother. If you need anything, you give us a call, okay?"

She flashed him a faint smile, removed her hand and walked away with her husband.

Trask turned to watch her go, rubbing his hand where she'd touched him. Just a moment ago, he'd felt as if he'd never feel normal again. But now...

Now he felt as if there just might be a sliver of hope out there after all.

"HE'S OUT OF SURGERY. He did just fine." A tall, beautiful African American woman rose as Quinn and Tara entered the surgical waiting room. "I tried to reach his parents, but I got no answer."

"I think they're in Branson, Missouri," Tara said. "They go there every spring, before the summer tourist rush kicks in." She rubbed her gritty eyes, surprised to find tears trembling on her eyelashes. "I want to see him."

"I know. They'll take him up to his room as soon as he's out of recovery." The woman offered Tara a gentle smile. "I'm Rebecca Cameron. I work with Quinn at Campbell Cove Security."

"Right. Owen's mentioned you."

Rebecca put her arm around Tara's shoulders. "Come on. I'll take you to his room."

The empty room looked so sterile. Tara found herself futilely wishing the hospital gift shop downstairs was open so she could at least buy a nice vase of spring flowers to make the place look more homey and welcoming.

As if she had read Tara's thoughts on her face, Rebecca patted Tara's back. "I suspect all he really needs right now is you." With an encouraging smile, Rebecca left her alone in the room.

It seemed to be forever later when a nurse and an at-

tendant wheeled Owen into the hospital room on a gurney. He wasn't exactly awake, but his eyes were fluttering
open and closed and his arms flailed weakly as he tried to
help the attendant move him from the gurney to the bed.

The nurse finished settling Owen and put his IV bag
on the pole beside him. She turned to smile at Tara. "Are
you Tara?"

Tara nodded.

"He asked if you were here when he first started coming out of the anesthesia."

Tara crossed to Owen's bedside. His eyes were closed
again, but when she took the hand without the IV, he
squeezed weakly.

"Tara?" he mumbled.

"Right here, Owen. Where else would I be?"

The nurse smiled at her again. "I'll be back in a bit to
check his vitals. You can stay in here with him if you want.
I could get you a reclining chair if you like. To make it
more comfortable."

"That's fine. Thanks. No hurry. Just when you can get
to it." She waited until the nurse walked out the door, and
then she bent closer to Owen. "You gave me a scare, you
big, brave idiot. Don't ever do that again."

His eyes fluttered halfway open, though his pupils
seemed incapable of focusing. "Admit it. You were impressed by my show of manly courage."

"Terrified is more like it," she confessed, her heart surg-
ing with relief to hear him making jokes. "I didn't need
proof of your strength, you know. I've always thought you
were the strongest man I know."

"No matter what my father thought?"

"By now, we both know he's a fool. So stop trying so
hard to prove it, okay?" She touched his cheek. "For the

dozen years you scared off my life span, you owe me big, mister."

His dry lips cracked into a lopsided, painful-looking smile. "Yeah? You got a payment in mind?"

She leaned even closer, lowering her voice to a whisper. "How about you marry me?"

His eyes struggled to focus. "Was that a proposition?"

"It was a proposal." She picked up the roll of tape the nurse had left on the bedside table after she taped down his IV cannula. Stripping off a piece, she wrapped it around his left ring finger. "See? I got a ring and everything."

A raspy laugh escaped his throat. He winced, and when he spoke again, his voice was hoarse but full of humor. "Why, Miss Tara, this is so sudden."

"Say yes, Owen."

"Yes, Owen." His eyes fluttered shut.

She drew up the chair beside his bed and sat there with a goofy smile on her face, her fingers twined with his.

OWEN WOKE TO sunlight angling through a window, falling across his eyes and making his head hurt. He turned his head with a grumble and found himself face-to-face with Tara.

She was just starting to wake, her eyes fluttering open. She gave a slight start when she saw him watching her. Pulling back from the bed, she laughed sheepishly. "Good morning."

He winced in pain as he shifted position in the bed. "That's a matter of opinion."

"Are you in a lot of pain? Do you want me to call the nurse?"

"No, please don't. She kept waking me up all night."

Tara brushed his hair away from his face. "Oh, come on, you slacker. You slept through the last couple of vitals checks. I was awake for all of them." She rubbed her red eyes. "God, I need about a week of sleep."

"How did you get the police to let you come here?" His throat felt as if he'd swallowed glass. Probably the breathing tube they'd have administered before surgery.

"Quinn sicced Tony Giattina on them. They didn't know what hit them."

"Tony's speaking to us after what we did to him?" He was surprised.

"Well, that's still up in the air." Tara touched his face, her expression gentle. "You look terrible."

"Thank you. You don't know how much better that makes me feel."

"I thought I'd lost you." Her fingers moved lightly over his forehead, her touch strangely tentative, as if she weren't sure whether she had a right to offer him comfort. "When I realized you'd been shot, I was so scared."

"I'm okay. Everything's okay." He put his hand over hers. As he did, he noticed a piece of tape wrapped around his left ring finger. A vague memory drifted through his brain. Tara holding his hand, talking about debts. But the rest of the memory eluded him, somehow distant and unreachable.

"I love you," she murmured, pressing her lips against his palm. "I was so afraid I'd never get to tell you that again."

"Oh, I already knew that." He gave a weak wave of his other hand, wincing a little as the IV cannula shifted in his vein. He was aching all over and felt as if he'd gone about ten rounds with a freight train, but a sense of peace began to settle over him. Everything was going to be okay now. His wound would heal and he and Tara would get their lives back.

"What are you smiling about?" Tara asked, rubbing her cheek against the back of his hand. He liked the feeling, liked the way it sent little flutters of life through his otherwise lifeless body.

"Just thinking that it's finally over. The truth will come out, one way or another, and we'll get to go back to our lives again."

"Do you remember anything about last night?"

"I remember running into Virgil and Ty. I remember getting shot. Then someone shot Virgil."

"Deputy Trask," she said, her voice darkening. "Virgil's younger brother."

Owen grimaced. "Poor bastard."

"What do you remember after that?"

"You holding my hand. Paramedics. Lots and lots of lights, and then it's a blank." He narrowed his eyes at her. "Did I miss something?"

"Quite a bit," she said with a wry half smile.

"I remember seeing you after surgery," he added. "If that's what you're getting at."

"Yes, I was waiting for you when you came up after recovery."

"You told me I owed you big."

"That's right." Smiling, she ran her finger lightly over the edge of the tape on his finger. "I also told you the payment I wanted."

He looked at the tape on his finger, then back at her face. What he saw in her eyes made his heart turn a little flip in his chest. "Did I agree to your terms?" he asked, emotion swelling through him to settle like a lump in his throat.

Tears glittered in her eyes. "Yes, but you were a little loopy at the time."

"So maybe you should tell me again. What do I have to do to even up things between us?"

A smile crept over her lips. "Marry me, Owen Stiles. Make me your wife."

He caught her hand in his, pressing it against his chest. "Why, Tara?"

She frowned, as if she hadn't expected the question. "Because I love you."

"You loved me yesterday and the day before that. But you weren't anywhere near thinking about marrying me. Don't make a big decision just because we've gone through a crisis."

"I'm not. I was already thinking about it before you were shot. It's just, staring down the barrel of a gun really clarifies things for you, you know? I realized that I might not get the chance to tell you that the one thing I wanted more than anything in this world was to live the rest of my life with you. To be with you in every way. It suddenly seemed so stupid to be afraid of having everything with you. I trust you completely. With my life. And with my heart." She stroked his cheek, the tears spilling down her cheeks. "I know now that we belong together in every way. I believe that with all my heart."

He had trouble pushing words past the lump in his throat. "So ask me again."

Her eyes met his, deadly serious. "Will you marry me, Owen Stiles?"

"I do believe I will," he answered, pulling her down for a kiss.

* * * * *

COMING SOON!

We really hope you enjoyed reading this book.
If you're looking for more romance
be sure to head to the shops when
new books are available on

Thursday 26th September

MILLS & BOON

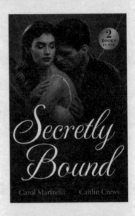

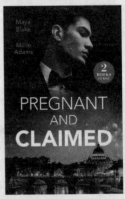

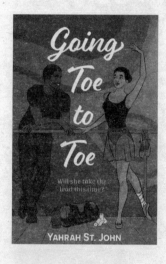

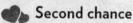
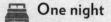

LET'S TALK
Romance

For exclusive extracts, competitions and special offers, find us online:

f MillsandBoon

X @MillsandBoon

⊙ @MillsandBoonUK

♪ @MillsandBoonUK

Get in touch on 01413 063 232